Critical acclaim for Frederick Barthelme's
Two Against One

"*Two Against One* is by far the most powerful, disturbing and interior of Mr. Barthelme's fictions, inviting us to be flies on the wall of a particularly shadowy and unwelcoming corner of its hero's psyche.... **The book is charged throughout with the voyeuristic fascination of a report behind enemy lines."**

—*The New York Times Book Review*

"*Two Against One* traces the minute thrusts and parries of a weekend in the trenches of the sex war.... Rarely has fiction confronted so scrupulously the darker sides of male sexuality—revulsion from messiness, the compulsion to separate sex from love, to have what Barthelme calls 'the body without the head'—and rarely besides have those matters been treated in pages so totally devoid of either literary 'psychologizing' or sexual ideology."

—Mark Muro, *The Boston Globe*

"Mr. Barthelme is anatomist and cataloger in minute detail of the current 'thirty-something' generation at its most vulnerable.... **One becomes curiously hooked, going back over a paragraph or page here and there to make sure no thought has been missed.** One gets drawn into the argument, which says quite a lot for Mr. Barthelme's powers."

—Colin Walters, *Washington Times*

"Barthelme is a relentlessly contemporary writer.... Many insights here are far more intelligent than the bromides that fill most fiction about love."

—Will Nixon, *Seven Days*

"Slick without being heartless and wise without sacrificing witty ... *Two Against One* is a sad comedy of modern manners, notable for its arch and acerbic dialogue.... A fine novel."

—H. Keith Monroe, *Winston-Salem Journal*

"Frederick Barthelme has written what seems to be the absolute divorce novel. This is a journey to the end of personality."

—Anatole Broyard

TWO AGAINST ONE

A Novel

Frederick Barthelme

COLLIER BOOKS
Macmillan Publishing Company
New York

Published by arrangement with Weidenfeld & Nicolson, New York, A Division of Wheatland Corporation

Collier Books
Macmillan Publishing Company
866 Third Avenue, New York, NY 10022
Collier Macmillan Canada, Inc.

Library of Congress Cataloging-in-Publication Data
Barthelme, Frederick, 1943–
    Two against one : a novel / Frederick Barthelme. — 1st Collier
Books ed.
    p.   cm.
    ISBN 0-02-030445-5
    I. Title.   II. Title: 2 against 1.
PS3552.A763T9   1989   89-7357   CIP
813'.54—dc20

Cover illustration and design by David Tamura

First Collier Books Edition 1989

10 9 8 7 6 5 4 3 2 1

Printed in the United States of America

For Don

TWO
AGAINST
ONE

1

EDWARD LASCO was on the screened porch of his rented house in a comfortable but not elegant older section of the town where he'd lived for the past fifteen years when his wife, Elise, who six months before had left him and moved to a nearby city to work in a psychiatric hospital, came around the side of the house and stood beside the screen looking in. She had on a business outfit—natural linen suit, knee-high boots, dark glasses with at least three distinguishable colors tiered top to bottom in the lenses—and she carried a slick briefcase, thin and shiny. Her hair was shorter than he'd seen it, styled in a peculiar way so that it seemed in spots to jerk away from her head, to say, "I'm hair, boy, and you'd better believe it." Edward had come outside with a one-pint carton of skim milk and a ninety-nine-cookie package of Oreos and a just-received issue of *InfoWorld,* and he was entirely content with the prospect of eating his cookies and drinking his milk and reading his magazine, but when he saw Elise he was filled with a sudden, very unpleasant sense that he didn't want to see her. It'd been a good two and a half months since he'd talked to her, and there she was looking like an earnest TV art director's version of the modern businesswoman; it made him feel that his life was fucked, and this was before she'd said a word.

"It's your birthday," she said.

This took Edward by surprise. He had not forgotten that it was his birthday, in fact he had spent the day debating with himself the

3

advisability of ordering, from an outfit in California, a complete, prepackaged, do-it-yourself dual-band satellite dish, antenna, feed horn, down converter, receiver, and positioner, and was still debating this purchase, trying to determine how long he might be interested in all this hardware, should he decide to buy it for himself for his birthday. He was startled, instead, in equal measure by his wife's presence and appearance. Edward wondered what she could possibly want. And, too, how Elise, who had been a plain but attractive housewife last June, had transformed herself since then into this triumph of art direction. He played with an Oreo, flipping it over in his fingers the way one might a coin—a silver dollar, perhaps—and looked at his wife, who hadn't moved, and said, "Well, that's right. It's my birthday."

"Yes it is," she said, still not moving.

"I'm forty," he said. "You'll be thirty-three, thirty-four next month, right?"

Elise did a little sniff, something not audible, but visible in the quick shift of her shoulders, the rippling of the thin blouse between her lapels. It was a gesture of recognition, note taken of his memory and of the formality suggested by his polite response. "True, but off the point," she said. "You're the birthday boy, and I'm here to help you celebrate." With that, she walked around the corner of the screened-in porch, along the length of the porch to the door, which was also screened, and which was hooked from the inside. Edward got up to unlatch the door.

"It's great to see you, Elise," he said. "Come on in." He noticed that the heels of her boots, tall, narrow heels, were coated with red mud from the yard.

When she came up the steps and onto the porch she had her briefcase clamped under her arm, so that she was able to hug him with only one arm. She kissed the lobe of his ear. "Happy Birthday, Edward."

"You smell funny," he said. "Not bad, I mean, you smell good. But it's like the ocean or something, the beach. You smell like people at the beach. It's nice."

Elise backed away and gave him a cocked-head look as if she didn't quite know how to read his last remark, or as if she were playing like she didn't know how to read his last remark. "I live at the beach now," she said. "I've been living out there for months; I moved out there with Roscoe, you remember Roscoe."

Roscoe was a local newspaperman who had gone back to graduate school and become a psycholinguist. Edward didn't know precisely what a psycholinguist was, that is, he had some idea what a real psycholinguist was, but he doubted whether that's what Roscoe was. He'd had little to do with Roscoe, met him at a couple of parties, gone to dinner with him once, but his impression was that Roscoe was some kind of SyberVision guy. He said, "Oh, the phoneme man. I remember him."

Elise dropped her purse on one of the chairs and walked into the kitchen. "That's right," she said.

Edward could hear her in there, opening and closing cabinets, inspecting the place. "What do you think?" he said.

"I think it looks great," she said. "I'm amazed at how clean you keep it."

Clean was one of Edward's special satisfactions. Since she left he'd grown fond of living alone, fond of solitude, and of the way the house was always clean. It was as if he had done it once since Elise left and ever since then it had remained clean. He remembered seeing a movie in which someone had described Indians as living light on the land, and he imagined himself doing that in this rented house. Nothing was ever out of place. He never moved anything. He was particularly pleased that when he came home from work every afternoon the house was exactly as he had left it that morning. He washed dishes daily, even though there were usually only three or four dishes to wash. He would scrape the leftover food into the trashcan, then rinse the dishes and place them in the new dishwasher, then turn it on and stand in the kitchen and listen. Sometimes he placed plates and knives and glasses in awkward places in the dishwasher, so that when he ran it, the plates and knives and glasses would clank together as the washer went through its cycles.

Edward had always been afraid of being alone, so he was surprised how much he enjoyed it. He did not watch television very often, but when he did, he'd gotten in the habit of using earphones instead of the speakers built into the television cabinet. This made the television program more intimate and, at the same time, allowed Edward to be aware of the quiet house—sitting in his favorite chair, with the long, curled cord leading to the earphones trailed across the room and over the coffee table. Sometimes he would leave one side of the earphones pressed to his ear and the other side slipped off his ear, the better to hear the room around him.

"I mean, it's real nice," Elise said. "It's so . . . clean." She had ventured out of the kitchen to the living room, and from there was moving toward the hall leading to the bedrooms. Edward followed, tagging along behind her. "This is what I'd call immaculate," she said. She looked into the bathroom and shook her head, backed out and flipped the light off and went down the hall to the bedroom that had been theirs. Edward was a little annoyed. There was something about the way she was moving through the place that was condescending, as if he were a child who had kept his room straight, kept all his toys in their proper places, and she were his mother just back from an extremely important bridge game. In the bedroom she checked the spread, fluffed the pillows, picked a curl of red cotton off the otherwise unmarred carpet. She said, "Well, it doesn't look like you need me. Maybe you'd consider coming down and doing my place sometime?"

"Probably not," he said. "Probably Roscoe would have a lot of psycholinguistical papers scattered around, and I'd have to be real careful of those."

"We're just friends," Elise said. "Don't get the wrong idea, I'm not sleeping with him or anything."

"You're living with him, but not sleeping with him."

"That's it."

"So who're you sleeping with?" he said.

"Other people," she said. "We're just friends. I told you already. He likes the beach, I like the beach, we're never there at the same time anyway." She started back through the house for the kitchen; he followed. She said, "What are you worried about? Are you worried that I'm not *yours* anymore?"

"I wouldn't say worried," Edward said. "I was just wondering. I assumed. You've been gone a while."

"Yeah, I know," she said. "A while is a long time. McCord said that. It was very stunning when he said it—we were together, remember?"

They were in the kitchen now. Edward opened the refrigerator and looked in. "Yeah, I remember. We saw that on television together. We were real young then."

Elise came up behind him and looked over his shoulder into the refrigerator, and she reached in and pulled an apple off the bottom shelf. She took a bite of it. "You know, this place is just like it was," she said. "Nothing's changed. Usually when a person leaves, the other person changes everything, but you haven't changed a thing—it's all exactly the way it was when I left. It's real eerie."

"I didn't see anything wrong with it," Edward said. "I mean, I don't use it that much anyway. The only thing I use the living room for is to walk through."

"You watch TV in there, don't you?" she said.

"I guess."

She was standing at the door between the kitchen and the dining room, looking through the dining room at the living room. "Well," she said, "at least you haven't gotten to the closed-drapes stage."

"No, I like them open," he said. "I open them every morning; I open those and the ones in the bedroom and the ones here in the kitchen." He was still looking into the refrigerator. There wasn't much there—some milk, part of a ham, orange juice, diet soda, apples, oranges, and bananas, six different kinds of margarine from a time some weeks before when he decided to test all the different margarines that were available, some rolls that had been in there several months, and a couple of open cans of pineapple. He was glad she hadn't made any remarks about the stuff in the refrigerator.

"The plants are gone," she said. "That's changed."

"They didn't die," he said. "I know you're thinking they died, but they didn't die. They kept dropping leaves all over the place, so I took them out. I had them on the porch and then, well, I don't know, I just didn't want them anymore. I gave them away."

"Who to?" She looked casual and comfortable in the house. Edward was surprised about that.

"Different people. I gave one to this woman who lives next door—you remember her—the old woman. I gave a couple to the Wilkies. That wasn't much fun. They came over here, both of them, on Saturday, one Saturday morning, and, I don't know . . ."

Elise shook her head. "Susan Wilkie, that's a great choice," she said. "What, you chose the recipients on the basis of breast size?"

Edward rubbed his eyes with the palms of his hands, laughing slightly. When he looked up Elise was smiling, too. "Well," he said, doing a kind of clownish shrug. "That wasn't the only consideration."

She finished her apple and went directly to the garbage, a brown grocery sack in the cabinet under the sink. "So here's what I think," she said, dropping the core into the sack. "I think I ought to clean up, take a shower, change some clothes. Then I think we ought to start having our party. I think we ought to go out for dinner, then maybe catch a movie. Is there anything on here?" She thought about that a minute. "Never mind. I've probably already seen whatever's on here. Maybe a movie's a bad idea."

"So you're staying overnight?" Edward said.

"Sure. We're husband and wife, aren't we? We're mates, aren't we? We're partners."

She was watching him to see how he reacted to this idea. He was trying not to give anything away.

She said, "We don't have to sleep together, if you don't want to. I can sleep in the guest bedroom."

"That's not a problem," he said. "That's not what I'm thinking of."

"What then?" she said.

"I was trying to remember what we did on my last birthday."

"We started to have a party, and then at the last minute you got upset and made me call everybody and tell them not to come. Don't you remember?"

"That doesn't sound like me," he said. "What did I get upset about?"

"I don't remember," she said.

While Elise was taking her shower, Edward sat on the porch and ate Oreos and drank milk and scanned the headlines in his magazine. His attention wasn't focused on the magazine, however, because he kept thinking about the way things had been when he and Elise had lived together. He remembered pleasant things and awful things in about equal measure. And he remembered feeling numb when she left. It wasn't as if they were really breaking up, as if the marriage were over, it was just that she wanted to work down there, and he couldn't leave his job, so they agreed to have this very modern relationship, and both of them were supposed to be satisfied with it. For his part it hadn't been particularly unsatisfactory. He had been bored and lonely and sad from time to time, but for the most part he was content with their long-distance relationship, content knowing he had a wife and that she was down there somewhere, out of town, working. The Roscoe development, which she had mentioned casually and then described as a friendship, didn't even bother him. He was surprised at his lack of interest in her. It wasn't that he didn't like her, or that he wasn't glad to see her, it was just that it was so peculiar to have her there.

When he went into the kitchen to put the cookies away, he could hear the shower running, hear her bumping into the wall occasionally as she turned in the tub. He went into the living room and stood at the front window, looking across the street at the ranch-style house there. There were three cars in the driveway, two BMWs and a Toyota. Then he looked up and down the street and in every driveway there were two or three or four cars, all relatively new, all clean, all glittering in the late afternoon light. The lawns were all carefully cut, and there were a few young trees, stark and elegant, waving a little with the breeze. A couple of houses down, three little girls, about five or six, were having a picnic on a bedspread on the lawn in front of the front door of their house. One guy, farther down the block, had some kind of hot rod in his front yard, and he was out working on it, working under the hood. Edward noticed a newspaper in the front yard of the house across the street and checked to see if his own newspaper had arrived. It had. A couple of front doors of houses had small advertising pieces attached to their doorknobs. Things from Pizza Hut. There had been one on his front door when he got home from work. Moving to the edge of the window and looking out parallel to the street, he could see the crooked stop sign at the end of the block. Mr. Orvatis, a neighbor when Edward and Elise moved in, had piled his 1953 Cadillac into the stop sign on a wet night in December en route to the St. Michael's school dance with four just-teenaged kids aboard—a small neighborhood scandal. Nobody was hurt. Mr. Orvatis was not asked to drive again.

Edward did not often stand at the front window and watch the neighborhood, but when he did, it was usually in the hope of seeing some of the neighborhood women, housewives, either carefully made up and carefully dressed and headed out for a shopping trip or a bridge game, or very casually dressed, jeans or shorts and T-shirts, playing with children, carrying in groceries, or working in gardens. Or running. The neighborhood women were given to running.

Elise appeared in the doorway behind him, the door between the living room and the hall. She had a towel wrapped around her and her hair was sparkling with water. She said, "Are my clothes still in my closet? I didn't bring anything except what I was wearing."

"In your closet, just like you left them."

For some reason, the sight of his wife nearly naked made him nervous. She was young and still quite pretty, even sexy, but he wasn't at all attracted to her. On the contrary, he was slightly repelled. He wished she had stayed in the hallway, out of sight, when she asked about her clothes. He had not really looked at her, just glanced, and then looked down at a pale square of light that was on the tan carpet in the living room. He started looking around left to right, trying to find out where the light had come from. This was odd since the only window in the room was the one he was standing in front of, and it was obvious that the light had come from that window. But the sun was going down at the back of the house, not the front, so this was a reflection of something, and he was trying to figure out what.

When she disappeared back into the hall, Edward moved over between the window and the square of light on the floor and intercepted the light, putting a shadow in it, and then sighted back up along what he took to be a line from the box on the floor through himself. He looked out the window trying to find the source of the reflection. What he found was an upstairs window in a two-story house, two houses down from the house across the street from him. He could not see anything in that window, only the brightness of the sun going down behind his house.

When Elise came out she was dressed in white shorts and a turquoise pullover shirt with a lot of beading on the front. An old shirt. She said, "Look what I found."

"A shirt," he said.

"Yeah, I know it's a shirt," she said, "but look what shirt it is. Don't you remember this shirt? This is my sixties shirt. I wore this shirt the night we went to the concert in Tulsa, don't you remember? Richie Havens, Country Joe and the Fish—all those guys."

"That was before we were married," Edward said. "I don't remember anything before we were married. The minute we got married, I forgot everything that happened before that."

She gave him a *that's real cute* look and went back into the hall, heading for the bedroom. Over her shoulder she said, "We can't go anyplace too formal. I don't feel too formal anyway."

They went to a barbecue restaurant in a nearby strip shopping center, a place called Smokey's, where they had eaten often when they were together. It was a small storefront about the size of a two-car garage, a counter running down one side, half a dozen cheap plastic booths on the other. There were a lot of windows in this place. Smokey was a pallid little guy in his mid-fifties who looked as if he ought to be selling eyewear in some mall optical shop. He insisted on coming out from behind the counter to give Elise a hello hug.

"Well, it's amazing," Smokey said. "You look amazing. What are you doing? You let him go around all the time by himself." Smokey poked Edward in the arm while saying this.

"How's Mrs. Smokey?" Elise said. She looked around the little restaurant. "Where is she anyway?"

"She's at art class over at the museum," Smokey said. He kind of shrugged and rolled his eyes at the same time, but somehow it seemed as if the two gestures weren't properly coordinated. "She's taken up art. She's going to be an artist."

"My brother says everybody wants to be an artist," Edward said.

"Your brother says everybody *is* an artist," Elise said.

Smokey laughed and patted each of them another time or two and then went around behind the counter and started cleaning his fingernails with a toothpick he picked up off the cash register ledge. "So," he said, "what's it going to be?"

"I want a sliced beef and a double order of beans," Elise said. "I've been thinking about your beans for six months."

"Same for me," Edward said. He and Elise took two of the red-topped stools at the counter, pulling napkins out of the dispenser to clean off the countertop.

Smokey moved over to the side and unlatched one of the big metal ovens and pulled out a slab of beef. He dropped the beef on a cutting board right in front of Edward and Elise and then started hacking at the meat with a knife as big as his forearm. "Yeah," he said. "She saw this show on TV. Next thing I know she's making these little things and leaving them around the house. Papier-mâché things. Clay things. One day I wake up and she's got all the furniture in the middle of the room, all the backs of the chairs to each other, everything facing out. I don't know. She said she was trying to disturb the space. She told me that's what art's all about, disturbing the space."

"Well, that's one way to look at it," Elise said.

"I wish she'd come back here and disturb the space in the kitchen," Smokey said, waving a knife toward the back of the room.

Elise did a little eye roll. "Yeah, she's a woman."

Smokey jumped back from the counter and held up his hands, one empty and the other waving the big knife, all this in mock apology. "Oh, don't get me wrong. She can disturb the space out here and I'll disturb the space back in the kitchen, it doesn't matter to me, one or the other, either way; I'll be the woman."

"Don't put any pickles on mine, will you?" Edward said.

Smokey was back at the meat again. "So where have you been?" he said to Elise. "Really."

"Here and there," she said. "I've been out of town a lot."

Smokey gave them a look, going from one to the other and then back again, and then nodded as if he knew what was being said. "Going for a trial sep," he said. "I get it. Me and Marge tried that in seventy-eight or seventy-seven. She went to live with her sister in a house trailer out on Camphor Lake. You know Camphor Lake?"

Edward and Elise shook their heads.

"I don't know," Smokey said. He was finished with their sandwiches by now and working on the beans. "It's this tiny place about fourteen miles out. West of here. You go down this unmarked road off Highway 59 and about two miles into the brush you come to this little junker of a hole. It's really dismal out there. There're about three trailers right next to each other and that's it. They got this lake that's about the size of a parking lot and about a foot and a half deep. They got seven fish in this lake, and every one of them's got a lot of scars in its lips where hooks were pulled out after it was caught and returned to the sea." He shook his head and snorted. Smokey slid two beat-up brown plates across the counter, stopping one in front of Edward, the other in front of Elise, and reached under the counter and pulled up two sets of silver, each tightly wrapped in a paper napkin. "Who wants a drink?" he said. He was already heading for a glass-faced cooler at the back of the restaurant.

"You got a root beer?" Edward said.

"I got a Barq's, Triple XXX, and a Hires," Smokey said. "But the Hires has been here about four years, so I don't recommend it."

Edward had a Barq's. He sat and listened to Elise and Smokey talk over old times, times when the four of them had gone out together, times when Smokey and Marge had come over for dinner, times when they had cooked out in the backyard of Elise and Edward's house. Smokey and Marge were a good ten years older than Edward, and Edward was almost ten years older than Elise, but they'd become friends anyway. Smokey had been, at that time, a not very successful art director for a not very successful advertising agency, a small agency, dealing mostly in local real estate developments. He'd been doing that for twenty years when Edward met him in the parking lot outside the apartments where they both lived then. Edward had been in his apartment at his window looking out over the parking lot when he saw this guy down below scrambling back and forth over the top of a Pontiac. He seemed to be drawing on it with a black crayon. Edward had called Elise to the window. "Look," he had said. "This guy out here—what do you suppose he's doing?"

"Looks like he's drawing a hamburger on the top of his car," Elise said.

"Yeah, I know," Edward said, "but . . ."

He watched the guy on and off all day. He watched the woman who brought the guy beer. He watched the drawing on top of the Pontiac take shape. By five o'clock in the afternoon, it was clear the drawing was not of a hamburger, but of some other kind of sandwich on a bun. It was a sketch, an outline drawing, a top view. The guy who had been doing the drawing was Smokey, and the woman who had been helping was Marge. Both climbed up on the trunk of the car and stood there looking at the drawing Smokey had done on the roof. They stood there on the trunk of the car, arm in arm, having a little trouble keeping their balance, and talked about what was on the roof. It was a sesame-seed bun; you could see the seeds on top of it. They stood there on the trunk of the car about twenty minutes and drank the remaining beer, and then went inside.

When they'd been gone about thirty minutes, Edward went downstairs and out into the parking lot and, on pretense of taking a casual walk out there, took a closer look at the drawing. He was a little nervous about going closer, because he didn't know where the guy lived in the apartments, he didn't know whether the guy could see his car from the apartment he lived in. He couldn't make much more of the drawing up close than he could from the window. At close range, from eye level, it didn't look like much at all.

The next morning Edward was at the window by eight-thirty. The guy was already on top of his car, but now he had paint. As the day went on, the drawing became a painting of a barbecue sandwich. It was a good likeness. About noon Edward went downstairs. The guy in the parking lot was sitting on the trunk of a car eating a piece of fried chicken off a paper plate. Edward introduced himself and said, "So. What're you doing, putting a sandwich on there? What's that, a barbecue sandwich?"

"Yep," the guy said. "Barbecue. I'm devoted to barbecue." He pointed at Edward with the chicken leg, sighting along it, as if he were going to throw it.

"I've been watching you from up here," Edward said, pointing to his apartment window. "It looks great from up there. Yesterday I wasn't sure what kind of sandwich it was."

"I saw you up there," Smokey said.

"So, what's the deal?" Edward said. "I mean, I don't mean to pry."

"I'm thinking of going into barbecue," Smokey said. "Right now I'm in advertising. I've been in advertising for twenty years, and I don't like it. I mean, parts of it are OK, they're just not my parts, know what I mean?"

Edward laughed. "Yeah, I know what you mean."

"Some of the other parts are pretty good," Smokey said. "They're the fun parts; I don't get to do those parts. What I get to do is this stuff with pictures of houses. I do the houses, you know, the houses you see in advertisements every Sunday in the paper. I do those."

So Edward spent his Sunday afternoon sitting on the curb watching this man painting a barbecue sandwich on the roof of his Pontiac. And Smokey turned out to be a nice guy, a little forlorn, a little sad, and oddly religious, but still more interesting than most of the people Edward knew.

They became friends. They had a lot of dinners together. Elise and Marge went shopping together. And on late nights around the dinner table, the four of them figured out just what were the chances of success if Marge and Smokey did what they wanted to do, which was open a barbecue joint. After a while the friendship had cooled somewhat, but the plan hadn't. Smokey had invited Edward to invest in the project, become a partner, but Edward had declined. In October, with a small black crucifix carefully out of sight in the kitchen, Smokey had opened his barbecue joint, and Edward and Elise became his first customers. The dollar bill that even now hung badly framed behind the counter was the dollar that Edward had used to pay for the first barbecue beef sandwich that Smokey had ever sold.

Edward stabbed his last couple of beans with his fork and thought how odd it was that Smokey was no more successful as a restaurateur than as an advertising artist. He wondered how Smokey felt about that now, several years later.

"Hey," Smokey said. He was wagging his knife at Edward. "Hey. So how do you like living alone these days, huh? Doing OK?"

"I don't get enough barbecue," Edward said.

"Hey, that's not my fault," Smokey said. "You can come over here anytime, you know what I'm saying?"

Edward smiled at him and nodded. "Thanks," he said, "but I don't get out that much."

"I don't think he ever goes out," Elise said. "When I went in the house today it was as if I'd never left—nothing's changed."

Edward said, "I should have been a domestic."

"You can do my place," Smokey said. "Marge used to do it all the time, but, you know, she's older now, and she doesn't do much of that. Besides, she's an artist. Artists don't vacuum."

2

IN THE car on the way home Elise was cold. Edward saw the goose bumps on her legs as they passed under the street lights, but he didn't turn off the car air conditioner. He thought it was stupid of her to wear shorts this late in the fall. In fact, during dinner there were many things that Elise had done that Edward hadn't liked. He didn't like her voice sometimes, the way she sounded when she was talking, smoking. The shrillness of it. The artificial excitement. The giggling. The way she sat on her stool. He'd spent some time looking at her skin, and little bits of bra. He thought it was tacky when other women let their underclothes show inadvertently, or not so inadvertently, without particular sexual intent, but the same tiny indiscretion in Elise made him loathe her, made him think her tasteless, sloppy, unfit. When they had lived together, he'd given her great lectures about propriety. She'd said he was a prude. He'd said it wasn't a question of prudishness, it was a question of taste. He said he had no objection to the artful display of underwear. This was a running argument that went on for years, reappearing and disappearing. He once even went so far as to get a Polaroid and take flash shots of the fragments of her underwear that showed. He made her bend over and pretend to pick something off the floor, or reach to get a book from a high shelf, and made her hold the pose while he got into position and snapped off a Polaroid. When they were out shopping he would point out women whose underclothes were all too apparent, women with too much cup, or brightly striped bikini underwear under thin white pants. Later, when Elise bought only long-sleeved blouses, and pinned the fronts of her shirts very high close to her neck, it became a kind of game for them, a parody of *Glamour* magazine's dos and don'ts. The care she took in dressing, finally, and the consistency she showed in hewing to the prescribed mode, eventually convinced him that she had internalized his views. So seeing her tonight, right back where she started from, was doubly unpleasant. This is what Edward was thinking as they were driving down Beautician Street, heading for the yogurt store.

"Remember when we used to just drive around?" Elise said.

Edward looked over at her and smiled, nodding. "Sure," he said. "Why did we do that?"

For Edward this question contained an unmistakable sense of loss and regret, brought back to mind all the lovely fall evenings when the two of them, fresh from fully equipped jobs and apartments and cars, all duly acquired and operational, the usual middle-class *amenities* covered, when the two of them, thus situated, would go out of a weekday evening, say around five, in the early fall, together in the car, a cream-colored Alfa Romeo Spider that Elise had acquired by luck from an uncle who had a taste for the Italian, and they would drive around, the two of them, as if they owned the joint. They drove mostly in the suburbs, where all the houses were alike, and all the office buildings were middle-sized and clad in green or bronze-tinted glass, and the shopping centers were new, with pristine asphalt and bright yellow parking spines patterning the smooth black lots like erratic backbones. They circled aimlessly through these sections of the city, sometimes silent, sometimes deep in conversation about "their relationship."

It was a thing they always liked to do—talk about their relation-ship. What he felt and what she felt. What she thought he meant by some remark he had made the day before. How she'd reacted when he gave her the extra bacon that morning. And finally, of course, how she felt about him, how he felt about her, hundreds of minutes of proclamations. There was contentment in those drives, a sense of

a world properly ordered, appropriately in control, and at bay.
Edward liked looking at the homes they passed, homes where small
hopes had been effectively met, thinking of himself both as an
integral part of that world, of having a home like that himself,
where the warm yellow light from the interior laced the edges of
the leaves of the chinaberry tree that stood just outside the glass,
and somehow, too, as a glider in that world, a planetary traveler
with no exceptional powers or capacities, and every good intention.
And often after they had driven for an hour or two through the
suburban neighborhoods, the mall lots, with their nice young
saplings popped into high curbed holes, in a way that reminded
him of vacuum-sealed toys—ray guns and Masters of the Universe
momentarily pinned like crazy butterflies on little sheets of cardboard with rounded corners, and hung like keys on pegboard
stands in K marts and K & B's—then they might drive straight out
of the city, into the pine-lined countryside where, if they were
lucky, some striking golden tree might break the green, or a brown
horse standing in a field alone might look up from its food to
whinny as they passed.

"Excuse me," Elise said. "What is it you're doing over there,
exactly?"

"Who, me?" Edward said. He was startled, caught, but pretended to hide it. "Nothing," he said. "I was thinking."

"You hate women, don't you?" she said. "I always knew you
hated women. I can tell."

Edward took both hands off the wheel and held them up in front
of him, Christlike. "Women? You're a woman aren't you? Do I hate
you?"

"Yes," Elise said. She was looking out the window on her side of
the car, looking at the worn-out shops with their dim lights in the
strip shopping center they were passing.

Edward watched her looking then looked himself at a water-bed
outlet, a candy shop, a very narrow Radio Shack with a fallen sale
sign strung between the brick columns in front of it. At the end of
the building there was a laundromat filled with a kind of pea-green

light that gave the place a swampy look. A couple of shapeless mothers read magazines while their boy children in striped T-shirts wandered in and out of the open doors. And there was one black guy, tall and thin, folding his clothes at center stage. "I love you," Edward said. "I've always loved you; I'll always love you. There's nothing I can do about it."

"That's bullshit," Elise said. "If you loved me, you wouldn't have let me leave."

"You wanted to leave," he said. "You hated it here, remember?"

"It's not that bad," she said.

"It's not that different," he said.

"I'm coming back," she said. "Maybe I'm coming back."

Edward stopped at an intersection, and they watched a flatbed truck with huge pieces of sheet steel, maybe forty feet long, go by in front of them. When the truck was gone, there wasn't any other traffic. Edward looked both ways and then ran the light. There was a time just after she left when he hoped she'd come back. He hoped her job would blow up in her face. He hoped she would fail. He remembered sitting on the couch in the darkened living room of their house for hours at a stretch, smoking cigarettes and keeping an eye on the white telephone that sat on the pass-through from the kitchen. He wanted her back then. He wanted her to need him to help her order her life. What bothered him most about her departure, about her not being there, was not the affection that he missed, not the attention, not even the company, but the idea that she was able to do it alone, that she could pay the bills and lock the house and close the blinds and get the car taken care of, that she could arrange the furniture and install the mini-blinds and tighten the little knobs on the kitchen cabinets. That without his help she could pick the movies she wanted to go to, decide what shows on television were worth seeing, hook up all the electronic gear satisfactorily, hang the pictures and deal with the Orkin man, and get the guy in to do the floor, and add and subtract with precision, and without his direction or advice. What bothered him was that she was separate from him, not, as he would have previously thought, had he thought about it, which he had not, a part of himself, a wing of his operation, subject in all things to his final OK.

That went on for months—the sitting, the smoking, the watching. Most of that time he was filled with loathing, as if she were an unpleasant and uncontrollable child. He was surprised by the intensity of this loathing. Once in a while, in those days, he let her see a little of it in telephone conversations when he snapped at her about one subject or another, but more often, he stuck with the party line, the sympathetic, caring, understanding Edward—"Yes, Elise. Whatever you think. I think you're doing the right thing." He wanted her to know how he felt, but he didn't want to have to tell her. If he had to tell her, then her response could not be genuine. He had been playing, in those days, a tough game, tougher than he was able to play these months later.

"You want to know how I know you don't love me?" Elise said. "I know because you don't want to make love to me. You haven't wanted to make love to me for a long time. Even when you made love to me you didn't want to make love to me."

"Sure I did," he said. "I liked making love to you. You were all right."

"We made love three times in the twelve months before I left," she said. "I have it on the calendar in my checkbook, I circled the dates."

"That isn't true. I'm sure it's not true," Edward said.

He wasn't sure at all. In fact, while the number might have been changed for rhetorical effect, the substance of her point was accurate. He didn't want to make love to her. He hadn't for a long time, but it had taken him years to decide that if you didn't want to make love it was better not to, even if in so doing you risked everything. Even if you made the other person feel unwanted, unloved, unattractive, sexually inadequate, emotionally cut off. He'd had lots of arguments with himself about it, telling himself that he ought to go ahead and do it, that he ought to just bite the bullet, close his eyes, fantasize, do what was necessary, and for a while he had done that, carried on as if it were for him an important part of their life together. But finally it had seemed more important to be able to tell her the truth. What it had come to was that it was more loving, more intimate not to make love to her than it was to do it when he wasn't much interested.

"You're crazy," Elise said. "You know that? You're just crazy."

"OK, I admit it. I'm crazy. We only made love three times in the last year we were together. I remember each and every one of those times. They were OK. They weren't the highlights of my life for that year, but they were OK. I'm not sure there were any highlights in my life that year."

"Poor baby. Poor, self-indulgent baby," Elise said.

Edward snorted and shook his head. "So I guess if I made love to you three thousand times a year you wouldn't have left town, is that right? Is that what you're saying?"

"No, that's not right," she said. "I'd have left anyway. I hate making love. Unless I can do it with a fifteen-year-old, I hate it."

"Oh, great," Edward said. "I really want to be in this conversation at this time. I've been looking forward to this all day long."

"Well," she said. "You're not going to get me on the soft shit anymore. If you don't want to make love to me, you don't have to. There are plenty of people out here who want to make love to me. That's not a problem."

"Yeah," he said. "I know them, they all work at the gas station."

She was quiet a second, then said, "Why don't we just go to the yogurt store and forget it, OK?" She pointed out the front window. "Why are you going this way, anyway? The yogurt store isn't this way. The yogurt store is on the other side of town, on Beagle."

"Moved," he said.

They rode in silence for a couple of miles, each looking out the window, watching the side of the street. It was a cool night, damp in the air, but not raining. Not even about to rain. Elise reached to roll down her side window, then found the electric window push button built into the armrest. He wondered if she was thinking how pretty things looked, how clean everything was, and if she regretted the conversation, the way it was going, and wished she'd never said anything about his not loving her. What she'd said about fifteen-year-olds was a joke between them, but there was truth in it. She'd had a couple of younger men and, while they weren't very satisfying emotionally, or intellectually, or *spiritually,* as she had said, in bed they were terrific. They had made her feel younger and more alive and more a part of the world, if only temporarily. They had made her feel as if she could watch MTV with impunity. But the young men had not done much for her heart.

Her last such affair had been with a graduate student in journalism who was given to writing long and excruciating essays in the school newspaper about the parking problem on campus. About the unfairness of it. About the inequalities in the distribution of the parking stickers. She'd told Edward all about it. David wanted her to move in with him, but he lived in a garage. It didn't occur to him that she might not want to live in a garage, that she might already be beyond garage life. It embarrassed her a little that she was so comfortable with David, that she could talk to him, that she felt with him that she was with her own kind. It bothered her to think that that was the kind she was—a little bit slow, a little bit earnest, and a little bit ordinary. She hadn't moved in with him. She hadn't even considered, for more than a few minutes, moving in with him. When she finally told him no, she wasn't going to move in with him, he offered to move in with her. She gave him a little handwritten note that said, "Miss Elise regrets that she is unable to do what is so kindly suggested." Left that note on the windshield of David's car one morning as she was leaving his garage. He didn't think it was funny. In fact, he came over to her house that evening and got her out of the shower and sat down for a serious talk in the bathroom. During this talk she opened a brand-new bar of soap, lemon-scented, and thought about Edward. Later, she called him on the phone to tell him about the end of her affair.

He was polite, cool, vacantly supportive. He'd told her about his one encounter during her absence, a woman he picked up in a restaurant. She worked there. He'd written her a note on the check, on the MasterCard bill, leaving his telephone number. She called.

They went out. She was a young girl, a freshman at the university. They had a long dinner at a restaurant Elise and Edward used to go to, and then they came back to the house. She'd gone into the bathroom and then called Edward to tell him she needed to borrow pants. She'd started her period during dinner. Edward had given her one of Elise's skirts. He'd reported that he was pleased when, after he suggested they make love, the girl declined, and he took her home. She promised to return the skirt at their next meeting, but there wasn't a next meeting. The skirt came in the mail two weeks later. Elise had laughed when she thought of the lack of ardor with which Edward must have pressed his case.

"Remember the girl," he said. "The one I picked up in that restaurant, the one that had so much trouble?"

"Like it was yesterday," Elise said. "The way you told that story, it was so awful. The poor girl. I mean, here she was, the lady in red, the mystery woman, your special angel, Edward. And you guys go out, and bang!"

"She was just a young girl," Edward said. "I felt sorry for her."

"You felt relieved," Elise said. "You may have felt sorry for her, but before that you felt relieved."

"True," Edward said. He nodded, giving Elise a sheepish grin. "I was off the hook. She was a nice girl. I wonder what ever happened to her."

"She probably went into nursing," Elise said. She looked up at the headliner of the car and put her hand on her forehead. "God, please forgive me for that. I don't know what got into me," she said.

There was more silence. They passed a shut-down barbecue place and a Shell gas station that was wall-to-wall stereo equipment inside. Two guys in Bermudas and floral-print shirts and straw hats with wide brims were in there being given the business by a small Indian fellow in brown slacks and a white short-sleeved shirt and a tie. Edward lowered his window just as they got caught by a red light about two blocks from the yogurt store. The air was thick and pasty. Edward said, "I think she was already in nursing." He stared out the windshield of the car, focused somewhere in the distance. "I think she told me that."

A minute later Elise had to tell him the light had changed. He got off to a jerky start and then changed lanes to be over on the right, where the yogurt franchise was. Elise said, "I don't think I want any yogurt. You want some?"

"Well," Edward said. "We're here."

"I don't know what's wrong with you, Edward," Elise said. She was slumped in her seat, her hands in her lap. "I mean, this girl was good-looking, right? What was her name, I forgot her name."

"Her name was Susan, and yes, she was pretty, and I was afraid if I touched her she would explode. Or I would explode. Somebody would explode. And then I'd have to clean up the mess."

Elise shook her head and let out a theatrical sigh. "You're a sick one, Edward."

"No, I mean a psychological mess," he said. "I wasn't talking about a mess mess."

She made retching noises. "Neither was I."

"Oh." He did a little closed-mouth parody of a smile. "I see," he said. "Well . . ." He slapped her bare leg. "Let's go in here and get some yogurt, what do you say? There's a girl in here that I'm really in love with. You'll like her. Come on."

He was out of the car quickly, and she a little less quickly. "Is this first-degree love, or what?"

"Absolutely," he said. He made a pumping motion with his arm by his side, pumping it back and forth like the arms that join the wheels of steam locomotives. "This is a major find for your husband."

"My husband," she said, hopping the curb. She made some kind of nasal noise and wagged her arms in a mimicked dizziness. "I think we'd better report our relationship to Guinness," she said.

At two o'clock that morning, Edward was standing at the bedroom window smoking a cigarette and looking out at the street. There wasn't much there to see. He had a towel wrapped around his waist. Elise was in bed asleep. He listened to her breathing and watched the tip of his cigarette out of the corner of his eye. A dog went by on the street, a black dog, trotting. As he watched, two cars pulled up. Then a third. Then a fourth. The street was suddenly a fiesta of headlights and taillights, backup lights, interior lights, blinkers. People started piling out of these cars. Tall, young people. Out of one car, four boys, out of another car, two girls, out of a third car, two more girls and another guy. They had the street nearly blocked. They were laughing and talking and punching each other on the arm, having a great time. It sounded as if a couple of cars had their radios tuned to the same station and turned up loud. The group, about ten strong, gathered in between the cars, sitting on the front fenders, chatting, laughing. Edward watched these people and wondered why they had chosen this particular spot to park. There was a streetlight nearby, but they weren't directly under it. They did not seem to be going into any of the houses on this block. And the way they had their cars in disarray, blocking the street, it looked as if they weren't going to stay long.

Up and down the street his neighbors had their lights out. There was a half-moon, bright in the sky, with one dusty gray cloud near it. He stepped away from the window a moment to put his cigarette out, and when he returned, the cars were pulling away. There was a kid kneeling in front of the last car, pretending to pray for his life. The others in that car yelled at this guy to get out of the street, to get into the car, but he didn't move. He just knelt there like a martyr, a saint, his hands pressed together and raised in prayer, his eyes toward heaven. Somebody pushed himself half out the window and yelled at this guy, pretending to be angry. The driver of the car did a couple of little jerks, letting the car roll an inch or two and then slamming on the brakes, making the car rock like a teeter-totter. It didn't have any effect on the kid in the street, he just knelt there. The driver flicked his high beams a couple of times and let the car slide forward until it just barely touched the kid kneeling in the street. No movement from the kid. There was a lot of yelling going on, waving of beer cans out the window. The guy riding in the

front passenger seat had the door open, and he was draped half in
and half out of the car. He had himself hooked up on the car
window like somebody on the edge of a pool after a difficult swim.
The driver let the car jerk forward and bump the kneeling kid, but
it bumped him much harder than the driver intended. It was
enough to make the kneeler break his pose for a second, but no
more. There was some yelling inside the car, some argument. Then
the driver put the car in neutral and gunned the engine. The car
wobbled a little, left to right. Then the taillights flickered and held a
steady bright red as the driver dropped the car into gear and let the
engine rev up against the brakes. At almost the same time, light
came on in two different houses across the street. The car inched
forward, and the guy in the street bent over backward as the
bumper pressed against him. Edward saw Wilson, or Watson—the
guy who lived across the street, two houses down—come out in
the front yard in his robe. Suddenly the brake lights went out, the
car jumped forward, there was a scream. Wilson or Watson started
running toward the street. Edward said, "Oh, shit." Reaching for
the telephone, he knocked over the lamp on the night table. Elise
woke up.

"What's going on?" she said.

"The guy got run over," he said. "I'm calling the police."

There was a lot of yelling outside now, people were running
around in the street, the other cars were back and car doors were
opening and closing, people were coming out of their houses.
Some kids were in front of the car, trying to lift it off the guy who
had been kneeling in the street. Watson or Wilson was there pitch-
ing in. The driver was still in the driver's seat, humped over the
wheel. Somebody was yelling at him to come out and help. Then
there were four of them at the bumper. They got the car lifted up
pretty well, although not off its tires. They rolled it backward, off
the kid in the street, who was just lying there now.

Edward gave his name and address, twice, to the guy who
answered the 911 hot line. Then he tried to explain what had
happened. "These kids were messing around, and one of them got

run over," Edward said into the phone. "It looks like they got the car off him. But he isn't moving. You're calling the ambulance, right?"

Elise was half standing, half kneeling at the edge of the window looking out. "Jesus Christ," she said.

Edward had to stay on the phone while the guy on the other end did something, and as he stood there he watched out the window, then shifted his focus to watch Elise watching out the window. In a couple of seconds he realized he was staring at her breast, her right breast, the one she always said was smaller. From that angle—he was behind her and to the right, he had her in silhouette—it looked quite large. Without thinking, he said, "Have you been doing something to your breasts?"

"What?" she said.

"Isn't that your smaller breast, there?" he said. "The right one? I was just asking if you had been doing something to them to make them, you know, bigger."

"What are you talking about?" she said. "You're crazy. There's somebody out here almost dead, and you're talking about my tits?"

Edward raised his arms in a gesture indicating he didn't know what he was saying either, in the process taking the phone away from his ear. "Right," he said. "What's happening now? Is anything happening?"

Elise got up from the window and came toward him, cupping her hands underneath her breasts parody-*Playboy* style. "No," she said. "Nothing's happening out there. Somebody just got run over out there, but it's nothing. My friend Edward is interested in my tits. They're real big and tender and sweaty." She was right next to him now, holding her breasts so that her nipples brushed against his bare chest.

He backed away quick, skirting her to the length of the telephone cord.

She started doing some kind of sexy dance to an imaginary rock 'n' roll tune. Lots of shoulder movement and hip movement and pelvic action.

Edward covered up the mouthpiece of the telephone and said, "Who's crazy now? Would you quit it?" He pointed toward the window. "What's going on out there now?"

"We don't know and we don't care," Elise said. "Come on. Fourth time's a charm." She was coming toward him again, and he was backing up, stepping up onto the seat of a chair. The room was mostly dark, but because of the window there was a kind of pearly light coming in from outside. It was like a blue-white glaze on her skin, coming from behind her, outlining her calves, her thighs, her butt, the curve from her hip to her waist, her breasts, the strong roll of her shoulder, and the gentle rise of her neck.

Elise continued her parody of sensual dance but at least stayed on the floor. The guy on the phone came back and asked Edward for his name and address, and Edward gave it for the third time, then hung up, but stayed in the chair. He stood there, the telephone hanging at his side, and watched his wife. He had two ideas: the first was that Elise was very attractive, the second was that her dance was not. It wasn't that the dance was cheap, nor that it was a sex joke she was using to make fun of him, to suggest his sexual world was garbage, his sexual tastes infantile. She was doing that, but that wasn't what bothered him. And it wasn't that she didn't do the sex part well. She did. But as he watched her hips sway, and her breasts bob up and down like odd, asymmetrical balls, as he watched the wispy translucent light curve across her skin, what he wanted was the body without the head. Without the face, without the eyes looking at him. In order to take sexual pleasure in the scene, he had to divorce himself from Elise, from their past. As he watched her dancing in front of him, he could not forget who she was, what she was to him, he could not forget that she was watching him watch her, watching his reactions, watching his face, his eyes, his mouth—he couldn't give up control of his own face, couldn't put it out of mind, and maintaining the control meant forgoing the sexual pleasure of her performance. He couldn't forget that she was back after six months, that it was Elise there dancing for him. He couldn't escape her *her-ness*. Things they had done together—arguments, and talk, caring, her needs and his, all the ideas, the moments of heartbreak and hatred, all the opinions, all the fights, all the affections—all these things were the subject of this dance. It was like a key to their entire relationship, inviting yet forbidding, lovely and sexy, and yet mean, mean-spirited, silly in a lovely way, and at the same time silly in a way that wasn't lovely, that was cheap and ignorant. There they were, sometime past midnight, sometime in the early morning hours, and outside some too-tough-to-be-believed kid had just been sat on by a car, accidentally, and they were inside, behind the junked-up brick walls of a rented tract home, and the wife was there dancing, playing with herself, and he was up in a chair talking to the police on the telephone.

"OK," Edward said. "That's it. Let's get the clothes on. You can quit now. We have to go out there, you know that, right? Elise?"

"What if I don't want to go?" she said. "What if I want to stand here and rub my nipples between my fingers like stiff little chicken hearts—"

She froze, her hands poised near her breasts, and she looked down at her nipples and then looked at Edward. Her shoulders slumped, the tenseness in her body dissipated. She stood a moment longer, then shuffled over to the bed and sat down on its edge. "Did I say that? Did I say 'chicken hearts'?"

Edward got down off the chair. "I'll get your robe," he said. "It's OK. It's really OK."

3

THEY HAD a meeting in the living room. Edward brought the robe and then they got Diet Cokes from the kitchen and went in and sat looking out the large window at the proceedings. The ambulance had cut its siren at the end of the block, rolling silently down the street to get the kid. It was one of those old-fashioned ambulances, the kind that look like hearses. There were a couple of police cars with their flashing blue lights. Edward had pulled the curtains on the picture window, and Elise sat cross-legged on the couch drinking her Diet Coke, smoking a cigarette, and gazing out at the scene. After a few minutes she said, "It's gorgeous, it's really gorgeous."

Edward said, "I know. It's horrible, but it is."

"I love it," Elise said. "I wonder how he is."

"I thought I saw him moving a minute ago," Edward said. "I saw his arms moving."

"That's a good sign."

"Yeah."

"Didn't crack his spine," Elise said. "What, was he running across the street or something? How fast was the guy going?"

"Oh, that's right," Edward said. "You didn't see it. No, what happened was that the kid was kneeling in the street. I mean, he was a kid out of the car, and they were messing around. They had stopped there. This kid went and knelt in the street in front of the car. They just nudged over him."

"Nudged?" Elise didn't take her eyes off the scene out the window, just nodded and blew smoke into the air. "Oh," she said. She carefully rounded the burning end of her cigarette in a large ashtray she held in her lap. "So, why was he kneeling there?"

"I don't know," Edward said. "Mercy, I guess."

"Drama," she said.

Edward rattled the last bit of soda in his soft-drink can. Outside they had the kid on a stretcher, and a little herd of people was moving toward the ambulance. Watson or Wilson, the neighbor, was on this side of the street, his back to Edward and Elise, standing with his hands on his hips watching the proceedings. Just outside the colorful front doors of the houses across the street, in the bright porch lights, there were women in housecoats.

"I like to watch bad weather on TV," Elise said. "It's even better on TV than in real life. Sometimes I wish they would just broadcast an hour or two of horrible weather. I like the snowstorms. I like it when you can't see anything. I like to watch the cars on the freeways, especially the ones that slide around. And all the street-lights get these halos, I like those. And surveillance, I like surveil-lance a lot. I like the infrared cameras. I wish I had one of those. I'd just turn it on and put it outside and watch TV all night."

"See what goes on out there," Edward said.

"I like plane wrecks, too," she said. "There was a great one in Dallas a couple of years ago, but the one I like best was that one in Washington, the one where the plane went into the Potomac on takeoff. That one was just . . . perfect."

Edward made a little noise like an electric motor and looked out the window at the almost clear scene there. The ambulance was gone, the police cars were gone, the kid's car was gone, most of the neighbors had gone inside. A couple of stragglers he could not identify stood beneath the street lamp talking. They were both men. They stood in the street at an odd angle to each other, almost ninety degrees, their heads bent, their hands in their pockets—both were wearing raincoats over what looked to Edward to be pajamas. One wore glasses. Both had messy hair, and both toed the street as they talked, kicking a foot this way, sliding a foot that way. The light falling on them from the street lamp had a greenish glow, draining their faces of color, making them look as if they were characters in some back-from-the-dead movie. A teen show. The street scene, which moments before had been crowded with anxiety and fear and danger, was now dormant and, except for these two men, a picture of domestic certainty and contentment.

"Maybe a plane could go down outside this picture window," Edward said, flicking his finger toward the glass. "Something small. A small private plane carrying people through the night. Maybe it could take out that guy across the street, the guy who's always burning stuff out of the trees in his backyard."

"The scorched-earth guy?" Elise said. "He still around?"

"Forever," Edward said. "He's there forever."

"What time is it? Is it about two?" Elise said. She resettled herself on the couch, sitting forward, the robe splitting nicely over her knee, and she tugged at the terrycloth modestly while she stubbed her cigarette into the ashtray. "I guess we have to negotiate," she said. "I guess we have to figure out what we're going to do."

"Why don't we just keep on doing what we've been doing?" Edward said.

She was inspecting the nails on her toes, hunched over, her arm wrapped around her leg, and the nails seemed to glow in the dim light of the living room. She looked up at Edward. "I'm sorry about this little scene in here," she said, jerking her head toward the bedroom. "I got carried away. Frustration, I guess."

Edward waved at her. Shook his head. "Forget it," he said. He felt lost and empty. "I don't have anything to say about our life. I mean, it's odd, but it's what we're doing. Living this way, I mean. But it's OK with me if it's OK with you."

"That's what I don't know," Elise said. She did a little thing that was a laugh and a sigh together. "I came up here for your birthday, but we haven't done any birthday things," she said. She shook her head. "I know you hate birthday things, but it seems like we ought to do some." She stopped a minute, then wagged a hand at Edward. "I'm sorry," she said. "I just got off on that. I guess it worries me. It's not the real problem here."

"What if there isn't a problem?" he said.

"Well, if there isn't a problem, we're in hog heaven," she said. "We're in high cotton. We've got smooth sailing. I mean, we light up our lives. Individually, and separately, we are a couple of happy motherfuckers. Ain't it grand and wouldn't it be lovely to think so."

"Pretty," Edward said.

She smiled and nodded. "OK," she said. "Fine. But look, we do have problems. I mean, that we never see each other is a problem, I think. Sex is a problem. What we're going to do for the rest of our lives is a problem. Is this what we're going to do for the rest of our lives? I mean, it's OK, it's not terrible, but . . ." She hooked her chin over her knee and wrapped both arms around that knee and rocked back and forth on the couch. "It's like I come up here after a long time, after not seeing you for a long time, and I don't know what to expect, so all the time I'm driving up here I'm wondering what this is going to be like, so I think about all the ways it could be when I get here, but when I *do* get here, it isn't any of those ways, it's just as if I was coming home from the grocery store, it's like nothing unusual is going on, and so maybe it isn't, but sometimes it feels like it is, sometimes when I'm down there, it feels like something real strange is going on, and then I come back here and it's like it's not. I mean, I come in here and spend the night with you and I don't even know what the deal is. It's like the deal isn't anything, I mean, we're just . . . married."

"We are married," Edward said.

"I know, but I don't know if you like me. Do you like me?" Elise said. She sat up, shook her head, and looked at the ceiling. "It's a stupid question," she said. "But I don't know."

She looked away from him then, at the carpet in the middle of the room, staring at it, tense and still. Edward could see the beginnings of tears in her shining eyes, and he recognized this as the moment he was supposed to get up and go across to the couch and put his arm around her and comfort her, but he didn't do that, he didn't want to do that. And it wasn't because he didn't love her, because at that moment he felt that he loved her, knew that he loved her. He was very happy that she was there in the room with him. He was excited by her, not in a sexual way, but excited nonetheless. He was touched by her. He watched her stare at the floor, thinking how wonderful she was. He wondered if the reason he refused to do what he was supposed to do was that he was afraid that if he did, the lovely thing he felt for her, right at the moment, would be lost. He recognized that if he failed to move, he risked bigger trouble an hour from now, or tomorrow. She might read his lack of movement as lack of interest, as a statement of his feeling for her. He imagined she had already done that, that she was sitting on the couch now, eight feet away from him, saying to herself, "Why doesn't he come over here?"

It was odd to him, too, that he was sitting there analyzing the situation. That instead of doing something he was watching and thinking and letting her play out her scene. For years after they had first gotten together, he wouldn't let her play out anything. He wouldn't let her pout, or cry, or feel sad, he wouldn't let her get mad and stop talking to him—he was always after her, right there, comforting or consoling or bitching or making fun, always trying to move her, forcing her toward resolution. He was *Father Knows Best* and Buffalo Bob, and Sister Charise—the supplier of whatever stern or stupid or sociopathic tonic seemed needed. It was something he did working out of his hip pocket, guessing all the time, reading her face, the way she moved her eyes, where she looked, reading the degree of authenticity in her smile, what she did with her hands, watching her posture and her movements, the way she rested her arm on the table, judging his performance by his sense of her comfort. They had had many talks like this over the course of their marriage, late at night, in darkened rooms, undressed or half dressed. He provided harsh reality when she got fanciful, provided optimism when the standard-issue dreck got her down. He figured he'd been a fair enough husband.

"OK," she said. "Let's go out."

"I don't want to go out," he said.

"You have to go out," she said. She was up off the couch in a swirl, redeploying her ashtray and her cigarettes and her drink, moving.

"I thought we were going to talk about stuff," he said.

She was already in the kitchen cleaning out her ashtray. From there she said, "What's to talk about? We're married. This is our life, Ralph Edwards notwithstanding. This is what we do. We are not retarded."

Edward, sitting alone in the living room, held his forehead in his hand and shook his head. "What?" he said.

"I said everything's peachy," she said.

"No, I mean the retarded business," he said. He got up and started for the kitchen. "What's that about?"

She was working over the ashtray with a paper towel. "Oh, that," she said. "That's nothing. It's just this friend of mine, this wonderful but occasionally out-of-tune friend of mine thinks this guy in this movie we saw was retarded. Which he wasn't, of course, but you can't explain that to my friend. This guy in the movie was just *extremely* sensitive. But my friend keeps saying, 'He's retarded,' and I keep saying, 'If he's retarded, it ruins the movie.' "

"Uh-huh," Edward said. "So, was he persuaded?"

"It's not a he, it's a she," Elise said. "And, no. She's a lunkhead."

Edward casually hiked himself up onto the kitchen counter above the dishwasher trying to conceal his relief that the friend was a she. "So," he said. "What's this movie?"

"You haven't seen it," Elise said.

"Right," he said. "But what's the name of it?"

She said, "*Man of Flowers.* It's an Australian movie, nobody's seen it."

"I can get it at the video store," he said.

"I don't need you to look at it and tell me if he's retarded or not," she said. "I already know he's not retarded."

Edward made a clownish, pained face. "I see," he said, drawing it out. "Are we being a little . . . sensitive?"

"Are we being a little condescending?"

"Well," he said. He shrugged. "I don't know. I would like to see it."

"I would like you to see it. You could tell me what you think, maybe settle this argument I'm having."

"I probably wouldn't have an opinion," Edward said.

"Oh, Edward, you always have an opinion. Somebody gets out of bed, you have an opinion as to whether they did it well or badly. If somebody walks across the street you have an opinion as to whether it's right or wrong."

"Well," Edward said. "Sometimes I know things."

"I don't think I want to go out," Elise said. "I wanted to go out a few minutes ago, but I don't want to go out now. Sometimes going out is wrong. Like when you don't have anything to do. We could go to the all-night store and get something for your birthday. That would be something to do."

Edward found a mosquito carcass on the windowsill over the sink. He waved at Elise to give him the paper towels. "I don't really want to go to the all-night store, but if you want to go, we can go. I don't know what you want to get me there for my birthday."

"Something inflatable," she said. She was looking through the kitchen cabinets. "Boy, you do keep a place clean, don't you."

Edward shrugged. "It's what I like to do," he said. "Do you want me to show you the new vacuum? It's wonderful," he said. "It has a headlight, a dirt-seeking headlight."

She nodded at him. "That's great, Edward."

"I really love it," he said.

This was absolutely true. He had bought the vacuum at Wal-Mart for eighty dollars on sale, marked down. He'd brought it home and unpacked it and put it together, thinking to himself how much he loved doing this. He'd sat on the couch with all the parts arrayed before him and carefully read the instructions, first in English and then in Spanish. His Spanish was not at all good, so what he really did when he was reading it in Spanish was read the Spanish words, pronounce them, and then look back at the English to see what they meant. Even this didn't quite work since he vaguely remembered that the Spanish words were in some other order, some other arrangement, so that it wasn't clear which Spanish word corresponded to which English word.

First he carefully looked at the diagram of the parts and checked to see that each part depicted in the manual had come in his box. He found the upper and lower handle sections, the main body of the cleaner, the hood assembly, the outer-bag assembly, and the throwaway bag. Looking at the drawing of the assembled vacuum, he checked the part names—headlight, hood, carpet-pile adjustment, cord-storage hook, spring hook, outer bag, handle bail, handle release, furniture guard—checking each part in the accompanying diagram. He noted that the headlight was available "only on certain models." He was particularly pleased with that.

After studying all the parts, and before beginning the assembly, he got an old towel from the bathroom and carefully wiped all the dust away from all the parts. Then he began the assembly. He put the handle together and thought how nice it was, how sturdy, and what a lovely color. He tried the switch, noting it was not the same switch he had previously encountered on this kind of vacuum. He wondered if this was a cheaper switch—it didn't seem cheaper. Then working closely with the manual, following each instruction in turn, he slowly went through the process of attaching the handle to the cleaner, attaching the outer bag to the vacuum's main body, attaching the spring handle, and the one pale green throwaway bag that had been supplied in the package. Once the bag was installed, he grasped the pleats on each side of the bag and pulled at them until the dotted line was entirely visible. Even though he worked very slowly, the assembly process went much more quickly than he had hoped it would. He wished there were many more parts to attach and, to that end, took out the vacuum attachments and proceeded to attach them, one after another, to the machine. Finally, having tested all the attachments as to their suction, he turned the machine off, unplugged it, and turned it upside down in his lap so that he could check the beater bars and brushes.

He puzzled for a few moments over the instructions he found in raised letters on the bottom of the machine—"Install side of belt nearest cleaner between ribs." He unlatched the metal plate so that he could have a better look at the belt and the drive shaft. There were two drawings on the bottom of the machine, not drawings, really, but reliefs, depicting the path of the belt and how it was to be arranged, how it was to be attached to the drive shaft and to the cylinder and beater bars. He studied these drawings and then fiddled with the brushes, noting that they were bright red and quite stiff. Then he relatched the metal plate, spun the wheels with his thumb to check them for alignment and looseness—all spun freely—and then he read the little plaque on the bottom, which specified amperage, bag type, and serial number for this particular model.

Then he sat there on the couch with the vacuum in his lap, both of his hands on the vacuum, and thought to himself how pleasant and peaceful it was that afternoon there in the room. After a few minutes with the cleaner in his lap, he lifted it up and put it on the floor, took the towel and polished up its bright blue cowl, carefully wound the new white cord around the upper and lower cord-storage hooks, snapped the semicircular plug retainer notch onto the cord, pushed the cleaner back a little, and squared it with the room, aligning it with the edge of the coffee table, and then sat back and read the remainder of the operations manual, with special attention to the section on pages 15–17 about replacing the headlight. Having done that, he lingered on the final page—actually the back cover of the booklet—to read the consumer information. Never let children use the machine as a toy. Keep machine on floor—not on chairs, tables, etc. Never vacuum in the presence of flammable or combustible liquids or fumes. Use machine and accessories only in manner intended by manufacturers. For optimum cleaning performance and safety, study and follow your operations manual—keep it in a handy and safe place for future reference. Having read the manual cover to cover, he sat there a little sleepy and content, the manual at his side, held loosely in his hand, his head lolling back against the cushion, and he regarded the new vacuum cleaner, appreciating its poisedness, the stark truth of it, eager to clean, clean, clean.

Elise yawned and tugged at her hair, pulling it away from her scalp and looking up at it through the tops of her eye sockets. "We could mess with this," she said. "Cut it into little animal shapes or something. Every time I get my hair cut this short I swear I'll never do it again."

"It's supposed to be easy," Edward said.

"Well, it's not," Elise said. "You mean, it's easy because it doesn't hang around all the time, but I still worry about it."

"Looks fine," Edward said. "Why don't we go to bed."

"We can't go to bed because we haven't solved anything," she said.

"We can solve tomorrow," he said.

"Tomorrow I have to go home," she said.

Edward was still on the counter, hands outside his thighs, looking at the floor, at her feet. He raised his eyes. He gave her a smile that he imagined might suggest she had said something wrong, but he wondered if that would get across. He held the smile and tried to imagine what his face looked like—his cheeks felt rubbery and bulbous, and he could just imagine the little creases where his mouth turned up at its edges. He knew this wasn't a genuine smile.

When she had left there was a lot of talk about *their* place on the coast. He had gone down a couple of times to help her get moved and get settled in. The first place was nice, pleasant enough, lots of windows, even a little bit of a view. Aside from the insects and the neighbors, Edward approved. But after a time she didn't invite him to come down so often, and he didn't invite himself. The first month or so after her departure they had talked on the telephone all the time, two, three calls a night. But that got old. Even before she had moved out they had stopped digesting their days for each other, and doing it on the telephone was even more ridiculous than doing it in person. So the calls, too, dwindled. And soon enough, when he went down, or she came up to visit, they just got in each other's way. It wasn't fun.

He remembered feeling awful about her being at the house this one weekend about a month after she'd moved out. She'd brought a whole box of work from her office, and she sat on the couch doing this work all night Friday, all day Saturday, most of Sunday. He'd suggested a movie, and she had declined. He'd suggested they go out to dinner, and she declined. Everything he suggested that weekend, she declined. He kept asking her if she was all right, and she kept saying she was fine. He'd asked her in every way he could imagine, tried to lead her into conversations, asked questions about her work, night life, tried to engage her in reminiscences, wondered aloud if he shouldn't come down more often, wondered how they were going to manage the Christmas holidays, even went directly at her with questions about her emotional state—was she happy? did she miss him? was she more comfortable without him?—and finally, he had accused her of infidelity with everybody from her employer to the operator of the health-food store she had mentioned she had found. She resisted all his efforts—"oppositional" was the word she used. But what she said was that she wasn't being oppositional, she was just a little bit withdrawn.

"Well, that's true," he had said. This was Sunday afternoon. She was packed and ready to go and the two of them were standing on the front porch saying good-bye.

"I'm fine. I'm really fine," she had said. "I love you, and—" She scanned the front yard and tapped her fingers on the steel trellislike support of the porch overhang. There were kids in the street riding pink Big Wheels. One kid on a tricycle looked as if he'd come out of a circus. Edward remembered a lot of neighbors being visible in their driveways, washing cars, washing animals, washing recreation equipment.

"And what?" he said.

"And I don't know what," she said. She gave the trellis thing a final smack, causing a short-lived, gonglike sound, then stepped up and brushed cheeks with Edward. "And I guess I love you." And then she strode, full of purpose, to her car. She didn't look at Edward again until she was in the street, pulling away, and then she turned for the slightest moment, pursed her lips, delivered her distant kiss, and was gone.

4

EDWARD WOKE up depressed and lonely. Elise was beside him, a hump in the covers. She was on her side facing away from him. Her briefcase was on the floor next to the bed. It was six in the morning. Light cut in at the edges of the windows, thin vertical slots that caught columns of flying dust. He hated the room. He hated how he felt. He felt like punching Elise in the back. He pushed up a little in the bed and leaned his head against the wall and looked at the saddle-back curve of Elise's waist. He twisted his head so he could see her head on the pillow. Her hair was twisted and flattened and bunched—it looked like toy hair. He thought for a minute about the events of the evening before, each recollection depressing him more than the last, and then, with a groan, he sat up on the edge of the bed facing away from her. He felt crowded and lifeless, and wished he were alone.

In another minute he was up, tying his robe around his waist, headed for the kitchen and the refrigerator. He got a Diet Coke out of the refrigerator, picked up his cigarettes off the counter, went to the front door, opened it, and got the paper, then went into the guest bedroom, into the back bathroom, and closed the door. He sat down on the toilet, lit a cigarette, pissed, and then opened the newspaper. He went through the headlines on the financial page, then got to the sports section. He hit the toilet handle, got up, shut the lid, and sat down on the fluffy white bathmat between the toilet and the tub. A small, papery ash on the floor next to the base of the vanity caught his eye, and he tore off some tissue to clean it up. He leaned back against the bathroom wall and looked at the bathroom door, at the doorknob. The door was not locked. He got up and locked the door, then sat down again. He wrapped the robe around him, covering his knees, and pulled a towel off the towel rack and flapped it like a blanket over his feet, ankles, and calves. He unfolded the sports section, laid it out over his legs, and stared at the front page.

He was glad there wasn't any natural light in the bathroom, that there were no windows. The only light in the room was from the two-bulb fixture over the mirror, and although that was the right kind of light, there was too much of it. He thought about getting up to turn off the light, but that seemed like too much trouble, so he just propped his arm on the closed top of the toilet and shaded his eyes.

Two hours later he woke up. Elise was knocking on the door and calling his name. "Edward," she said through the door. "Are you in there? What are you doing in there? Come on out. Roscoe is coming up, I just talked to him on the telephone."

For a moment Edward was lost, he didn't know where he was. Time had slipped away from him. He didn't know whether it was evening or morning. He didn't know what day it was. All that came back to him quickly, however, and he got up and said, "Be right out," then turned on the water in the lavatory.

"Are you OK?" Elise said.

He grunted at her then leaned over the sink, resting his forehead on the spigot. Ricocheting drops of water hit him in the face. Elise said something else, but he couldn't make out what it was because all he could hear was the water running. Without moving anything but his arm he reached out and opened the bathroom door. He turned his head a little so he could see. "I'm fine," he said to Elise.

She was standing back a little from the door, clutching herself, arms folded across her chest, her hair wet. She had red rabbit-head slippers on her feet. They were slippers his mother had given her two years before at Christmas. Silly things. A kind of family joke—that Christmas five pair of such slippers had changed hands, not all of them rabbits. They had given his mother a pair of antelope-head slippers, and his father a very peculiar pair of fish-head slippers. And at the Christmas Eve exchange of gifts, when all his family was gathered, there magically appeared two other pair of similar slippers, as if these slippers were the great middle-class joke that everybody got.

"I found them in the closet," she said, looking down at the slippers he was staring at.

"This is the first time you've ever worn them," he said.

"It's not because I don't like them."

"How could you not like them?" he said. "They're big red rabbits."

"They hang heavy on the toe," she said.

"As what does not," he said, turning back to the sink. He cupped his hands and filled them with water and then doused his face. He did that a couple of times, carefully spreading the water up over his forehead to the hairline, then down under his chin. Then he dried off. "Roscoe's coming?" he said. "What time is it?"

"Eight," Elise said. "How long have you been in here?"

"Six," he said.

"You didn't hear the phone?"

He shook his head and came out of the bathroom. She backed up, then followed him through the guest bedroom back out into the hall and into the kitchen.

"I think he's just lonely down there," she said.

Edward was thinking how lovely Elise was with her wet hair and her rabbit slippers. Surprised at how nice it was to see her there in the morning, especially given how he'd felt two hours earlier. It was typical of his life with Elise, when he'd had a life with Elise, that he would like her one minute and dislike her the next, that he would find her heartbreaking and lovable and then turn around moments later and find her repellent. Now, after half a year of the quiet life, of nothing ever out of place, of the carpet pile in the house disturbed only along those paths from kitchen to living room to bath to bedroom that he always walked, it was not entirely unpleasant to have gone through this small emotional turnaround. He liked being in the kitchen with her, he in his robe and she naked except for her funny feet.

While she was grinding the coffee, he came up behind her, opened his robe, and laid himself across her back, pressing himself up against her ass. He wrapped his arms around her, feeling her breasts, and laid his head sideways on the nape of her neck. She went on with her business with the coffee but did not try to break the connection with him. After the coffee was ground and in the filter in the machine, she took the pot out of its seat and did a sidestep toward the sink, and he went with her, step for step. Then it became a kind of game, they moved around the kitchen as if joined, his stomach to the small of her back. It was funny, and awkward, the bells on the rabbit slippers jingling as they moved across the kitchen floor to the sink, back to the coffee maker, across to the refrigerator, to the cabinet where the bread was kept, back to the refrigerator. He would not let go of her. They moved in a rocking motion like a big waddling bear, and when she was not ferrying something from one place to another, some food or utensil, she clasped her hands over his on her chest, as if through that touch to give him some remote-control direction, as if she were the woman in *Aliens,* and he the huge hydraulic machinery.

"So," Edward said. "I guess we have to face the new world." He backed away from her and closed his robe, tying the belt in a tight knot.

"We don't actually have to face it," she said. "We could kind of peek at it." She gave him a look on that.

"Why is he coming up here?" Edward said.

"I don't know," Elise said. "He wants to see me. We've been having some trouble lately, you know."

Edward was looking at her back, at her shoulder blades, at how smooth her skin was. "You've been having some trouble lately," he said.

"Yeah," Elise said.

When they were living together, he was occasionally taken over by this extraordinary dread, this sense that his life was finished prematurely. That he had reached the end thirty years too soon. And now, in the kitchen, on this short visit, he felt that again. He had tried to explain it to Elise, tried to tell her about it, how it felt, tried to explain what it was like when all of a sudden you sense that nothing is moving. That you will see the same backyard, the same tree trunks, the same cars going by on the same roads, the same light slanting the same way in through the same windows, that there is no change in your future. He had said it was like having a cold, a permanent cold or flu, the kind of disease you had in childhood, it always made the light switch seem like it was moving away and up, as if it were in Dr. Caligari's house. And that it would always be there, that way. He hated feeling it. And it just zipped through him, and by now, already, it was gone. Things were all right again, except there lingered in his imagination the memory of that crushing stoppedness.

"What are you doing?" Elise said. "Why are you looking at me that way?"

"What way?" Edward said.

"There was this look on your face," Elise said. She was turned toward him now, pointing at his face. "It was like something out of *The Exorcist*," she said, pretending to laugh, but not really laughing. She turned away, went to the refrigerator, and got a cup of yogurt. "I don't know," she said. "Forget it."

"Just then?" he said, using his right hand to point at his left shoulder as if he were pointing back through time.

She waved and spooned yogurt into her mouth.

"I'm not real steady this morning," he said. "Things have been jumping back and forth."

"Emm," she said, nodding and cleaning the spoon the way a kid is supposed to clean a spoon of cough syrup.

"It's about you," he said. "About you being here."

She nodded a second time, seeming not to react to what he was saying.

"It's like last night was OK," Edward said. "And then this

morning I hated you when I woke up. I didn't want you to be there. And then when you came to the bathroom it was OK, and then in here it was OK, until a minute ago. Then it was bad again."

"I see," Elise said.

"Now it's OK again," Edward said.

She gave him a polite smile and opened the cabinet under the sink to throw away her empty yogurt cup. "That's good to hear," she said. "Keep me posted, will you?"

5

"SO I'M tooling along the highway at eighty and then all of a sudden everybody stops. I mean, I'm halfway between there and here, and there isn't anyplace to go, there isn't a town for miles, and everybody stops, and I'm behind this big truck—Griffin Industries. So people start getting out of their cars and walking across the road to see what's going on, but of course, you can't see a thing, just a line of cars. Pretty soon everybody's getting out of their cars. They all look like businessmen of one kind or another. I mean, they're all curious about what's happening. The cars are coming at us the other way, they're getting through, but our way, we ain't moving. I'm watching in the mirror and behind me this one guy's out pointing up ahead, like he's explaining what's happening to some other people that are back there. So I'm sitting there, and there are bushes over on my right, and suddenly this train roars through there, big train. And some people in the line are turning around and going the other direction. I don't know where they're going. We're on the highway in the middle of nowhere. I mean, I'm figuring if they're going the way I'm going, they got no business turning around, because there ain't nowhere to go back there. These people are talking to each other in this real interesting way, they're signaling and making gestures with their hands—you've got strange bedfellows out here."

Roscoe had hit the front door talking, telling this story about his trip up from the coast. The three of them were standing in the living room. The door was still open. Roscoe was lanky, affable-looking. He had on Weejuns, khakis, and a long soccer-style pull-over shirt. Edward made a move to shut the door, and Roscoe went on with his report.

"So after a while I'm sitting in my car, not doing anything, and I see in my rearview window, here comes this woman in this blue dress. Now this woman looks like she ought to be in an office building somewhere, you know, typing or something, getting coffee for the boss—" He stopped and looked at Elise. "I don't mean all women are like that," he said. "Just this woman. I mean, that's the way she looked, know what I mean?"

Elise nodded and rolled her hand in circles telling him to speed it up.

"Anyway," he said, "she's carrying a map. She walks past me to this group of people in front, waving her map, then they all gather around and try to find what she's looking for. That goes on for a few minutes, and from where I am I can see this guy's giving her the once-over, know what I'm saying? While one of them's talking to her, pointing stuff out on the map, the other two are checking out her attributes. Anyway, they get finished with that and she hightails it on back to her car, which is a few back from me. I watch her go, me and these other guys. She does this little wobbly walk with her feet very close together, and it makes her rump bounce. Then I'm watching her in the rearview mirror and this guy gets out about two cars back, and he's got his Casiotone with him. He's got it strung around his neck somehow, and he's playing away. I get the window down, and he's playing something that sounds like 'Begin the Beguine.' The woman with the map is standing back there right next to him talking to another girl, and some guys in yellow sweatsuits have come up, and they're standing there, too."

Roscoe was talking to Elise more than Edward. Edward was just standing there, listening in.

"So everybody's turning around now," Roscoe said. "I'm sitting out there in my car, and this guy turns a U-Haul around about half a dozen cars ahead. And what I'm wondering is how many of these people have to go to the bathroom as bad as I do. In the rearview the girl who was back there has pulled out, replaced by a guy in a brown Nissan who is using *his* rearview to watch himself pluck his mustache."

Roscoe tugged at his shirttail, pulling it down. It was a real long shirt.

"So there was a wreck on the highway, is that it?" Edward said.

Elise reached out and gave Edward a little pop on the nose. "Hey," she said. "Take it easy there. Let the man tell his story."

"Yeah, Edward," Roscoe said.

Edward backed up, holding his nose. She hadn't meant to hit him hard, but she had, accidentally. She'd caught him with a fingernail. It had split the skin. His nose was bleeding a little. He had his fingers cupped over his nose, so his voice sounded like he had a cold. "That's real nice, Elise," he said. He took his hand away from his nose, looked at the blood, and put the hand back.

Elise snorted and rolled her eyes, then came across the room after him. "Come on," she said. "I'm sorry. I didn't mean to do that. Are you all right?"

"Is he all right?" Roscoe said.

Edward sat on the arm of the couch and tilted his head back as if he were trying to stop a nose bleed. "Yeah," he said. "I'm fine. Thanks."

Elise was kneeling on the seat of the couch next to Edward, trying to get his hand off his nose. "Let me see," she said.

Edward used his free hand to keep her away. "No," he said. "It's nothing. Don't mess with it. Finish the story, Roscoe. What happened?"

"I'm going to get some peroxide," Elise said, heading out of the room. Then from the hallway, out of sight, she said, "Is it still in the bathroom? Is it still where it always was?"

Edward bobbed his head. "Exactly," he said. He was wondering how he had gotten involved in this project, this particular set of circumstances, how he had managed to have a wife and not have a wife at the same time, how his wife happened to have a boyfriend who wasn't a boyfriend, how the two of them managed to live together while he lived alone, how they happened to come see him on his birthday, how everything that was supposed to be perfect and beautiful, the sex-love-marriage-family system, the source of all good and the protection against all evil, the cornerstone of the culture of which he was part, and the cultural foundation of all civilization from the time of Christ to the then present moment—how it was, exactly, that the successful navigation of this simple system had eluded him so entirely.

Roscoe was at the bookcase, paying careful attention to a two-inch-high blue satin camel, stuffed, that Elise had given Edward once, years before, after a visit to a peculiar Chinese restaurant in Bogalusa, Louisiana. The people at the restaurant could not explain why they sold tiny embroidered blue satin camels, but they did, and Elise had bought one, as a memento of their trip. Roscoe was looking at the underside of it.

"It's a camel," Edward said.

"Huh?" Roscoe said. "Oh, yeah. I see that." Roscoe quickly put the camel back where he had found it.

"So," Edward said. "How's the linguistics game?"

Roscoe was standing with his back to Edward, reading book titles, his head canted to one side. "What?" he said. "Oh, I don't know. Gave it up. I'm into micros. Selling them, vertical market stuff, mostly."

"Oh," Edward said.

"Well, not really," Roscoe said. "I mean, I'm just starting. I'm a late starter."

"Me, too," Edward said.

Then Elise came into the room, bristling with medical supplies. She had isopropyl alcohol, peroxide, cotton balls, Band-Aids, Q-Tips, zinc ointment, Bacitracin, an Ace bandage, and a small bottle of Mercurochrome. "This ought to do it," she said. She got Edward to sit on the seat of the couch while she arranged her equipment on the couch's arm. Then she went to work. First she cleaned his nose, top to bottom, front to back. She did this with a cotton ball dampened with alcohol. She discarded the ball. She went from there to Q-Tips.

Roscoe, who was standing to one side and watching, put a hand over his ear, kicked his head sideways, and said in a bad Howard Cosell voice, "The world of Angelo Dundee . . ."

"OK, OK," Elise said. "Go on with the story. Where were we? You were on the highway, I remember."

"My story has lost some of its beauty somewhere," Roscoe said.

Edward looked at him from under Elise's hands. "No it hasn't. Go ahead. You're on the highway. All the cars are stopped. You have to go to the bathroom."

"He's acting up, Elise," Roscoe said.

Elise pulled back from Edward and gave him a look. "You *are* acting up, Edward."

"All right," Edward said, doing mock contrition, his head dropped to his chest. "I'm acting up. I admit it. I don't know what happened. I was just sitting here, and then, suddenly, I started acting up. I can't explain it."

"I can," Elise said. She bent close to Edward, her nose almost touching his, and looked into his eyes.

Roscoe took the cue. "I'm on the highway, right?" he said. "It's seven in the morning, I'm fifty miles from anywhere. Traffic is stopped, nobody's moving. I'm there and there are all these truck drivers and businessmen and secretaries—I mean, it's amazing what's coming out of these cars. So I'm out there, maybe thirty minutes, and yes, Edward, I *do* have to go to the bathroom. In fact, it's becoming increasingly important. I spend some time looking at the sky. That doesn't work. So . . . time wears on." He paused a minute, then said, "I don't want to do this." He picked up his suitcase off the floor. "I just want to go to my room, if I could."

"That would be a jump over here to the hall," Elise said, gesturing toward the hall door with her thumb. "Take a right. But come on, Roscoe. You can go to your room later."

"I want to bathe," he said. "It's a dumb story. I don't know why I started it. I was nervous. What happens is after a while we get rolling and I feel better. I figure I can make the Welcome Center at the state line. We get going pretty good, we're doing thirty. I bang on the damn wheel I'm so happy. So we go like that half a mile and then I'm stuck on a bridge."

"What?" Elise said. She was trying a large Band-Aid across Edward's nose.

"I pissed in a towel," Roscoe said.

"What?" Elise said.

"That's it," Roscoe said. "Right there on the bridge," he said. "I felt like some guy in a war movie. You know, he gets his foot shot up, it gets infected, he's in the jungle, and the enemy is everywhere, all around him, incoming sailing over his head, deadly insects whizzing through the air, the screams of the brightly colored birds echoing in his ears, and he's limping, half dragging himself back toward camp, and he knows he won't make it alive with that foot. He knows he's only got one chance to live. He takes out a screwdriver he happens to have—he's a tank mechanic, maybe—and he commences to hack off his foot with the screwdriver."

Elise shut her eyes and shook her head. "I don't know what that has to do with you pissing in a towel."

"He bit the bullet," Edward said. "He did what had to be done." Edward got off the couch and went over to Roscoe, trying to give him a high five. "Way to go, Sparky," he said.

Roscoe didn't quite understand what Edward was doing, so at first he stuck his hand out as if to shake hands, and then he flattened the hand, palm upward. Edward, meanwhile, recognizing that Roscoe wasn't going to get his hand up for the high five, swept his own hand downward, as if to slap Roscoe's. But while Edward was correcting, Roscoe was finally raising his hand to accept the high five. The result was waving arms. This went on for a second or two, up and down, until both men stopped, stock still, there in the living room, and each of them, very carefully, very slowly, reached out at about shoulder height, and did what amounted to a demure patty-cake.

Roscoe nodded. "Thanks," he said.

"What is this?" Elise said. "You guys remind me of The Two Stooges."

"This is male hand stuff," Edward said.

"Yeah, well," Elise said. "It sucks. What about breakfast?"

"I have to go to my room first," Roscoe said. He turned around to Elise. "Are we sharing a room or what?"

Elise said, "I'm *his* wife, Roscoe."

"Hey," Roscoe said. He held up his hands as if to assert his innocence. "I know that. Just asking."

Elise pressed all her nursing supplies to her chest with one hand and looped her free arm through Edward's, walking him toward the hall. "It's OK with you if Roscoe stays a day or two, isn't it?" she said. "I thought we'd all stay here a couple of days. The three of us. I mean, we don't have to if you'd rather not. I just thought it would be nice if we did."

Edward had his free hand on his nose. "It's OK," he said.

"We could get to know each other a little bit," Elise said.

"I feel like I know Edward already," Roscoe said.

Edward stopped and looked at Roscoe. He guessed that Roscoe was a little better than thirty. He was maybe a trifle too earnest, but other than that, friendly enough. There was about him something so nonthreatening as to be threatening, as if Roscoe had carefully calculated what type of public performance would convey an easy security, a sense that Roscoe was not the enemy. And Edward guessed that the next, more personal dimension of Roscoe was a duplicate of the surface, that Roscoe was, in fact, not an enemy, but a man wearing a mask that was a perfect likeness of himself.

6

ELISE CHANGED her clothes in the bedroom. Edward sat with her, listening to the sounds of Roscoe in the shower off the guest room, listening to the water rush through the pipes. He didn't like watching Elise dress. He remembered times when he had wanted to be with her, when he had wanted to touch her, when just a glimpse of her breast was enough to make him forget everything else and think only of sex. Times when he thought of her body as extraordinarily lovely, sexy. Times when her efforts to bring him sexual pleasure—not the efforts themselves, but the *fact* of the efforts—so distorted his perceptions that he thought he might just burn up. Times when they had made love and he had felt so much in love with her that he had forgotten what he did not ordinarily forget—the awkward and almost inevitably disappointing physical mess of lovemaking. He remembered brutal sex, mean sex, sex so cheap it made them both freaks. He did not remember much happy sex, sweet, kind, or gentle sex.

"You're thinking about fucking," Elise said. She was facing away from him, facing a mirror, looking at him in there. She had on white cotton underpants, women's underpants designed to look like men's. She clutched a shirt to her chest, covering her breasts. "I can tell. I look at you and can tell what you're thinking. I always hated this look you get on your face when you think about fucking. You look like you're in pain."

He stared at her back. Stared at the two narrow hollows, one on

56

either side of the ridge of her spine. "I was remembering," he said. "Some of the stuff we did wasn't pretty."

"We did what you wanted," she said.

He nodded. "We did what I could," he said.

The shirt was unbuttoned, but she put it on over her head anyway. "I don't buy that," she said. "That's your usual bullshit."

"Maybe," he said. "It doesn't seem that way to me." He fingered the Band-Aid on his nose, flattening its edges. The Band-Aid was not well stuck. "You were there, too," he said. "You did half of it."

"I did more than half," Elise said.

"More than half," he said.

"That doesn't mean I'm responsible for it," she said. "There was like this understanding. I understood. If I wanted sex this is what I could have." She had started buttoning the shirt at the bottom so the top buttons were still undone. In one quick movement she opened the shirt and cupped her hands under her breasts, a reprise of her performance of the night before, only this time she held the pose for just a second, and gave him an ugly look. "I took it," she said.

He sat there for a minute without saying anything, watching her close the rest of the buttons on her shirt. Finally, he said, "I apologize."

"That's good," she said. "Make it worse." She pulled on a pair of black jeans that she had gotten from the overnight bag Roscoe had brought for her. Then, looking at herself in the mirror, she said, "It wasn't so bad. You don't know what goes on out there. I could tell you some shit."

"Like what?" Edward said.

"What they do, what they expect," she said. She snapped the fly of her pants and then smoothed her hand over her rump. "What I did."

"You mean you did worse stuff than we did together?" Edward said.

"I guess it depends on how you look at it," she said. "I did some stuff I regret. I don't really regret anything we did."

"I don't think I want to hear this," he said.

She was satisfied with the way she looked and turned away from the mirror, grabbing her purse off the table. "You probably do," she said. "But I don't think you will. We did that already, anyway."

"We did?" Edward said.

She waved her hand. "Come on," she said. "Let's forget it. It was a long time ago. We haven't done anything for a long time."

"It hasn't been that long," Edward said.

She did a sigh, a big one. He could see the anger she felt. It was just under the surface. She didn't want to get into it, whatever *it* was. When they used to argue, she would say, "I don't want to get angry," and Edward always thought that was very odd—he would try to tell her that either you were angry or you weren't, and that if you were, it was unlikely that not talking about the anger would make it go away. She said he was a jerk, that he should shut up, that he just didn't know when to shut up. And later, when the moment had passed, each of them acknowledged that the other was probably right—Edward admitting that it was a good idea to let some stuff go, Elise saying she wished she could just say what was bothering her.

The longer they were together the thinner her patience got. He'd come to recognize this tone in her voice, this ready-to-get-ugly tone that made him feel she despised him. When he first felt this from her, he couldn't understand it, he'd never seen it before, not from Elise. Later he figured it always happened when he said something about something she had done or was doing. She was interpreting his comments as instructions, and she was finished with instructions, especially his. He tried to say they weren't instructions, that he was trying to help out, but she countered that they had always been instructions, that even if they were disguised as helpful remarks, beneath that thin tissue they were orders. He had a hard time with that. He couldn't figure out whether it was true or not. He had grown up in the world of *the better idea*—that was his family's system. It wasn't love, or affection, or support, or help, it was whoever has the best idea wins. And there was no particular stigma attached to losing, so that the system revolved around the losers' eagerly awaiting the next contest, the next chance to match wits, the next opportunity to go up against the big guys. The big guys were, of course, the parents. And in truth, what Edward did not notice until rather late in his life was that his father, almost invariably, had the best idea. Edward went through his entire childhood and adolescence thinking his father was an extraordinarily bright man, and it wasn't until he was well into his twenties that he realized that this brightness was pockmarked with blind sides, things not noticed, things not taken into account. But whether the world of his childhood was actually the ideal of the better idea or the more likely world of *sometimes* the better idea mattered less to Edward now than the fact that, whatever world it was, he still lived in it. Thus, when he commented to Elise about the way the table was set, how the fire was laid, what ought to be done about the furniture, he *believed* that what he said was entering an open discussion of possibilities, and that if what he said was the best available idea on the subject—and he believed it was, more often than not—then what he said would be done.

Elise had come from a quite different family, had been coddled and ignored at turns, and was neither inclined nor equipped to embark on major arguments about the position a lamp ought to occupy in a room. And so, for the first eight years of their marriage, Edward, like his father, had won an inordinate number of domestic disputes. In the eighth year Elise had discovered this great defense. She refused to participate in the contest, arguing instead the primacy of individual rights and opinions. This came to be known, by Edward's hand, of course, as the Fuck You defense. And Edward, already shaky about the better-idea idea, and nervous about the correctness of his relations with women in general, and with Elise in particular, and unable in any case to penetrate her resolve, had simply quit pushing. But he wasn't sure it was a good idea. He wondered if she was just bullying him, if he was just rolling over.

"I hate it when you get angry," he said. They were in the living room, walking single-file toward the kitchen. He was behind her.

"I'm not angry," she said. "I just don't see any sense in talking about what we did six years ago. We had this life, we did these things. Some of them were pretty messy. So what?"

"I'm just feeling guilty," Edward said.

She gave him a look over her shoulder. "For stuff that happened six years ago?"

"No," he said. "Because I don't want to do it anymore."

"Nobody's asking you to do it," she said. "Jesus. What a Catholic."

Roscoe poked his head out of the hall doorway. "I'm almost there," he said. "What's the dress code on this deal?"

"Jesus," Elise said.

"A true yuppie would not ask this question," Edward said.

"Gotcha," Roscoe said. He disappeared back down the hall.

Elise opened the refrigerator, stared in for a minute, and shut it again. She opened the cabinets next to the sink. She closed them. She went around the kitchen opening the cabinets, looking in, closing them.

Edward said, "I know nobody's asking me to, but I feel bad anyway."

She stopped messing with the cabinets and turned around to face him. "Fine," she said. "But do me a favor—keep it to yourself. It's still a touchy subject for me. I've almost got it through my head, after five years, that you can love me and not want to sleep with me. I mean, it's just conceivable that that's possible. Barely. But this is a new idea for me, a very strange idea. I'm working on it. I've been months down here in this crummy little apartment, trying to figure this out, trying to get with the program. It would be real helpful to me if you didn't wallow around in it so much. OK?"

Edward stared at Elise. She was radiant, powerful. She seemed to frighten the air around her—it had pulled back a little bit, leaving a space between her and the rest of the world. There were tears in his eyes. He was grinding his teeth to keep the tears under control. He crossed the room and put his arms around her, first the right, then the left, and he put his head down on her shoulder. He had her arms pinned at her sides. She didn't move, she was limp, she made no effort to return the embrace. He breathed in her scent, plain and clean, felt the warmth of her neck against his, felt how solid she was, how sturdy, then he started to rock back and forth, left foot to right foot, then thought that was an affectation, a self-conscious and unnecessary effort, and so he stopped rocking and stood still, his arms around Elise, there in the middle of the kitchen.

Roscoe wanted to drive, so they went in his car. His car was a goldish BMW. Edward rode in the back seat. They had some trouble figuring out where to go for breakfast. At first Edward tried to steer them to a new place he'd seen written up in the city magazine, the kind of place he wouldn't ordinarily go to, but then he couldn't find it and nobody wanted to stop and get a magazine and find out where it was. Elise suggested a place she and Edward used to go, a place called The Locomotive Sandwich Shop, and they drove over there, but the building had been replaced by a gas station, one of those new kinds that is a grocery store and gas station combined. Roscoe thought they ought to try a mall, one of those where they have eighteen different kinds of food in little booths, but Elise pointed out that it was only nine o'clock and malls weren't open yet. They thought they might go to the airport, but nobody wanted to drive that far.

As they drove, one of them would point at a place out the window, and the other two would groan and make faces.

"Why don't we get some frozen stuff and go home?" Edward said. "I mean, go back to my house. We could get French toast, waffles, muffins—any kind of muffin you want. We could get some premixed pancake stuff, some of those eggs that come in milk cartons, some Sizzlean, stuff like that. We could do an all-frozen thing."

"We could get some frozen potatoes," Roscoe said.

"We could have some Swanson frozen fried chicken," Edward said.

"Yeah," Roscoe said. "I love that."

"I don't," Elise said. "Let's go to that drugstore. You know the one, it's really a fifties drugstore, but it's pretending to be an eighties remake of a fifties drugstore."

"Highland Village," Edward said.

"Right," she said. "Let's go there. How do you get there from here?"

Edward gave Roscoe the directions. They went there and got a booth in the back. Edward sat on one side of the booth, and Elise sat on the other. Roscoe ordered pancakes and bacon, Elise ordered French toast, and Edward ordered a chicken-fried steak and mashed potatoes with brown gravy. He tried to get some peas, but the waitress, a skinny woman in her fifties, had to go ask the cook if he could do peas, and when she came back she told Edward they didn't cook peas before lunch.

"You used to have peas twenty-four hours," Edward said.

The waitress gave him a distant smile and said, "I used to have a lot of things twenty-four hours. But I'm older now, I've only got sixteen hours in a day."

"I know what you mean," Edward said.

"I'm really sorry about the peas," the woman said.

She retrieved the stained, single-sheet menus and swept away, her severely starched pink uniform a reluctant traveling companion.

Roscoe, who had the inside seat in the booth, turned sideways, leaning against the back wall, and said to Edward, "So. How're things going? How do you like living alone?"

"It's good," Edward said. "It's real quiet. I like being alone."

Roscoe shook his head. "Not me," he said. "Getting this place with Elise was the best thing I ever did. I mean, we've got plenty of privacy, but I like having somebody else around sometimes. When I was living alone, you know, before?" He shook his head again. "I used to run around all the time trying to find somebody. Anybody. I was always going over to people's houses, people I didn't like, or didn't want to talk to. It was awful. I've always envied people who like to be alone."

"Some times are better than others," Edward said. He was looking at his knife, trying to figure out whether the stains on it were water stains or food stains.

"So, what do you do all the time?" Roscoe said.

"He reads magazines and watches TV," Elise said. "He doesn't really watch it, he flips through the channels. How many channels have you got, Edward?"

"Thirty-eight," Edward said. "I don't flip as much as I used to."

"It's real annoying," Elise said. "You sit down there and it's like watching somebody's slides. You get a minute of The Bangles, thirty seconds of Regis Philbin, some sexy black singer on the black channel, a glimpse of a Chuck Norris film on Showtime, some kid movie on HBO, Australian-rules football for about ten seconds, *Magnum*—he tends to watch more of *Magnum* than he really should." She smiled at Edward, patted his arm. "Really," she said. "It's how he gets connected to the world. But he's afraid to watch anything very long, because he's afraid he'll miss something else. A lot of people do that, though."

"Yeah," Roscoe said. "I do that all the time. I know what you're talking about."

Edward decided they were food stains on his knife, and he started looking around for another one. He got up and got a set of silverware from the next booth.

"You used to watch a lot of nature shows," Elise said. She turned to Roscoe. "He'd sit there for hours watching anything with an animal in it, any kind of animal, he'd watch it."

"Me, too," Roscoe said. "I like those. I saw one where a bat was having a baby—that was pretty disgusting. They lick their babies a lot. They've got faces like raw meat."

"I think I remember that," Edward said.

"He likes to look at the women," Elise said.

"Women are really pretty on television," Edward said.

"Yeah, but they don't really look like that," Roscoe said. "I knew this girl—an actress and, I mean, she was pretty, but nothing like she was on television. I mean, she was kind of dumpy in real life."

"You liked what's-his-name until the Bo Derek incident," Elise said. She still had her hand on Edward's arm. "Edward is very protective of Bo Derek."

"I saw that," Roscoe said. "She was real nice and he was a jerk, right? I bet he regrets that."

"Let's call him up and ask him," Elise said.

"So," Roscoe said. "What do you do? I mean, you just go home and sit there every day?"

"Pretty much," Edward said. "I like it. I like to listen to the refrigerator." He looked at Roscoe and decided from the expression on his face that his interest was genuine, that he was just gathering information, so Edward felt he ought to make an effort. He said, "It's real serene, restful. There's not a lot of unnecessary movement around me. Sometimes it's not great, but I don't bore easily. I used to get bored all the time, but I don't so much anymore."

"I wish I didn't," Roscoe said. "I do such stupid stuff when I'm bored. It's like—it's like I'm not smart enough to figure out something interesting to do."

"Do the small stuff," Edward said. "That's my advice."

"I want a hobby," Roscoe said. "Remember hobbies?"

"That would be good," Edward said.

"We report all of Edward's hobbies to the Institute for the Scrutiny of Remarkably Short-Lived Phenomena," Elise said.

Edward did a closed-mouth smile, flaring his nostrils. "I try," he said.

"You did pretty good on the electric race cars," Elise said. "That lasted a couple of weeks. And the dish." She shook her head. "No, I guess the dish didn't last very long."

"You had a dish?" Roscoe said.

Edward nodded.

"Yeah, it was a real special one," Elise said. "It didn't pick up any signals."

"I was trying out the KU band," Edward said to Roscoe. "So I bought this little dish about three feet across, but I couldn't ever get anything on it."

"So he jumped up and down on it, finally," Elise said. "Taught the dish a lesson."

"Well," Edward said. "It wasn't working. If it had been working, I wouldn't have jumped on it."

The food arrived. The waitress with the independent-minded outfit had plates stacked up her arms. She stood at the edge of the table for a minute figuring out how she was going to put the plates down without unbalancing the whole system. She had big and little dishes. She started to put down a plate of regular toast, but everything started wobbling, so she froze. They had to take the plates from her, one by one. She called out each order and nodded at it on her arm and then nodded at the person who had ordered it. When she was unloaded she laughed and said, "I guess I'm just an old pack-horse."

"Thanks very much," Elise said. "I think we've got it now."

The waitress didn't want to leave. She was apologetic about the customers having to serve themselves. "I'm real sorry," she said. "I've been doing this since nineteen fifty-six, so you'd think I'd be able to get it right." She reached over and moved some of the plates around on the table, putting them where she thought they ought to be. "Oh, sometimes I make two trips, but I really don't like to. I have them load me up in the back, and I just come on out. You got everything you need here?"

"We're fine," Elise said.

"I could use some more syrup," Roscoe said.

"Why, honey," the waitress said, giving him a mock stern look. "There's a whole pint of syrup right there in that syrup dispenser." She pushed the syrup dispenser a couple of inches toward him. "I don't know what you're going to do with it, but I'll get it for you."

"He doesn't really want any more syrup," Elise said.

Roscoe picked up the syrup dispenser and wiggled it, holding it up to the light. "I guess you're right," he said.

The waitress, who had her name—Jeanette—embroidered into the white oval that was itself sewn onto the uniform just above the left breast pocket, said again that she would not mind getting more syrup. "You know," she said. She crossed her arms over her chest and then brought one finger up to her lips. "I believe that you young people today eat more pancake syrup than we did when I was your age. I believe that's true. Yessir." She nodded, absentmindedly rearranging one more plate on the tabletop, and then silently moved along the row of booths back toward the kitchen.

Midway through breakfast the gray day turned into a haze of slanted lines and shiny drips, of reflections of city blocks in bubbles the size of pencil erasers, of tires buzzing on suddenly blacker streets, of glistening water abacuslike on loopy telephone wires, of stamping feet and squeaking shoes, of lights—head and tail and stop and street—blistering prettily, of the relentless sound-hash of rain.

In the booth across the aisle from the huge plate-glass window of the drugstore they all stopped talking and watched. People on foot outside hustled by. Cars coming into the intersection did little diving stops, their noses dropping suddenly, their backsides slipping out of line with the already still cars in front. At the Exxon station on the near corner self-serve patrons stood up on pump curbs and stretched awkwardly to keep the nozzles in their holes and, at the same time, to get a little protection out of the slim overhangs.

Roscoe broke the silence. He was staring out the window, the last inch of his final rasher of bacon locked between thumb and forefinger, about to go into his mouth, when he said, "Everybody likes the damn rain so much now. Nobody used to like rain. Only I liked rain. When I was a kid I used to go out in the backyard and sit in a cardboard box when it rained. I thought I owned it, I thought it was my idea—the rain, not the box."

"It always happens that way," Elise said. "You find something, you like it, and then twenty minutes later everybody else likes it, too."

Roscoe ate the bacon. "Yeah, I know," he said. "It takes something away from it. I can remember my mother standing on the porch in this shirtwaist dress, this blue dress she always wore, watching me out in the rain. We'd stay like that for a long time, maybe forty feet apart, she on the porch, and me in the yard, looking at each other. She always stood there with her arms folded.

The dress was short-sleeved, so her arms were bare, and it was like she was folding them for warmth. Sometimes she'd stand inside the screen door, leaning against the doorjamb, so to me she looked real shadowy and dark. I'd take things with me out there, a towel, a magazine or comic book, and sometimes I'd make trips into the house for supplies. If I had a real good box, a big one, she'd let me take a bedspread and a pillow out there. And if we had rain that lasted a couple of days, after the first day I'd build a box for the next day. I'd get a door in there, and a little window—one time I remember it rained for about three weeks, and I built this great box that had Saran Wrap over the windows and had a shelf in there, and a cardboard floor. She let me take the portable radio out that time. I stayed in that little house a couple of days, I mean in the daytime. We brought it into the garage at night. Finally, it was getting kind of dilapidated, and I left it out one night and some stray came along and used it as his doghouse. We kept the dog after that. Called him George."

"I like it best at night," Elise said. "It's late and you're trying to go to sleep, and you're real tired, and all the lights are off, and what you hear is this breath sound, only it's everywhere. I even went out and bought a tropical rainstorm record once. Remember that, Edward?"

"Still got it," Edward said. "I think. It's a rain *forest,* isn't it?"

"Right," she said. "Forest." She tapped at her mouth with her napkin, then slipped the napkin onto the table under the lip of her plate. Picking up her purse, she said, "You guys about ready?"

"I think we ought to stay here," Roscoe said. "I don't feel like moving."

"I don't think I could endure any more of this," Elise said. "I mean, we do have the problem of there being two of you and one of me."

Roscoe slid out of the booth and clapped Edward on the shoulder. "I love it when she's direct, don't you?" he said.

Edward put an arm around Roscoe. "Hey," he said. "We're swell. We're peachy. What's the big deal?"

"Oh, fuck you guys," Elise said. She turned around and headed for the door. Edward and Roscoe shuffled along behind her.

At first no one talked in the car, then Roscoe broke the silence. "I hate this car," he said. "I've always regretted buying it. I liked it for about four days."

Elise gave him a sidelong look. "We all want to hear about you and your car," she said.

"I forgot I wasn't supposed to talk about the car," Roscoe said. He caught Edward's eye in the rearview mirror and raised his eyebrows as if to say, What's going on?

Elise had gotten suddenly surly. It wasn't clear what she had gotten surly about. Maybe she hated Edward, maybe she hated Roscoe. Maybe she hated both of them. Maybe she just didn't feel well. Maybe being there with Edward was too awkward, or not awkward enough, or maybe the way Edward and Roscoe got along—and they had gotten along, which surprised Edward him-self—was upsetting to her.

"OK, Elise," Edward said. "What's the deal? What are you pissed about?"

In the front seat, she put her hand over her forehead and blew out some air, blew it out through pursed lips, so that it sounded like a small tire failure. "I'm not pissed about anything," she said. "I just don't want to hear about the car. Or the rain. Or the history of syrup." She turned around to look at Edward. "Sometimes it just gets to be too dreary, you know what I mean? We go out to breakfast and you order chicken-fried steak." She shook her head and blew more air out, this time through her nose. "The moment for chicken-fried steak has gone, Edward. But even when I say that, I'm thinking, well, maybe it's all right to eat chicken-fried steak. I mean, it's like the three of us sitting back there, in that drugstore place, like we're one big happy family or something. It turns my stomach."

"What do you want us to do?" Edward said. "I was doing fine until you came up here yesterday. You come in and you pull your usual, and then Roscoe shows up, and . . . shit, Elise."

"You'd have had a better birthday if I had stayed home?" Elise said.

"Yeah," Edward said. "It would break my heart to have to spend my birthday alone. I like it a lot when we pretend I'm ten."

"I am ten," Roscoe said.

It was a funny thing to say, and a funny time to say it. He was talking more to himself than to the other two. But once he'd said it, he looked in the rearview mirror to see how Edward was going to react.

Edward looked at the back of Roscoe's head. He could tell Roscoe was looking at him in the rearview, but he didn't want to look back, so he stared at Roscoe's hairline, behind his ear, down to his neck. Roscoe was real clean-cut, Edward thought. Probably got the job done at some place called The Hair Also Rises, a little niche in a mall somewhere, where a plain-looking twenty-four-year-old woman with spiked hair and an inclination to unbutton her shirt, a woman with a lot of bangles, traded stories with her pals while she turned unsuspecting citizens like Roscoe into half-wits, hair-wise. And he probably tipped her big, so secure did he feel when he stepped out of her chair. She'd have a funny name, like Fen or Pola, and he'd mention her in casual conversation with his co-workers, and they'd mention their hair people, too. Nobody would tell anybody that the headdress looked like hair by Ronco.

Elise was looking straight ahead, tracing her lips with her thumb. She said, "He is. He's not lying. That's why we get along."

"He's what?" Edward said. "Ten? He looks older than that to me. He looks like he might be thirty. Maybe more. I bet he functions like a thirty-year-old. Don't you, Roscoe?"

Roscoe shrugged. "I guess," he said. "Sometimes."

"That doesn't make any difference," Elise said. "That's not what we're talking about." She reached over in the front and patted his leg. "We like him ten."

"Good," Edward said. "That's great. Like away." He turned sideways in the back seat, putting his feet up on the leather. He was sitting behind Elise, facing the driver's side of the car, looking over his shoulder at the frosted back window. "We got here a ten–year–old with a BMW," he said, addressing an imaginary audience outside the rear window. "He's getting along real nice with my wife. She makes him biscuits and he cleans up his room. It's an all–star relationship."

Roscoe checked the mirror, then turned to Elise. "I think I'd better drop you guys off and go to a movie or something."

"Tell me which one you're going to," Elise said. "So we don't run into each other."

"That's cute," Edward said. "You folks are so cute together. I don't think I ever saw anything so cute in all my life."

"Come on, Edward," Roscoe said. "You were being nice at breakfast. What happened?"

"My lovely wife, Daffy, wanted some fireworks," Edward said.

"My esteemed husband has difficulty distinguishing between the cherry and hydrogen bombs," Elise said.

"Wait a minute," Edward said. "Was somebody just clever? I mean, if we're going to be clever I got to stop off at the house and get my monkey ears."

"Monkey ears?" Roscoe looked in the mirror and squinted at Edward, and Edward squinted back.

Elise said, "I don't know why you're complaining anyway, Edward. You don't want it."

"It?" Edward said. "Dear God, we're not going to talk about *it*, are we? Here in this car on this rainy day? Why don't we talk about your period instead? When was your last period? Was it a big one or a little one? What's your feeling on PMS? Are you having PMS right now? What's your sense of the optimum dimension for the male sexual organ? Speaking here in terms of circumference as well as that other dimension."

Elise sighed and shook her head and then, almost under her breath, she said, "Mine eyes have seen the glory . . ."

"Thank you," Edward said. "Thank you. My mother thanks you. My father thanks you. We all thank you."

There was a short silence then. Roscoe and Elise looked straight ahead out the windshield. Edward looked straight out the side of the car. Then, very slowly, Elise turned, just her head, rotating it as if it were mechanical, pausing a moment when she looked at Roscoe, then turning her head farther until out of the corner of her eye she could see Edward in the back seat. She held her head that way for a minute, looking away and then back to him, moving just her eyes, and then she turned her head—even more slowly this time—back to the front of the car.

The rain was trashing the windshield. You couldn't see a thing out of it. The wipers were just flailing at the glass, flapping back and forth like two thin animals with their tails caught in traps. They drove a couple more minutes in silence and then made a turn on the street that was the entrance to the subdivision where Edward's house was. They all watched the water splash. Then Roscoe said something. "Tiny," he said. "The tinier the better is what I hear."

7

ROSCOE AND Elise went to a noon movie at the mall, together, and Edward stayed home. It was a pleasure to have Roscoe and Elise out of the way. He had changed clothes as soon as they had come in from breakfast, and when they left he changed again, this time into his bathrobe. The robe was a two-year-old ratty pale blue Ralph Lauren terrycloth job that Elise had given him. He liked it. He spent most of his time at home in it, routinely changing into it when he came in from work, using it as his main dress for the weekends. It had been repeatedly ripped up and repaired, sewn back together by hand a half-dozen times, most recently the week after Elise moved away, when Edward had taken it down to her apartment and asked her to fix the pocket and belt loop on the left side. She had resewn the robe and returned it on one of her visits. They had tried, of course, to remove the Lauren insignia, but they had failed. By now the pony and rider, which had been discreet to start with, had been rendered a harmless off-white—testimony to the power of Clorox, since, of course, the emblem was thread, which does not readily give up its color.

After he watched Roscoe and Elise drive off into the rain, Edward went into the bedroom, put on the robe, straightened a few of Elise's things, then went into the kitchen for a cold drink, then retired to the couch in the living room, where he sat and realized for the first time in a while that he still had the Band-Aid on his nose. He peeled the bandage off, carefully folding it in half so that the two sticky faces were pressed exactly together. He put the folded Band-Aid in his robe pocket and left his hand there, playing with the Band-Aid as he thought how peaceful the house was when only he was in it.

It seemed to him that the things in his house were the most patient things imaginable. They were just sitting there, or standing there, awaiting his attention. They would not move unless he moved them. They would not require him to answer their questions, or respond to their remarks, or perform for them in any way. And yet there they were, at attention, ready to be turned on, or sat in, or looked at, or moved, or rearranged, or opened or closed. These were just ordinary things, lamps and baskets, chairs and tables, books and magazines and pictures. He didn't think of them as very quiet living things, he didn't attribute to them any of the characteristics of living things, on the contrary, they had about them the magic of things for which living or not living is not an issue. They were just there. Poised, but not imposing. What he had noticed, however, was that when there were other people around, these same objects were not so interesting to him. Somehow, in the company of people, these objects lost their specialness. Their haunting character. That aspect that was best explained by saying that when only Edward was in the house, the things there could just as well have been parts of a three-dimensional photograph through which he occasionally walked. It wasn't a matter of security, exactly, for he knew the things could not protect him from harm, but there was the sense that their stability through time provided for him a defense against time, a language with which he could have a conversation with time. He was sitting there on the couch on this Saturday afternoon thinking this, and thinking how screwy it was to be thinking this. And, at the same time, thinking that this kind of thing was exactly what he liked to think.

One of the things he liked to do, for example, was to move a single object in the house just a little bit. He might move the salt and pepper shaker set from the left to the right side of the old wooden bowl that sat in the middle of the dining table. So that when he looked in the direction of the table from his position on the couch, he would see the shakers on the right of the bowl instead of the left. This would be the only thing he would change in the house for days. Thus he would have the opportunity to consider the shakers in that position versus the shakers in their previous position. And he would have the time to recognize the dissimilarities, the change, which he took to be time's part of the conversation.

Obviously, when Elise was living there, this kind of play was not possible, because there was no way to be sure that Elise wouldn't come in and move things around to suit herself. And in fact, when they had lived together, that is exactly what she did. The way she lived in a place was much less structured than the way he did, and objects were always popping up in odd places, so that some afternoon he would come home from work and find her half-pound cloth-enclosed solid rubber wrist bands, the ones she wore while exercising, perched casually, like modern black candleholders, on the stove. Or a chair might have been moved, the prints of its legs still visible in the carpet. Or a shirt might be over the back of a chair, or the Tunturi exercise bicycle might be turned around so that its front wheel, instead of facing the bedroom door, now faced the bedroom window. None of these things, and no things like them, had much bothered him when she lived there, but since her departure he had noticed how much better he liked the house when such things did not happen unbeknownst to him. He might move the bicycle, or leave some socks out, or twist the television set, angling it toward the couch, and that was OK. It was even OK, he thought, when they did it together, when they were both involved in the change, or even when they were both present when the change took place. What he didn't like was the order of things disturbed without his knowing of the disturbance.

At that moment, the telephone, perfectly in position on the edge of the counter in the kitchen, rang.

Edward got up off the couch and went to answer the phone. "Yes?" he said.

"Who is this?" the caller said.

It was a woman. Edward held the mouthpiece of the telephone away from his face a minute while he tried to figure out who it was. He did not recognize the voice. He couldn't place it. He thought about the office and the neighbors—nothing there. He thought, Old friend? Wrong number? "Who do you want?" he finally said.

"It's not a question of who I want," the woman said. "You must be Edward."

Edward nodded. "Maybe I am, and maybe I'm not. Who's this?"

"A friend of Elise's," the woman said. "You don't know me. Is she there?"

"No, she's not here," Edward said. "I mean, she's here, she's in town, but she's not here now. May I tell her who called?"

"Well, yes," the woman said. "But it'd be more to the point if you told me how to get to your house. She is staying there, isn't she?"

"Yes," Edward said. "But are you sure we're talking about the same Elise? I mean, I don't know who you are."

"Well," the woman said. "My name is Lurleen and I really hate meeting people for the first time on the telephone. Don't you? Elise and I live in the same apartments and we work together. She told me she was coming up here. I know Roscoe, too. I know about you. Elise talks about you."

Edward tightened the belt of his robe. "Oh," he said. "Well. Hi, Lurleen. Does she say great stuff about me or what?"

"I've heard worse," Lurleen said. There was a little pause, and then she said, "No, just kidding. She thinks a lot of you."

"I think a lot of her," Edward said. "We've been together a long time. Some of the time we're not actually together, but . . . you know what I mean."

"She's doing real well," Lurleen said. "Her job, her whole life—I think she's doing real well."

Edward squinted at that, looking across the room at the clock on the stove. "Well," he said. "That's good. I'm glad to hear it." He liked the woman's voice, but he didn't much like being told how Elise was doing. He always wondered about people who presented themselves as if they were more intimate with someone, some third party, than you were. Especially if the third party was your wife, or your lover, or your brother. It was as if these people had to let you know how intimate they were with the person you had in common. He said, "Elise can take care of herself, she always could."

"Don't I know it," Lurleen said. "She's an impressive woman. She has all the tools."

"Yeah, I think she's the best pure halfback in the draft," Edward said.

"What?" Lurleen said.

"Nothing," Edward said. "Just a joke. So what you want is directions to come over here, is that it?"

"That would be nice," Lurleen said. "I'm at the mall. Where is she, anyway? Is she coming back?"

"She went to the movies with Roscoe," Edward said. "She should be back in about an hour. Maybe two."

"That's perfect," Lurleen said. "That means I have time to look at shoes. I don't know whether you know it or not, but you've got some pretty good shoe stores here in the mall." She did a little laugh. "Shoes are one of my things," she said, putting a special spin on the word "things." "I'm shoe crazy. Ask Elise."

"Everybody is," Edward said. "You don't need to be ashamed."

"Hey! Who's ashamed? My shoes are my children. Every one of them a twin. We don't talk about being ashamed where I come from."

"Sorry," Edward said. "I just meant—"

"I've got an idea what you meant," Lurleen said. "But it's OK, everything's OK. Maybe you could just tell me how to get there, so when I finish I can come over."

Edward gave her the directions and said it was nice to meet her and then they hung up. He figured he had at least an hour before anyone showed up, so he got a fresh Diet Coke and went back to the living room and sat down. He was uncomfortable sitting there, so he went into the bedroom and got into bed. He drew out the black wool sock that he kept under his pillow, and he draped that over his eyes to keep out the light. He thought of Oblomov for a moment, remembering the time in college when he had read the book and had been so smitten by it that, like the title character, he had decided to stay in bed, permanently. He managed it for a little more than a week, after which the idea seemed better in mind than in practice.

Instead he learned the art of the nap. In a radical political maneuver, very unpopular at the time, he endorsed the views of then President Lyndon Baines Johnson on the nap. Not surprisingly, this endorsement stood him in good stead with his live-in companion, a religious/sexual fanatic named Kinta, whose view of human life centered on the idea that you'd better damned well be doing something sexual every single waking moment of your life, or else you were in big trouble. The president's nationally televised thinking on the subject of the nap, that you had to take off your clothes to take a decent one, dovetailed nicely with Kinta's ideas and opinions, not to mention her purposes. Edward had lived with Kinta just over two months. She was a gorgeous, small, dark woman who never said anything that Edward understood, in spite of the fact that whenever she was not making love, and much of the time that she was, she was talking. Kinta explained things. And no matter what she explained, she always started in the middle, and ended not far from there—after many suns had passed over the mountain.

Years after he had spent the two months with her, he had run into Kinta in a shopping mall in Louisiana, in Lafayette, and when he asked how she was, she said she was "stuck in the mud." At first that was all she said or would say about herself, and her reticence startled Edward, who had expected a five-year history, including names, dates, places, articles of clothing, stories about food, allusions to whole sets of beliefs, the kind of flying-apart-at-the-seams report that he had years before understood to be her stock-in-trade.

Kinta had married a doctor. Over coffee she explained that he was a very nice man, that his name was Richard, that he was fond of children, that he owned a DX7 synthesizer on which he played Windham Hill–style music in his spare time, that he drove a Mercedes, that they had a lovely house with plenty of glass, and that she felt very safe with him.

"He's a state trooper," Kinta had said. "And it's nice, you know, when something happens, to have a doctor right there. It's not like when you go to the doctor, where you think the doctor knows what he's talking about. But it's still nice. He can explain things, get prescriptions—it's OK."

"So what's the 'stuck in the mud' business?" Edward had asked.

"It's just that I feel as if something has been evacuated from my life," Kinta said. "Nothing ever made any sense, but I used to understand things anyway. Now, it's different. I have a lot of things to do, and I do them. It's like there are places I'm supposed to put my feet, one after the other, and I do that, and everybody I know thinks I really mean that, or if that's not what they think they don't say anything about it, and everybody is enormously well-to-do. I used to really hate it. I tried fucking the gardener, I thought that might help. The gardener was this young kid named Chuck Monet. One afternoon when he was leaving the house I just went outside and got into his truck. He knew exactly what to do. We went to his apartment and fucked for eight hours. Richard was out of town, so I could have stayed, but I got Chuck to take me home anyway. I took a bath and went to bed. I was in bed almost asleep when Chuck called to see how I was. I told him we wouldn't be needing his services anymore."

"I see," Edward said.

"I told him to forget about it," Kinta said. "I told him what had happened between us hadn't really happened between us but between him and the person I see in the mirror, and that she had really enjoyed it, but that I didn't think it was the kind of thing that would improve my marriage. I told him how sometimes people go one direction in order to get to a place that's another direction."

"How did Chuck take it?" Edward said.

"He wanted to have a baby with me," Kinta said.

"Yeah," Edward said. "Everybody wants to do that. Every time I turn around people want to have babies with other people."

"It's what we like," Kinta said. "Or else we can't think of anything else to do. Sometimes I don't know which it is."

"So, after the gardener, what?" Edward said.

"Well," she said. "After the gardener I settled down. Sort of. I figured it out. It's like you're sick. Like, when you were sick? You stay in bed all the time. After the first couple of days you feel fine. Unless you try to get out of bed. So that's what it's like."

Edward nodded his understanding, and the conversation had gone on a few more minutes before Kinta's husband, a good-looking young guy in good-looking clothes, with an engaging smile and an attractive six-year-old daughter, found them there in the Bun Shoppe. Kinta was very apologetic. Richard was very apologetic. She introduced Edward, everybody was very pleased to meet everybody else, and then the little family trod off, slump-shouldered but hand in hand, toward Bethlehem, the temporary gift-wrap and decoration shop that had been set up for Christmas in the center of the mall.

Edward had watched them go, staring at their backs, with mixed feelings of sadness and envy and amazement.

Elise found him. She had been in the bookstore buying books for his parents for Christmas. She had read in *USA Today* that older people like books and protection more than almost anything else, and had decided that she and Edward could afford his parents at least one of the two things. She said, "You look like you've been hit by a truck."

He said, "I ran into an old girlfriend from Texas. One I told you about—Kinta."

"The stargazer," Elise said.

"Not so much anymore," Edward said. "She married a doctor, a guy named Richard. I met him, too."

"Well," Elise said. "It sounds like you had a big time."

"Kinta fucked the gardener," Edward said.

"Don't tell me," Elise said. "I'll bet he was real good. It's all that plant massage they do. They get their hands down there in the dirt, and they start wiggling them around, and they start yanking on the roots, and they straighten things out. They get that scent on them, you know? They got them suntanned bellies—they got permanent sweat on there. They got that open shirt so you can see that stuff glistening. It's hard for a girl to resist. A girl's got to work real hard just to keep her eyes in her head."

Edward regarded his own belly, which was somewhat larger than it ought to have been, and completely covered by his shirt, a dangerously tasteful oxford cloth from Brooks Brothers. "I believe my wife to be slightly miffed," Edward had said, pretending to talk to an overweight young man with golden hair who was sitting two booths away and appeared set on eating an entire banana cream pie. The kid was wearing one bandana around his neck and another around his leg, and his complexion was very red, as if to suggest a heart problem. He looked at Edward when Edward pretended to talk to him, and he smiled at Edward and nodded. His nod was real vigorous, a parody of itself.

"Wrong," Elise said. Then she, too, turned to the guy with the pie. "Wrong," she said again. And the kid with the pie nodded at *her*. He agreed with everybody.

Edward sat on the edge of the bed thinking about Kinta and thinking about the other girlfriends he had had, thinking she was the only one of them that he still liked. This struck him as odd, since he had had his share of girlfriends, a dozen serious ones, maybe, variously intelligent, attractive, sexy, interesting. Of them, Kinta was the only one he much thought about. A couple of times a year she would pop into mind, he would wonder where she was and what she was doing, who she was with, how she was getting on. He had her phone number, and once in a while he called, but most of the conversations were short, sometimes slightly bitter. For a time after the Lafayette meeting he'd called more often, and she'd been pleased to hear from him.

They talked sex on the telephone. They talked about making love together again the way they had years before. A couple of times they had masturbated together on the telephone, pushing each other with intimate details, fantasies, porn stories. In one of those calls she had described how it would feel to have him screw her. Her description had been so vivid that he could actually feel the penetration she described. It was remarkable, and after that call was done—they always hung up quickly—he had called her back to ask if it had been as feelable, as *real* for her, and she had said yes, and they had laughed about it like two lovers in bed after a stolen morning intimacy. The sex calls died out after that. He tried to keep them going, he called her weekly, but she told him the same thing she had told the gardener, only more directly. "I have a good life with Richard," she said. "This stuff was OK until it started seeming like we were really doing it, and that fucked things. It makes me feel like I haven't got enough."

Edward tried to persuade her that it was OK, that it really wasn't such a terrible thing, that it did not have major implications for her life with Richard. She wasn't convinced. She said, "I don't screw anybody but Richard anymore. If I start screwing people then I start thinking about screwing people and pretty soon Richard is history. You remember how I used to be, don't you? I've changed all that. It's an act of will. You can call, I like talking to you, but not about this stuff, OK?"

Kinta held the line, the frequency and intimacy of their telephone conversations diminished. He thought about her sometimes, felt fond of her, but he did not call her very often. He had tried a couple of other old girlfriends, interested in having sex with them on the telephone, but in one case he had no luck at all, and in the other a rather lukewarm response which ended abruptly when the UPS people brought a package to the ex-girlfriend's door. The package was chrome barbells. The woman had to get off the phone.

Lurleen was heavyset, wearing an orange jumpsuit and high-top Reeboks, and she gave Edward a phony little smile when he opened the door. "Howdy," she said. "I'm Lurleen. You're Edward, right? You don't appear to be dressed."

He was still in his robe. "I was resting," he said.

"Well, that's OK," she said. "Is Elise back?" She was tugging at odd parts of the jumpsuit. "God, I hope Elise is back."

"Any minute," Edward said. He stepped away from the door to let her in. "Why don't you come inside and sit down? I'll change my clothes and we can wait for her together."

"That'll be fun," Lurleen said.

Edward left her in the living room while he went back into the bedroom to change, and when he came out she was sitting in his spot on the couch. There was, of course, no way for her to know that it was his spot, but it upset him nonetheless. He thought about sitting on the couch with her, about taking the seat at the other end of the couch, the end where he never sat, but instead pulled a cane-backed Cessca chair from the dining table and sat there. Lurleen was thumbing a magazine, huffing at the articles, or the pictures, or both. It was *Time* magazine, so Edward took her huffs to represent her opinions of current events, of things cultural, sociological, and political. She gave no indication of wanting to talk to him, so the two of them sat there, she in the living room and he ten feet away at the dining table, his chair turned to face her, without speaking. Edward didn't want to bother her, but on the other hand, he didn't want to be impolite. He said, "So, how are you? Would you like something to drink?"

"Sure," she said, without looking up. "How about a beer? You got any beer?"

"I don't have any beer," Edward said.

"Oh, that's right," she said. "You don't drink. That's very health-conscious of you." She looked up and gave him a quick, dry smile.

"I used to drink," Edward said. "All it made me want to do was drink more. I mean, it's not like eating, where you eat enough and then you stop." He made some hand gestures during this little speech.

"I love drinking," Lurleen said. "If I didn't drink, I don't know what I'd do."

"There may be some wine," Edward said. "But if there is, it's been there a while. You want me to look?"

She gave him a dull flick of the eyes and shook her head. "I don't imagine it's absolutely necessary," she said.

They stopped talking again. Edward noticed that the light fixture in the corner, the standing floor lamp, had been moved a little toward the window. He tried to remember if he had moved it, but he couldn't remember. He got up and started across the room to move the lamp back to where it belonged, but then thought Lurleen might find that odd, so he did a quick detour into the kitchen for his cigarettes. He kept his cigarettes in a cabinet in the kitchen so he wouldn't smoke so much. When he returned Lurleen was at the window, looking out into the front yard. She turned around and frowned at the cigarette.

"You don't seem to have much to say to me," she said. "Am I bothering you? Do you want me to leave or something?"

Edward was a little startled by this remark. "No, of course not," he said.

"I can leave if you want me to leave," Lurleen said. "All you have to do is say so."

"I know that," Edward said.

"So?"

Edward shrugged, and then affected what he thought was a playful voice. "So I guess my house is your house," he said.

"I really would like a beer," Lurleen said. "Is there a convenience store nearby?"

Edward returned the dining chair to its place at the table and then cut across the room to retake his traditional position on the couch. He had the impression, on looking at Lurleen, that she thought this bit of business was peculiar. She gave him what he thought was a puzzled look, a kind of Lettermanesque squint, and a twisting of the mouth, and a raised eyebrow all at the same time. As if she were saying, "What the hell are *you* doing?"

He did a little self-conscious wave and said, "It's where I sit."

"Ah. I see," Lurleen said. "It's where you sit. I forgot for a moment that you're a guy living alone—you've probably got everything in its place and a place for everything, right? You've probably got a little nightshirt for the toaster."

"Wait a minute," Edward said. "Have we got a problem here? What's the deal?"

"Nothing," Lurleen said. She was fidgeting a little, as if she felt she'd been too aggressive. "I just want everybody to be happy. I don't think anybody ought to be coerced into anything."

Edward did the comic's routine of looking around for somebody when it's obvious that there isn't anybody there. "Somebody under siege here?" he said. "Is there some duress around here somewhere? What are you talking about?"

"Hey," she said. "I'm not talking about anything. That's what I do, I go around not talking about anything. That's my standard thing. Things are going great for everybody. Take me for instance. I've got my aerobics, my very interesting employ, my apartment—what could be better? And I've got friends. Elise."

"Elise is on your team," Edward said.

"That's it," she said. "Elise is on my team. Of course, she's not the only one."

"No," Edward said.

"I'm on there, too," Lurleen said.

8

WHEN ELISE and Roscoe got back at four, Lurleen and Edward were on the screened-in back porch drinking Heinekens. There were a half-dozen empties on the table. "Hey," Edward said as they came through the house. "Have a beer. Have a couple of beers. Hey, Elise. Lurleen's here."

"I'm here, I'm here," Lurleen said. She waved both hands up in the air over her head as if she were a political figure acknowledging a crowd. Only she had her back to Elise and Roscoe. "We're watching this rain," Lurleen said. "We've decided this rain is very beautiful. We like particularly the way it just comes down, from the sky, just, like—drip, drip, drip." She popped Edward on the upper arm. "Right?"

"Right," Edward said. "And we like the shiny parts the best."

"Yeah," Lurleen said. "The shiny parts are great."

Elise bent to kiss Edward's cheek, then did the same to Lurleen. "Some of my friends have been letting their hair down," she said.

"Well," Lurleen said. "Maybe a little."

"What's all this stuff on the floor?" Roscoe said. "Looks like hair."

"Roscoe made the hair-on-the-floor joke," Edward said.

"Yeah, that's a good one," Lurleen said. She twisted her head, looking back over her shoulder at Roscoe. "Howdy, Cowboy. How's it hanging?" She turned around to Edward, hitting his arm again. "Sometimes we call him Cowboy to give him kind of a boost."

"Hiya, Cowboy," Edward said.

Elise took Roscoe's arm, the two of them standing behind Edward and Lurleen, who were still sitting at the table facing the backyard. "Dear Roscoe," she said. "It appears as though our friends Edward and Lurleen have decided to be somewhat abrasive upon our return. I do not think it is our duty and responsibility to endure too much of this particular personality disorder. On the other hand, we *are* staying here."

"All of us?" Edward said.

"Sure," Lurleen said. "I, and Roscoe, and Elise, and you. We is all of us so deeply in love with one another, our fates inexorably intertwined, that we are decided to live together as one. Beginning today. At a theater near you."

"I like it," Edward said. He banged his bottle on the table two or three times as if applauding.

Lurleen did a big smile and nodded, accepting the applause. "These is the facts in the case."

"What's all this on the floor?" Roscoe said.

This time everybody laughed. Elise put her hands on Edward's shoulders and bent around to look into his eyes. "Hello, Edward?" she said, almost singing. "Do you think I ought to call the doctor?"

Because she was in such an awkward position, Edward could, and did, latch onto her in a Valentino-style embrace, pulling her farther over his shoulder, her head almost on the table, and once he had her there, he made loud smooching noises and then kissed her squarely on the lips. Elise didn't fight it. She didn't exactly participate, either. She just held the position, twisted over his shoulder and onto the table, bracing herself against him with one hand and the table with the other. When Edward released her she didn't move at all, she held the pose. She gave him a polite smile, then did the same for Lurleen and Roscoe. "Will there be anything else for you, sir?" she said, sliding away from the table, limping, holding the contorted pose as best she could, as if that were her natural condition.

"Give him a side o' grits," Lurleen said.

"Don't want no grits," Edward said. "They eat your teeth."

"That's nothing compared to what they do to the lining of the large intestine," Roscoe said. He pulled a wire-frame deck chair off a stack by the porch wall and sat down across from Edward. "I hate this weather," he said. "I wish I'd stayed at home."

"And gone to jail for stealing the hogs of Curl Trenary," Lurleen said.

"OK," Elise said. "We're shifting into the lamentation mode." She took Edward's bottle off the table and finished the beer that was in it, then put the bottle on its side on the table and spun it. The neck ended up pointing at Edward. "Looks like it's you and me, Bub," she said.

"How come you always get to pick?" Lurleen said. "Edward and me were getting along great until you guys came back. A couple more beers and I'd have had him on the bedroom floor."

Elise gave her a creepy smile. "Not unless he was picking lint," she said.

"What, I'm not a woman?" Lurleen said. "I'm a woman. I have drives and desires. More than you, I'll bet. Sometimes *I* want to go eat at a fish restaurant. Sometimes I like to think *I'm* pretty."

"Yeah," Roscoe said. He put an arm around Lurleen's shoulder. "We'd like to express our solidarity on this matter."

Lurleen shrugged his arm off her shoulder. "Don't be hanging on me," she said. "I was accidentally being serious."

"You are pretty," Elise said. "You're as pretty as any of the rest of us."

"Now wait a minute," Edward said.

"Well, thanks a lot," Lurleen said. "I feel a lot better now."

"Are we talking about physical ugliness?" Roscoe said. "Or spiritual? I mean, the way I figure it there are only about three good-looking people on the planet. Both of them women. Then we got a bunch of people who are pretty good painters. I mean, you get far enough away and everybody is gorgeous."

"Oh, that's pretty," Elise said. "Roscoe hates women just like Edward. The two of you ought to join a misogynist club."

Edward folded his arms over his head as if to protect himself from blows. "Here we go," he said. "It is true that on several occasions I have spoken unkindly of women. More precisely I have spoken unkindly of certain women, of certain kinds of women. Certain characteristic behaviors, as noted by me, have been reported. And it is further true that I have commented, from time to time, negatorially as regards the wearing of leggings or similar by certain women whose physical characteristics themselves are, in my view, a commentary on the wearing of leggings. In particular, I have characterized that space which comes to exist in the leggings at or near the crotch as a quote crawl space quote. I have further noted the amount of foodstuff that in the normal course of things comes to rest and-slash-or gets lodged on the surface of a legging in and around the aforementioned crawl space, here speaking of cake and cookie crumbs, the tiny colored beads people use for the topping of festive eats, and so on, and so on. I have also mentioned hairs, so-called floaties, specks of ash, and those particles of unknown origin so small as to have not warranted naming." By now Edward had settled into a deep baritone, a rolling, cadenced, Burtonesque mimicry of the good Archbishop at Canterbury on a singularly terrifying day sometime after the Middle Ages. He was singing. "But it is not my belief that these reports of cheesy jetsam settling itself on the stretchy loins of certain women constitute an indictment of all women, nor, indeed, a derisive view of womanhood. On the contrary, it is my firmly held conviction that when the smoke has cleared, when all the old wounds have been muscled off the front pages of our internal newspapers, and when the new wounds have been licked into submission, what we will discover, to our amazement, is that women are like people."

"They suck," Elise said.

"I didn't say that," Edward said.

"Edward," Lurleen said. "Dogs are like people. Women *are* people."

Edward sat up and unwrapped his arms, and gave Lurleen a patient smile. "Yes, Lurleen. I believe that to have been my point. Forgive me for trying to make it slightly more intriguing by clothing it in something other than pointedness. I sometimes forget that some of you women may sometimes have some difficulty with possible interpretations of some of the language that is sometimes used to perhaps articulate possible thought."

"I hate those things, too," Roscoe said. "Leggings. They look great on seventeen-year-olds, but on adults they look desperate and sad."

"I don't want to just talk about leggings," Lurleen said.

"Leggings are like Nicaragua," Elise said.

"My thinking exactly," Edward said.

"What's for dinner?" Roscoe said.

Lurleen got up and started back into the kitchen. "Why don't you have any children? You should have some children. It's great, you get to clean their litter boxes, put their little food in their little bowls, take them to the vet."

"Where are you going?" Elise said. "Why did you say that?"

"I've got to clean up," Lurleen said. "Is it OK?"

Elise followed her into the house. "Sure," she said. "I'll show you the way. Roscoe took a bath in there this morning, but he's usually clean as a whistle. The thing about Roscoe is that he doesn't have any hair on his body."

"That's disgusting," Edward said, calling after her. Then he turned around to Roscoe. "Is that true?"

"No," Roscoe said. "But I knew a guy once who didn't have any hair on his body. Not one single hair. This guy didn't even have eyelashes. He was a real good architect, or something, but he was more famous for not having any hair on him."

"I don't think that would be so horrible," Edward said.

Roscoe pushed Lurleen's chair out of the way and then slid his own chair around so that he and Edward were sitting on the same side of the table. He said, "I think I ought to have a beer. Then we could sit out here, two men, drinking beer and talking."

"What would we talk about?" Edward said.

Roscoe got up and started toward the kitchen. "I don't know," he said. "Hunting, women—what about civics?"

While Roscoe was getting his beer, Edward did not take his eyes off a gray two-by-four that was leaning against a pine tree about sixty feet from his back door. He was thinking that it was probably a bad thing to live alone, that although he preferred living alone, there were probably ways in which it was unhealthy. He wondered what those were. He also guessed that his living alone was some kind of phony living alone and not real living alone. That was because of Elise. It wasn't that he anticipated her return—he wasn't sure he thought she would ever come back—but that he imagined that she would not ever leave him. That they were connected, and that it was terminal. She would go on living someplace else, and he would go on living here, and they would go on being married. Ordinarily, a ridiculous idea. So why wasn't it a ridiculous idea in this case? That puzzled him. It didn't feel ridiculous. It didn't even feel unusual.

"Something's got to be done," Roscoe said, stepping out onto the porch again, a beer in each hand.

"What?"

"They're in the back bathroom showering or something," Roscoe said. "Giggling. I went in the bedroom there to get another shirt, and I heard them. The water's running. I put my ear up against the door. I couldn't make out what they were actually saying, but I could hear them saying something. I don't think they could hear me."

"Roscoe," Edward said. "I don't think you're comfortable here. You don't look comfortable. You don't act comfortable. You say things like 'The women are back there showering together and we've got to do something about it.' " He stared at Roscoe thinking that he didn't really dislike him, even though he had some reason to dislike him. Roscoe was very *amiable*. Roscoe was always trying to please, and entertain, and be friendly, and keep things going smoothly, and more often than not he succeeded. But Edward had the impression that something was lost in this process, some thought or feeling, that some substance was put by, sacrificed to etiquette. But somehow you could always tell he was playing this role of a person who was not acting, which may itself have been a further refinement of the disguise. The result was that Roscoe always looked like a man grimacing too much on hearing of the death of someone he'd never known. Still, Edward liked him well enough. Edward said, "What should we do about the women in the shower? We could go in there and bust their faces. We could go in there and tap on the door and say, 'Yoo-hoo.' We could remove their fingers with a chain saw. What do you think we ought to do?"

"I guess you're right," Roscoe said, wiggling the neck of his beer bottle near his mouth. "I guess it's not going to hurt anything. I wasn't really suggesting that we go back there and do anything. I was just saying that."

"Being one of the guys, huh?" Edward said.

"Yeah. Yeah, I guess," Roscoe said.

"I guess it is pretty strange," Edward said.

"That's what I meant," Roscoe said. "I don't think it happens that much in America. You know, among women who aren't lovers."

"Lesbians," Edward said.

"Yeah, that's what I mean," Roscoe said. "Lesbians. I mean, lesbians do that all the time, but, well, you know what I mean."

Roscoe finally took a drink. The rain had stopped, but everything was still dripping, and the clear gray of the daylight was giving way to the denser, more closed slate of dusk. Through the trees that bordered the backyard and separated it from the empty lot on the other side of the block, Edward could see a couple of street lamps, cold and blue-white against the thick sky. He tried for a minute to match the drips as they fell off the edge of the roof with the sounds that he heard. He didn't have much luck.

Edward asked Elise to take a walk with him. She told him it was raining. She told him she had just gotten out of the shower. He told her that was an hour and a half ago. Lurleen told him that wasn't the point. Roscoe said he thought it was a good idea, that they ought to take a walk together. Elise told him she had to work on

Monday, she couldn't afford to get sick. Lurleen said they should just stay in the house, that if Edward had something private to say to Elise, they should go into the bedroom and close the door. Edward said he thought it was embarrassing to have to ask his wife to go for a walk. Roscoe said he knew where Edward was coming from. Elise told him that she really didn't mind going for a walk, that it wasn't the walking part that bothered her. Lurleen told her that she ought to at least give Edward a chance. Edward said that he was tired and he really didn't want to go for a walk anyway. Roscoe told them that whenever he saw two people walking in the rain, a couple, he was quite touched. He told them that Elise never took walks with him. "Sometimes when she goes out running, I go with her," Roscoe said. "But then she goes off and leaves me there. I mean, she walks with me for a while, ten or fifteen minutes, and then she starts running, and there I am left alone out in the middle of nowhere."

"It's not nowhere, Roscoe," Elise said. "It's only a couple of blocks from the apartment. Besides, you could run, too."

"Of course I could run," Roscoe said. "That's not the point. The point is, we agree to go out for a walk and then you start running."

"She likes to run," Lurleen said.

Roscoe waved his hands. "That's fine," he said. "I can understand that. I can live with that. Just don't tell me you're going to take me out for a walk and then start running."

"He doesn't like running," Lurleen said.

Roscoe walked toward her, staggering, Frankensteinlike, his hands outstretched as if to wring her neck. "Lur-lee-een," he said.

"Roscoe the Magnificent," she said, batting his arms away from her. "Stop. Edward has some stuff he wants to talk to Elise about."

Roscoe quit playing. "So, fine," he said. "Let them talk." He turned around and looked at Elise, pointed to Edward. "Why don't you go for a walk with this man?"

"He just wants to get her alone," Lurleen said.

All three of them turned around and looked at Lurleen. The phone rang. Edward left the guests staring and went to get the phone.

It was Kinta. She was calling long-distance from a pay phone at a Gulf station in Slidell, Louisiana. It must have been right on the highway—in the background Edward could hear the cars whizzing by. Kinta said, "I'm leaving Richard. He's a stupid motherfuck. He's been slamming his dainty little secretary. All this time. I'm out here trying to do good and avoid evil, and he's up there with his little tykette. So, Edward? So, I'm coming up there and I'm going to fuck you 'til the cows come home." There was a pause, and then she said, "Edward?"

"Hi," he said. He wasn't surprised by the call—except for this weekend, he had talked to Kinta more recently than he had talked to Elise—but the proposition shook him a little. He said, "Sounds great. Oh! Hold on a minute. . . . What's that in the backyard?" He leaned away from the telephone mouthpiece and made some mooing sounds.

"Don't start that crap with me," Kinta said. "I mean, I can get you off right here. You want me to? You want me to show you? You want me to tell you what I have on?"

"Take it easy," Edward said. He glanced over his shoulder at the people in the living room, then went around the counter into the kitchen. The stretching telephone cord knocked over a salt shaker, spilling salt on the countertop. Edward said, "Wait a minute, OK? Hang on." He hooked the telephone receiver on the refrigerator handle, stepped back across the room to straighten up the shaker, picked up a pinch of salt in his right hand and threw it over his left shoulder, then swept the rest of the salt onto his palm and rinsed his hand under the tap. He got the phone again. "Now," he said. "Where were we?"

"I want to be somebody's dingbat," Kinta said. "I'm itching all over. There's this good-looking black guy down here at the gas station. He likes the way I move, I can tell. He wiped my wind-shield. He had a big wet rag. He went back and forth. He did it good."

"Stop," Edward said. "OK? Just quit fucking around and talk to me a minute."

There was a little pause on the telephone, then Kinta said, "Oh. OK. I found out he's screwing his secretary and I'm leaving him. I took the car and I left. I got here and then I realized I didn't have anywhere to go. So I called my friend Edward."

"And you're at a gas station?" Edward said.

"Yeah," she said. "I'm standing out here and I'm cold and I'm wet and I hate men."

"Well, I'm glad you called me," Edward said. "You won't have any problem with me."

Kinta either didn't notice, or let it go. "I'm driving up there right now," she said. "I'm moving in for the duration. I won't take no for an answer."

"No," Edward said.

"That's pretty direct," Kinta said.

"I can be direct," Edward said. "I got Elise here, and her boyfriend, and some other friend of hers, a woman named Lurleen, and what I don't need right at this moment is Kinta."

"Well," Kinta said. "That's *extremely* direct."

"On the other hand," Edward said. "I could be wrong. You could lively up the place."

"I could, but I wouldn't," Kinta said. "I'd be a good little girl. I'd behave myself. I'd be the wounded party. Your women would love me. I'd put on a little show for the guy and he'd love me, too. Then, when they weren't looking, blam! I'd have you squealing."

"Oh, Jesus," Edward said.

"Well, I would," she said.

Edward could hear her laughing away from the telephone receiver. He liked her laugh. It was nasty, and unblinking, and private. He said, "OK. Come on."

"Great," Kinta said. "I'll be there in fifteen minutes."

"What?" Edward said.

"Just kidding," Kinta said. "But it's OK if I come up there? Really? What about all those people? Maybe I should stay at the Holiday Inn. Do you have a Holiday Inn there?"

Elise came into the kitchen, Lurleen trailing behind her. Elise raised her eyebrows at Edward as if asking who was on the telephone. Then Lurleen said, "Who is it?"

Edward put his hand over the mouthpiece and said to Elise, "It's Kinta. She's coming up here."

"That's fine with me," Elise said. She started opening the cabinets where Edward kept the dishes.

"Who's Kinta?" Lurleen said.

When there was more than one person around, Lurleen had this way of talking that was like talking to all of them at once, a knack Edward had never picked up. "Old friend," he said, his hand still over the mouthpiece.

Elise turned around and made a fist with her left hand and put her right forefinger inside the fist, then she held both of them up for Lurleen to see.

"Oh, great," Lurleen said. She pointed at Edward. "I don't know what you see in this scumbag. I don't know why you even bother to come up here. What is he, some kind of hero or something? The next time you start talking about moving back here, I'm going to do I don't know what."

Edward was telling Kinta what to do when she got to town, but he looked at Lurleen, and then looked sideways at Elise. "Why don't you just call when you get in," he said to Kinta. "Take the second highway exit and stop at a gas station and call. OK?"

"You told them, didn't you?" Kinta said. "I can hear it in your voice. They are standing right there and you told them. What did they say?"

"It's fine," Edward said. "It'll be great."

When he got off the phone Elise said, "I don't really want her in my house. I mean, I know I shouldn't care, but—"

"It's not really your house, exactly," Edward said.

He was surprised that he'd said that, surprised that he felt it. While saying it he had worried about how she would react, worried that it would hurt her, but, having said it, he could see that he needn't have worried. She was giving him a rock-hard look, expressionless, direct, as if to say, 'Why, you're a dumber fuck than

I thought you were, aren't you?' He returned the look, but he didn't feel nearly as tough as he wanted to. Then he thought that maybe her expression meant 'Yeah, I know, and it's horrible, isn't it?' That idea scared him. The confrontation was easy, it was a game for him, but if the look was resignation, no recourse, he thought he might be out of his league. That's when he realized that it wasn't his house, or that he didn't think it was his house, that no matter where she was or what the status of their marriage, the house was a place about which she would always have a say. He figured it applied to this particular house, that if he moved, too, then his new place would be more his than theirs. It seemed odd to him that he was so devoted to keeping things in order, and yet, when she came in, he pulled back and allowed her to mess things up. And he wondered why he didn't insist, why he was content to trail after her, picking up cigarettes and glasses of water and cleaning ashtrays and throwing away little bits of trash, little pieces of envelope-flap found on the kitchen countertops or in that little indentation where the cabinets met the floor. He wondered if he was just afraid. Or foolish. And he reminded himself that she was not messy, that she always cleaned up after herself, finally, and the picking up after her that he did could easily be seen as obsessive, a parody—virtue run amok.

"Well," Elise said. The muscles in her face softening to childlike doubt, her voice going to a stammer. "It's sort of my house, isn't it?"

He loved her when she said that. In someone else he might have seen it as manipulation, but with Elise, he had to squeeze his teeth together to keep from crying. She meant it. For fifteen years he had been enthralled by this one little move of hers, this one moment when she revealed how unsure she was of what she was saying or doing, when she laid herself completely open right in front of him. No protection, no defense, no effort to keep up appearances, no aggression, no hostility—no guile. With that small, innocuous question, she had shown her strength.

"Never mind," she said. "I don't care. Let her come. Is she coming today? Where's she going to sleep?"

"Where am I going to sleep?" Lurleen said.

"You can sleep with Roscoe," Elise said.

Roscoe was just then coming in from the living room. "Who can?" he said.

"I'm sleeping on the couch," Lurleen said. "I've already tried it out."

Elise shrugged at Roscoe. "Sorry," she said. "I tried."

"Gee, thanks, Lurleen," Roscoe said. "That makes me feel really good. I mean, you could wear clothes and everything. I'd wear clothes."

"What about your toenails," Lurleen said. "Have you seen your toenails recently?"

"I'm going to my room," Edward said, starting across the kitchen.

9

THEY HAD the following things for dinner: one Le Menu Yankee Pot Roast frozen dinner, one sliced Butterball turkey sandwich on Roman Meal bread, one pair of Sara Lee cinnamon and raisin bagels lightly toasted and topped with cream cheese, one peanut butter and jelly sandwich on white bread, served with a small dish of Borden's chocolate ice cream and half a glass of milk. Kinta had not shown up. Edward was increasingly uncomfortable with his guests, a discomfort he unsuccessfully attempted to mask with a number of suggestions as to what they might do, these ranging from renting a movie at the nearby video store to playing board games. He did not, however, have any board games for them to play. But as he thought about that, board games became more and more interesting to him. And he wanted nothing more than to sit with these three people, four should Kinta arrive, and play a long, slow game of Risk, Monopoly, or perhaps some newer game that he didn't know the name of, but that he would be able to find if he went to the store. Preferably a game using money, colored tokens, and the ownership of property. Gusher came to mind, a game he remembered from his childhood. He tried to describe to his guests the play in the game of Gusher, but he couldn't remember how it was played.

They were all just sitting around the kitchen. It had turned dark outside, the rain had stopped.

"I'm going shopping," Lurleen said.

"Oh, great," Roscoe said. "Where are you going? Can I go?"

"I'm going to the mall," Lurleen said. "And yes, you can go if you want to."

"This is all very convenient, you guys," Elise said.

"It may be convenient, but it's also true," Lurleen said.

"Do you sometimes get the feeling that our little lives are getting littler and littler?" Roscoe said.

Elise waved at him. "So long, Roscoe. Take it easy. Glad you could come. Come on back anytime. Say hello to Grandma."

Roscoe and Lurleen were gone in a hurry, leaving Edward and Elise perched on the kitchen counters. They sat there without moving for a long time after the front door closed. They didn't look at each other.

Edward was thinking about history. About how it's used to overlook the present. That he should be thinking this was reasonable since, in a small way, that was what was happening between him and Elise. They had been together for so long, done so much together so many times, that it seemed as if there were nothing left to do but sit and stare away from each other. When he had the impulse to do something, or say something, he was quickly flooded with references—other times and places, other circumstances, things he'd said or she'd said years before, things he'd done or she'd done, the time when such-and-such happened, or when so-and-so came to town—and it seemed as if everything he was doing was a repetition of something else he had already done. It seemed to him that too much of what he read was somebody laboring mightily to show that, whatever the subject, it wasn't new or unusual, that all these other people had done it before and usually they had done it better. He did not doubt that, and was even willing to grant, out of politeness if nothing else, that when *it* had been done before, it had been done better. But so what? He was not there in time, he was here. He did not imagine that Nolan Ryan spent many hours analyzing his fastball in the context of the great historical fastball, Walter Johnson or somebody. Probably Nolan Ryan went out and threw *his* fastball as well as he could throw it, every time. And that's all. The things he had to deal with were things in the present, not things in history—from humidity to the care of his cleats. For Edward, this model applied across the board, from his situation with Elise to the "New American Cinema," and history was essentially anecdotal and supplementary, the pleasure in its curiosities—a little sideshow, a collection of once vital doohickeys. He thought all of this while he was sitting on the kitchen counter, thinking that he did not know what he should say to Elise right at that moment. Not only that, he didn't know what he wanted to do, where in the house he wanted to be, or if he wanted to be in the house, what he would like to be doing with his hands or feet, what he would like to be touching, or tasting, or seeing, he did not know whether he wanted to be with her or without her, whether their situation there in the kitchen was particularly uncomfortable or particularly comfortable.

"I read something that said there are a lot of people doing what we're doing," Elise said.

"Sitting on kitchen counters?" Edward said.

He'd looked up when she started talking and now she looked up and caught his eyes. "Cute," she said. "No, I mean, living the way we live. People staying together but living apart. People with other people in their marriages. People with two husbands, or two wives, or extra children picked up God knows where. It said this was a growing phenomenon in our culture."

"Is that right?" Edward said. "Do you sometimes feel like things aren't really growing, that they've been there all along and that people are starting to notice, or talk about them, or something like that?"

"I don't know," Elise said. "I just thought it was interesting. It's like we're finally coming to the end of the fifties."

Edward nodded and pushed himself off the countertop. "It's been a long decade," he said. He went across the kitchen to where she sat on the counter, pressed between her knees, and put his head on her shoulder. "I miss you," he said.

She held him for a minute, her arms around him, her knees

locked on his hips, and then she said, "We seem to do a lot of this in the kitchen. Know what I mean? I'm not complaining."

"It's the heart of the home," he said.

"So," she said, pushing him away slightly. "I guess what we've got is open planning, right? You here, me there?"

"It's the rage," he said. "You told me yourself. It's in the papers." He backed away.

"All right," she said. "Come back here, will you? I don't know what else to do. Do you want me to move up here again?"

Edward was across the room, leaning against the dishwasher. "Is that an offer? I mean, do you want to come back?"

They had gotten to this point before, mostly on the telephone, when one or the other of them was having a particularly bad day. He'd ask her, or she'd ask him, and no one would answer.

"I guess I'm going home tomorrow," Elise said. "I'll leave you here with the lovely Kinta. Let her see to all your needs."

"Let's don't get my needs into this," Edward said.

"They're already in," Elise said. "Up to here."

"Why don't we just look at this as a two-house situation," Edward said. "Is there some reason we can't do that? Sort of take it easy, be friendly, and—"

"Then you turn her nipples into pinball flippers," Elise said. "Yeah, that's a great idea."

Edward gave her a look that started out mock-stern, but then slid into something he imagined looked more like a foreigner trying to understand the English language. He held that look, waiting for Elise to say something more.

"Well," she said, shrugging. "Not the flippers themselves, but the little buttons that control the flippers. You know what I mean."

"So what do you care?" Edward said.

"So it's not you if you're humping Kinta," Elise said. "I mean, it's not chaste. What would you do if I were out there humping Raul Allegre?"

"Haven't you been?" Edward said. "Who is that guy you've been hanging around with, anyway?"

She didn't smile at his little joke. He nodded his apology, then said, "I'd accept it. I accept Roscoe. I accept whatever you do just as long as you can come back and tell me you love me, and make me believe it. If I don't believe it, it doesn't work."

"So, do you believe it?" Elise said. "That I love you?"

"Well, it's situational," he said. "Sometimes I do, sometimes I don't. You want the tabulated results? The tabulated results say, on balance, yes. Love, or something like love. Only it's not the same exact love it used to be. But I don't mean by this that it's a lesser love."

"You mean, a different love," Elise said.

"Yeah, I guess," Edward said. "It's kind of an abiding prefer- ence." Talking about this made him fidget. He was checking the tops on the spice jars in the spice cabinet, and he found a lot of loose spice dust around the edges of the spices, and he got a paper towel to clean that. Love was not something he wanted to talk about—it was too complicated, too vague. Except in retrospect, there was no way to measure it. It wasn't that it was impossible for him to say one of the obvious and correct things one said about love, it wasn't that he didn't know what those things were, and it wasn't that one or another of them might not apply to the moment—about three of them had already occurred to him as appropriate—but it was that there were so many things to say, so many of them contradictory, that locating a single-syllable answer, a yes or no, indicative of that feeling he had for her was too easy—the answers never stopped coming. One after the other, each a modulation of the one before. He believed that she loved him; he did not believe this; he did not care. He loved; he did not love her; he did not care. She makes a face, she doesn't like something he said, she doesn't love him. She makes another face. . . .

"I know," Elise said. "It's a stupid question. It doesn't mean anything. Sometimes I sit down there at my apartment, and it's late at night, and I'm thinking about you—about us—and I wonder what it comes to. I mean, isn't it just a question of whether or not we're willing to continue . . . associating? I mean, sometimes I think that there are other questions, questions about big emotions and everything, but I'm just as lost as you. I like living alone, or living with Roscoe, which is the same thing. Someday I'll tell you about the day Roscoe and I tried to make love."

She stopped a moment and thought about that, doing a kind of internal hemming and hawing. Then she said, "No, maybe I won't. He was real nice. He was sad one night. He didn't want to do it. I forced him to try. I don't know why. He was OK until I started taking his clothes off. Then he went south."

Edward said, "I thought you weren't going to tell me about this."

"I'm not telling you," Elise said. "I'm just remembering. He was like some sad little kid. I was crazy. This was before he started living there. We were like friends, like go-to-the-movie friends, and that was OK—I was real comfortable with that for a while. I was screwing the guy who lived next door, but he had a wife, and screwing was about the only thing he wanted to do anyway. Me, too, I guess. I wasn't too happy." Elise looked into the refrigerator, squatting down in front of it and pulling out the drawers at the bottom. She found a spotted orange and sniffed it, holding it to her nose and then holding it away so she could look at it. "It's got gangrene," she said, waving it back over her head so Edward could see. "Let this be a lesson to you. When they get to this stage you throw them away." She tossed the orange at Edward, startled him, he wasn't quick enough to catch it, so it hit him in the shoulder, bounced off the countertop, and landed with a tiny thud on the floor next to the dishwasher.

"Great job," Edward said, bending to clean up the mess the orange had made on the floor.

"You don't have to clean it up right now," Elise said.

"Why wait?" Edward said.

Elise stood up and closed the refrigerator. "I don't think I could live with you anymore," she said. "Not the way you are now. Were you always this way?"

Edward cradled the remains of the orange, heading toward the garbage can, his hands dripping. "I don't know what you mean," he said. "I just think it's easier to clean things up than to leave them."

"But," Elise said. "It's like that's the most important thing to you. It's like nothing stands in the way of your cleaning up."

He dumped the orange in the trashcan and then got some paper towels, wet them, and started wiping in circles around the spot on the kitchen floor where the orange had hit. "Is that a complaint?" Edward said.

"I don't know," she said. "I guess so. I'm afraid if we ever started to make love again you'd want to be cleaning up along the way. You'd be out there with the Viva ready to get the perspiration, and some Kleencx for the saliva. You'd have a Dustbuster for the broken body hairs. You'd be kissing one nipple and drying the other. And stroke after stroke—"

"OK," Edward said. "That's enough. I get it."

Elise grinned and did a little pout. "I didn't get to the Handi Wipes," she said.

"Hang on to them," Edward said. "You can use them to humiliate me later."

"I'd rather make love to you later," she said.

"It's the same thing, isn't it?" Edward said.

Elise did a little whistle and shook her head, backing up until she was pressed against the kitchen cabinet. "Time to die," she said, in a distant, babylike voice. Then she flapped her outstretched hands and tiptoed out of the kitchen doing high-pitched bird noises, squeals and hisses, science fiction stuff.

10

EDWARD FINALLY got his walk, though he had to go by himself. He didn't like to walk. He remembered that about a block from the house, just about the same time he remembered there were holes in the bottoms of the shoes he was wearing. He could feel the water in his socks. He was getting confused. In twenty-four hours since Elise had shown up he was already thinking about living with her again. He was thinking of ways in which they could live together and not live together at the same time—adjoining apartments, or a big house with separate entrances, separate services, separate homes. He didn't know why he was thinking about that. It didn't make sense to him that he would have been so content without her there, and then, when she showed up for a day, that he would be ready to think about living with her.

He walked in the middle of the street. There was no one out. Most of the porch lights were off. He was cold, his feet damp, he had his hands in his pockets, and he shuffled down the center of the street, sometimes looking at the bulging tar crack where the left and the right halves of the road were joined, sometimes looking up, straight into the distance, into the hard, pointed perspective of shrinking streetlights. He did not feel real good. He started talking to himself, saying he didn't know what was going on. Then he started talking out loud—he wasn't talking in a whisper, but it wasn't far from that. "I just don't know what's going on," he said. "I don't know what they're here for. I don't know what I'm supposed to do. What are my options? I could do anything. I could tell them to leave. I could ask them to stay. I could marry Kinta. I could move down there with Elise. Kick Roscoe out. I was doing fine until yesterday. Maybe I'm still doing fine. That's right. I'm still fine. All I have to do is wait until tomorrow, and then everybody will leave. And then things will be just like they were yesterday."

He saw something leaning against the base of the streetlight, and went to see what it was. It was a business card, carefully propped up against one of the huge bolts that held the street lamp base. He picked up the card. In the middle was the name Jimmy Robinson, and underneath that, in small capital letters, it said "PERSONALITY," and under that there was a telephone number. He put the card in his pocket and then wiped his hand on his jeans. "I wish I could go home and go to bed. I wish that when I went to bed I wanted to be there as much as I want to be there when I'm not. I guess I could go to the office." He stopped a minute and looked up and down the road at the houses. "I wonder who lives in all these places. I wonder if any of these people are as screwed up as I am. Sure they are. The law of averages says they are. They're all just like me." He pointed at a house with a red Buick in the driveway. "There lives Edward Lasco, or equivalent." He cupped his hands around his mouth and pretended to shout toward the house. "Hey! Edward! Why don't you come out and walk this street with me? We'll have a great time. Later on you can come over and screw my wife. Or one of her friends. Or one of my friends. What do you say?"

He was backing down the street now, looking around at the other houses, wagging a forefinger at one after another. "I know what you guys are doing in there. Don't think you're fooling me. You're all in there wishing you were someplace else. All you women are in there looking at Arnold Schwarzenegger's chest, or somebody else's chest, thinking about when you were twenty-three. And the men are doing the same thing, except you guys are looking at Catherine Mary Stewart or somebody like that. But it's too hard, isn't it? I mean, you've got your robes on, you've got dry socks, you've got your picture books and your forty-five-inch rear-projection TVs, and it's just too hard to get up out of that old chair that you like so much, and go out and find Catherine Mary Stewart. Well, I think that's OK. It's probably smart. You're probably doing the right thing. The fact is that Catherine Mary Stewart doesn't give a shit about you. There's only one of her, anyway. Not nearly enough to go around. It's not a terrible thing, what you're doing. It's OK. Just keep on. Just think—Monday morning you get to take a bath, you get a nice clean shirt, you get in that nice car and drive to the office, and everybody's real friendly, they tell jokes, it's great. You'll walk in there and there will be that girl that's sort of like Catherine Mary Stewart, and she'll look at you in this real interesting way, this way that you can imagine is something about what would be possible if . . . It's fine. Don't worry. Don't be afraid. So what if you're fat? Everybody else is fat, too. I really mean it. Listen, your son doesn't hate you, and whoever your daughter's fucking, she's fucking because she thinks she loves him. She doesn't, of course, but that doesn't matter. She needs the practice. And it's OK for you, too, you don't have to want to screw Margaret, or whatever her name is, that woman you've been living with. I mean, she's a nice woman. She does a lot of shit that has to be done. She's right there with you. That's probably more important than the other stuff she does. She's with you and you're with her and that's the way it is. And that's enough. You can do the whole shot on that alone. Listen to me, I know what I'm talking about."

A voice came off a darkened porch Edward was passing. "You all right, buddy? You need some help?"

Edward waved in the direction of the voice. "Yeah. I'm fine. I'm out here having a little round-table discussion. Thanks." He kept moving, talking much more softly. "See there? There's a nice guy. Another one. They're all over the place. In every one of these houses there's a nice guy. I mean, hell, I'm a nice guy. We're all nice when you get to know us." He took the business card out of his pocket and propped it up against another street lamp just as it had been propped up before. "There," he said to the business card. "Now somebody else can get you. I feel like I've done a good thing. I'm your wind." He stopped and looked back up the street in the direction from which he'd come. He hadn't been counting the blocks so he didn't know how far he was from his house. "I should probably go back," he said. "They're probably waiting for me. All my friends. They're probably all sitting around the living room, talking to one another, having a good time, wishing I was there." He waved back up the street. "Kinta's probably arrived. Boy, am I missing out on it now. I could just walk back up there, go in, and be pressed to everybody's bosom just like that." He tried to snap his fingers, but it didn't work, so he tried again. The second time he got a phony-sounding little snap that reminded him of a kid trying to snap his fingers. Before he tried the third time he licked his finger. Then he got a great snap. "There you go," he said. "I knew you could do it, Edward. You can snap your fingers as well as Sister Elizabeth Andrew."

Sister Elizabeth Andrew—the fourth grade at St. Teresa's. He could still remember her walking into a classroom, the wooden beads on the long rosary slung from her waist clicking together as she moved. In memory she was not so much a person as an entity. A presence. She wasn't nearly as colorful as some of the Catholic nuns about whom he'd been told, she had not disciplined her children by requiring them to smack her outstretched hands with a ruler while she cried out, "Strike the hand of the bride of Christ." No. She had been a whistler, which is another nonphenomenon. She had been cheerful and kind, and only occasionally stern, on which occasions she could snap her fingers with the force and the sound of a bullwhip. Edward did some quick figuring. Thirty years before, Sister Elizabeth Andrew had been about fifty. That made her eighty, or dead. He said, "Oh, Sister? Are you still there? Or are you in heaven above?" He looked up at the sky. There were stars up there. "You're up there, aren't you? I know you're up there. You're watching, aren't you, Sister Elizabeth? You're getting ready to snap your fingers at me right now. I know. You're cleaning your glasses on your habit, flying across the sky, watching me. Well, I'm all right. I'm doing all right. I didn't do one bad thing today. OK?

Why don't you just settle on down here like a flying saucer and talk to me, look at me through those gold-rimmed glasses of yours, with that look of yours. All that kindness and understanding and holding the line. I guess now I can say that I loved you, within the appropriate bounds, of course. You should not be offended when I say that I was not much curious about what was there under the habit. I may have wondered about the breasts, I admit it. But it was scientific curiosity. I mean, in those days all the breasts stuck out like crazy and yours were flat as refrigerator cookies. How'd you do that, I wondered. I didn't understand. And they can say what they want, but when you messed up my hair, or pressed my head to your hip for doing something good, I wasn't thinking about anything more intimate. Now, on Miss Robbie, the lay teacher we had as a substitute sometimes, there were thoughts. I mean, she had the legs, remember? She had that blond hair like Veronica Lake. And she wore that perfume. So, now that I think about it, there were a lot of thoughts, all of them confessable. And those were the days before panty hose, you'll recall."

Edward was walking again, talking to the sky, remembering Miss Robbie's red lipstick, her fine skin, her lemony hair—her walk, which said she was a pistol. Miss Robbie had been the first woman about whom he'd fantasized, whose skirt he'd imagined pushing up over thighs to reveal the dark circles of the tops of hose, whose panties he had longed to kiss. And she had been the first woman to teach him a lesson. Late one afternoon, the three o'clock bell fast approaching, she had been in the process of reminding the class of the homework assignment, and Edward had been smarting off in the usual way, and Miss Robbie had, just when the bell began to ring, thrown a chalk eraser at him. She'd caught him on the side of his head, and he'd picked up the eraser—the other students were by now out of their desks and leaving the room—and he had thrown the eraser back at her. An impulse. And he missed her by a mile. But she didn't like having the eraser thrown back at her, and required him to stay after school, and got the principal, and told the principal, Edward found out later, that in addition to throwing the eraser, Edward had, in front of the other students, called her a "goddamn son-of-a-bitch slut." The principal, a fat nun named Sister May Grace, had taken Miss Robbie at her word, and had insisted on a conference with his mother and father, and had devised the suitable punishment that for six weeks Edward went to school every day in the convent. He sat in a room the size of a Pullman sleeper from eight in the morning until three in the afternoon, doing assigned work. No recess, no lunch, no playground. From the window in the room he could see the children playing. He had told his parents that Miss Robbie was lying, that he hadn't called her anything at all, but either they had not believed him, or they had been unwilling to argue the case. Thirty years later he still didn't know which it was. "On the eraser thing," he said, pointing at the sky. "I want you to know I didn't call that woman anything. I *did* throw the eraser at her, but I didn't call her anything. And I'm not blaming you for putting me in the convent for six weeks. As a matter of fact, I didn't mind it too much. I kind of liked it. But I know it wasn't your doing. It was Sister May Grace. I know that. And I understand that you were not in a position to rectify the situation, even if you wanted to. But I'll bet you knew Miss Robbie was lying. I'll bet you knew that. And I found out later that she *was* a slut, that she was screwing some guys on the football team or something. I don't really remember the story now. I didn't find out until I was in the eighth grade. She was full-time by then. So even if I had said what she said I said, which I didn't say, I would have been right. So this is just to set the record straight, OK? In the eighth grade a lot of the guys were talking about her tits. She had the kind with the funny nipples, you know, the kind that are like a second mound on top of the first mound of the breast. I don't know what you call those, but that's what she had, according to them. So anyway, that's the story. I don't know why you people hired that woman anyway, I mean, it was clear what she had in mind from the way she walked. It was clear what she liked. If I'd been you people I wouldn't have hired her. I mean, *I* would have hired her, but if I had been you I wouldn't have. Too much blouse, know what I mean?"

Edward stopped walking and looked at a puddle. He thought the puddle was real pretty the way the light bounced off it and everything. He stood there looking at this water for several minutes. This puddle was in a chuckhole in the street. He didn't know why it was called a chuckhole. The puddle was maybe a foot and a half wide and a foot long, filled up to within about two inches of the surface of the street with dark gray water. In the water's slick surface he could see the reflection of a street lamp, the dark sky with the darker trees in front of it, the moon so tender and pale, the reflections of gibbering black telephone wires, curly gray half-clouds dashing across the reflected moonlit sky. He squatted down and dipped his finger in the water. The water was cold. He moved his finger through the water, slowly, so as to minimize the disturbance of the surface of the water. "So," he said. "I guess I have to go home now, right? I mean, it's written, right? Oh, woe is me." He stood up and shook the water off his finger, and dried the finger on his pants leg. "Something's wrong with me, that's for sure," he said. "Look at this night. It's a beautiful night." He gestured this way and that, pointing out the things he was talking about as he talked about them. "There are some lovely trees. And there are nice houses. There's one, and there's another. And then, above them, the clear night sky, with the twinkling stars twinkling. And below me this fine pavement, pavement of the first quality, fine concrete appropriately curbed, and these handsome street lamps, full of this aggressive blue light that seems to go where no man has gone before, in under the tree limbs, in under the eaves of the houses, irradiating the darkness, revealing, revealing. It's a wonderful light. And here I am in the middle of it, standing here, displaying, as my old pappy used to say, human emotions and aspirations, as he said once, and this land is my land, these are my tired and weary, what a career I have, and what a beautiful wife and child, and so I can trot back to my lovely home, down this street I share with my fellow human beings, each of us with our assigned tasks and responsibilities, each with some little stone block to carry around in our feelers, our glistening, caramel-colored buttocks wobbling behind us." Edward turned back toward the house. "My apologies," he said, now addressing the world at large with a sweep of his hand. "I don't know what happened there. I just got carried away. I was thinking of ants, see? You know those ants on television shows about ants? Where the ants all crawl around carrying these little pieces of sand or whatever it is that they carry, and the backs of the ants, the pointed, sort of teardrop-shaped part at the back, is always this kind of light brown and it's always shining. So I was thinking about that." There were headlights coming at him, so he moved over to the side of the road, to the curb, to the sidewalk. "Now," he said. "Here comes somebody. Perhaps this is my savior? Christ in a Crosley. There are not many of us who remember the Crosley. And, on Christ, even fewer. But I have, myself, done the research. There was a Christ. He did some amazing shit. But it must be said that in those days, there were many people who did many amazing things. After my lifetime of research it's fair to say that Christ was the Iacocca of his time. But I mean no disrespect by this—Lee Iacocca has, at least, got sense." Edward stopped and stood on the sidewalk and shook his head. "I think maybe I had better go on home and get into my PJs."

11

THE CAR was Roscoe's, Elise at the wheel. She pulled across the street and stopped next to Edward. Her driver's door window came down with an electric whine. She said, "Are you having a crisis? What are you doing out here?"

"Addressing the loaves and the fishes," Edward said.

"Ah," Elise said. "With what result?"

Edward said, "The loaves remain loaves, the fishes, fishes."

"Well, get in the car," Elise said. She patted the seat next to her. "It's time for you and me to have a little talk."

"OK," Edward said. He started to walk around the front of the car but suddenly the street was full of cars, three or four coming in each direction. He had to wait by the right-hand headlight until the road was clear. When it was, he got in the car.

"Aren't you cold out here?" Elise said. She ran up her window. "I'm freezing."

"It's sort of interesting to see you," Edward said.

Elise turned to look at him. "You, too," she said. "So where do you want to go? You want to go to the mall? What time is it?" She looked at the clock on the dash. "No, it's too late for that. We can go to the all-night grocery store."

"I don't like grocery stores as much as I used to," Edward said.

"That's too bad," Elise said. "You used to love grocery stores. We used to go play in them, remember?"

"Better days," Edward said.

"Aw," Elise said, making fun of his indulgence.

"I didn't mean it that way," Edward said. "I meant that I remembered them fondly."

"You meant it exactly that way," Elise said. "Back then you remembered some previous days fondly. Back then you were suffering a great loss, as I recall."

"Yeah," Edward said. "But not at the same time as I was playing in the grocery store. Anyway, we were still new to each other then."

"Then we got over being new to each other," she said. "It was still OK."

"It's OK now, isn't it?" Edward said.

"Yeah, it's fine," she said.

They rode in silence for a few minutes, then Edward said, "OK. The grocery store is OK. Take a left up at the light. I'll take you to the future store."

At the light she said, "The way I see it we have a couple of options. I can move back up here. You can move down there. We can stay the way we are. What do you want to do?"

Edward said, "We're picking up a lot of baggage, you know what I mean? You got Roscoe. You got Lurleen."

"You got Kinta," Elise said.

Edward nodded. "I got Kinta."

"I think we ought to just quit," Elise said. She was staring ahead at the back of a Buick, in the rear window of which there was a "Baby on Board" sign. She pointed up ahead. "I think we should join this dialogue," she said. "You know the 'Baby on Board' stickers, and then the other people who have the 'Nose Bleed in Progress' stickers—this is the great American dialogue, apparently."

"That was nineteen eighty-five's dialogue," Edward said. "I failed to participate."

"Yeah, me, too," Elise said. "I participated in my heart, though. I said things here in the car. I remarked to my friends, when I had friends, about these signs in the backs of cars. I interacted to the extent that I looked at the signs when they appeared in the drugstore on racks. I thought of a few cute ones myself, of course. I saw the stupid piece that TV comic did about these signs. I spent some time wondering what in the hell these people thought they were doing, putting these signs in the backs of their cars. Now that I think about it, Edward, I guess I participated fully in this dialogue."

Edward said, "My shoulders ache."

"I think you're getting a cold," Elise said. "From all this walking you've been doing. Are your feet wet? Never mind, don't answer that. It's an unfair question."

"Yes," Edward said. "My feet are wet."

"Does it sometimes seem a little risky, the way we're living?" Elise said. "I mean, not seeing each other? I come back here and it's like I never left. Why don't you move down to the coast?"

Edward looked at Elise. "What would you do with Roscoe?" he said.

"Roscoe could be a friend of yours," she said. "He's not so bad."

"I didn't say he was bad," Edward said. "In fact I kind of like him. But I'm still jealous."

"You hide it well," Elise said.

"Like when?" Edward said. "Like this weekend? I didn't have much choice. Suddenly, you were there. Then he's there. What am I supposed to do? Then, in comes the fat girl. Now, *she's* got opinions. She's got ideas about the way people should live. She's got her own view of things. She doesn't say much about this view, but you can see it in her eyes, in the way she looks at you, in the little expressions she gets on her face."

Edward looked out the window, suddenly realizing that they were headed out of town. "Where are we going?" he said.

"I'm taking you home," Elise said.

"What do you mean?" Edward said. They were on the highway headed south. They went under an overpass and, against the sky, Edward saw the tall red, white, and blue sign of an Exxon station. Apart from that all he saw was trees. "What, we're going to the coast? We can't do that, Elise. Come on. There are people back at the house. It's ten o'clock at night."

"It's eleven. And I can do anything I want." She thought about that for a minute. "Well, within reason," she said. "We're going to pick up a hitchhiker, if a hitchhiker appears, and the three of us are going down to my house. No, wait a minute, forget the hitchhiker. Just you and me, just like old times. Besides, we need to have a talk. I need to have some time alone with you."

Edward tried to get comfortable in the seat of the car, couldn't, thought about all of the times he and Elise had settled their problems driving. It seemed to have this effect on both of them. In the car she suddenly seemed more beautiful, more interesting, more lovely; he felt more connected to her then, as if it were the two of them against the rest of the known world, and he was glad she was his partner.

He looked at her in the driver's seat. She was relaxed, watching the road, her face creased with bands of light from oncoming cars, dotted with reflections from her own dash lights. He didn't know why he had let her leave, or even *if* he had let her—he didn't know whether if he had tried to stop her from leaving he could have. He tried to remember why she had left in the first place, what was the point, what she hoped to achieve. They hadn't had big fights or anything like that. Things had just gotten duller and duller. He'd been depressed, taking a lot of Valium, and she'd been depressed, out of a job. They'd gone through the motions, kept up the appearances of marriage—they'd eaten dinner together, watched TV together, paid the bills together—all the little rituals. Meanwhile, things got duller and duller.

A lot of times, when they were in the house together, say early in the morning, or late in the afternoon, or even at night, Edward wished she weren't there. He wished he didn't have to look at her clumsiness, at the slow way she did things, at the mess she always made. But he tended to overlook it, telling himself that it was his fault, that he was depressed or upset about something, or simply bored. He had figured that all couples went through that—the point at which you are getting on each other's nerves so thoroughly, so completely, so constantly that there doesn't seem to be any relief from it, and so you just steel yourself, go through the motions, do what you have to do—what you can do, with as little interplay as possible. And all that trying had itself produced another layer of awfulness—these two people working so hard just to live under the same roof.

Edward said, "OK. Where do we start?"

Elise had been concentrating on the driving, and as she turned to look at Edward she let off on the accelerator and the car slowed noticeably. "Are you ready to start already?"

"I'm thinking about it," Edward said. "I'm remembering it. We had this horrible time, back in the summer. We hated each other. OK, no—we didn't hate each other, but we didn't like each other very much. It was hard to be together."

"Well," Elise said. "That seems to have passed. Hasn't it?"

"I guess so," Edward said. "I mean, I remember being upset about things, but I don't feel upset about them now."

"Right," Elise said. "Same with me. But we're half a year away—you wouldn't expect the same things to be bothering us."

"Right," Edward said.

"I mean, I'm still messy," Elise said. "Wait until you see the apartment. But so what? I do the best I can. I don't mean to be messy. Are we going to dump the marriage because I'm messy?"

"I don't know," Edward said. "I don't think so."

"We won't call it that, anyway," Elise said.

"I've got no interest in dumping the marriage, particularly," Edward said. "I mean, what's the percentage? I'd have to go out there and look for another woman. I don't want another woman, you understand, but I'd feel like I had to go out there and look for one."

"I know," Elise said. "I feel the same way."

"Yeah, but you've got Roscoe," Edward said.

Elise sighed. "Yes. Roscoe's a friend. Roscoe's a mate. He's a companion. But it's not quite the same thing."

"I don't know why not," Edward said.

"I don't either," she said. "I mean, it's close. It's real close. But it's more like you're my brother and he's my friend. I think that's because we spent all that time together, all those years."

"There isn't that much difference between a brother and a friend," Edward said.

"No," she said. "Not that much. But some. A little." She turned around and looked at Edward. "But don't get the wrong idea," she said. "I like him. I'm committed to him. He goes where I go."

"So you're telling me that if we do something, it's three of us not two of us?" Edward said.

"Yes," she said. "Can you live with that?"

"Shit, I don't know," Edward said. He was watching out his window a white cloud that grazed the horizon. It was a long, thin cloud, gauzy, and it seemed to slide along the sky in the same direction they were going. "So you're talking about three of us being married," he said. "Only I didn't pick him."

"Yeah," she said. "I don't like it either. But I didn't set out to do it this way. I mean, it just happened."

"It just happened," Edward said.

"I know it sounds stupid," she said. "I don't know how else to describe it. It's the way I feel. I don't have to live with him or anything, I mean, he could live somewhere else, nearby. I don't think he'd mind that. But he has to be part of our, you know, family."

"I don't think you're going to sell me this," Edward said. "You're not doing a very good job of selling it to me now." He thought for a minute, watching the road disappear under them. Then he said, "You're crazy. I guess I figured he was just in it temporarily. A temporary friend for you while you were living down there. I don't know what I figured. But I didn't figure what you're telling me."

"Well, I haven't told you everything," Elise said.

"Oh, great," Edward said. "I look forward to hearing the next part."

"OK," Elise said. "Here goes. You remember when I lived here, when he lived here, too, when he was at the university? Well, I had an affair with him. I never told you about it. This is about a year and some ago. Things were not all that great with us. I don't know. So I had this affair. We did all the usual affair stuff. We met a lot in strange places, motels, cars, parks. We had a lot of sex. I don't know, sex was driving me crazy then. I thought I was in love with him. I was going to leave you, I wanted to leave you and go off with him. He didn't want that. He said no, I shouldn't do that. This is before his wife was killed. She was in that car crash, remember? Anyway, when that happened, the wreck, that was the end of our affair. It stopped on a dime. He had all this guilt. It was really horrible for him. Anyway . . . never mind. So, our affair stopped. That was about, I don't know, six, eight weeks after we'd started. Are you listening to this?"

Edward was listening. He wasn't reacting, which surprised him. He didn't feel terrible. It was as if the events she was talking about were in another time. It was like a TV movie, or an experiment. It was long gone. He was thinking that he liked her, and that he was glad she was telling him all this. And he was thinking how odd it was to be in Roscoe's car in the middle of the night on the highway headed for her apartment a hundred miles away, with her telling him about an affair she'd had with Roscoe a year before. How odd it was to be so cool about it—it wasn't that he didn't care about her, it wasn't that he was numb. It wasn't like that at all. What kept occurring to him was that he trusted her. That if she had an affair with Roscoe, then she probably had good reason, needed it, and that made it OK. This was a revelation. He kept saying to himself, "Do I really feel this?"

Edward said, "Yeah. I'm listening. I don't feel terrible."

"You don't?" she said, turning to look at him.

He turned his head to look at her. Then he shook his head. "No," he said. "Maybe I'm not jealous. I used to be jealous as hell, didn't I?"

"You want the rest of the story? There isn't much more. When I left you, I went down there, and then I ran into him, and he was still hurting about his wife. We started going out. It was just fun, this time. I mean, it wasn't an affair. I mean, it was an affair, but it wasn't an affair like the other affair. It was like we were much older. I mean, you know how I told you about trying to make love with him? That's true, we did try. It was not good. This was last summer, I mean. We haven't tried since. But we get along fine, so I asked him if he wanted to move in, and he wanted to move in, so he did, and then we've been living together since then, and it's all very sort of comfortable. I mean, I care for him in this really extraordinary way, I care about him, I care what happens to him, I care what he thinks. It's like I'm getting to take care of him, the way you took care of me, you know what I mean?"

"The way I used to take care of you," Edward said.

"Right," Elise said. "That's what I mean. He thinks I'm wonderful. It's like we're an old married couple, Roscoe and me. So, whatever happens, Roscoe's in. Unless he takes himself out."

Edward watched the side of the road, listened to the engine, listened to the tires on the concrete, listened to the wind blowing around the edges of the car's glass. He wondered if this was why Elise had come up, to tell him this. He wondered why it had to be so formal, why she had to talk about it as if it were a contract. He figured she wouldn't have made this big play out of it if it had just occurred to her, she had to have been thinking about it for a while. Finally he said, "This is what you came for, right?"

"I thought you ought to know," she said. "It's a change in things. The way we've been going, it's as if we're still married and we live apart. And I think that's true, but there is this other thing, this Roscoe thing. I don't know how else to talk about it."

Edward said, "Well, you could have left it alone. You didn't have to say anything about it. I mean, that's the way we're living anyway, isn't it?"

"Yeah," she said. "But you didn't know it, not really."

"Well, fuck you, too," he said.

"I'm sorry," she said, her voice going hard and cool.

There always came a point in their conversations when Edward recognized that her patience was gone. He could hear that point in her voice. She'd say something, and it would be perfectly clear that they weren't going to come to a consensus about whatever it was they were discussing, that she had her view, that she was sticking to that view. Whenever he heard that note in her voice, he knew they were not headed for a negotiated settlement. It was something he envied in her, that ability to control a conversation by the tone of her voice. Once or twice, early in their relationship, he had tried to push beyond it, tried to force her hand, and he had found out that she was serious—once she had left him, and once she had slapped him in the face with a videocassette she happened to be holding. He envied her because he never got to that point. He tried to put out the same signals occasionally, sometimes even getting away with it, but he knew, even if she didn't, that for him it was a kind of game, a performance, a rhetorical device.

The point of her "I'm sorry" wasn't whether or not he could handle a relationship in which Roscoe appeared in the role of . . . what? other man? husband two? but how they were going to talk about this relationship. Her point was that they were going to talk about it sensibly or not at all. That meant good faith assumed—he had to take her seriously, and at her word, and she would do the same for him. It was her way of saying that she was *caught* in this thing, that she wasn't just fucking around, or being indulgent, or having the time of her life.

Edward straightened up in the seat and took off his shoes, then his socks. He propped his bare feet up on the dashboard over the vents. "Hit the heater, will you? Just for a minute, OK?"

She did, and he got his feet dry, and they rode through the night in silence, she watching the road and he watching her watch the road. It was a divided highway, two lanes each direction separated by a forty-foot gully of tall pines and scrub bush. He could see only flickers of the headlights going in the other direction, and the only light on their side of the highway was from their lights, and the reflections of those in the trees surrounding the highway. He was glad she was driving.

Out of an old habit, he checked the fuel gauge, and the temperature gauge, and the oil gauge on the BMW, craning his neck to get a look at the tilted panel on which the gauges were mounted. Everything was OK. He put a hand out and tucked it in under her leg, between her thigh and the seat cushion, remembering a videotape he'd made on one of their trips through Louisiana. It was the middle of winter, and they were driving late in the day. He shot all this videotape of Elise driving, listening to tapes of Laurie Anderson and Philip Glass. The sun was going down and there wasn't enough light, so the pictures were dark and eerie, and the music fit right in with the car sounds and the road sounds. He got the dashboard lights, and the long white strip of highway in front of them, and her hand on the wheel, and finally, the sun going down behind the black trees alongside them—he'd shot that out her window, and then since they were going eighty miles an hour, the trees looked shredded, almost on fire with the brilliant orange of the sun behind them, spread out through the searing low red clouds, every bump in the road reflected in the video.

After that trip he'd sometimes come home and find her looking at that tape. It was childish and crude, but it had this melancholy that was particularly affecting—she loved all the long, tedious close-ups intercut and distorted by the wobbly camera, the incomplete parts of her, the sound of the car, the awkward, loud, repetitive music. It was like some kind of religious ritual, that tape, mesmerizing the viewer, but it seemed to work only for him and Elise. They had tried showing it to Marge and Smokey, but after a few minutes Marge and Smokey got restless and started fidgeting, started asking for drinks, started wondering what was on the other channels, started wondering what else they had on videotape. That disappointed Edward because he thought the tape was beautiful, touching. He made the usual jokes about how you had to have been there, and then took the tape off, resetting the television for the cable channels and giving Smokey the remote control. Later, when the guests left, he and Elise sat down and watched the complete tape, two hours, beginning to end, sitting side by side on the wicker sofa they had then, holding hands, speechless.

He moved his feet a little so the hot air could go up his pants leg, and he said, "So you're in love with him, right?"

Elise took a long time before she answered. The question hung out there in the car, mixed with the sounds of the tires on the night highway. She didn't take her eyes off the road. Finally she said, "I don't know if I'd say that. I don't know what that means. I don't deal in that kind of shorthand anymore. I just don't want to be without him. I want him around. Life is too short. He's too decent to let go. I don't know, maybe I'm getting old, but I don't see any reason to separate yourself from people you're close to." She turned around and looked at Edward. "I want you to understand this, you know what I mean? Like, it may not be exactly love in the same sense we used to talk about love when we were twenty. But it's close enough. For practical purposes there isn't that much difference."

"And what about me?" Edward said. "I don't want to be pushy here, but . . ."

"I don't want to live without you either," she said. "But I have more confidence about you, somehow. I don't think you're about to file for divorce. I guess you said that, didn't you? But even before you said it I knew it. It's like romance isn't such a big issue anymore. I don't know what the issue is, but I know what it isn't. At least for now. I mean, who knows? Tomorrow you could be out there bonging some nineteen-year-old, calling it love. I don't think it's likely, but it could happen."

"I wish it would hurry up," he said.

She smiled at him and then patted his wrist, leaving her hand on it when she was finished.

"Let me see if I've got this straight," Edward said. "You kind of love him and you kind of love me, and you want to go on loving both of us. Is that it?"

"That's sort of it," Elise said. "I'm not sure about the 'kind of' business in his case, and I'm sure it's wrong in yours, but, generally speaking, yes."

"And we're going to do this forever?" Edward said.

"Stupid, isn't it?" Elise said.

"Does he know about this?" Edward said. "I mean, does Roscoe know?"

"Yes," she said.

"And he likes it?"

"You've got to know Roscoe," she said. "He's scared to death. His life's been a mess. His wife got killed in a car crash. What he wants is something with a little order in it, something that he can count on from here on out. Being swept away isn't uppermost in his mind, not even, as far as I can tell, very important to him. It's a little weird, I know." She stopped a minute and cracked her window to change the air inside the car. Then she rolled the window up again. "Maybe it's not weird at all," she said. "Maybe it's just a quieter kind of thing without all the sweat, and hot lights, and the thumper music. Maybe it's more civilized."

"I'm going to have to think about this," Edward said. "I guess I figured you were coming back. I mean, I guess I thought you would do some time down here and then move back. Just you. Did I say that already? A lot of times I say things and then when I hear myself say them it sounds like I've already said them. Anyway . . ."

"Yeah, I know," Elise said.

Edward rolled his head on the headrest so he could see her. She glanced over at him. He said, "You know what?"

"It's messy," she said. "Really."

12

ELISE'S APARTMENT wasn't a mess at all. It was open, airy, done in decorator pastels, with high ceilings and ceiling fans, lots of glass, and not very much furniture, every stick of which was carefully placed. It wasn't an architect's delight because the finishes were cheap—sheetrock and off-the-shelf moldings and lousy carpentry and sliding glass doors and all the other shortcuts in detail that make it possible for apartment developers to squeeze the last dime out of their investments. Still, it was cuts above the usual, and Elise had made it better than that. The walls and carpet were blue, the ceilings white. Edward was amazed. "It's real nice," he said, looking around. "I wouldn't have believed you could do this blue."

"It looks like a bordello," she said. "But you get used to it. I asked them if I could paint it, but they said I couldn't." Out the windows and between the other buildings in the development— half were condos and half apartments—Edward could see the marina and beyond it the bay. She had a couple of Eames chairs from the fifties, those potato-chip chairs, with the original wooden legs. And she had a table that looked like it was made by a madman. The colors were bright, crazy like Memphis, only this was handmade and hand-painted, with two legs made out of tree limbs that had been done in stripes and spangles, a third leg made out of a very pointy pyramid, and the fourth leg a sheet of wood covered in galvanized metal. The top was half solid, hard black rubber, and the other half black and white vinyl tile. Then he found a fifth leg, bolted on next to one of the others, the pyramid one, and it was a real leg off one of those fifties aluminum-legged kitchen tables, the kind that always came with the green or yellow imitation marble linoleum tops. The rest of the furniture was plain and direct. There were a few old pieces, Mission style, that might have been Stickley. It was an odd mix but it looked wonderful—playful, funny, and comfortable all at the same time.

Elise was clearly nervous about how he was going to react to it. She went into the kitchen calling over her shoulder, "You want something? You want a Coke, or a drink? Courvoisier?"

Edward laughed at that. "I'll have a Diet Coke," he said. "If you've got one. Where'd you get the table?"

"Bizarre, isn't it?" she called from the kitchen. "I found it in this junk shop. I figure it must have been a prop for some kind of little theater thing or something. It wasn't real sturdy when I got it, but I put some nails in, strategically, until it worked." She came out of the kitchen carrying two Cokes. "Don't worry," she said. "It's clean. I scrubbed it before I brought it in the house."

"It's pretty crazy," Edward said. "I like it."

"Good," she said, sitting down.

They had driven the last forty minutes without a word. Elise had driven fast, and it had gone quickly. Edward hadn't felt like talking about Roscoe and Elise and himself anymore. He didn't know what to say about it. He didn't know how he felt about it. It seemed to him such a curious idea that three people, three adults, with ordinary jobs and regular lives, might elect to live in this way Elise was proposing, that all he had in the way of responses were rote things—it's impossible, it'll never happen, how could it ever happen, nobody lives like that, people might get themselves into it for a while, but nobody sets out to do it. And then, of course, he wondered why not, and supplied himself with the obvious answers to that. None of it terribly thinkable, but they'd been living it for half a year with no debilitating or crushing consequences.

He had, from time to time since she'd gone, wondered if he just didn't care that much about her anymore, wondered if his affection for her, his love, was more a matter of record than of pressing need, but he'd wondered about that less frequently than even he would have thought—he was in love with her, although, just as she had said, it wasn't the kind of love he had learned about in high school, or the love that was in the movies, or the love that was on TV, or in the magazines, or in the poems and stories that he had read and that he still read from time to time—it was something more delicate and difficult than that, something that could not easily be reduced to a moment of high passion, or intense loneliness, or desperation of any kind. He caught himself thinking this and worried about how mystical-sounding it was. He had learned from his father to distrust what could not be readily explained, and he had learned from his mother to distrust his father. The inexplicable, according to her, was no less actual, or present, or true than its more readily accessible sibling. She had used this argument, to Edward's knowledge, principally to defeat his father in arguments about ordinary household questions—furniture and furniture arrangement, where the kids should go to school, what they should be allowed to do, what they shouldn't. Thus Edward had learned the limits of reason, of rational discourse, of explanation and analysis, and logic. As he got older he warmed to the idea of the inexplicable. He noticed that explanations, as a general class, tended to diminish the explained. The language, even brilliantly and imaginatively used, seemed always to fall just short of the experience it sought to describe. Often, when he was at the university, he noted that the efforts of his professors to describe a painting, or an idea about painting, or, in another class, the power of a particularly clever business strategy almost always fell short of the fullness of his appreciation of what was being described. In the very few cases when an articulate and imaginative professor had attacked a problem, the explanations, while quite lovely and moving, often had less to do with the picture, or text, or idea being discussed than with their own internal workings, and this rough recognition had bothered him since that time, so that now, all explanations and analyses were seen by him, by definition, as guesses, nothing more—shooting at a flea with a howitzer from a distance of three hundred yards while bouncing on a trampoline mounted crooked on the flatbed of a huge truck lumbering up and down a steeply sloped hill cluttered with boulders, tree trunks, and holes, and topped with a furiously dense tall forest. Blindfolded.

This view made things hard for Edward, since his sense was that a few people did things and everybody else busily explained what had been done, but over the years, he had found several socially acceptable covers for his skepticism. He could play cowboy and dig his toe in the dirt, or he could pretend to be playing devil's advocate, or he could present himself as naive, or he could play the game straight, building upon a received explanation for some phenomenon a new explanation that extended the previous by including in it some little thread that had been left untended in the original. He used these devices interchangeably and whimsically, but most often fell back on the cowboy, playing dumb, both in the sense of not knowing and in the sense of not speaking. So that now, in Elise's apartment, a hundred miles from home, when faced with the idea that his wife wanted to have two husbands, that in fact she already *had* two husbands, he found himself not only more receptive to the idea than one would imagine, but also intrigued by it—he wondered if it was an interesting idea, if there were possibilities intrinsic in the marriage of three childless adults that might make such a relationship workable, or even preferable, to the more conventional one. He was thinking about this and watching Elise put the finishing touches on a fire she was building in the fireplace, a fire built around a Duraflame—one of those guaranteed-to-burn-for-three-hours logs made out of sawdust and wax—and two thoughts occurred to him: I really like this woman; this is a very funny idea.

Elise looked up from her fire and said, "How about some pancakes? I've got the good microwave pancakes here. I bought the bad microwave pancakes first, and then I bought the good microwave pancakes. It's a trial-and-error thing."

"I've got a microwave," Edward said.

"I know," Elise said. "I saw it. It's a Panasonic."

"I'm a little late getting into the microwave thing," Edward said.

"Me, too. This place has a built-in microwave, so that's when I started. Do you want the pancakes?"

"I don't think so," Edward said.

"Oh," Elise said. The fire was going now, and she was sitting on the floor in front of the fireplace, rubbing at the smudges of charcoal on her hands. "Me either," she said. "They're really not that good. They taste kind of . . . manufactured."

"So tell me what the right kind is," Edward said. "So when I go back and buy some, I buy the right kind."

"Pillsbury," she said, without looking up. There was a smudge the size of a quarter on the side of her right forefinger, and she was working on it with her left hand, with her thumb. "So, what do you think?" she said.

"I think you have a wonderful place. I think you're wonderful. I think Roscoe's OK." Edward stretched out, put his hands behind his head, and watched the ceiling fan twirl. "Sometimes I mention Roscoe, and I really don't want to," he said. "Like just now. I wish it was just you and me, sometimes. I mean, even if you were living down here and I was living up there, I still wish it was just you and me. It makes things so much simpler, you know what I mean?"

"Things have been pretty simple for the last six months," Elise said. "I remember when we tried to talk to each other all the time, it was telephone conversations when neither one of us had anything to say, so we just sat there on the phone, listening to that hiss." She shook her head. "That wasn't good. It's like when I moved down here I wondered what we were doing, but then after a while I didn't wonder anymore, we were just doing it. I was doing it. Do you know what I'm talking about? It's like that's the way things were."

She looked at Edward and he thought he saw sadness in her eyes, a kind of resignation he hadn't seen before. He thought he saw a lot of things in her eyes—isolation, determination and commitment, a clear demarcation between her and himself, between her and the rest of the world. He couldn't stop himself from seeing Elise as a lovely, defiant figure, worn and lonely, a kind of latter-day samurai, romanticized just as the movies had romanticized the samurai, but lacking the certainty that made the samurai's life tolerable. He thought it was that she did not know what she was fighting for or about, and then he realized that it wasn't that she didn't know, but that he didn't. As he looked at her sitting there in her living room, looking up at him, he thought it was remarkable that she had left him, literally packed up and moved out of the house, without leaving him in the sense of terminating their marriage, or their relationship. He looked at the fan again. "I know I must have asked you this," he said. "But why did you move out? I don't remember. I don't mean that you shouldn't have, or anything like that, I just don't remember why you did."

Elise stared at the fire while she talked. "I remember what I told you," she said. "It was pretty close, but not that close. I think after the big affair with Roscoe I thought something in our life was gone, that something had changed irrevocably, that things would never be as they had been and so I'd better get out. It was like, for me, I had to start a new life. I didn't really want to, but I had to. So I was trying to get out quietly, smoothly. I was determined that if we had to split up we weren't going to do it stupidly, the way everybody else does. We weren't going to have a big screaming match, a huge, bitter divorce. I was thinking I'd get out of there, and you'd find somebody else, and I'd find somebody else, then we could just quietly dissolve the marriage, one afternoon. See, I really thought it was finished."

She turned around and looked at Edward, and he looked back and saw the reflection of the fire in her glassy eyes. He nodded at her.

She turned back to the fire. "That's what I thought at first, anyway," she said. "I hated it, and I hated the way I was doing it, but it was the best I could manage. I felt guilty and stupid. I was mad at Roscoe, but I was madder at you for somehow getting me to want to have an affair with him. It doesn't make a lot of sense, maybe, but that's how I felt. Like you had let me go. I was thinking I would be off by myself somewhere, and have a little life, and work, and watch TV. I thought maybe after a while I'd find some guy that I liked and wanted to be with. I guess I really wanted that. It's hard to explain how it feels when somebody holds you, especially when you've been brought up to be held." She turned around and smiled at him. "Holding is not your long suit, in case you didn't know."

"I do a kind of mental holding," he said.

"Mental doesn't get it," she said. "Not for me, or didn't, anyway. I love it when somebody makes love to me. The frightening thing is, it doesn't matter what the circumstances are." She made a face and waved her arms around, as if having difficulty explaining herself. "It's like once you get to the point of actually making love, it doesn't matter *how* you got there. He's on top of you, or behind you, or underneath you, and all you think about is how it feels to have this man pouring so much heat into you. Even if you're doing all the work, you're still on the receiving end of the thing." She stopped for a minute and thought about that and then said, "That was part of it. I don't know how to describe it any better than that. It's like doing it with Roscoe reminded me. I mean, I felt guilty and horrible, but I also felt I deserved it. I was worth it. Now it seems as if Roscoe and me were never anything but friends, and I know I always thought you couldn't have a sexual relationship with a friend, but what happens is that you forget about the friend part, I mean, you just slide into it, and for a while you're a Paris slut, or a teenager at a beach party, or you're with a stranger, or you're punishing some man you used to know, or you're punishing all men by turning yourself into what they want most. I don't know how it happens. I'd go to lunch with Roscoe, and I'd say something, and he'd say something, and pretty soon we were talking about sex, and pretty soon after that we were getting the check and heading for his apartment. We talked about love a lot, but I don't think either one of us cared that much about it. No, that's not right. I cared about it, but I probably told myself that's what it was, with Roscoe, love. I mean, now it seems stupid, but then it seemed perfectly correct and reasonable. I was trying to do what he wanted, trying to be what he wanted me to be, and while we were having the affair, I guess that's what I was. And when that was over, when Ginger died, and he just couldn't play anymore, couldn't even talk about making love, much less do it, and when he didn't want to see me anymore, it killed me. Some days, when you were at the office, I just walked around the house all day long, touching things. They didn't seem like they were my things anymore. Sometimes I'd masturbate all morning, or all afternoon, or both. It was like I was a visitor there with nothing at all to do. Sometimes I'd go out and ride around in the car and I'd look at the buildings and I'd wonder, 'Where am I?' "

Elise got up on her knees, with her feet still crossed behind her, and stretched to get the poker from the stand that held the fire tools. She opened the mesh screen in front of the fire and slapped at the oak log that was balanced on top of the fake log, using the hook on the back side of the head of the poker. The fake log crumbled and fell through the grate and flamed curiously. "Oh, shit," she said.

"That's all right," Edward said. "They all do that. It's good for the other log. Close it up."

She put the poker back where she'd gotten it and closed the screen. "Anyway," she said, rearranging herself on the floor so that her legs were straight out in front of her and she was leaning back on her hands. "I mean—" She stopped suddenly and looked at Edward. "Are you sure you want to hear all this?"

"Yes," he said. "I didn't know I was going to hear it, but I want to."

"That feeling didn't go on for too long. I decided that I'd do what I'd always done, you know, with the plants, exercising, reading stuff, shopping. So I did that and it was OK. I mean, it wasn't really OK, but I could get through it. I could keep busy. I didn't care about any of it, but I knew what to do. You remember I used to come down here to go shopping? You probably don't remember, but I did. Only sometimes I didn't go shopping, I'd come down here and sit on the beach, or sit in a bar or a restaurant looking out at the water. One time I picked up this guy and we went to the

Motel 6, and then I didn't want to make love with him, and he got real mad and started shoving me around in the room. And, I don't know, I thought to myself, 'You're too old for this,' so we had sex, only he didn't want to make love to me, all he wanted to do was kiss me between my legs." She shook her head, remembering it. "I mean, I got interested, and I wanted him to make love to me, I wanted him to fuck me, but he wouldn't do it. That was a crazy day."

Edward said, "I'll bet." He coughed the second word. The rain had started up again. He heard the low rush of it, the pattern of the drops from the eaves hitting the deck, the sound like a woodwind chime—constant, but spare. He was eager to hear Elise's story and, at the same time, hurt by it. He wanted details even though he knew that each detail would hurt. "I hate to hear this, I hate you telling me this, and I want you to tell me everything. Not Roscoe, but this other guy. I want to know how it felt when you touched him. I want to know how you touched him."

Elise got up off the floor and headed for the kitchen. "Well, that's enough of that," she said. "Want a Coke? Want some ice cream? Want a whole head of lettuce?"

Edward followed her into the kitchen. "Come on, Elise," he said. "You're talking to me."

She opened the refrigerator. "That's not what you're interested in," she said.

"I'm interested," Edward said. "I want you to talk to me." He reached past her and got a ring of pineapple out of an open dish on the second shelf of the refrigerator. He ate it and started to lick his fingers, then thought again and held the fingers out for her to lick. She shook her head.

Elise poured herself a tiny glass of milk. "So he was this black guy, and his cock was nine feet long, and I begged him to fuck me, and he did, finally, in the ass, and I loved it, and we lived happily ever after." She gave Edward a quick, condescending smile. "That's the whole story."

He wiped his fingers on his jeans. "OK," he said, turning to go back into the living room. "So don't tell me. Don't tell me anything."

This time she followed him. "What I want to do is tell you what I want to tell you," she said. "You asked me why I left. I'm trying to explain it. I mean, all these things are involved. Everything's involved. I've had a lot of time to think about it. I don't want to get sidetracked."

Edward squatted down in front of the fireplace and opened the fire screen. She was behind him, stroking his hair.

"Not right now, anyway," she said.

"Right now is when I feel like it," Edward said.

"Well, I'll tell you again later," Elise said. "How's that? I'll tell you every single thing that I can remember. Everything."

"You won't, though," Edward said. He shut the screen and stood up, then turned around and gave her a hug. "It doesn't matter," he said. "I am interested. I do care."

"You get the prize for phony," she said.

He looked at her to see if she was being mean or friendly, and it was friendly, so he sat down again in his chair and waited for her to go on with the story.

"So that's what I was doing," Elise said. "That kind of thing. There was some other stuff. And then I started feeling odd because you didn't notice anything. You remember how you used to be? I mean, if I was out of pocket for ten minutes, you were all over me. But by that time you weren't, and I hated that, but I wasn't about to tell you. I used to look at you at dinner, or in bed, or just sitting around, and I'd be thinking, 'Why doesn't he know what's going on?' " She shook her head. "I hated you for what had happened to me, what had happened to us. It wasn't so much the sex, the absence of it, although that was a part of it, as it was the feeling that not only did we not have sex, we didn't have anything else either. You weren't even mentally holding me anymore."

Edward said, "I guess things got a little dry there for a while."

"I was also thinking a lot about myself," Elise said. "I had always pretended to like myself, but what was really going on was that I

was envying everybody else, I mean, *everybody*. So I was thinking maybe I should *be* somebody else, and you were in the way. I mean, with you I had to be me. The same me I had always been. So everything was flying apart and there I was with you pretending it wasn't. Finally I just started doing it, whatever I wanted. I guess it used to be that I didn't ever think about what I wanted. I was too busy worrying about other people, about my parents, or about you, or about Roscoe, or about somebody I was working for—I could *do* peon. But I didn't feel like that anymore, I felt my life was shredded, I was all raw meat flopping around out there, naked all the time. That's when I started yelling at you, remember?"

"I remember," Edward said. He took off his shoes and felt his socks. They were still wet. He moved down onto the floor and cocked his feet up in front of the fire, on the hearth. "I remember the first time you yelled at me," he said. "You were in the closet. You were squatting down on the floor doing something, looking in the files or something, and I was trying to tell you how to do it. And you started screaming."

"It was a Saturday," she said.

"You'd never screamed at me before," Edward said. "You'd yelled at me, but you'd never screamed like that. Your face was red, and you were spitting, and you said you hated me. Over and over, you screamed it. I just cried. You'd never done that. You'd never said that. I mean, you'd said it, but it had been phony. That time it was true. I felt the way you loathed me. I think that was when everything changed."

"For you?" she said.

He was rubbing his eyes, using the pads of his forefingers to wipe away the sleep. "Yeah," he said. "It went on, too. After that you didn't have to scream to make me feel that. I could see it coming up in your eyes, or I could hear it in your voice. What is funny is how much it frightened me. I lied like crazy if I saw that coming. Except it wasn't really lying, it was more like rationalizing, looking real hard to find the bright side, letting other stuff slip by."

"I noticed that," Elise said. "It was amazing, both of us there letting this stuff go by, not commenting on it, not bringing it up. It works, but it's strange. I spent a lot of time looking at you, trying to figure out what you were thinking. We did all the usual stuff and said all the usual things, but we were thinking other things. I didn't like you much. I didn't think much of you. Anyway . . ." She leaned forward and stared at a large scratch on the top of his foot. She rubbed it with her thumb. "What is this? This doesn't look good."

"I dropped a speaker on it," Edward said. "I was vacuuming the living room, and I did all around the speaker, and then I felt guilty for not doing under the speaker. So I was picking it up with one hand to move it and it slipped."

"It looks like it could use some peroxide," she said, rocking backward and up onto her feet. "Hang on a minute."

Edward watched her go up the stairs thinking that it had been a long time since anyone had played doctor for him twice in the same day, and that he hadn't missed it. Then he had a little argument with himself as to whether or not he had missed it, thinking on the one hand that it was rote and ritualized so thoroughly that it was meaningless, and on the other that in spite of its mechanical aspect, it meant a person was propelling herself through space on his behalf. And then he thought maybe he was overdoing it, taking things too seriously, that it wouldn't hurt anything to let her doctor the cut on his foot, even if the cut on his foot didn't need doctoring. He wondered why he was reacting so strongly to it and decided it was because she was in her wife role, had slipped into it without his noticing, and was giving her typical flawless performance. He thought about her picking up the guy in the bar, he tried to imagine it, tried to picture her sitting in a darkened room with her elbows on a cold polyurethaned tabletop, tried to imagine how she felt— equal parts freedom and fear. He imagined she didn't have to try too hard to have a good time, to make herself attractive, imagined how she had laughed at the guy's jokes, how she touched his arm at the bar to tell him she was ready to go. He could even picture the motel room with its stocky mirror and low, rattan-front K mart dresser where she dropped her purse and her jacket. He closed his eyes and saw them standing there pressed against each other. Elise teasing him and exciting herself with every move.

When she came down the stairs with the peroxide and the Band-Aids he told her what he had been thinking.

She said, "Don't be a jerk, OK, Edward? Just let me do your foot." She knelt on the floor and turned the peroxide bottle upside down on a cotton ball, then swabbed the skin around the cut. "It wasn't terrible. I mean, I wasn't in terrible shape. It wasn't a terrible life. It was eerie because I felt so strange, because I was doing such strange stuff. So I left. I was also doing all this stuff about being able to take care of myself, I mean, I figured out that I had never done that, and I was thirty-something. I mean, I had sort of done it, but I hadn't really done it. You know what I mean?"

Edward watched her. She was talking to his foot. "I guess," he said. "You hadn't really done it."

"Don't make fun of me," Elise said. "You guys always get to take care of yourselves, even if you have wives and friends and families—we only get to play like we're doing it. That grates, know what I'm saying? If you're a woman there's always somebody taking care of you. Even if you try to get rid of everybody taking care of you, there's somebody taking care of you. I mean, you can't escape it. Think about that. It's awful. Anybody you're connected to you're connected to in this subordinate way. I don't want to fight about it—people have been making fools of themselves fighting about it for years—I just want to understand it, see how it works, see *why* it works." She was about finished with his foot. She was pressing down the edges of the Band-Aid she had put on. "You know," she said. "I stayed out of the movement because everything that was done in the movement seemed panicky and stupid to me—not that it wasn't right, but that it wasn't the issue. I mean, maybe all of it taken together makes sense, means something, I guess I think that's true, but piece by piece it was a pathetic little joke that we were all playing on ourselves. It seems to me that the rules are pretty simple—you do good work and you get along fine, you do great work and you get along even better. So if you're not getting along very well, it's probably a good indicator of the quality of what you're doing. I mean, that seems simple enough, right? Then you start looking at the anomalies, at the men who aren't doing much but are getting along great. That's what burns everybody's ass. All these shit-brained men getting along great, making big money, giving all the orders, ruling the world. So then all my beloved sisters went out and said, 'Hey! We can be half-assed! We should be rich and powerful and famous like these guys.' The logic, of course, is irrefutable. Perfectly correct. Only we missed the point somewhere. It's a kind of cultural grade inflation. Everybody wants to be an A student, so . . . why not? Hey!"

"So you came down here to do great work?" Edward said. "Is that it?"

"No, I do mediocre work just like everybody else, but this other thing interested me. I was interested in seeing if I could take care of myself, if I could feel like I was taking care of myself. But it didn't really work. I always knew you were up there, so I really wasn't free of that. And then there was Roscoe. And even though I was taking care of him in a certain way, in spite of his passive exterior, he's still a man, so sometimes I wondered if he and I weren't just playing at me taking care of him, so the long and short of it is that I never got there, and after a while I forgot about all that anyway. The subordinate part became less the defining characteristic of my womanhood, something only skin-deep, superficial, an accidental by-product that existed mostly in manners, made things easier, and that nobody paid much attention to. It's an uncomfortable position to occupy, because you can't talk about it with the girls, since they want to talk about equal pay for equal work, and of course I agree with that, but then they want to extrapolate from that, they want to generalize about social and political equality, and of course they are right there, too, but only if the goal is to get to the top of the heap of the not-very-good. They don't want to hear about this other question. And it doesn't matter anyway, since now all the women are jumping on the hardworking husbands, the well-kept homes, and instead of fighting for not being required to have children, they're fighting for maternity leave. They'll get it, too. You guys are such wimps."

"Why, thanks," Edward said. "Gee, that's great to hear."

"You are," she said. "The odd thing is that when little boys grow up they don't ever lose the kind of silliness you associate with boys, but when little girls grow up they become women."

"Yikes," Edward said.

"If they grow up," Elise said. "Anyway, so I'm out here trying to see what it's like, and I have concluded, after extensive study, that I will never know. That there will always be somebody ready to help. Which is a good thing and a bad thing at the same time."

The phone rang and she got up to answer it. She stood in the kitchen talking, and Edward listened from the living room. She was talking to Roscoe. He wanted to know where she was. He wanted to know why she was where she was. He wanted to know when she was coming back. He wanted to know how Edward was taking it. Edward didn't like listening to her end of the conversation, so he went upstairs to go to the bathroom, even though there was a bathroom right there, off the entrance to her apartment. The upstairs was pretty much like the downstairs—bare and elegant. He looked around, went through the dresser, went through Elise's closet, looked through her things in the bathroom. Nothing of Roscoe's, but nothing of his either.

He went down a short hall and opened a closed door. Roscoe's room was barer than the rest of the house. There was a double bed and box spring on the floor in the middle of the room, a Masters of the Universe castle used as a night table next to the bed, a couple of stacks of paperback books, a half-dozen clip-on lamps clipped onto windowsills and curtain rods, an eight-foot-high pencil cactus, and a low wooden desk with a portable computer on it up against the window. Edward looked through the things on the desk, and then crossed the room, went around the corner, and looked in the closet at Roscoe's clothes. They were very carefully organized. He owned a lot of socks, and most of them were white. Roscoe's bathroom was orderly, too—fresh white towel, a clean tub, an empty woven-wood wastebasket. For the first time Edward noticed how peculiar it smelled in the apartment. It was fresh paint, new carpet, new furniture—all combined to make a scent that he stood there for a minute puzzling about, until he concluded that it was nice, that he liked it. He walked back into the center of Roscoe's room, sniffing. He liked the room, too. It reminded him of a lot of rooms that he had had, and that he and Elise had had, in the early days of their marriage. There was something about the humility of these objects—they did not pretend to be more important, or more valuable than they were. They did not even hope to be. The bedspread was ordinary, the desk was cheap, the lamps were drug-store specials. It all reminded him of himself. Whoever bought the things for the room, and he imagined it must have been Roscoe, had bought them knowing that every choice was important, that even if you didn't have any money you could come out OK if you resisted the impulse to buy the first thing that came down the pike. It was how he and Elise had operated for years, how he still did, more or less. He stood at the window and looked out at the tall masts in the marina, at the odd assortment of colored lights there, thinking that the problem between him and Elise was that they didn't need each other, that they could function quite competently and comfortably each without the other, and once they had done it, inertia itself was working against the repair of the marriage. They would just slide into the future in separate lives.

"Checking out the competition?" It was Elise. She had come up the stairs without him hearing. She was standing in the doorway to Roscoe's room, leaning against the doorjamb, watching.

"I was looking for a letter to his mother," Edward said. "You know, where he explains everything. I was thinking I could use that against him down the road."

"If I were you I wouldn't mess with his mother," Elise said. "She's old line. Major stuff."

"I wasn't going to mess with his mother," Edward said. "I was going to mess with him. See, I was going to take the letter, and I was going to use it against him in some way. I was going to study the letter and find in it certain revealing notations. Wrong things that he wrote there that you didn't know he wrote there. I was going to get us all in a conversation, and then I was going to say them, and look at him real hard."

"You were going to show him up to be the rude and vainglorious cretin that he is, is that right?" Elise said. "And the letter was the smoking gun. I see." She started coming toward him across the room. "It's a splendid idea, let's look together."

"Won't work," Edward said. "Everything here is about R-Base Five Thousand, vertical marketing of financial packages, local area networking, specialized word-processing for the aircraft-leasing industry. There's not a thing here about his mother."

She hooked an arm through his and walked him out of the room, then walked him down the stairs, back to the fire. She said, "Well, what's happening up there? Kinta arrived. She's scaring Roscoe to death. On top of that, he's afraid she and Lurleen are going to go after it. Lurleen's already made two labia remarks. I said you'd call Kinta later. He wanted to come down here, but I told him we'd be back first thing tomorrow."

"We will?" Edward said.

"Sure," Elise said. "We have to take up our duties."

"Well, why don't we take them up tonight?" Edward said.

Just as soon as it was out of his mouth, he wished he hadn't said it. It was an awful moment. She was coming toward him, she was being friendly, even loving, the way she had come upstairs and walked him down, the way she had hooked her arm in his, happy to have engineered this time alone for them, to have kept Roscoe and the others at bay—that satisfaction was apparent in the way she moved, the way she talked, her tone of voice, the way she touched him, the way her eyes looked. He'd recognized all that before he'd said it, and he wondered now if he'd just said it out of cruelty, some perverse delight in going against her, some childish refusal to accept a new mood if he didn't initiate it. He had said, in effect, "If we're going back tomorrow, why don't we just do it now?" and she had instantly pulled away from him, shrunk from him—remarkable the way she became smaller, more distant, the way the sheen in her eyes dulled. She was already recovering, he could see that, but the blow had been felt and that made him feel wretched. He said, "I don't know why I said that. I guess I'm nervous. I haven't been away from the house overnight since you left. I'm sorry."

"Not to worry," she said. She was reaching for the fire tools. "We can go tonight if you'd like."

"No, I don't want to go," Edward said. "I think I just said that because you looked happy. Too happy. I don't like to forget the mess we're in. For a second it felt like we'd forgotten that, like we were together and everything was OK."

"And what's terrible is that it's only tonight?" Elise said.

"I guess so," Edward said.

She grinned at him over her shoulder and poked at the fire. "It was OK there for a minute, wasn't it? You and me coming down the stairs like that? It was real nice." She finished with the fire and put the poker away, then closed the fire screen. Then she turned around and sat on the hearth with her back to the flames. "It's too bad it only lasts about twenty seconds."

"Why don't we forget it," he said. "Why don't you just finish telling me why you left?"

"I mean, I left," she said. "You know, why does anybody leave? You leave. It's too much for you. You think maybe if you leave something will happen. What's interesting isn't why I left, but what we're doing now. Are we going to be able to go on doing it? Is there any reason not to do it? I mean, how do we feel about it? How do you feel about it? How do I feel about it? And then the thing with Roscoe, that came up, and I didn't see that coming, and that makes the thing that much more complicated. How does he feel about it? And what are we all *doing* together? In what sense are we together? We're just people who rely on each other, I guess. But we don't do anything together, we never see each other, we never talk to each other—you're just there in my head all the time. And maybe I'm there in yours. I mean, when I talk to people, I talk to them like we're still married and live together."

"I know," Edward said. "I do that, too. Even to people who know we're not. I think they must think we're pretty strange."

"So," she said. "As Uncle Jack says, now is the time to accelerate the demystification of the ground situation. What we've got here is a clear contiguity disorder. Coupled with a mythopoetic reduction in the marginality of things."

"Oh, God," Edward said. "You've been reading books again."

Elise hung her head in mock dishonor. "It's true. I admit it. I read a book."

"Well, hurry up and let's watch some TV," Edward said.

Elise popped her head up, a pretty grin spreading across her lips. "What's on?"

13

ONE OF the things Edward liked least in the world was the feeling he got when he was out somewhere—at the office, or shopping, or in a restaurant—and he went into a public restroom, and, glancing at himself as he passed the mirror, he found bits of food on his face. This had happened to him Friday at the office, and it was the second time it had happened to him recently. To have it happen twice in such a short space of time was enough to suggest that his connection with reality was somehow diminished from what it had been previously. For some reason, he connected the increased incidence of these food discoveries with his life without Elise.

This is what Edward was thinking—remembering—while bathing in Elise's tub. They had watched a half-hour of news on television, after which Elise had decided to exercise. She had a stationary bicycle, the sound of which annoyed Edward, had always annoyed Edward, and so when she said she was going to ride the bicycle, he said that he thought it would be a good idea if he went upstairs and took a bath. Her tub was an ungainly thing, not even the standard-issue white porcelain, or even white fiberglass, but some marble construct almost three feet deep and shaped like an inverted cone. Edward supposed the designer had two thoughts in mind: (1) that the marble would make the tub a snazzy item, and (2) that he would make up in depth what he lacked in length. Edward sat in this tub with water up to his armpits and his feet on the tub wall ahead of him, somewhat above his line of sight. It was as uncomfortable a tub as he could imagine, and it was ugly to boot, a kind of brown marble that he had never before seen.

Nonetheless, he was pleased to be in a tub, any tub. He was fond of tubs, and fond of bathrooms in general, but his fondness was usually limited to his own tubs in his own bathrooms. Now and then an alien tub would strike his fancy, if his high standards of cleanliness were met, or if he was terribly tired, but those cases were infrequent. Elise's bath met the cleanliness test, and it was kind of his, anyway, being hers, and it was pleasing to him in spite of the tub, though he was not sanguine about the way the water felt. It was soapy. When he dunked his hand in the water and then pulled it out and rubbed his fingers together, it felt as if there were a thin film of soap between the fingers. He couldn't recall if this meant that the water was hard water, or soft water, and after thinking about that for a second concluded that it was probably soft, though *slippery* and *sticky* would have been modifiers more to the point. Nonetheless, the water felt good, as water always did. When his feet got cold he put them down in the tub even though this required bending his knees back close to his chest, well out of the water, which, in turn, meant that his knees got cold. He tried crossing his legs, one over the other, bent at the knee underwater, but could not get his legs and his feet in the water at the same time.

Still, outside of his own tub he could not imagine any place he would rather be. It was silent in the bathroom except for the ticking of the clock, the rippling of the water as he moved in it, the odd sound of the flesh of his buttocks dragging across the bottom of the tub, sticking to it and then pulling away. He wet his left hand, shook it, then dragged it over his face, down his neck, and then sat feeling the barely moving air cool his skin. Thinking over his situation, he thought he probably would not move down here, move in with Elise and Roscoe, but he felt comfortable with the current arrangement, saw no reason to change it, and looked forward to getting everyone back in place. That meant him at his house, Roscoe and Elise here. He didn't know about Kinta—he was looking forward to seeing her, looking forward to having sex with her, but he noticed that his interest was more clinical than passionate. He supposed that he would grow more passionate as the event grew nearer. He remembered that he was supposed to call her, so he got out of the tub, did a quick dry, wrapped the towel around himself, and went into the bedroom looking for the telephone. It was on the bedside table, and it had a twenty-five-foot extension cord so he could stretch it right back into the bathroom. He did that, then got back in the tub and dialed his own number. Roscoe answered.

"Hi, Roscoe. It's Edward. Is Kinta there?"

Roscoe hesitated, as if he wanted to say something, then decided against it and said, "Yes. Just a minute."

Kinta got on the phone. "The fat girl's headed your way," she said. "We had words. She said I did all my thinking with my twat. I thought that was pretty ugly, a pretty ugly thing to say. I told her I had a healthy attitude about sex, and that her attitude wasn't healthy. I told her I didn't go to bed at night with socks on my tits."

Edward sighed. "I see," he said.

"She thinks women are badly treated. She thinks I give women a bad name. She stalked around here like some kind of a barn, swaying back and forth, and read me the riot act. It was funny, really. Poor Roscoe kept giving me signals the whole time, telling me to shut up, telling me to leave her alone. But I couldn't. I hate that kind of simpering, self-righteous, nickel-and-dime martyrdom. The only thing worse is when they're *not* loud-mouthed farts like Lurleen. You know what I mean? When they're pretty and nice and sweet and closely reasoned—the 'my body, right or wrong' crowd." Edward heard her lighting a cigarette, heard her blowing out the first stream of smoke, then she went on. "So anyway, watch out. She left half an hour ago, maybe more. Apparently she's got a thing about your wife. Roscoe says she wants to save Elise from you."

"From me?" Edward said.

"Right," Kinta said. "That's why she came up here in the first place. She's not a man-hater, she's a you-hater. It must be stuff that your wife told her or something. She's coming down there to be sure you guys don't work something out. Is that what you're doing?"

"No," Edward said. "We just started driving. She wanted to come down here, I guess. It's OK. It's been nice. We talked about a lot of stuff—why she left, for example."

"Why did she?" Kinta said.

"She had this big affair, and then she felt there wasn't anything left between us, and there's a lot of internal stuff about wanting to feel independent, or responsible—self-reliance, that sort of thing. She says women can't ever feel that because they're women."

"True," Kinta said.

Edward was trying to rearrange himself in the tub and slipped and splashed water all over the telephone receiver. "Oh, shit," he said. "Hang on." He pulled the towel off the towel rack and dried the phone, then settled back in the tub.

"What's going on there?" Kinta said. "Is there water nearby?" She laughed a little at her joke.

"I'm washing away the sins of the day," Edward said.

"I get the fire department to do that for me," Kinta said. "They get those big hoses, and the ladders, and the trucks, and the sirens, and those spotted dogs—you know those dogs?"

Edward didn't say anything. He sat there listening to Kinta wait for him to respond.

"OK," she said. "Sorry. Not funny. So you're coming back tomorrow?"

"That's the plan," Edward said. "That's what I hear, anyway. Will you stay?"

"Hey! Sure," Kinta said. "I'm in for the duration. I got nowhere else to go. Besides, I've got your entire bed for the night. I'm going to rub myself all over it. You're not going to believe it when you get back."

"Please," Edward said.

"Sorry," she said. "If it's OK with you, I'll stay a few days. I really am leaving Richard. It's not because he's fucking this girl, although that does piss me off. It's more like I'm just tired of him. He's not funny, or interesting, he always does the same shit, I know all his routines—he's at the end of his line. I mean, he's just going to do this stuff until he's eighty. The same stuff. It's OK, but I don't want to watch it. It doesn't get me like it used to. It's the same for him, too. I'm dead meat to him."

"I don't know about that," Edward said. "I don't see you as the dead-meat type. But we'll talk about it. Me, I'm just taking a little soak here. You have my permission to take a soak there. I recommend it."

"I'm taking Roscoe out," Kinta said. "Dancing. Hit the clubs. Make out in the mall lot. Stuff like that. Then we soak. Me and Roscoe."

"Fine," Edward said. "That's fine. That's perfectly fine."

"Actually, we're not," Kinta said. "But he's OK, he's real nice. He's kind of like you. What's the story on him? He lives with your wife?"

"Yep," Edward said.

"Well, that's modern of them," Kinta said. "But they're not like lovers or anything, right? He said they were friends. Is that right? Do we believe that?"

"I believe it," Edward said. "He's the lover I was telling you about. I shouldn't say that. But as to belief, yes."

"And you'll be miffed if I sleep with him before I sleep with you, right?" Kinta said. "That would be unseemly, wouldn't it?"

"Yes, I think so," Edward said.

"Just checking," Kinta said. "I guess after the gas station I can wait a day or so."

"Kinta," Edward said.

"Just kidding," she said. "The guy at the gas station was fifty and he had hair growing on his hair. I mean, I'm as liberal as the next gal, but too much hair is too much hair. It was Centers for Disease Control time down there. You'd need a chopper to clean the guy up. I stayed in the car the whole time. Except when I was calling, I mean."

"I'm relieved," Edward said.

"I really just want you to hang on to me for a while," she said. "I don't think I'm quite the hot item I used to be. I mean, I'm still probably too hot for you, but I'm not like I was. No, that's wrong. I am like I was, just not as often as I was. I'm getting along in years, I think. Remember when we used to do it on the telephone?"

"I remember. It was terrific. It was very . . ."

"Sexy," she said.

"Right," Edward said.

"I tried it with some other guys. Nobody liked it. Nobody understood it. They all wanted me to come over right away. I told them that was the point, I'm not coming over. They didn't like it."

"I'm hurt. I thought it was me and me alone."

"Yeah," she said. "That's why you called all those old girlfriends. You told me about that, remember?"

"A fatal mistake," Edward said. "Besides, I was just checking it out, trying to see if it was sweeping the country. It was. Still is, I think."

"Not here. I mean, I like it well enough, but it's not what it was. I think I have a conflicted libido."

There was a sudden silence on the line. She didn't say anything, and neither did he. On his end Edward heard that hissing noise that starts off real low and then rises until you can't imagine anybody on the other end of the phone being able to hear you, then stops abruptly, reopening the line.

Kinta said, "It's nice to talk to you, Edward. I like you. There aren't many people around I like anymore. There must be a lot of people around that I would like, I just don't know who they are, I never meet them. Anyway . . . I guess I'm going to talk to Roscoe about this situation you guys are in. Get up to speed so that when you come back I can tell you how to do it. He already told me something about it. It isn't a simple thing, is it? No, don't tell me. Let me work it up."

"Have at it," Edward said.

"I think it's interesting. Seriously. If Richard had come to me and said he wanted to have this other woman in our marriage I might have gone along with it. But he didn't want me to have anything to do with her. I mean, it wasn't like the two of us becoming the three of us, you know what I mean? It was him and her, and, when he couldn't get to her, it was me. I'm not complaining, I had my share, just not recently. It'll be a wonderful thing if you can make it work. How are you on the jealousy angle?"

"Fits and spurts," Edward said. "I don't see them much. This is the first time since last summer. Maybe I'm mad about that, her leaving me alone all that time. I mean, I'm not really mad, or maybe I'm mad internally. Maybe I just think I ought to be mad."

"You tried to get in touch with her? Since the summer?"

"No," Edward said.

"Oh. That's a strong case, then, isn't it?"

"It's not like I never thought of that, Kinta," he said.

"I think we all ought to move down there into some kind of commune," she said. "Extended family. I like it. You don't mind, do you? I mean, me including myself? I probably wouldn't do it anyway. Never mind."

"You're welcome," Edward said. "I like you, too."

"You do?" she said.

Edward took a minute before he answered, letting the question hang on the line between them. Finally, he said, "I do. I'm really glad you're here. There."

Now it was her turn not to talk. He listened to her breathing. He got the soap out of the soap dish and dipped it in the water and worked up some lather one-handed. After a while she said, "Me, too." And then it was as if neither of them had anything else to say. They sat silently on the line for another half-minute, and then she said, "So I'll go now."

"OK," Edward said.

"I'll see you tomorrow," she said.

There was another silence, this one awkward, and then they both said good-bye at once. Edward thought it was a bad ending to their conversation, but started to hang up the phone anyway. He had the handset about halfway to its cradle when he heard her say "Good night" again, her voice ridiculously tiny coming out of the phone a foot and a half away, and he froze, holding the receiver out over the cradle, waiting for the hard click of their disconnection.

Lurleen was hot. Edward could hear her all the way upstairs. He had taken another twenty minutes in the tub after talking to Kinta, and then, when he was getting out, he heard the doorbell. He got dressed in a hurry, pulling his clothes on before his skin was fully dry, getting angry in the process, but he didn't go downstairs. Instead he got a computer magazine from Roscoe's room, propped up the four pillows on Elise's bed, and sat there reading and waiting to be called. He read about desktop publishing, about laptop computers, about the average access times of fifteen different hard disks. After that he spent most of the time looking at ads and listening to Lurleen and Elise downstairs, trying to make out their conversation. He couldn't, quite, so when he heard Lurleen say something about screwing, he crept to the top of the stairs and listened harder.

Lurleen was saying, ". . . so you can't give in. You may want to give in, but you can't. It's not fair—to yourself, to any of us. You know what I mean. It's a self-worth thing. I see you bending over backwards, slipping into the role you're trying to lose. I mean, I have the same problem. Men start talking to me at the office and I'll do anything for them. They're nice and I'm gone. But at least I've recognized the problem—I'm trying to find my center and they're not helping."

"I think you may be overreacting," Elise said. "I mean, we just drove down here and that's all. I know what you're talking about, I'm aware of it."

"That's the worst of it," Lurleen said. "You always think you've got it under control—we all do. And then, Wham! You can't be lonely. You've got Roscoe. What about him?"

"I like Roscoe," Elise said.

"You told me you loved him," Lurleen said. "Not more than two weeks ago. You sat right there."

Edward rubbed his eyes, rubbed the sleep out of them, kept on rubbing and listening.

Lurleen said, "Maybe I'm coming on too strong here. It's your life, I know that, and I respect that. I really do. But . . . I've had so many friendships with women ruined because of the men they're with—I mean, I want a man, too." There was a break in the talk. Then she continued. "I do. Don't look at me like that. I don't do pelvic tilts four nights a week for nothing. The last guy I had—you remember that guy? I met him at the record store? Kind of a furry kid, a graduate student or something? I screwed him and screwed him, and I thought, you know, maybe he'd fall in love with me. Maybe I could make it love. When I wasn't screwing him I was typing stuff for him, cooking him dinner—all the rest of that. So three weeks into it he wants a night out with the guys, then he wants one to go play guitar somewhere, then he has to go out of town suddenly. After a while I was chasing the son of a bitch and I couldn't even find him. What I'm saying is, you get this stuff into your head and you end up believing it, you know? He was out with some blonde cunt he found at the sporting goods store. Little Miss America, little Miss Barbell. I don't know—maybe I'm just complaining because I can't get a guy to stick with me for more than twenty minutes, and you've got two."

The conversation stopped and Edward started to retreat to the bedroom, started feeling scuzzy for eavesdropping, but Lurleen began again.

"I don't know what you're going to do about this Kinta person—is that her name? Is that some special name she made up or something? When I see women like that I can't even imagine that I am one. Showing her little titties off to Roscoe—she was prancing around like she was on HBO. She *is* a woman, so I try to understand, but it ain't easy. They all go for it, you know what I mean? And she plays to it. And you try to talk to her and she treats you like 'Oh! You're here, too? Are you staying long?' "

Edward was sitting with his back to the balustrade, leaning against the turned posts that held it in place. He rubbed his back against the knobs in the posts. It was interesting hearing Lurleen talk when she didn't know he was listening. She was more sympathetic that way—to him she'd been only strident and bossy, a rather unpleasant-looking person with a manner to match. He could easily imagine the difficulty she had with men. It wasn't the looks—he'd known plain women, homely women, even a few major-league ugly ones, and all of them had figured out a way to have some kind of satisfactory relationship with a man. Sometimes it was surprising how people matched off, how an unattractive woman would turn up with a remarkably handsome boyfriend. For Lurleen, though, the looks were just the beginning. Her feminist stuff was off-the-shelf, untempered by experience, or compassion, or understanding. Ironically, practically all she ever talked about, as far as he could tell, was men. She had given Elise a book called *Men Who Hate Women and the Women Who Love Them*. She was big on the books—sixteen men to avoid, the power of sexual loving, the me book—all the titles carefully contrived by marketing geniuses to whet the appetites and balm the egos of menless women. She fell for it, built a life around falling for it. This puzzled Edward, who had assumed that those books were for high school dropouts or similar, that a graduate degree built in protection against their seductive messages—how could she take them seriously?

He was still thinking about Lurleen when Elise came up the stairs and found him on the landing. She started to say something out loud, but then caught herself and whispered, "Why don't you come downstairs? Join the party?"

"Is it safe?" Edward asked.

"I wondered what you were doing up here," Elise whispered. "Have you been listening all this time?"

"The last few minutes," Edward said. "From the point where she said you were hurting yourself and all of womankind. That was just before you said you were in love with Roscoe. Two weeks ago. You said that."

Elise bent down to kiss him on the forehead. "I said it tonight," she said. "Didn't I? Will you come downstairs now?"

"I'll bring my book *Women Who Give Self-Help Books to Other*

Women and the Other Women Who Accept the Books Without Remarking on the Probable Value Thereof."

Elise rolled her eyes. "How many times have I told you you don't have to nail every foot to the floor?" She tugged at his arm. "You've got to come down here, I can't do this alone."

So, for the second time that night, she led Edward downstairs, arm in arm. It seemed to him that she was making a show of their closeness this time, pressing against him, clinging to him more closely than she had done the last time, hugging him as they went down the stairs step for step.

As soon as they hit the ground floor Lurleen said, "It's the notorious Edward. Much heralded. How are you?"

Her voice was cool. She looked right at him when she talked to him, stared at him. It wasn't a pleasant look, but something closed and defiant, as if she hated his guts and didn't mind him knowing it, didn't mind telling him.

"That's me," he said. "How are you? How are things up at the front lines? Kinta get in?"

Lurleen gave him crossed eyes and maximum dumb. An opinion. "Yes. Kinta arrived in tiny white shorts and a halter top that looked as if it might fit a five-year-old, all under a suitably wrinkled men's jacket. She's a real superior being. You must have gotten her out of a magazine."

Elise gave Lurleen a dirty look. "Kinta's a little bit strange, but she doesn't mean any harm."

Edward shrugged at Lurleen. "Yeah. She's OK. I like her. We get along."

"I'll bet you do," Lurleen said. Then, spreading her arms in a windmilling gesture, she said, "But hey! If that's what you want—"

"She's pretty," Elise said. "She used to be. Is she still pretty?"

"She's great if you like inflatables," Lurleen said.

Elise did a give-me-a-break face.

"You must have had the metal to the pedal coming down here," Edward said.

"You mean 'pedal to the metal,' " Elise said. "You put the pedal to the metal, not the other way around."

"I knew that," Edward said.

"I don't want to go back to my apartment," Lurleen said. "Is it OK with you if I sleep here tonight?" She was talking to Elise, ignoring Edward.

Elise said, "Your apartment's only fifty-five feet away."

"I know," Lurleen said. "But last night I had this horrible dream. There was all this supernatural stuff whirling around in my apartment. I woke up stuck in the sheets. The guy next door was an exorcist or something. In the dream. He kept coming over to borrow peanuts. I had an endless supply of peanuts in the dream."

"I'm not saying a word about that," Edward said. "I'm not even thinking about it."

"He's Mr. Nice tonight," Elise said. "Just like I told you, Lurleen."

"He's fine," she said.

"How about something to eat?" Elise said. She had been holding onto Edward since they came down the stairs, and now she released him in the middle of the room and headed for the kitchen. "I'll tell you what we've got."

Edward and Lurleen followed her into the kitchen, and the three of them spread out looking for snacks. Lurleen was under the counter next to the dishwasher. There were only pots and pans under there, so she must have been figuring on cooking her snack. Edward found a Nestlé's Crunch ice cream bar in the freezer compartment of the refrigerator, stuck down behind seven quarts of frozen yogurts. Elise was at the far end of the room holding two cabinet doors open, staring into the cabinet. Edward asked her if the Crunch bar was the same Crunch bar he'd left when he helped her move. Without looking she said it probably was. He tore open the bag and blew into it, then pulled out the Crunch bar.

"I think we need to get some things straight," Lurleen said. "Where is the pizzelle maker? That's not what I want to get straight, but I want to know where it is."

"Gave it to the Salvation Army," Elise said, again without turning from the cabinets.

"You gave them the pizzelle maker?" Edward said.

This time Elise turned around. "Yes," she said. "Is there something wrong with that?"

Lurleen gave her a look and then shook her head. "It's just this picture of all these poverty-stricken people in their unpainted, unheated, broken-down shacks, dressed in rags, ponying up to this pizzelle maker—it's plugged into the light socket next to the bare bulb, see—I don't guess a pizzelle maker is high on their list of necessities."

"I think it's OK," Edward said.

"Well, they're not in rags, anyway," Elise said. "Edward gave them about three thousand dollars' worth of Perry Ellis shirts last year. Not to mention three pair of brand new Johnson and Murphy loafers. Not to mention the blue wool Ralph Lauren suit that was the best suit he ever owned—I mean Edward, not Ralph."

"My favorite suit," Edward said.

"I had my heart set on pizzelles," Lurleen said. She stood up and closed the cabinet door with her knee. "What kind of cereal have you got?"

Elise scanned her cabinets and said, "We've got Froot Loops, Rice Krispies, Honey 'n Bran, Cap'n Crunch, Rice Chex, Wheat Chex, Golden Grahams, Puffed Wheat, Choco Bears, Nutri-Grain Wheat, Nutri-Grain Bran, Grape-Nuts, Post Toasties, Sugar Frosted Flakes, Mister Midnight's Wheat and Honey, Mungo-Mungo, Motorballs, Space Krisps, Monster Bits—"

"Aw, come on," Lurleen said, crossing the kitchen to the cabinet in front of which Elise was standing. "You don't have any Monster Bits. You don't have any Motorballs. You're just making all that up."

Elise went into her totally stunned routine, flapping her arms and wobbling her head back and forth, her tongue lolling out of her mouth, her eyes rolling. She stumbled backward until she bumped into the wall and then stood there, pressed against the wall, shaking.

"Oh, shit," Lurleen said. She was standing in front of the cabinets, holding the doors just as Elise had held them. She turned to Edward and said, "They're all here."

"Nah," Edward said. He took a step up behind Lurleen. The cabinet was wall-to-wall cereal. He couldn't remember all the cereals she'd named, but since the cabinet held about thirty boxes of cereal, and she hadn't named thirty different brands, he guessed they were all there. He turned around and gave Elise an are-you-a-little-too-weird-to-be-believed look.

She had stopped shaking and was in big contrition, shoulders slumped, head down, body limp. "I like cereal," she said, chin on her chest.

"Oh, that's really great," Lurleen said. "She likes cereal. This isn't cereal," she said, pointing to the cabinet. "This is religion."

"I like to try things," Elise said. "I mean, ones I haven't tried before. When I get on the cereal aisle, I guess I go a little crazy."

"I don't remember you doing that," Edward said.

"It's new," Elise said. "It's sort of a new thing I've been doing."

"Hmm," Edward said. He finished off the Crunch bar and deposited the cleaned stick in the paper bag in the cabinet underneath the sink.

Lurleen said, "I think it's reprehensible. You're never going to eat all this cereal. Nobody's going to eat this cereal. One thousand blind children couldn't eat this cereal."

Elise seemed to take offense. "Sure they could. Look—" She shouldered Lurleen aside and started pulling boxes down from the shelves. "Half of these are empty. Half of them are almost empty."

Edward said, "I'm going back upstairs. I'm going to read the computer magazine I was reading."

"What, are you trying to sneak away?" Lurleen said. "Don't you think we should have a talk, the three of us?"

"I don't see any reason for the three of us to have a talk, no," Edward said.

"Oh," Lurleen said. "La-di-da. I was just getting warmed up to work on this situation you've got here."

"What do you care about it?" Edward said.

"I don't know," Lurleen said. "I just care. I care about Elise." She stopped and looked at Elise and then looked back at Edward. "Or maybe I just don't want to be left out."

That surprised Edward. She was serious and defiant, challenging him to make a joke about it, challenging him not to take her seriously. He hated people who could do that, who could be in the middle of an ordinary situation, a situation governed by some version of normal social rules, and could, if the mood struck, change the entire experience with a single remark. He hated the people who could do that at will, not the ones who did it accidentally. It was as if Lurleen had found the key that she thought would allow her entrance into the relationship with Edward and Elise and Roscoe. He could see by the look on her face that she wasn't going to let it go.

She said, "I feel like you guys have this private world that I can't get into. I mean, I try to be a good friend, I try to be supportive and caring—if you guys get back together I don't want to be lost out here."

Elise put an arm around Lurleen's shoulder and gave her a hug. "Nobody's going to get lost," she said.

"This is bullshit," Edward said. "Come on. I know how you feel, but—"

"Let her up, will you, Edward?" Elise said.

A couple of things occurred to Edward. One was that he didn't like being direct with people he didn't know very well. Another was that Lurleen was an uncomfortable person to talk to, one of those kinds of people who act like they know everything, and then, when you deal with them on those terms, they turn around and start playing vulnerable and alone. He knew as soon as he started being solicitous she'd turn around and box his ears. And he didn't know why the woman was there in the first place. Why Elise had befriended her. She was nosy, intrusive, manipulative, self-righteous, insensitive, and unimaginative, and yet Elise was patting her shoulder, rubbing her arm, telling her everything was going to be all right. And he was feeling guilty for having said her self-revelation was bullshit—that made him mad.

He put on a kind of childlike voice and said, "Are we being a little self-centered, Lurleen? Are we inserting our nose into someplace it doesn't belong? Are we being a little presumptuous? Are we having too many opinions? About things that don't involve us? Why are we driving back and forth across the country when we could be at home minding our own business? Do we want to be more important than we are?"

Elise shut her eyes and shook her head.

Edward went right on with the litany. "Do we wish we had more interesting thoughts than the thoughts we really have? Do we sometimes sit at home alone and think, 'Why not me? Why aren't I queen of the May? Why doesn't everybody love me?' Do we have some trouble with other human beings in the world having their own ideas? Having their own lives? Do we sometimes think that everybody else is real dumb and we're not? Do we sit there and think how pathetic they are? And then do we get real compassionate and think things like 'They're doing the best they can'? And then, after we've been compassionate—and we *like* being compassionate, don't we?—do we get real liberal and say, 'Different strokes' or, 'It takes all kinds'?" It was while searching for the next refrain that Edward realized he was making a lot of ugly faces at Elise and Lurleen, but mostly at Elise. His recitation had started out as a lesson, but somewhere along the way had turned into an attack and, at the same time, a personal report, a confession—most of his nasty questions were made out of things he'd sometimes thought about himself, things he did, about the way he regarded other people, and especially about the way he had been thinking about them since Elise left. So he suddenly realized that the faces he was making, which he had imagined were taunting reflections of the ugliness he was uncovering in Lurleen, were, in fact, reflections of his own bitterness, distrust, disaffection. He had gone too far again.

The women were standing there at the other end of the kitchen staring at him, their faces blank, their eyes dulled, cheeks slack. Neither one of them showed any reaction to Edward's performance. He realized all this in a second, and it paralyzed him. He got the last distorted look off his face, but that was all he could do. He stared at the women. They stared at him. He was aware of the light in the kitchen, the shimmering blue-white fluorescent light. Out of the corner of his eye he caught the distorted reflection of a clock in the chrome of the faucet. He noticed the wallpaper—fat flowers dangling off a segmented vine. There were three cereal boxes on the countertop behind Lurleen. Where was the toaster? He suddenly wanted to know where the toaster was. He figured it must be behind him, on the counter behind him. Lurleen was wearing high heels. There was a scab on Elise's right hand, just above the knuckle—she still had her arm around Lurleen. They were together. The two of them. He wanted to open the refrigerator.

Then the heater kicked on, and as quickly as his paralysis had set in, it disappeared. He reached for the door handle on the refrigerator.

Elise said, "Lurleen, I'd like you to meet my husband, Edward. Edward, this is Lurleen."

14

THERE WAS a big debate about whether or not to put another Duraflame log on the fire. Elise read the instructions on the package and reported that it specifically said not to add logs to a fire-in-progress. Lurleen said it didn't make any difference, they should just throw it on. Edward said they didn't have much fire anyway, and the instructions probably meant not to add the log to a successfully "burning" fire, on the idea that the thing might just explode or something.

"You think that's it?" Elise said.

"That's my guess," Edward said. "All you've got there is mush. You'll probably have to put some paper in under there to get it started."

"It'll be fine, Elise," Lurleen said. "Throw the dude on there."

They had gotten the snacking done, and Edward, made sheepish by his performance in the kitchen, had decided to stay downstairs and not go anywhere and read. Lurleen was on the edge of the brick hearth to one side of the fireplace. Elise was on the floor, on her knees, with the Duraflame in her lap, and Edward was sideways on the loveseat, his head propped up against one arm of the thing, his legs strung out on the other. After a minute of indecision, Elise opened the fire screen and dropped the new log on the grate.

"So . . . what's the question?" Lurleen said. "I don't quite understand what's going on. I look at you two, and you seem to be getting along great. What's the problem? Why don't you just move somewhere together? I'll go with you." She slid down the hearth a bit, bumping into the fire tools, knocking the poker out of its seat. It left a shadow-image of itself in the carpet where it hit. "Sorry," Lurleen said. She got after the ashes on the floor. "Maybe we better start at the beginning. You guys were living up there in that house, happy as a couple of logs, everything real cozy, everybody getting along fine, and then . . . ?" She turned to Elise. "You started having the thing with Roscoe, right? This was last spring?"

"Sometime," Elise said. "A long time ago. Everything seems to have changed since then. It's like everything is different than it was. I mean, a lot of the things are the same, but I don't feel the same."

"Me either," Edward said. "It's like I passed into another dimension. It's like that guy's joke—you know, he says he went out of town and while he was gone somebody came in and stole all his furniture and replaced it with duplicates. Or maybe it's not like that at all, but it's something. Something's different. I don't look at the days the way I used to."

"Well, that's interesting, Edward," Lurleen said. "What makes them different?"

"I'm alone all the time, for one thing," Edward said. "And the stuff I do is easier than it used to be. I don't mean my work, I mean stuff around the house. Dinner—stuff like that."

"It's easier for me, too," Elise said. She gave Edward one of her earnest looks, one of the looks that meant it really *was* easier for her, and that she wasn't just parroting what he had said. One of the looks that meant she was not hurt by his saying that things were easier for him.

"I guess it is harder when two people are living together," Lurleen said. "I've never lived with anybody, so I don't know that, but I can imagine that if two people are living together it's harder to get anything done."

"You're always waiting on the other guy," Elise said.

"You're always picking up after the other guy," Edward said.

He rolled his head to the right so he could see Elise, and they exchanged looks, each acknowledging the other's remark and apologizing at the same time—Edward thought the apology part was real nice, the way it was all done with the eyes, with the caught glance, and the tiny shrug of the eyebrows as he and Elise looked away from each other. He thought it was nice that they had this routine down, that they knew how to say to each other with the tiniest gesture what would have taken five minutes of back-and-fill to get said otherwise.

Lurleen noticed the private business between them, did a huff, and said, "OK, none of that. What's that mean? Does that mean you guys were being nasty to each other, but you really don't want to be nasty to each other, because being nasty to each other at this time seems not very useful or interesting, not to mention redundant?"

"Yes," Elise said.

"So you're agreeing you're not going to fight, is that right?" Lurleen said.

"That's what I'm agreeing," Elise said.

"Count me in," Edward said.

"Good," Lurleen said. "I hate it when people fight. I used to have to watch my parents fight all the time. It was always the same— they'd argue, and argue, and argue, and then my mother would cry, and then it would be over. It happened every time. She had this terrible weapon she would save until she absolutely had to have it, and then, when she was sure she was losing the fight, she'd start crying. It was really a beautiful thing. I used to wait for her to do it. My father would sort of forget everything else, everything he'd been saying, all the ugly things he was saying to her and about her, when she started crying, as if it didn't matter."

"She manipulated him," Elise said.

"I don't think so," Lurleen said. "I mean, I don't think she used it in that way, I don't think she was thinking about it, waiting for a chance to use it. It just happened. She did fight dirty, though. She was tough—most of what I know about my father I know from listening to these fights. I know about girlfriends and drinking and sexual tastes—one of the things you don't want to know about is the sexual tastes of your father, I guarantee—I know a lot about him."

Edward had his hands over his eyes. "I don't think I want to hear this," he said.

Elise reached out and patted Lurleen on the forearm. "I think Edward wants to indicate that he doesn't want to discuss this particular subject, so could we move on?"

"Where're we headed?" Edward said. He raised his head off the arm of the couch and looked at the two women. "I think I'm going to be ornery. Is that OK?"

"Be all you want to be," Elise said. "You can be Roy Cohn for all I care. You can be Roy Cohn's close friend."

"OK, OK," Lurleen said. "That's enough of that. So the story is you"—she pointed to Elise—"were screwing Roscoe in a major way, and then Roscoe's wife got blown up in a plant accident? Right?" She stopped for a second, waiting for Elise to reply, but when the response wasn't immediately there, she waved it away. "Never mind, whatever. So then you came down here."

Elise turned to Edward and grinned. "She's good, isn't she? She ought to be a scholar at the University of Southern Baptist Hospitality, Chronology Department. Look how she's pinning things down for us here. She's getting all the facts straight. I mean, before long she's going to know exactly what happened. She's going to know every *i* we ever dotted, every *t* we ever crossed. I mean, this girl's got a career of striving for excellence in front of her. We can probably set her up in a special Institute for Southern Baptist Hospitality Studies, from whence she can ramificate the engenderments of affections—the calls, so to speak—that we, you and I, have used upon occasion for the rearticulation of syntagmatic deciduation, if you take my meaning, make a list of those, and then turn her razor-eyed but very polite Southern aristocratic attention to the pause, a unit of meaning crying out for some attention in my book."

"I was just asking," Lurleen said, doing a loopy shrug.

"I know that you were," Elise said. "But I got carried away, as I sometimes do in our conversations. And"—she cocked a finger at Lurleen—"the guy in the movie is not retarded."

"Oh," Edward said. "I heard about this. Where is this movie? Do we have this movie here?"

"We have the movie," Elise said. "But we can't watch it. The thing's broken."

"She always says that," Lurleen said. "I wanted to show her the part that proves the guy is retarded, and she told me the thing was broken. I mean, I admit it would be a better movie if the guy wasn't retarded, but he is."

"Is not," Elise said.

Lurleen made a big show of rolling her eyes and heaving a brace of small sighs. "So," she said to Edward. "How come you guys don't sleep together anymore?"

Edward, who was still on the couch with his hand over his eyes, felt muscles in his body twitch, things went tight, speeded up in his head, and he ran down half a dozen quick answers in half a second. He felt jittery, the way he felt when he went to the doctor and had to strip and sit naked in the room waiting for the doctor to return. He hated that Lurleen knew about Elise and him, that they didn't sleep together, that they didn't make love—it made him feel pathetic: not only was he not a real man, he was not even a real person. Stupid stuff, he knew that, but he felt it nonetheless, felt like the kid the girls laughed about in high school, as if the authority with which he presented himself to the world, and which, more often than not, was accepted unchallenged, were abruptly thrown into focus and shattered, the public skin flaking away instantly but in slow motion to show a pitiful, retiring nub of gristle, wet and rubbery and featureless—a penis. His.

He said, "What do you mean? We make love. We've made love before. We know how to do it. We just don't want to anymore. Tell her I know how to fuck, Elise. I mean, you don't have to tell her that I'm good, but tell her I know how."

"He knows how to fuck," Elise said. "I know I don't have to say this, but he's OK."

"Thank you," Edward said.

"He's very insecure about this," Elise said to Lurleen. "He

doesn't want anybody to know. He's probably real mad that I told you." She turned around and looked at Edward, who had removed his hand and was looking at the ceiling. "Are you mad, Edward?"

"Who, me? Mad? Just because you've told everybody in the world that I'm a guppy made flesh? Hell, no—I'm fine. It doesn't bother me at all."

"Guppies fuck like crazy," Lurleen said. "Haven't you ever seen them in those tanks slipping around on each other?" She caught a signal from Elise, stopped talking for a second, then said, "Oh, that was dumb. I'm sorry, Edward. I mean, it's true, but I'm still sorry."

"OK," Edward said. "So I'm not a guppy. I'm some lower life form. Something south of the Vienna sausage. Or maybe I'm a pale reflection of something south of Vienna sausage. I'm in the party-weenie area. I mean, can we move right along through here?"

"Are you really that upset about it?" Lurleen said.

"He's not upset about it, he's upset about you knowing it," Elise said.

"Right," Edward said. "Striking a blow for truth, the devoted wife mistakenly machetes her impotent husband's loosely dangling apparatus. Good work, darling."

"Oh, come on," Elise said. "It's not as if you never screwed me. And it's not like you don't screw other people. I mean, you screwed that girl in nineteen seventy-nine, didn't you?" She instantly started waving her hands at Edward as if to stave off his reply. "Sorry," she said. "I could *not* stop myself. I'm sorry. I apologize. The truth is that you're totally capable. Totally. You don't screw me because you don't want to." She did a tiny shrug for Lurleen, and said, "I mean, it doesn't make sense to me since everybody else wants to. . . ."

"Yeah. Me, too," Lurleen said. "We've got lines at our doors. You stand around my house and all you hear after midnight are little pebbles that the romantic young men are tossing at my windows."

"It's OK, Edward," Elise said. "Really."

"Are you guys about finished beating me up?" he said. He swung himself around so that he was sitting upright on the loveseat. "I'm not that upset. If I was upset, I wouldn't do it. I mean, I'd fuck you until your liver screamed. I'd practice a lot. I'd get it down to where I could do it with my eyes closed. I'd paint it red and circle it with neon and rent one of those light-bulb signs that makes the big arrow, and I'd have that pointing at it all the time, and I'd get me a pair of bulge-oriented slacks, you know? I mean, I'd terminate and stay resident if I was that upset about it. But I'm not upset. I'm all right," he said. "I'm cool." He looked at Lurleen and Elise and they were both looking at him so he gave them a little shake of the head and a wave. Then he said, "Just don't tell anybody else, OK?"

The three of them went out to look at the water, at the bay, because Lurleen insisted that it was a good idea, that they needed a break. It was a short walk—they went through two parking lots and around the edge of a private marina full of small sailboats, all alike. The bay was fed by the Gulf, was big enough so that it looked as if it might as well *be* the Gulf. After they circled the marina on the wooden boardwalk that led to the slips, they climbed a rise in the land and walked along the edge of a low, six-foot bluff that edged the water. There wasn't any beach, only a jumble of hat-size rocks and the usual garbage—wood and paper and plastic—that collects at the edge of bodies of water. Developers hadn't gotten to the property adjacent to Elise's complex—it may have been city property or an old shipbuilding yard, a small one, a repair yard. After they climbed through the first fence there was a thin inlet and a single-file footbridge with only one handrail. They went over the bridge and then stopped to survey the property—it had been cleared once, a long time before, but, like the water's edge, it had accumulated its own debris: high weeds and saplings; forty-foot trees dumped there when the next plot was cleared, held up at angles by sun-whitened branches as big around as lamp posts; huge rusted steel pieces—plates and angles, hunks the size of cars bolted together, fittings for the big diesels. There were stacks of U-shaped concrete castings in the weeds, there were masts and booms strewn like giant pick-up sticks, piles of one-and-a-half-inch reinforcing rods, a couple of railroad-car natural-gas tanks next to each other sixty yards inland from the water, and, beyond those, a three-story corrugated metal building, its roof out in places, parts of walls gone, its huge doors open to the channel coming in from the bay.

The ground was soggy, and where there weren't weeds the mud glistened in the reflected night light—it came over the trees surrounding the property, from an insistent moon creased by a few ragged, black-bottomed clouds drifting lazily east. At the far side of the property was a Cyclone fence like the one they'd come through to get in—topped with barbed wire, pushed over in places, and, in other places, with chain links cut and pulled back so that sections of the fence hung off the structural steel pipes like rips of webbed paper. Beyond that fence there was a dense forest that stretched along the curving shore maybe six city blocks, ending abruptly on a point of land where a set of new, bright condominiums was haloed in the mists surrounding it.

Edward picked up a threaded nut bigger than his fist and showed it to Elise. "This is OK," he said. "I didn't know it was here, this place. Did you?"

"I've seen it," she said. "I never came in before."

Lurleen sat down on a prefab concrete stoop. "I just want to sit here. We don't have to talk. Anyway, I've been thinking. You people aren't so strange. I mean, I think you're in love with each other, love in the old-time sense."

"What's that?" Elise said. She squatted down about ten feet from Lurleen, picking white pecan-size rocks out of a waterlogged cardboard box that had split its seams. The rocks were spilling out on the ground.

"That's pioneer stuff," Edward said. "Old-time love." He took rocks from Elise and tossed them out toward the bay. "Right, Lurleen?"

"I'm serious," she said. "I've figured this out. It's because you're in love that you don't have to live together; you don't need it—I mean, it's a spiritual thing. It's like you're not even two people anymore. You're one person in two different places."

Elise laughed. "Yo, Edward," she said.

Lurleen gave her a mincing smile. "I don't want to get into anything here, OK?" She turned to Edward and nodded as if to assure him that she didn't want to get into anything.

"Me neither," Edward said.

Elise said, "We're already in it. We can't get out."

Lurleen was marking the concrete steps she was sitting on with a triangle of metal she'd found. "For me, sex has always been like it's supposed to be, like it is in the movies. I mean, you're in love and you have sex." She stopped again, this time tapping the metal on the concrete step. Then she said, "I guess that isn't true either. I wasn't in love with the basketball player. And, oh yeah, I wasn't in love with the mechanic, and I certainly wasn't in love with that other mechanic."

"Two mechanics?" Elise said.

"One was foreign, one domestic," Lurleen said, then she laughed. "Just kidding."

"What time is it?" Edward said.

"About three, I think," Lurleen said. She stood up and brushed off her backside. "You know—I know other people like you. In fact, I know two couples like you. I'm beginning to think you people are the wave of the future."

"Who are the others?" Elise said.

"You don't know them," Lurleen said. "Well, you met one of them, one of the couples. Martha and what's-his-name. You remember, they came to see me last summer, just after you got here? He's tall, thin, steel-rimmed glasses? Lead-colored? You remember?"

"Is he the guy with the big feet and the red tennis shoes and the real short legs?" Elise said. "He's about eight feet tall, but only about two feet of it is legs?"

"Yeah," Lurleen said. "He works for *Newsweek* or something. I don't really know him, I only know Martha. I've known her since college. Anyway, she told me about the arrangement they have. They haven't been together fifteen years, and they're not married, but they live together. They've been living together since her husband left her—Mike. His name was Mike. Anyway, they just like each other so they live together. For a couple of years they've been doing that. She said she doesn't want to be out there looking for something that doesn't exist. I don't know what his story is. So they live together and say they're lovers, but they're not. I'm the only one who knows that, though."

"So what do they do?" Elise said.

"Cheat," Lurleen said. "They're at my house for a week, and they're like a married couple. The way they talk to each other, the way they argue, the way they arrange things, the way they divvy up responsibilities, things they do for each other, the way they talk about things they used to do—they make this public effort to *pretend* they're lovers, but when they're in private, they *are*, so why are they pretending, see what I'm saying?"

"Like lovers," Edward said.

"Exactly," Lurleen said. "I mean, they're lovers, for all practical purposes."

"Except one," Elise said.

"Yeah, but that's the point," Lurleen said. "That one doesn't matter. I mean, it matters to me, but it doesn't matter to them. What Martha told me was that they have assigned nights. They go out. Separately. It's like this mechanical thing. They do it once a week, and they do it on the same night. She goes out, and he goes out, and neither of them comes home until the next night. Then they don't ask any questions, they pick up exactly where they left the day before. They don't always go out with other lovers, either. Martha said sometimes she goes to a movie and then goes to a hotel for the night. She doesn't know, but she assumes he does the same thing."

"I don't think that's odd," Edward said. "I've heard about people living that way. Or something like that. It makes sense, after a while."

"Speak for yourself," Elise said. She threw a handful of rocks into the concrete channel in front of them, listening to the splashes as the rocks hit the water. "I mean, I was tired of us when I moved out. There wasn't anything to hold me there. I was glad to get away. But so what? When I left I didn't know I'd be sitting here now. And what does that mean, anyway? We're only here tonight. Tomorrow I'll take you back, and I'll come back, and we may not see each other for another six months. It's not like we're living together the way these people she's talking about are living together."

"I don't get the point," Edward said.

"The point is that you're saying this is the same as that, that both are correct and reasonable and ordinary things to do, that they 'make sense,' as if they're normal."

"I didn't say that," Edward said. He shrugged, did some wagging back and forth with his shoulders. "Maybe I meant that, but I didn't say it. Besides, your idea of *normal* is exaggerated. We lie a lot about what we do, people do, I mean, and that's where we get this idea of something being normal—we all repeat what we've heard. I can't figure out why, but we do. I mean, we have all this stuff about marriage and family and love and romance, and as far as I can tell, all of it is powerful and true until you're about thirty, if you're lucky, and after that it's shit. I don't mean it's terrible, marriage and all that—in fact I don't think it's terrible at all, necessarily, just that it isn't what it's said to be—and I don't mean by *that* that it isn't as good as it's said to be, but that what it's said to be isn't an accurate representation of what it is."

"Whew," Lurleen said. "The man should go on *Merv Griffin*."

"*Merv Griffin* doesn't exist anymore," Elise said.

"Well, he should go on the Indira Gandhi show, or whatever that is, that black woman who killed Phil Donahue." She turned to Edward. "You mean you think behind all those doors in all those houses on all those streets with all those streetlights, all those brick houses, with all those Chevrolets in the driveways and children's playlike motor vehicles bumped into the porch columns, and all those yellow bug lights by the doors, you think in all those wood-paneled dens and blue-tiled bathrooms, in all those master bedrooms with the king-size beds and the separate closets and the cheap curtains over the windows, that what is going on is not what is said to be going on? That those people don't *believe* what they say they do? That they're just saying it for some reason?"

"Yes," Edward said.

"What's the reason again?" she said.

"The reason is, you can't tell a woman you've been living with for twelve years that the sight of her backside—or her broiled chicken, for that matter—gives you the willies. You may like the woman fine, but if you tell her something's wrong you've got to talk about it, worry about it, explain it, and worst of all, do something about it. On the other hand, if you say everything's OK, and she says the same, then both of you can go about your lives without much difficulty. When somebody asks, you say you're happy, love is grand."

"You really believe that?" Lurleen said.

"He believes it," Elise said. "I've heard it a thousand times. I heard it especially when he was in cynic school."

"If you don't believe it you're from Mars or someplace," Edward said. "They're like us, they're doing the same things we're doing, thinking what we're thinking, feeling the same—which means that while you're out getting screwed by Roscoe, so's a quarter of the population. Another quarter is doing the screwing, and the remaining half is wishing it was doing one or the other."

"Or courting Kinta on the telephone," Elise said.

"Right," Edward said. "Or maybe, for some people, it's too much trouble, or they feel too guilty, or cheap, or they don't want to disrupt things, or they'd rather noodle around doing whatever they like—gardening, office politics, cooking and cleaning, shopping. . . ."

"That's like me," Lurleen said. "I'll go months, sometimes longer, without thinking about romance, and I'm perfectly content, and then I suddenly get crazy—blam! I want to be a spy or something. I want to be a sex bomb. So I go to bed with some guy who tells me he has herpes, and I tell him I don't care, and for weeks

all I want to do is go to bed with this guy, or somebody, anybody—
I get real excited about it and I start thinking that I'm young and
free and hot, and I'm living high."

Elise said, "What's that got to do with what he's saying?"

"He's saying love can be anything, and I'm agreeing," Lurleen
said. "Something like that."

"I thought he was saying love is phony," Elise said. "What were
you saying, Edward?"

"I wasn't saying anything," Edward said. "She asked if I thought
the people in the houses who appear to be happily mated are, and I
said no, at least as to the public version—love, marriage, family, so
on. They may be OK, but that's coincidental—it's easier to say
you're OK than it is to worry about it. People are private, that's
what I'm saying."

"So they're caving in?" Elise said.

"You're not," Lurleen said. "You're separating."

"They are, too," Edward said. "Only they're doing it at home.
That's what I'm saying." He rubbed his forehead and yawned. "And
if that's not what I'm saying, that's what I ought to be saying."

"I wish you'd say what you ought to be saying and not all the rest
of this shit," Elise said.

Edward sighed. "See, here's what happened. Lurleen said she
knew these people. I said the way they live makes sense. You said I
was confusing them and us, using them to say what's going on
with us makes sense. I said I wasn't." He thought a minute, then
said, "I could have been doing that, because if you live with
somebody a while, pretty soon she looks the same all the time, she
smells the same, she acts the same, she does the same things when
you have sex, she does the same things when you don't have sex,
she says the same things whenever you say whatever the same
things you say are, you have the same arguments, the same mild
disagreements, she likes macaroni and cheese, for God's sakes, she
likes the magazines fanned on the coffee table, and you like them
stacked—I mean, you're looking at thirty years of walking through
the room and finding the magazines on the coffee table this way you

don't want them, thirty years of unfanning the magazines. She's looking at thirty years of unstacking the magazines. And that's not all. After a while you want to feel a body that feels different. You want to kiss some lips that don't feel like hers, you want your head on a shoulder that doesn't feel like her shoulder—it's not that you don't like her shoulder, her shoulder is fine, it's just that something else is wanted. You want a shoulder run by a brain other than her brain. She does, too. It makes sense. That's just the tip of it. So we don't live that way, we're lying. It's not a question of maintaining other values, it's a question of lying. And the reason we lie is not that we want to maintain these other values, anyway, it's because it's easier. The maintenance is a by-product, a killer waste that makes people imagine that things are better than they are, that things are possible. I mean, ten minutes ago *we* believed it. We thought that."

"Ten minutes ago?" Elise said.

"Ten months, then," he said. "What's the difference?" He walked up the steps Lurleen had been sitting on, stood on the top step. "One time I asked my mother, who was in her seventies then, how it was for her, how the years between my age, which was thirty-five, and hers, had been—I was feeling lousy and I said something like I hoped things were going to get better, and she said no, it just gets worse."

"Your mother said that?" Elise said.

"Yes. I asked why she hadn't told me sooner, and she said she figured I would find out soon enough. But this was my mother, you know what I mean? She had a regular middle-class life. She wasn't beaten up, or raped all the time, she didn't go through seventeen husbands, she always had something to eat, she had a decent house, she had a family, a husband, but when I asked her at seventy-five, she said it gets worse. And she's a Pollyanna, not given to self-indulgence or cynicism—she's always finding ways for things to be OK. But all those years when she was helping me in school, or driving car pools and making lunches and putting them in brown bags, when we were going to the pool at Rockland Elementary, when she was listening to my father's dinner-table tales of business intrigue, when she was teaching—all that time what she was thinking day to day was that her life was getting worse. Her best year, she said, was when she was fourteen. After that everything was a slide. Sixty years of slide."

"That's horrible," Lurleen said.

Edward looked at her, then at Elise.

"Hi, Mom," Elise said.

15

WHEN THE two women went inside to go to bed, Edward stayed out in the shipyard. He wasn't tired. He wasn't happy. He felt that his dissertation on love and life was a little embarrassing, a joke. Which is not precisely to say that he thought what he had said was not true, but to say that it lacked something in the way of polish, intellectual decoration, style. Sitting on the stoop that Lurleen had abandoned, from the top of which he had pontificated, recalling his mother in the black leather chair she had sat in when she said it just got worse, he wondered exactly what she had meant. He wondered how it had gotten worse for her—he remembered photographs of her in the 1920s, at a desperate-looking beach backed by drab clouds. She lay on her stomach on a towel, her frizzy dark hair splayed by the wind, her smile careless and adventuresome. It was a picture his father had taken, a step in his courtship of her, which was a process Edward thought he understood—his mother young and impressionable, lovely, eager to enjoy herself and her life, and to prosper spiritually as well as materially, suddenly found herself sought and besieged by a wild man, which is what Edward knew his father had been in those days, knew from the first-person accounts of both his parents and, as well, by the simple process of extrapolating from what his father was when Edward was growing up. So, his mother: a city girl from a decent family in the middle of the middle-class of the period, a pretty girl with an older sister and no father—he had died when she was quite young—a young girl with taste and imagination and some—but not too much—respect for the conventions, and with aspirations, too—she had not gone away to college in those days to find a husband, she had gone to learn, to find a career, to make a life. Edward tried to imagine her a young woman, bright and quick, her principal equipment the startling, somewhat haunted good looks, and a droll wit that, in spite of her attempts to control it, drove away more men than it attracted. There was, in Edward's imagination, something of the farm girl about her, too—the fairness, the even temper, the endurance. His father must have seemed to her an odd mixture of charm and boorishness, of insistent reason and tantalizing wickedness—he was a gambler, a reckless boy from out of the West, an overachiever whose self-reliance and disregard for the rules and regulations set him apart, even while his common sense pulled him up short of the death-wish set. They would have been a terrific pair—clever, funny, intriguing, ready for anything just as long as nobody got too seriously hurt, as long as all that was wrecked was the car or the dance floor or the hotel room. He was out of lumber and construction and real estate, she was out of education; he had the raw power, the drive, and she had the culture. They worked together. Edward sat in the shipyard and remembered that picture of his mother on the beach, thinking that what she must have meant was what he had experienced—that although moment to moment his life included its fair share of highlights, of the feeling that life-in-the-world is a splendid and singular blessing, the overall sense of his forty years, seen in close-up, was a sense of diminished possibilities, of the denominator of things being lowered step by step, of narrowing and cutting off and limiting and forsaking. That afternoon on the beach at nineteen she was happy, and it was five years past her best year. And he remembered her happy in other photographs, remembered her *seeming* happy, anyway, and remembered from later years, after he was grown and capable of remembering, her perfect laughter in the kitchen or at the dining table or on the lounge or out in the pleasant summer evening on the brick patio. He remembered her in a striking black business suit of the fifties, languorous and inviting against the porch wall of their house, her hair the color of dark ashes. In that photograph, and in fifty others he had known all his life, pictures he could flash through his brain at will, she had the poise and the manner of a movie star—elegant, unconcerned, openly sensual. He remembered these photographs and thought about what his mother had said to him and tried to put the two images of her together without resorting to the easy explanation that what had started out as an engaging and enriching lark had turned, in later years, into an essay on the virtues and dangers of concession. She had wanted to be a teacher, but she was a teacher only for a couple of years. She had wanted to be an actress, but she appeared in only two plays. She had wanted to have a family, and she had done that, and well—Edward had two brothers, both older than he, more successful, and both as in love with her as thoroughly and completely as he was.

As he thought of that, it occurred to him that perhaps having the sons in love with the mother was not the measure of a successful parenthood, that the brothers loved the mother too much, that this love somehow cut them off from their world, their women—then he thought that was silly, it was a routine comparison, inevitable, the results not taken too seriously. Besides, if you had a half-decent mother, the new women didn't stand a chance anyway.

Edward came down off the stoop and walked away from the bay, along the channel toward the building. He could see through the building, the bright street lamps on the other side, on the road that passed in front of the property, the dull blue light cracking through the trees and slinking into the building through the open bays of which he could see shadowed machinery up against an unmarked gray background. When he actually got inside the building, he could see perfectly, but the air was dense the way water is dense, the space seemed filled from its concrete floor to the bar-joists and the torn-up roof, filled with a delicate coolness finer than mist but no less perceptible—there wasn't anything there in that room, except this peculiar air he felt all around him, close, as soon as he walked in, air that put a slight pressure on his skin: he felt as if his whole body had been gloved. "Howdy," he said, listening for whatever echoes might come off the walls. Some did, though they were partial, like the narrow shadows that outline objects when they're close to a surface. "My name is Edward," Edward said. "I'm in tiny apes and dragons—how about you?"

No answer.

"OK, I know you're in here," Edward said. "Reach for the sky." He made his hand into a child's play-pistol and slowly swept the building left to right.

Nothing moved.

He made that hashed clicking noise you make to simulate the TV version of the cocking of a gun, and then, his arm straight out into the darkness, he discharged the gun twice, then a third time, doing muffled reports with his mouth.

"Safe, at last," he said, holstering the imaginary pistol under his left arm.

There was a chair there. He sat down. Something fluttered briefly in the rafters above him. He said, "Hey, Mom! It's not so bad! Come on."

He wished she were there with him, wished he had a big, comfortable chair for her to sit in—she could have a newspaper in her lap, and they could have a conversation, and when the conversation slowed, she could go back to her paper, read another story, read another headline, and Edward would listen to the small, amused guttural sounds she'd make as she discovered things she found curious or wretched or clever. And every time she found something, he'd ask, *What is it?* and she'd tell him. Sitting in the big, hugely padded, preferably tasteless, nondenominational chair— something worse than a La-Z-Boy, but on that model—with her feet up on the pop-out footrest, her head back against the leather headrest, canted to one side to look around the partially closed newspaper at him, sitting eight feet away in a blond wood school chair, the same chair he was sitting in now, she would tell him what she found amusing, tell him what she thought about the world. *Buckle up, Edward. Bear down. Take a hit. Try again.* Not in those words, of course. Hers would be sweeter, gentler, kinder, more sympathetic, more forgiving—wearier. But that would be the message; that was what in seventy years she had found worth repeating.

Edward looked into the blankness of the building at the spot where his mother would have been sitting had she been there. He knew what she would say about Elise: Stick with her, make it work. But it hadn't worked all that well for her, though she never once blamed his father, never once said the man was a beast. Nor was Edward sure, finally, that he was. Maybe in his thirties and forties, maybe even into his fifties, when he was still persuaded of his own genius, when by his own account he could do no wrong. Maybe then he was cruel and stupid—in those days, the last stages of *the better idea,* Edward's father had been his own one true Church, with his own canon, his own liturgy, his own incessant and selective reason. But Edward didn't know much about that period in their lives, he had been too young, too concerned with his own interests and inclinations to carefully record or even identify the qualities of his parents' interactions. He felt guilty about it later and spent hours trying to reconstruct scenes from his childhood, details of the dinner table, trying to remember the tone of the conversation, the subject of the conversation, whether it was a monologue or a dialogue, whether his mother had been participant or spectator— his recollection was the latter. And then the question: Was his father too strong for her, or was she treating him like a child having a tantrum, a thirty-year tantrum? He had taken much from his father, much of his personal initiative, his will to do things as fully as he could do them even if it was ridiculously hard, his capacities for analysis, and most of all, imagination. But since twenty, Edward had tried to avoid taking his father's worst features as well, even to the point of consciously recognizing and avoiding behavior that he identified as his father's. Still, over time, his resolve wore thin, and by forty he saw himself very much a replica, all his efforts to the contrary notwithstanding. He and Elise used to talk about it, used to identify things he said, arguments he made, procedures he insisted upon as characteristic of his father—"You sound like your father" and "That's something your father would do" became show-stopping arguments, and they were used liberally and effectively. Finally, Edward came to accept the idea that he would *be* his father long after his father was gone and, with that in mind, strove less to avoid his father's mistakes than to emulate his mother's patience and understanding.

Thinking of his life with Elise, he wasn't sure how well he had done. Roscoe had moved in with her and Edward had not even raised his voice about it—the lack of emotion surprised him, but he didn't know whether to see in it a characteristic of his father or his mother. Was he defiant or enduring? He didn't know. Early in their relationship, when Elise left him because he was seeing another woman, her departure had killed him. On other similar occasions in their years together, those times when the prospect of their continuing marriage seemed less likely than the probability of divorce, just the thought of living without her had been crippling. This time it wasn't. Maybe he hadn't allowed himself to believe the current state of things was more than a temporary affair, another act in the endless light drama of their marriage. Maybe he could not even *imagine* himself without Elise, thought that what Lurleen said was true, that he and Elise were one person, and maybe that was so deeply felt, so *known,* that he simply did not feel the emotional stress of their separation. Maybe it hadn't hit him. But in that tin barn in the middle of the night on a piece of land of undetermined ownership a hundred miles from his house, what struck him most powerfully was the level of his disconnection, not from Elise or from his marriage, but from everything else. Here I am, he thought, on this wood chair in this metal building, and what am I doing? Thinking about my mother, father, family, thinking of times past and things lost. Why am I not at the disco? The club? Some big party? An opening? A movie theater? A knock-your-eyes-out eatery? Why am I not putting my children to bed? Or looking at my children already in bed, sleeping? Doing a little take-home work from the office, still in my shirtsleeves and tie, while the lovely wife pretends to finish up in the kitchen when in fact what she's doing is waiting for me to complete my work so that we can go upstairs together and look in on the children. Where are these damn children? People around me are going pell-mell to get the children, the pets of the eighties, and where are mine? Why don't I have a few? Is it because I can't control them? Because I'm . . . scared? Because if I had some I'd have to be interested in their lives, and I only want to be interested in mine? At this point he jumped up and said, looking back at the chair as if he were still in it, his voice sudden and mock-stern, "Edward!" He sat down again, staring at an imaginary person standing where he had been standing. "It's not funny," he said. "It's a mess." Up again, taking the other role, he said to the chair, "You're a jerk, come on, self-pity is not attractive—you're like everybody else, OK? They're all out here as stupid and self-centered and hopeless as you. Get off it. You want to disco, disco. You want to vie for the title of Mr. Mozambique, that's OK. But don't simper." He was walking around the chair now, circling it, talking to it. "You don't like to disco, Edward. Besides, people don't disco anymore—where've you been? They're out in the parking lots. I mean, the professors are tucked away in the tree-lined lots outside the mall, in their Volvos, with their teenaged honeys, doing hair pie in the back seat, the better to recapture the good times—you remember the good times, don't you, Edward? Little yellow Sun records, rolled-up short-sleeved white shirts with those real wide collars, the bop, the slop, the hands up under the furry pink sweater in Roxanne Carpolino's parents' garage, there against the Hotpoint washer-dryer combination? You remember all that, don't you? That's what counts. You want it, you got it. But, hey, just don't mince and simper, OK? You're doing a fine job. Everything is all right. Listen to me. Your mother's wonderful, your father's wonderful, all your brothers and sisters are wonderful, everybody's wonderful, including you. OK?" Edward put his hands behind him and paced back and forth in front of the chair. "Here's what I think. Are you listening, Edward?" He stopped and looked at the chair for a minute, then continued pacing, his footsteps ringing in the building. "I mean, what's the big deal? You have all these feelings. The feelings are complicated. There's not much you can do about that. If they weren't complicated you'd be bored silly." He looked at the chair. "If you want to know what I think, I think some of the brain must be gone. Some of the little cells have taken a powder. Or did we say that already?"

Staring at the chair Edward could see himself sitting there, could see the roll of his shoulders and the thickness of his chest, and the white oval of his head tilted slightly forward. This was disconcerting because Edward was not an out-of-body person. He rubbed his eyes and reminded himself that he was alone in the building, and then, taking a last look around, he walked out the way he had come in, into the abandoned yard, across the yard to the fence, through the fence and around the marina, across the parking lots, to Elise's house.

When he got inside, Elise said, "There you are. I was about to send a posse out after you." It was an expression she had picked up from his mother.

He said, "I've been sitting in that barn thing over there. Talking to myself. Where's Lurleen?"

"She went home. After your sweeping indictment of practically everything she decided you were a wonderful person, and she went home."

"Yeah," Edward said. "I guess I was painting with the big brush again, wasn't I?" He took a couple of clownish swipes at the ceiling as if he were using a broom for a paintbrush.

Elise laughed—one of her pretty laughs—and said, "Well, it was good for her. She has put down the burdens of her former beliefs re our marriage and will follow us to the ends of the earth." She raised an eyebrow and then smiled. "Here," she said, doing her version of Edward's big brush act. "Let me help you with this."

Then they were both wheeling around the room with their imaginary brooms, swatting at the ceiling, swishing the walls, making up sound effects, the splash of the would-be paint as it hit the Sheetrock, then small explosions, then bigger ones, and in a minute a full-scale predawn attack on a foreign capital complete with whistling rockets, dive-bombers, ack-ack guns, thundering bombs, and the remarkably cheerful squeals of the wounded and dying.

16

LURLEEN WAS there early Sunday morning for microwave pancakes, microwave bacon, microwave eggs. These were real eggs cooked in shallow plastic cups—a kind of fried egg redux. The three of them sat around a thin breakfast table Elise had made out of some black metal sawhorses, Storehouse variety, and the top of a table that she and Edward had once owned, the legs of which had been lost somewhere along the way. Lurleen looked rested and relieved, and she was a little too eager to talk. "So," she said. "You guys have a great night, or what? Did you stay out there long, Edward? These are great eggs, aren't they? Have you ever seen eggs like this? I feel much better this morning. I'm glad we had our talk last night." She mounted a sliver of egg on a piece of toast, put that in her mouth, and then, while she was chewing, pointed at each of them in turn with her fork. When she'd swallowed, she said, "We're a team, right? I mean, we get things done."

Elise's apartment was pretty in the morning. Edward liked the way the light came in through the Levolor blinds, the way it striped the silly blue walls, which were lovely *because* of their silliness, not in spite of it. Sitting at the table listening to Lurleen and watching Elise nod at her, scanning the rooms he could see from the makeshift table—the kitchen, part of the living room, a second room that was identical to the living room in size and shape but that Elise had set up as a gym—he went through a quick cycle of feeling, starting with the notion that it was a nice apartment and she had a nice life without him, then it wasn't a nice apartment, it was a decorator's pathetic attempt to inject his misguided taste into the drab lives of the project's renters, in this case his wife, then it was an OK apartment, charming precisely because of the decorator's folly, then it was just plain blue, an accident that did not reflect on Elise in any way, then it seemed sort of empty again, bare and hollow and full of so much sad hope, as if it were waiting there for a life to be lived in it. Out of nowhere he said to Elise, "Why don't you just come back home?"

That stopped the conversation. At first it was very tense around the table, but that tenseness gave way to a kind of curious, almost disinterested, consideration. Elise and Lurleen chewed their ways through, eyeing him and occasionally eyeing each other.

Finally, Elise said, "Why don't you come down here?"

"It's blue," Edward said. "It's all blue."

"Paint it," Lurleen said.

Edward hadn't intended to open this conversation, to throw the three of them into it, but he knew he had, and now he had to get them out. He imagined himself the Muhammad Ali of husbands, most of the time floating like a butterfly, occasionally stinging like a bee. He thought stinging was what he had done a minute before, and now—floating time. He said, "So, what do you think? Coral? Maybe something in a nice puce"—he made a face that meant he didn't think puce was such a good idea—"I'm thinking there isn't such a thing as a nice puce. I'm thinking if we go with puce, we're going to have to accent with aquamarine."

"I don't want to move back up there," Elise said.

Edward did a reverse nod, lifting his chin in a short jerk to acknowledge her remark. He was thinking: her turn. He was thinking: Let's don't do anything dramatic here.

"OK," he said, nodding more than he had to, making fun of his agreement by burlesquing it. "That's fine. That'll be fine. That'll be OK. Sounds good to me. I can go with that. Sounds like a strong statement of deeply held convictions. I like it. It has that special something. That—" He started wagging his hands in the air as if trying to locate the word he wanted to use to describe the special something.

Elise knew the routine. Having given what she had got, she backed off, smiled, and said, "So . . . let's send it up to the boys in fulfillment. See what they say."

Lurleen, who had watched this tiny exchange with wariness, suddenly relaxed and said, "Hey! That's all right. Way to go, guys. Way to pull it out of the hat!" She reached out and patted Elise on the arm, nodded at Edward, then got up to take her plate to the kitchen. "What I think we ought to do is go back up to Edward's and check out Roscoe and Kinta. Maybe go to a movie or something. Maybe go skin diving."

Edward gave Elise a small, tired smile, and she returned it exactly, as if in the moment they both realized and accepted the trouble they were in, and realized, too, that they didn't want to be in trouble, but that it was going to be with them for a while.

Lurleen hollered from the kitchen, "I'm going to rinse these, OK? I'm just going to clean up a little." She didn't allow any time for argument. Water splashed in the sink.

As if the water were a cue, Edward and Elise leaned forward at the same time, both of them putting their elbows on the narrow white tabletop, staring at each other, bringing their faces close together. Edward said, "She's rinsing."

"She's doing a fine job," Elise said, and she smiled in this way that Edward remembered he loved.

At close range her eyes were like the representatives of a peaceful, compliant nation—he couldn't help but think how close her eyes were to her brain, and that made it a kind of funny, lovely moment, because as he looked into her eyes, he saw the linkages to her brain, saw the brain itself, literally imagined a soft, whitish lump trailing stringy tendrils out to her eyes, saw it as what he loved, and as divorced from her body. He brushed her cheek with his and said, "You won't believe what's going through my mind."

She shut her eyes. She was enjoying the touch, the feel of their skins together. In a lovely, playfully resigned voice she said, "Yes, I will. Let me guess—laser optics, Bolivia?"

17

THEY LEFT the apartment at eleven. Edward and Elise in Roscoe's car, heading back up the highway they had come down the night before. They weren't talking much. Lurleen had changed her mind a half-dozen times about whether she would come with them, finally deciding that she wouldn't, that, as she put it, "You guys have a handle on this now. You don't need me." Edward had thought when she said it that she was mighty optimistic.

In the daylight, the town where Elise lived wasn't very pretty. The highway that split the place in two was bordered on both sides by gas stations and convenience stores and restaurants and nurseries—and these weren't slick, modern, glitzy examples of the breeds. These were low-down, on-the-cheap rehashes: a U-Haul rental place in a former car wash; a video store in a building that still had a purple silhouette of a woman in some kind of aerobics pose on its side; a movie theater in an otherwise empty strip shopping center; a couple of huge blue cedar–sided apartment projects with no cars around them; and hundreds of those tiny prefab wood-siding shacks that you buy off a lot, thrown up along the side of the highway to advertise Bird Heaven, Strings & Things, International Wholesale Outlet, Rug-O-Mania, The Bomb Squad—Edward liked that one—with its "Fireworks to Suit Every Occasion" slogan in Chinese-looking letters under the name, Rent-My-Tux, Hair by Gordie, and the strangest one, a small black building that had "Moose Parts" in crude, handwritten red letters on its roof. When they'd passed it, Edward wasn't sure if it said "Moose Parts" or

"Mouse Parts." On top of all this, the state was working on the highway, so there was a lot of paraphernalia associated with street repair everywhere Edward looked—the bright pink cones, the big earth-moving equipment, piles of construction supplies, and, even on Sunday, legions of seedy-looking workers in their Day-Glo pink vests.

"I don't want to be overbearing, snot-nosed, and stupid," Edward said. "But how come every one of these guys seems to be doing his best to look like that guy in *Nightmare on Elm Street?* I mean, I understand that they're going to get dirty, but couldn't they get dirty in little white suits?"

"Don't be a pill, Edward," Elise said.

"What?" he said. "I'm supposed to be nice about them because they'll do this work? Here. Look at this guy."

They had slowed down because three lanes merged into one up ahead, and they were passing a place where some guys were standing around the back of a concrete truck. Edward was pointing at a huge man, six and a half feet tall, wearing two T-shirts, a boys' department plaid flannel shirt, his vest, a pair of lime green sweatpants held up by a kid's two-gun cap-pistol rig, in the holsters of which he had, on one side, a walkie-talkie, and on the other, what looked to be one of the thickest sandwiches Edward had ever seen.

"Jesus, Edward," Elise said.

"Take a look at the stomach," Edward said, looking the other way. The man was about five yards in front of their car. His stomach slid out from under his T-shirts, rolled out over the top of the gun belt, which wasn't actually buckled, because it was too small, but was tied together with a length of yellow rope, and hung out over the sagging sweatpants like the furry snout of an elephant seal.

"I think it's cute," Elise said.

Edward made a retching noise. "I'd hate to see his tits."

Elise let out a disgusted sigh and shook her head, deliberately not looking at the guy Edward was talking about. She was up close behind an Oldsmobile, in the rear window of which a six-year-old kid was making faces, stretching her mouth, putting her fingers in her nostrils, making thumb-and-forefinger circles around her eyes. Elise made faces back at her, making noises with each face.

"What are you doing?" Edward said. "What if the guy looks in his mirror?"

Elise banged the steering wheel with the heel of her hand. "Why, he'll probably come back here and beat you up. He'll probably rape and mangle me. It'll be a horrible thing."

Edward rolled his eyes. "I'm sorry," he said. "We were doing OK there for a minute."

"That was before sociology," Elise said. She brushed at her hair, then stretched to look in the rearview mirror, picking at the top of her skull, trying to get the hairs there to stand up. Then she said, "We're still doing OK." She turned around to look at Edward. "Really, we are."

That was the last thing she said for a couple of minutes. The road opened up into a four-lane divided highway, two lanes each way, and Elise took the left of her two lanes so she could pass the slower cars, including the Oldsmobile with the face-making kid. She also passed an ice cream truck that had a lot of tinkling bells on it, and some guy in a Ryder Rent-A-Whole-New-World truck who was talking into a tape recorder. It wasn't long before Elise and Edward were isolated, sunk in a channel of high pines, rolling along twenty miles over the speed limit. Elise settled back in her seat, set the cruise control, opened up a pack of gum, and took out a stick.

Edward said, "Are you avoiding me? I mean, are we not talking?"

"No, we're talking," Elise said. "You go first. You want some gum?"

Edward waved off the gum. "Why don't you," Edward said. "Go first, I mean. I always go first, and half the time it turns out it's all me."

She glanced at him.

"That's not a criticism," he said. "I mean, it could be a criticism, but it's not. I didn't mean it that way. I just don't know what the fuck is going on. I don't know what I'm doing. I was out there last night thinking about my mother—I love my mother and everything, but . . ."

"I haven't talked to your mother in a long time," Elise said. "How is she? Is she OK?"

"She's fine," Edward said. "She's down there in Florida—she and my father are probably out fishing or something. He's probably telling her how to do it right now."

"I don't know why you don't relax about that stuff," Elise said. "I mean, that's their system. Some people have real liberal, squeaky-clean systems, and some people don't. That's theirs."

"I know. I should know that by now." Edward looked out the window on his side of the car. "I'm sorry, Dad," he said. "You're real strange, and I love you. But if I have to hear one more Triumph-of-the-dad story I think I'm going to scream."

"Can't do it, can you?" Elise said.

"What?" Edward said.

They were riding in the right lane and had to slow for a solid black RV that was touring in the road ahead of them. This was a real showpiece RV, complete with the perfectly tailored spare-tire cover over the spare tire on the rear deck. "The Seans" went diagonally across the tire cover. Elise swung out into the passing lane and pulled up alongside this RV, and Edward could tell at once that it wasn't an off-the-shelf item. There were, ranked behind the front wheel well, rows and rows of identical decals, each depicting a flaming chicken leg, arranged on the side of the van like kill stickers. This was a chauffeur-driven RV, and about halfway back there was a large observation window that extended well below the vehicle's belt line. In that window there sat a man in a business suit, a very elegant man, reading. He looked up as they passed, and Edward caught his eye, and the man smiled politely and nodded, and turned back to his book. Edward said, "That looks like a wonderful man. Did you see him?"

"Yeah," Elise said. "But what about the stuff on the side there— it looks as though he downed a lot of chickens."

"He's a great warrior in the battle against the pernicious elevation of the drumstick," Edward said.

Elise pulled back into the right lane and reset the cruise control. Although it was only midday, there wasn't any sun, so the empty highway ahead of them was bathed in shade. There were a lot of squeaks and rattles in the car, and the wind noise was considerable. They swept past a hitchhiker, a young woman sitting on her knapsack at the edge of the road with her hands over her face. Edward said, "So, what's this I can't do?"

"Leave your father alone," Elise said. "Whenever you say something nice about him, you say something bad about him at the same time."

"He taught me how to do that," Edward said.

"Your job was to forget it," she said. "Anyway—it doesn't matter. I don't want to talk about it. It's better what you do than what some people do. Some people treat them like children— fathers I mean. I met this one guy at work, he went in and took Polaroid snapshots of his father when his father was dead, because he wanted to be sure, he wanted proof that his father was dead. That's the way he wanted to remember him."

"This a new boyfriend, or what?" Edward said. They were doing seventy-five in the right lane; suddenly the guy in the Ryder truck, the guy who was talking into the tape recorder, steamed by them. "What's with him? What's he doing there, a love letter?"

Elise watched the yellow truck slide back into the right lane in front of her. "I figure he's one of those guys who's in the middle of a big argument, and he's carrying on the argument there with that machine, and when he gets where he's going, he's going to send the tape back to the person he's having the argument with. Either that or it's songs."

"He's probably lying," Edward said. "He's doing a whole tape of lies, one after another, strung together, each lie elaborating the previous lie in some splendid way. I don't know why I said that. Oh . . . I do know why I said that. It's because I've been lying recently."

Without looking, Elise said, "You never lie."

"No," Edward said. "I've been lying recently, and I don't know why. Three or four times in the last week I told people lies for no reason at all. Somebody called me up and asked me if I had this magazine, and I had it sitting right there in front of me, and I told them I didn't have it. It wasn't that I didn't want them to have the magazine—that's the funny part. I just wanted to lie."

Elise turned and gave him her outer-space look.

"I know," he said. "You see what I'm talking about? It's not as if I have to lie for any reason, it's not as if I'm protecting myself from something terrible that might happen to me. Or maybe I am— maybe things are slipping away, and I'm pretending to be on top of them the way I used to be."

"So, what lies have you told me?" Elise said. "Since Friday?"

"I don't know," Edward said. "I don't remember what I told you. Did I tell you anything that sounded like a lie?"

"Don't ask me," Elise said. "It's hard for me to imagine you lying. You were always the guy who caught lies before they were even out of people's mouths. You were the guy who hunted down the uncommitted lie. It used to happen to me all the time. I'd be about to lie to you about something, and you'd catch me before I even got it out. I used to think it was uncanny the way you did that."

Edward nodded his response, groping around trying to find the lever that would allow the seat back to recline. He found it and dropped the seat about two notches, giving himself more room in the cramped passenger side of the front seat of the BMW. He watched the trees glide past out the window and then focused on the ones in the distance, then gradually turned his head, tracking them closer and closer until he was watching them out the side window again. He liked doing that because it was visually disconcerting; he wondered if it would make him sick if he did it enough. He felt kind of sick already—drained, rolled over, kneaded, weak. He thought he might have the flu. Or maybe he had lost his taste for the Elise problem, maybe, for the moment at least, he didn't care. He said, "I guess this has been a lousy weekend, huh?"

"Well . . ." Elise thought a minute, not looking at Edward, but at the road, tilting her head this way and that as if mentally rehearsing the events of the weekend. "It wasn't all that bad," she finally said.

"I liked our walk. I liked talking to you. I liked that thing last night, or was it Friday night, with the guy in the street. I liked being in your house."

"I liked it when you came and got me with the car," Edward said. "I guess I liked that. I'm not having such a great time, really. I think I'm having a stress experience. My weekends are usually a lot simpler than this one. I go to the movies or something, I go to the mall, I watch TV, I buy a magazine, sometimes I clean—I guess I don't clean as much as I used to. I think I clean a lot, but I really don't clean as much as I used to. I like it better when I clean more. But a lot of times, now, I'll look at the rug and think, *I could vacuum this rug,* but then I think I'll have to go and get the vacuum out of the closet, and I'll wonder if I wrapped the cord up the way you're supposed to, because if I did, it's real annoying to unwrap it, and then you've got the bag problem, you don't remember when you last changed the bag, so there's a risk that if you go in to get the vacuum cleaner you'll have to change the bag, which makes vacuuming the rug much harder, because you don't want to change the bag, but then you think that you probably *ought* to change the bag anyway, because the vacuum cleaner works a lot better when the bag is new, and then you think of all the different plugs you have to plug the vacuum cleaner into in order to vacuum the whole house, and you think that if you're going to vacuum this particular rug, you probably ought to vacuum the whole house at the same time or else this particular rug will be cleaner than the rugs in the rest of the house, and if that happens then things will get out of balance, rugwise, and everything will go piecemeal—you'll have one ashtray that's full of cigarette butts and two other ashtrays clean, you'll have one real good bathroom and one bathroom that's about like a gas station, and some room will be better than some other room, so pretty soon you'll let that other room go entirely and just use it as a junk room, and pretty soon after that you'll want to close it off from the rest of the house, and then after that you have the probability of some other room becoming more messed up than the rest of the rooms, and then you'll want to close that room off, and you can see where that leads, can't you? Sometimes I think I'm just like those people who buy a brand-new couch and then cover it with that plastic junk, I mean, I'm afraid to do anything in the house, because if I do anything then I'll have to clean it up, and I'll get all obsessive about cleaning it up, and then I'll have to clean up the whole house. I mean, I've got a problem in this area, don't I?"

"Major," Elise said.

"I'm serious," Edward said. "Everything's connected to everything else. If you do one thing then you have to do *every* thing. When you left, about the time you left, I used to try to cook for myself. So I'd decide I wanted to have a steak, and I'd go to the store to get this steak, and I'd think I had to have a baked potato, so I'd go over to the produce section to get a potato, and then while I was over there I'd see all the vegetables, so I'd decide I had to have a vegetable, and then there was bread and salad and dessert and something to drink and pretty soon I've got eighty dollars' worth of dinner, not to mention four and a half hours to cook it, and when it's cooked, it's not very good, and, of course, I have to eat at the table with a full place setting, which means the laundry, and if I used the white napkin that means that everything white in the house has to be washed, including the sheets and the towels, which means I have to go back to the store and get some unscented Clorox, and then when I get in the car to go to the store I notice that the car is low on gas, so I have to take the car to the gas station before I go get the Clorox, and while I'm at the gas station I notice that the car is real dirty, so I have to get it washed, and, you know— it never stops. You do one thing and you're sunk. That's why it always scared me to death when you'd go out to work on the flower bed."

"I don't know why you worried," she said. "I was doing the digging."

"Yeah," he said. "Every time you wanted to plant a fig tree you were out of commission for a week. You'd come back from the nursery with diagrams." He rattled an imaginary piece of paper at her, then did a magician's hand flick as if the paper vanished. "This is not a criticism. I understand why you came back with the diagrams. But whatever happened to jam it into the ground, and if it lives, fine?"

"Whatever happened to you like-a me like I like-a you?" Elise said. "One of the things I've noticed about you since I left is that a lot of things you say about me are not criticisms."

"Sorry," Edward said.

"Don't worry about it," she said, giving him a sympathetic smile. She touched his shoulder, then put her hand behind his neck, inside his collar. "It's how I know you love me."

"I do, don't I?" Edward said.

"I think so," she said. "When I'm down there alone or something, I always think that you love me. I think about where you are and what you're doing, and I think you're not doing anything to hurt me, and—it's more than that, it's as if one of the questions you ask yourself before you do anything is, 'Will this hurt Elise?' I like that."

"It makes for a lot of guilt," Edward said. "In the gray areas."

"I know," she said. "But it's real nice, because you're not one of those people who says, 'This won't hurt Elise if she doesn't know about it.' I hate people like that. I mean, they're not willing to do anything for you. I don't think I understood about that until I lived with you." She squeezed his neck, sliding her thumb back on one side and two fingers on the other until she had a pinch of flesh that she gently released. "See there? I learned something from you."

Edward said, "I hate the past tense. I hate the way it sounds. It feels as if everybody's gone, and I'm in this city, one of those desolate cities that's been evacuated, the kind you see in all the atomic-attack movies. Except it's more like a fifties atomic-attack movie—it's black-and-white, it's got those buildings in it, it's got all those old cars parked on both sides of the street. Beige cars and gray cars. You can tell they're beige, even in black-and-white. Sedans. Newspaper racks with those steel tubes attached to them where you're supposed to drop your money."

"So I'm still learning," Elise said. "Like crazy."

Edward smiled at her, reached up and circled her wrist with his thumb and forefinger, and took her hand off his neck, drawing it over his shoulder. He didn't have the full weight of the arm, she was moving the arm, too, so it felt to him as if he were moving one of those cantilevered, perfectly balanced lamps, or a robot's arm. He held her hand alongside his face, touching her knuckles to his cheek, then turned a little and brushed his dry lips over her fingers, nibbling at them, pressing and releasing his lips on the first joints, then opening his mouth slightly so that the wetter, more interior part of his lips would stick to her skin; then, holding her hand in place, he drew his head back slightly, allowing his lips to open a little so that the delicate connection between them was stretched, the skin of his lips and of her finger drawn to each other until the pressure of his small movement tore the two skins apart. He made a sound then. A muffled popping sound, the kind of sound that's made by a distant marimba lightly struck. As they rushed along through the high, thin pines, he did each finger in turn, and with each new contact he put off as long as possible the coming apart.

He was looking out over her hand, slightly to his right, at the road ahead of them, focused at some indeterminate distance, someplace out there in front of them where there wasn't anything to focus on, where there was nothing but clear, quiet air. He was thinking of Elise, the particular taste of her skin, of her fragrance—not a perfume or cologne, or even a soap, since she could not use scented soaps, or wear perfumes. He liked it that it was her hand he was kissing, her skin, he liked it that she had about her this particular kind of unaccented freshness, although to him it was no less an artifice than it would have been if she had dabbed herself with Chanel. It wasn't the smell itself that enthralled him, but its association with her, that she had decided years before to stick with herself, more or less, as she had come out of the box. And it wasn't the choice that particularly interested him, but that it was her choice.

He had, over the term of their marriage, come to know her by the result of that choice, by her fragrance, by the way she smelled, and so acutely did he identify her particular scent that he could always tell by holding her, by hugging her, if anyone had touched her. If she had shaken hands with a woman where she worked, Edward knew it instantly when she came home, even though she may have washed her hands several times in the interim; if she had hugged someone, Edward smelled it immediately when he hugged her. In fact, one of her early affairs had been discovered in just this way. She had come in from work in an ordinary mood, on an ordinary evening, and set about the preparations for dinner, and Edward had come in from work himself, and hugged her, recognized the change in her scent, and asked her if she was having an affair. She had denied it, of course. She denied it for weeks. Finally, when she was ready, she acknowledged the affair, acknowledged that he had discovered it on the day of its first realization weeks before.

In his affairs, one of the hundred small, awkward messes he found telling was the absence of Elise's scent—on a towel at a lover's apartment, on a lover's pillow, in an embrace, on the back of a lover's neck. He didn't find the other smells unpleasant. On the contrary, he found them engaging, variously touching, intriguing, but in each case the scent was not Elise's, something he couldn't stop himself from noticing.

He had been holding the wrist and kissing the fingers for several miles when Elise said, "Thanks. That's nice." She retook control of her arm, turned her hand over, and rubbed his lips with her forefinger, rubbing from one side to the other, slowly, as if making a shallow, moon-shaped mark absentmindedly in dust while carrying on a conversation about something else entirely.

Edward felt his lips balloon and flatten as the pad of her first finger moved back and forth, and, at the same time, felt the movement of the car, felt that he and Elise were moving in concert, and that movement was in contradiction to the movement across his lips. In order to touch him that way, she had turned her hand so that her other fingers grazed his nose, intruded on his cone of vision, and in a minute he opened his mouth, allowing her finger to fall to his teeth, then in between them, and then he held her fingertip with his teeth.

"Ow," she said, pulling the finger away from him.

"That couldn't have hurt," he said. "That was a nip. That was a love nip."

"Well," she said. "Don't."

Edward rolled his head around the headrest and said, "All right." He patted her shoulder. "I'm glad you don't have any shoulder pads on. I don't like shoulder pads. I especially don't like them when people carry their purses on their shoulders, and they have shoulder pads, so that the pad pinches up like some real bad hicky, some distort-o-thing. I feel embarrassed when I see that."

"It doesn't count," she said. "You don't count. I mean, if some-body lets you see that, then you can rest assured that they don't care what you think about anything. So there's no reason for you to be embarrassed. You can be disgusted. Not embarrassed."

Edward raised an eyebrow at her. "I've seen it on you," he said.

She grimaced, holding her drawn mouth and swinging her eyes back and forth like a parody of somebody looking for an escape route. "Well, you didn't let me get the whole story out."

"It's OK," Edward said. "I can take it."

He watched Elise drive. She looked relaxed and comfortable, in control, and he had this idea that she never looked more comfort-able than when she was driving on the highway. She didn't smile, but she didn't frown either. Her face was placid, quiet, uninflected. He couldn't tell if she was thinking or if she was just drifting as she drove. He turned around in time to see a dead dog on the side of the road, its feet jutting up as if the dog were stuffed. It was some kind of spotted dog, a mutt with large black and white spots, so that it looked like a tiny cow. The dog was in perfect shape, it wasn't one of those that had been crushed. It must have been hit, and then it must have bounced, landing on its back with its feet up in the air. And it froze that way. The image of the dog lingered with Edward for a while after they passed it.

He started thinking about Roscoe, about what Roscoe was doing with Elise, about what Roscoe was doing living with her but not sleeping with her. He disliked the thought of their intimacy, but he wasn't much disturbed by the idea of their living together, having breakfast together, doing their wash. He calculated that Roscoe and Elise did everything but sleep together, that for all practical purposes they lived as man and wife, which made them like the couple Lurleen had talked about, and something like him and Elise for the last couple of years before she moved away. But he figured that he was still Elise's husband, that she felt that way, and he thought it must be hard for Roscoe to accept that. Roscoe hadn't shown any scars that suggested such difficulty, but Edward assumed they must be there.

He was thinking about times when he was very young, when he and some other boy in high school were infatuated with the same girl. The issue was always: Who is going to choose? Roscoe didn't have any inclination to force that issue, and Elise didn't seem to be troubled, which left him. He wasn't going to demand that Elise leave Roscoe and come live with him. Sometimes he wanted her to do that, but he didn't want to ask. There was something wrong with asking.

Remembering what she had told him about Roscoe's wife, about the car crash, Edward wondered what Roscoe did about other women—whether he had them or not, whether he had affairs, whether he ever disappeared for a night or two. Then he thought it was very odd that that question had never come up before, odd that he didn't know the answer to it. He swiveled his head and looked at Elise, and she was staring straight out the windshield, so he didn't bother her. For a minute he wanted to ask, then thought it didn't matter what Roscoe did, that it could be one of only a handful of things—one-night stands or maybe a regular, occasional girl, or men, or prostitutes, or some combination of those, or nothing—what if it were nothing? In any event, if Roscoe made no demands on Elise, and if their intimacies were not so much shadows of sexual and romantic longing, but were of another kind that Edward associated with long-married men and women, if they were intimacies built around comfort and ease, around a sense that each knew the other as completely as the other could be known, around the idea that the world is not a swell place, and if you find somebody you can get along with all the time, it's probably in your best interest to stay with that person, to keep that person with you, then, as awkward as it might be, he couldn't immediately think of any reason for the three of them not to try to carry on more or less in the manner that Elise had suggested—a marriage of three. He couldn't think of any *reason*.

What if he didn't like seeing Roscoe touch Elise? What if he didn't want to see them hug or kiss or hold hands? They had done those things on Saturday at his house, as chaste a set of touches as he had ever seen, but touches nonetheless. What if he didn't want to see them touch? What if he didn't want them to be that fond of each other? What if he wanted to be the person with whom Elise felt intensely at home?

This resistance to the three of them together was not particularly gripping, he wasn't aching, the sight of Roscoe did not turn his stomach, he did not wail to God in the middle of the night about the unfair way he had been treated, but neither was he deeply engaged in the situation. He wasn't seeing them every day. He wasn't having dinner with them, bumping into Roscoe in the hall of his house, he did not have to dress and undress in front of Roscoe, he did not have to say to Roscoe, because he was there, and Elise was there, things that he had said only to Elise. And if they did something like this, how could he pick up and go to the movies on Saturday afternoon with Elise, how could he sit on the couch and hold her, how could he sit in bed and talk to her—she had herself swept him away to her apartment the night before; wasn't that an admission of the impossibility of the arrangement? And how would it be to be at home with Roscoe and Elise on a rainy afternoon when Elise was more interested in Roscoe than she was in him? He and Roscoe trying to top each other, trying to out-joke each other, trying to out-sympathize each other, trying to beat each other at the game of Lover.

Edward reached down and pushed his shoes off his feet, first the left then the right, then he looked up and said to Elise, "You OK?"

She gave him a small nod and a glance, fatigue showing up around the edges of her eyes. "Fine," she said. "It's not much farther."

Edward put his feet on the dashboard, catching its curve in the bottom of his arch, wiggling his toes to freshen them. What remained with him was that Roscoe seemed to have agreed to the proposition already. Roscoe was as bright as anybody else, so presumably he had already thought about all the things that Edward was just beginning to think about. But Roscoe had a slightly different situation: he had lost a wife. It was as if his person were gone, and he had made the decision that nothing was left to do but to attach himself to some other person. There was strength in that choice, a kind of evenness, a view of the world that wasn't too far from his own. Still, it was a crazy idea. What if they wanted to make love, Roscoe and Elise? He and Elise would not make love, and Roscoe and Elise would. Even if it were not so much making love as having sex, how would he feel? Bad. The only possibility was for them to abstain. But that wouldn't work, because Edward would know that they wanted to make love, and in Edward's world, wanting was the same as doing. The damage to a relationship was first seen in the mind of the doer, the relationship was compromised the instant the doer moved the prospect of the infidelity out of the mental category fantasy and into the mental category possibility. He figured everybody had that line, knew where it was, knew when it was crossed. Thinking about this reminded him of a woman he had known once who had told him she had not slept with somebody, had sworn up and down she hadn't slept with this guy, only to tell him sometime later that what she had not done was *fuck* the guy—what she had done was every other sex act known to man. Edward had been in the vulnerable position of wanting very badly to believe that she hadn't slept with him, hadn't had sex with him, but hadn't been able to believe it when she told him that she hadn't. Finding out that she had was unpleasant, if not surprising, but the discovery of the legalistic bit of word play she used to maintain her innocence so enraged him that he went to the store and bought a box of four-inch-long nails and a hand ax with a flat butt, and returned to her house and hammered all of the nails in the box into her dining room table, one after the other, stopping occasionally to proclaim "I'm not *hammering* anything into your dining table," and to brandish the ax at her, showing her that it was an ax, not a hammer.

18

A GIANT eighteen-wheel truck roared by, and Edward leaned to the side to check the speedometer. They were doing seventy-five, which meant that the truck was probably doing ninety. As he leaned toward Elise, she stiffened a little, glanced at him out of the corner of her eye without turning her head, as if she felt herself being threatened.

He said, "I was thinking about stuff. That's not why I'm leaning over, I'm leaning over to check the speedometer, so I can guess how fast that truck is going. But before that, I was thinking about stuff."

She went into her purse, which was standing on the emergency brake lever between the seats, and said, "What stuff?"

"You and Roscoe," Edward said. "And me. The three of us. I don't see it."

"Look again," Elise said. She was peeling another piece of gum that she had gotten out of her purse. "That's not what I mean." She put the gum in her mouth, biting off half-inch sections, one after the other, until all the gum was in. "I mean, it *is* what I mean, but I don't mean it to sound that way. I want to be nice about it—no, that's not it either. I want to be loving without giving up reason."

"You want to be persuasive," Edward said. She flashed him a we-could-do-without-that look.

"Sure," she said. "That, too. But what I want you to understand is that I'm not exactly free to do anything else. I mean, to do anything without Roscoe—and I don't want to mislead you, so I have to say that even though this sounds as if I might prefer to do something without Roscoe, that's not exactly the way it is. I mean, sometimes it is, but what I'd really rather do is have him be part of our team."

"Oh, I see," Edward said. "It's a team concept. That's great, I always wanted to be on a team."

She sighed. "I know—it sounds so stupid. I wish I could tell you how it feels, make you feel it. I think if you felt it you could understand. It's like, Roscoe's part of me. He takes care of me, I take care of him—we look out for each other."

"We can't both take care of you," Edward said. "If we both take care of you, then you've got one more person taking care of you than you really need. We'd be running into each other all the time. He'd decide to surprise you with dinner the same night I decided to surprise you with dinner. We'd make reservations at two different restaurants, same night, same time."

"You could do that," Elise said. "Or you could talk to each other and kind of go in together on the deal."

"I don't want to go in together," Edward said.

She said, "This isn't an ultimatum. But the situation is what it is. I can't make it something else. Maybe after a while it'll be something else, but I don't even know that. I know how weird this is. I mean, what do you think I do down there all the time? I mean, do you think I just watch TV and exercise? I spend all my time thinking about, you know, this idea about the three of us, and I think, 'what a dumb idea.' But I don't have any other ideas. I've been away from you and I don't like it. That's why I came up, I wanted to see you, I wanted to talk with you, I wanted to spend some time with you."

"What, a weekend?"

"It's something," Elise said. "I mean, I don't want to jump on you, but I feel like being with you a little bit. I want to feel you caring about me, and I want to care about you, or try—this stuff is so impossible to talk about. I feel this real deep link to you. And sometimes I want to swim around this huge link and polish it up. And then, at other times, I just want to be alone. Make my own way. And part of being alone and making my own way is my relationship with Roscoe. I have this link to him, too. Maybe it's not the same link, and maybe it's not as big or as deep, or something, but it's no less real, and since it's not really hurting my link to you, I can't let it go."

"What if it is hurting your link to me?" Edward said.

"That's the point I'm trying to make," Elise said. "It's not. That's the thing I've learned. There was a time when Roscoe and I were hot and heavy, and I thought it might, but I figured out that it doesn't."

"You can figure all you want," Edward said. "But it doesn't apply to me."

"It would if you understood," she said. "That's the whole point. I want you to understand."

She was crying a little, a tear forming at the outside corner of her eye. Edward said, "Don't do that, please. Come on, Elise. I'm trying. You give me this thing that seems ridiculous, and you tell me you know it's ridiculous, and then you tell me you want to do it anyway, and that you want me to want to do it, and then you start crying when I tell you it seems ridiculous."

"I know," she said, wiping her eye with the back of her hand. "I feel dead and trapped, I let myself get into this situation, and I can't get out without cutting my life in half. Maybe I should have just called you or something. Maybe we don't have to do anything about it."

"I'm not itching to do anything about it," Edward said.

"I am," Elise said. "I have this idea that we could all be sort of OK together. I mean, we're friends, Roscoe and I are friends—why shouldn't we all be together?"

"Because I'm not in love with Roscoe," Edward said. "If I were in love with Roscoe, it would be easy."

"What if you liked him?" she said.

"I can't like him, Elise," Edward said. "How can I like him? You're in the way. Besides, I don't like men. They smell funny, too much body hair. They think wrong. They're too big."

"And you're competing with them, right?" Elise said.

Edward sighed and readjusted himself in the seat. "I guess so. I don't know, let's just forget about it. Let's think about it. I mean, do you actually want to do something about this, or do you want to just keep on doing what we're doing and say that this is what it is?"

"I don't want to rush into anything," Elise said. "But I would like to see you more often."

"You can see me," Edward said. "I'm a tired old guy. I'm up here in the house all the time. But this isn't what you were saying last night—you were long on self-discovery, short on mates and mating."

"Is this a walk-and-chew-gum problem? I mean, Roscoe's not going to hurt you. He's not taking over for you. He's not doing anything much except coming along for the ride. You act like we're about fourteen, and it's a big deal that he's seen me with my pants off. I keep thinking that you don't understand the thing, because if you understood it, you wouldn't be upset. You couldn't. But then I explain it, and you seem to understand it, and you're upset anyway."

"Great," Edward said. "You're a real sweetie pie. Why don't you get a carload of boyfriends? A tactical unit that can surround you at all times, circle you, tell you how wonderful you are, be real friendly all the time, rub you down, pay you money—thirty or forty guys, maybe. You can give them little smiles, pat their little heads. That'll be great. I'll be wanting to join that unit right away."

"You can make anything into a farce," Elise said. "It's harder not to."

"Yeah, I know," Edward said. "And that's the hardness proof. Discredited nineteen fifty-one, Leipzig." He rolled down his window and left it open a minute to change the air in the car, then he rolled up the window and turned to Elise. "So," he said. "Do you want to start again?"

She shook her head. "No," she said. "I think we can stop there, try again later."

There was high-angle sunlight in the car, coming in through the tops of the windows on Edward's side, exciting the dust, drawing a sharp shadow line up the thigh of his faded jeans. He wasn't ready to end the conversation, but if Elise wasn't going to play—he wondered if she said the same thing about him to Roscoe that she had said about Roscoe to him. *Just along for the ride*—Edward didn't know whether that was strategic understatement or tact, or her idea of the new world definition of love. He wondered if she said it about him, too. Or maybe she was just self-conscious. Or lying. "Along for the ride" was a curious thing to say about somebody you intend to spend the rest of your life with. Still, looked at another way, it was admirably plain, matter-of-fact, sort of the pioneer view of things—rugged, unadorned. He liked that in her, the willingness to cut the crap, but it was risky, because in simplifying her description of her connection with Roscoe she increased the probability that it would be misunderstood. He was certain that she did not mean that her feeling for Roscoe was flimsy or temporary or casual— although casual was what was suggested by her remark; no, what she meant was that she liked Roscoe well enough to want to stick with him, which is to say about as much as you can like anybody, but at the same time she wanted to say that liking Roscoe that much didn't reduce or diminish how she felt about him. But there was something else in what she said and the way she said it, something about her view of things, the world—it was detachment, she was detached, as if she weren't in the world at all, but sort of *right next to it.* Or maybe she suddenly got old in her head, and she was self-contained, and the normal ways of doing things didn't seem to make any sense anymore, because they were all based on assumptions she didn't share. Or maybe she was just crazy.

Edward said, "So what's wrong with plain old marriage, one man, one woman? Two kids, bungalow, fence."

"It kills people. Dries them up. They get tight and small. They end up doing all this stuff, making up all these rules, and they're not rules that you make up because you want to, they're rules you make up to protect your perimeter. So the idea is that you destroy the perimeter yourself, in advance, by having a third person involved. Then every time you start getting real uptight, you've got two people telling you to get with the program. If it's only one person, it's so private that you can control it, but if it's two people, you have to listen."

"You have data on this?" Edward said.

"It's just an idea," she said. "It sort of makes sense, doesn't it?"

19

KINTA WAS the first one out of the house when Edward and Elise pulled into the driveway. She came out slow and with bare legs, and stood alongside the left front fender, waiting for the travelers to get situated and get out. She gave Edward a thick-lipped smile through the windshield, and he waved with his left hand while opening the door with his right.

"Somebody loves you," Elise said in a singsong half-whisper.

Edward was just stepping out of the car when she said it, and he stopped, poised between the car and the driveway, turned his head and looked back in at Elise.

She gave him a pert smile. "Honesty is the best policy," she said.

He nodded, got out of the car, going around the front to say hello to Kinta. They hugged and kissed, and although he pictured the kiss as being very proper, as seen from a third person's point of view, Elise's point of view, he knew from the feel of it, from the softness of Kinta's lips, from the little dart she did with her tongue—just enough to graze his lips with the tip of it—that she meant business. He wondered if this meant she had some larger scheme in mind, something slightly longer-range than she let on.

She pulled away from him quickly, seeming awkward, and took a step toward Elise's door, which was now open. Elise was coming out.

Edward watched the two women embrace—they did a full-scale, forty-second hug—watched their faces while they had their arms around each other, looking for a clue in each case as to how they felt about each other, about being there in Edward's front yard, hugging, about Edward, about everything. He was interested to see that Elise's face showed no signs of the warning she'd issued in the car moments before. She looked like she was genuinely pleased to see Kinta, pleased to hug and be hugged. On her side, Kinta looked slightly desperate, squeezing her eyes shut, putting more muscle into the embrace than it asked for, pressing her head hard against Elise's shoulder, against the curve of Elise's neck. It was as if this hug was big stuff for Kinta—she had some things to say with it, and she wanted to get them right. Elise, who had been a little surprised at the fierceness of Kinta's attack, instantly regained her poise and returned the hug in kind, the only signal of her mixed feelings in the hard line of her jaw over Kinta's shoulder.

It was when Elise went back into the car for her purse and Kinta leaned over the top of the open door that Edward first realized two things: one, she had on one of his shirts; and two, under it, all she had on was panties, pale green, opaque, and shiny. Both parts of this realization made him more nervous than he wanted to be, and he wondered if that was Kinta's intention, her idea of strategy. It was as if the one social error, wearing his shirt, were not enough, so she had decided not to wear pants to heighten the effect. Edward was flattered, of course. Had he not been with Elise, the sight of the pale, pretty skin of her thighs might have excited more than embarrassed him. But at that moment he wished to God that he'd never even met Kinta—his embarrassment was for himself, not for her, and it was, he reckoned, a reflection of how he felt about Elise—that he was afraid of her, that he was afraid of what she thought, that he was afraid that if she thought he and Kinta were a hot item or were about to be a hot item, she might give up on him, lose her interest entirely, and satisfy herself with her friend Roscoe. As quickly as he thought about the fear, he felt foolish and wished he could just let people do what they wanted to do without feeling responsible for half of them, and indebted to the other half. It zipped through his mind that he should not be afraid of Elise, that he should be able to take the pleasures of Kinta—Elise had walked out on him, number one, and number two, to Kinta, her state of relative undress wasn't anything special.

Elise was back in the car, sitting in the seat fishing through her purse, and Kinta was pressing herself against the outside of the BMW's door. Edward thought he ought to go up and pat Kinta on the rump, that doing that would be an appropriate therapeutic intervention for himself, but even as he imagined himself moving forward, his right hand cupped and ready, he knew that he wouldn't do it, and he tried to decide if that meant he was governed by his fear of Elise or some version of propriety, or only that he had the common sense not to make a difficult situation any worse than it already was. He also wondered, since he had encountered situations before in which he had attributed ideas and opinions to Elise that she had later denied, whether in fact her reaction to Kinta's performance was the same reaction he imagined her having. Maybe she just shrugged it off, maybe she didn't read anything into Kinta's appearing in her underwear other than "That's Kinta."

His view of Elise was that she was immensely strong, spiritually powerful, and that she could endure any adversity. So in their relationship he had always viewed her as the tough guy, while he had seen himself as the weaker sex, and, as might have been expected, over the term of their relationship he had done most of the swashbuckling, public and private, while she had contented herself with the role of shrinking violet.

He was thinking about that and looking at the gap between Kinta's legs at the point where his shirttail stopped, when Roscoe stepped out of the front door, which was slightly behind Edward and some distance to his right, and said, "Telephone."

Edward pointed at his chest and said, "Me?"

"No," Roscoe said. "Elise. It's the Midnight Cowgirl."

"Tell her I'll be right there," Elise said, getting out of the car.

Edward trailed her back into the house, with Kinta at his side, and when Elise went into the kitchen to get the call, with Roscoe standing by, Kinta caught Edward's shirt and pulled him to one side in the living room, behind a wing-wall that separated that room from the dining room, and out of sight of the kitchen. She put her arms around his neck and pulled his face to hers, paying off the promise of their little peck by the car. He was too nervous about Elise or Roscoe coming back into the room to enjoy Kinta's kiss or the pliant way she arched her body to his or the pressure she put on him at the inside of his upper thigh. He was as busy unwrapping her arms as she was wrapping them around him, around his neck, around his waist, around his thighs, smoothing his butt with her hands. When he took her hand off his ass, she switched his grip and put his hand at the top of her thigh, just at the point where the panties met the skin.

He was having a hard time. Kinta's rough play was typical and engaging—the sudden intimacy, the eagerness were hard to resist. He let himself drift into the embrace a little, then he popped out, listening for Elise's voice, listening for odd sounds in the house that might suggest Roscoe on the move. Hearing none, he went back to Kinta. He was like somebody on the border of sleep, headed for morning. He repeated this a couple of times, picking up bits of Elise's conversation with Lurleen—it was full of dull, short sentences: Elise fending off an interrogation. He felt guilty.

Kinta got the lobe of his ear in her mouth and licked it, running her tongue around its edge, then nipping it with her teeth, then coming up on her toes and pushing the tip of her tongue into his ear. "You like me, don't you?" she whispered. "I know what you like." Still at his ear, she reached down and slid his hand, which had remained where she put it on her thigh, between her thighs, holding his fingers against the damp fabric between her legs. "Kinta wants to fuck," she said. "Kinta wants to make you a big man."

That was too much. Edward yanked himself out of her grip, using real force, enough so that she tripped and had to grab for the wall. He stepped around her, out into the double door between the living and dining rooms, and looked into the kitchen, where Elise and Roscoe were standing face to face, a few feet apart, while Elise talked on the telephone.

Kinta was giggling, leaning against the wall in front of him now, her arms folded over her chest, laughing in short, soft spurts. Edward caught the rippling in her shirt, then, self-conscious because she was looking at him look at her, he looked her in the eye and made a clownish face. "I'm sorry," he said. "I mean, it's just, you know, right now, and everything."

"You're so scared," she said. Then, as if to push her point, she opened her mouth and rubbed the tip of her tongue with her second finger, resetting herself up against the wall so her back was flush and her legs open and straight; she bunched the shirt at her stomach with her left hand, at the same time tightening the panties, now completely visible and creased, and in one movement she sucked her finger, withdrew it from her mouth, ran it down between her legs, twice, back and forth over her tightly bound labia. Then, without another word, she pushed herself off the wall, gave Edward a very polite kiss on the cheek, and disappeared into the hall that led to the bedrooms.

Edward stood there without moving, staring at the spot that Kinta had just vacated. He exhaled and shuddered, rolling his shoulders to take the small satisfaction of relaxing. He was tired. He wanted to go to bed. He wanted everybody to be gone.

After a minute he stooped down to pick up a magazine that was on the floor, then he put the magazine back in the stack of magazines in the bookcase against the far wall, and then he picked up a pair of Kinta's shoes, hooking his first and second fingers into the backs, and picked up two glasses off the coffee table in front of the couch, and got a folded newspaper off the couch with another finger from that hand, and kicked the corner of the rug so it would lie flat, and walked into the kitchen to put the glasses in the sink.

Elise was still on the phone. "I don't know, Lurleen," she said. "Yes, it was. Yes, it is." She caught Edward's eye and gave him raised eyebrows, then shook her head. "Tonight, I guess. Yes. No. Roscoe looks like he hasn't slept for a week. Edward's cleaning up. Everything's one hundred percent normal."

Edward put the glasses in the right-hand sink, then opened the cabinet under the sink and dropped the newspaper into the garbage bag, and then, as he was walking past Elise out of the kitchen, he reached up with his free hand, his left, and traced his forefinger across her lips.

She gave him a silent kiss.

He stopped in the dining room to look at the mail that was on the table where he had left it Friday when he came in from work. He went through the envelopes one-handed, then restacked them and headed for the bedroom with Kinta's shoes. He stopped in the living room and stooped down to straighten the rug that he had tried to straighten with his foot on the way to the kitchen. He picked up a couple of bread-colored crumbs off the floor there, dropped them into an ashtray, and was almost to the hall door when Kinta came out, dressed this time.

"Is this better?" she said. "Do I look like a matron? Do I look like a wronged woman? What did you guys do down there?" She took the shoes out of his hand and crossed to the couch and sat down there, dropping the shoes to the floor. She patted the couch. "Come sit down and tell me all about it. Is Elise ever getting off the telephone? Is it that other woman, the fat woman?"

"Too many questions," Edward said.

She shrugged. "Sorry," she said. "How about something simple. How are you? You look good. You look a little beat-up, but you look good." She waved toward the corner where she had gone after Edward. "I'm sorry about all that stuff. I was just playing around."

Edward was relieved, because it seemed as if Kinta had switched back to her regular-person mode. He opened one of the magazines and tore out one of the tear-out subscription cards, then went back to the ashtray in which he had dropped the crumbs and picked out the piece of purple gum he had seen in there when he'd deposited the crumbs. He put the gum on the card and then folded the card four times, and then said, "I'm OK. I'm not great, but I've still got my legs."

"What?" Kinta said.

"Nothing," Edward said. "I was just thinking about this guy I know. This football player. People all over the country are thinking about him. He lost his legs in a fire in Arizona. This was last year sometime. People at the office talk about him, everybody asks about him—it's an awful thing. And I was just thinking that it hadn't happened to me, thank God."

"What I think about whenever anybody I know has something bad happen to them, is that the odds against me are getting worse," Kinta said. "This girl I know had both her breasts removed last month. I hadn't seen her in two years, and she sent me a card to tell me she had both her breasts removed. That was all she had to say. There wasn't anything else in the card. It was hard even to imagine writing a card like that."

Edward nodded and held up the folded subscription card with the gum inside. "Let me put this away," he said.

Elise had just hung up the phone. She and Roscoe were talking, moving toward the part of the kitchen that couldn't be seen from the living room. Edward did some heavy coughing going in. "Lurleen OK?"

"She's fine," Elise said. "She wanted to know everything that happened on the drive up here."

Roscoe was standing in front of the sink and at first didn't understand what Edward wanted when Edward stood in front of him. Then he got it and stepped aside and reached down and opened the cabinet door.

"Thanks," Edward said. He turned to Elise. "Kinta got her clothes on."

"Are we in the way here?" Elise said. "I mean, we don't have to stay."

Edward dropped the gum into the garbage and nodded at Roscoe, then smiled at Elise. He regretted the smile, because he imagined it looked phony. It felt phony. "No, I want you to stay. Please stay," he said. That was sort of true, even though minutes before he had been wishing everyone was gone. He was usually comfortable with Elise, if nothing else, and right at that moment in the kitchen what he was looking for was comfort, ease of movement, a sense of being at home. Then he thought he was probably lying, that he didn't want Elise to stay, that he was right the first time when he had thought, out in the living room, that he wished everyone were gone.

He imagined himself alone in his house, in his blue bathrobe, sitting on the couch and flicking through the TV channels with the remote control. Maybe reading a computer magazine, like the one he'd been reading at Elise's apartment. His house looked a little shabby to him in comparison with hers. He didn't like the shabbiness of the place, it wasn't one of those clever things that argues that someone prefers the flaws of his or her life to the perfection of somebody else's. He was a little bit embarrassed by his house. He had already noticed the stains by the air-conditioning registers, the nicks in the walls, the stupid sheers he had been meaning to take off the front window—what bothered him most was the ordinariness of the house. Elise's blue walls were at least not ordinary.

Part of it, of course, was that he had been gone overnight, and Roscoe and Kinta had been in the house, and they had—unintentionally—slightly altered the order of things, so that now Edward saw the house not as this perfect pattern in which he usually lived, but as a fifties tract house with low ceilings, dirty walls, cramped rooms, badly painted moldings, stained carpeting, and a generally run-down look. His usual affection for the house was gone, replaced by this nasty, critical eye that recorded every paint chip or water stain as a testament to how poorly he was doing without Elise. Which led him to think about the thing he and Elise had talked about in the car—the competition between him and Roscoe—and to wonder if the real competition wasn't between him and Elise.

Edward sat down on the couch in the living room next to Kinta. She smiled at him. A polite smile that said, "I've got my shit in order, what about you?" He didn't like the smile. It wasn't because he thought she was trying to taunt him—he didn't think that. He didn't like it because of the kind of thing it was: polite. Why did he have to have someone in his house who thought that polite would get it? Why didn't she know that polite was not enough, that she had to do more, that she had to work harder than that? She was over thirty. She ought to know better. He said, "Lose the smile, will you?"

The nastiness of the remark caught him. He didn't want to be nasty to Kinta, and as soon as he was, he felt worse than he had before, when he had just *thought* the smile was unpleasant. At the same time, he experienced some relief, some little bit of comfort knowing he didn't have to sit there on the couch with Kinta *thinking* he didn't like her stupid smile. Also, having said something about it, he noticed that he didn't object to the smile so much anymore.

Her face had toned up immediately, the moment he spoke, going from comfortable to protected to hurt in the space of a quarter-second. But that left Edward sitting on the couch with a hurt woman. She was trying to cover it, but it was there, it was clear, she didn't know what to say. He had caught her off guard.

Kinta said, "I'm just feeling awkward. I feel a little out of place. It's been a while since we've seen each other, and I don't know what to expect."

"What to expect about what?" Edward said.

"Coming up here," she said.

"I told you on the phone that things were fucked," Edward said. "I don't know what you expected—what, you figured you could fix everything? You were going to do it all with your cunt?"

"My," she said. "We do know how to be mean, don't we?"

Edward shrugged. "OK," he said. "Sometimes I feel mean stuff. Sometimes I say it just to say it, just to get it out. Don't you ever do that?"

"No, I don't do that," Kinta said. She leaned over and straightened her shoes on the floor, then sat up and cocked a knee on the couch between them. "But it's OK," she said. "I've seen it before. It falls in there under the *He doesn't mean what he says* heading. It's either that one or it's the one about *It's my party and I'll cry if I want to*. When you're a woman, you learn this stuff. Men are always saying stuff they don't quite mean, so you learn to wait a couple of beats to see what they say next." She thought about that a minute, then said, "Sometimes you have to wait more than a couple. But, it's all right. We do it better than you do. You're better at ice hockey. In fact, ice hockey is something you guys do extremely well."

"In my defense," Edward said, "I want to assert that there are only so many brain cells, and they're up there working as fast as they can, they're running as fast as their little legs will carry them. I mean, the spirit is willing, you know what I mean? But I've got brain cells all over the lot trying to catch this stuff before it gets out of my mouth. And I've got these other brain cells, the bad brain cells, they're in there working under the cover of darkness, and they're sneaking this stuff out. So you've got the brain-cell wars going on. You've got the brain-cell wars happening."

"You don't have to apologize," Kinta said.

"I apologize," Edward said.

Elise started in from the kitchen, talking the minute she crossed the border between kitchen and dining room. "So, what are we going to do now? I mean, we're all here, except for Lurleen."

"She'll probably be here before dark," Roscoe said. He had followed Elise from the kitchen. They stood there, side by side, in the doorway between the living room and the dining room, looking for all the world like a couple.

"I was just being mean to Kinta," Edward said.

"It's true," Kinta said. "But he didn't mean it."

"What did he mean?" Elise said.

"He meant he was unhappy," Kinta said. "He meant that he was suffering a sudden conflation of these little black arrows of unhappiness. You know the ones? They use them on TV for commercials."

"Is that what those are?" Roscoe said.

"Yep," Kinta said.

Elise led Roscoe into the living room, and they took chairs facing the couch. "It feels like a morgue in here," Elise said. She looked at Edward. "Does it feel like we're all dead? And we're just sort of sitting here?"

"Dead ain't nothing like this," Kinta said.

"This is like a TV movie of dead," Elise said.

"I don't know why all of you people are talking about dead this way," Edward said. "I don't feel any deader than I did yesterday."

"It's slack," Elise said. "It feels slack around here. It's just, like, after the drive and everything."

"We should do something," Roscoe said. "We could go to the movies or something."

"That's a good idea," Kinta said.

"Vortex goes to the movies," Elise said. "I don't like it. We'll suck everybody else in the theater into this thing, and then we'll all be dead. Everywhere we go, people will have the life sucked out of them. We'll be known everywhere as the Osmotic Vortex. Trees will fall down when we come around. Birds will sit on their backs with their feet in the air. Butter will melt."

"Well," Roscoe said. "Let's go buy something. We could do that. Maybe a baked potato or something."

"That's a bad idea," Kinta said.

"You got any more ideas, Roscoe?" Edward said.

"I don't know. We could get some of those plastic bins. You know, the ones that come in different colors. The stacking kind."

"I like that," Kinta said. "We could buy a lot of them and build a huge house or something. We could build a storage wall."

"I feel like somebody's put this stuff all over me," Elise said. "It's clear and thick and gooey. You can see right through it. It's like only our heads are sticking out. We're sitting here in this room, and we're covered with this stuff, and only our heads are sticking out."

"I know what you're talking about," Roscoe said. "I can feel it in my shoulders."

"Is it going to rain today?" Kinta said.

Everybody looked at Kinta. "Yo," Edward said.

"I was just trying to vorticize a little," Kinta said. "I figured—*rain*, you know."

"I get it," Elise said. "She means maybe it will rain, and then there will be more of this tricordial membrane covering us. It'll be darker in here. We'll all feel even more dead than we do now."

"Edward doesn't feel dead at all," Roscoe said. "I'm not sure I really feel bad, myself. I mean, I was sort of angry that you guys went down there and everything, but I'm over it now. When you got back I felt better."

Edward looked at Kinta. She said, "I didn't touch him. He missed Elise, that's all." She turned around to Roscoe. "Will you tell Edward that I didn't touch you, please?"

"She was fine," Roscoe said. "We had fun. We watched a movie. We had popcorn. It was OK."

"See?" Kinta said.

"You're crazy," Edward said. "I don't know what you think I'm thinking, but I'm not thinking it."

"He'll think it later," Elise said.

"So, what did you guys do?" Kinta said to Elise. "Down there?"

"What did we do, Edward?" Elise said.

"Why are you asking me? You were there. We sat out in that place for a long time, and then we went in and went to sleep, and then we had breakfast, and then we came back here."

"No," Kinta said. "I mean—what did you decide?"

"What did we decide?" Edward said. He looked at Kinta and then at Elise.

Kinta said, "You don't want to talk about this with all four of us here, is that right? The relationship, and everything?"

"What's to talk about? Roscoe's got a new wife. I live alone, quietly. You've got nobody to screw."

"He's starting again," Kinta said.

"Give it a rest, will you, Edward?" Elise said.

"And let's leave my wife out of it, OK?" Roscoe said. "Elise is my friend, not my wife. I had a wife, but she was hit by a truck." He stopped with that and looked at the others, and then he squinted and suddenly adjusted the way he was sitting. "She was coming back from some little town and she had car trouble about ten miles out. She got out of the car. She was dressed up—some kind of thin dress and heels."

"Roscoe—" Elise said.

"So this truck was coming along at about seventy-five miles an hour, one of those big trucks, an eighteen-wheel truck. It was still light, but it was dusk, that heavy, thick kind of light that happens at dusk. It was like, about to rain. So everybody had their lights on. So she stumbles there on the side of the road, loses her footing or something, tries to get her balance by taking a step out toward the highway. The guy in the truck swerves, a reflex, and suddenly he's got the truck going sideways, the back coming around, and in another couple of seconds my wife and the car are cut in half. By the time I get there, they've pretty much got it cleaned up. Traffic is flowing normally. Ginger is covered up, by the side of the road. Everybody is patting me. Cops are patting me, ambulance people are patting me, state troopers are patting me. It's a long time ago. It starts to rain a little, very tiny drops that seem to be far apart. It's getting darker and all the trees are black, and car lights are glittering on the highway. There's a trooper out there who still has his glasses on, his wide-brimmed hat, and he's motioning the traffic by, which he shouldn't have to do because the lanes are clear, but the people are all going fairly slow, to see what happened. So everybody starts leaving. They've got a new truck to get the old truck out. They've got a wrecker for what's left of Ginger's car. They've got an ambulance, cops are leaving. People are saying to me that I ought to go home now."

"Right," Elise said. She got up out of her chair and tapped Roscoe on the shoulder and then pointed at Kinta and Edward. "Let's go. You people ready?"

Kinta got off the couch, picked up her shoes, and headed for the bedroom. "I need to get my purse," she said.

Edward said, "Where are we going?" Then he got up off the couch.

"It's time to buy," Elise said. "We'll get a lot of those plastic stacking things. We'll get some deck chairs. We'll get some new microwave cookware. Maybe we'll get a new cutting board. I don't know, I just feel like getting out." She tugged on Roscoe's arm. "Are you OK?"

"Sure," he said. "I was just talking because Edward said that thing about you and me. I mean, I was just trying to clarify things." He got up. "Wouldn't you rather go to a movie?"

Kinta came out of the hallway, snapping her purse shut. "I could go to a movie," she said. "What's on?"

"I don't want to go sit in a dark place for two hours," Edward said. "Why don't you guys go. I'll stay here and rest. That's what I really want to do."

"I think I'll stay here with Edward," Roscoe said. "I don't much feel like going out."

"What's everybody cutting out on the deal for?" Kinta said. "I've got my purse and everything. I'm ready to go." She turned around and looked at Elise. "Hey, Elise? Are you caving in, too?"

"No. Let's go," she said. "We can go to the mall. You can tell me all about Richard." Elise put an arm around Kinta and glanced at Edward. "And then you can tell me about your plans for our friend."

20

As soon as Elise and Kinta left, Roscoe went into the back bedroom. He said he was going to take a nap. Edward went into his bathroom and turned on the water in the tub. He liked the water rushing into the tub. He undressed and sat down cross-legged on the cotton bathroom rug, leaned against the wall, listening to the water. Then he felt chilly, went out into the bedroom and got his robe, and put it on, went back into the bath and sat down on the floor again.

The bedroom door was shut, so he left the bathroom door open. He leaned against the wall, and against the tub, his left arm up on the edge of the tub as if it were out a car window, and he watched the steam coming off the water, thinking about Roscoe. Thinking how peculiar it felt to have Roscoe in the house. To be in the house with just him. For a minute his problems didn't seem like problems—he could not take seriously that he and Elise and Roscoe were all going to live together in a new, three-way marriage. On the other hand . . . maybe they were already doing it. He could see himself living alone, occasionally visited by Elise and Roscoe. He wondered if that wasn't ideal—it was so much easier alone. Maybe he didn't like it as much as he thought, but it was easier. He wanted to think about himself and Elise, about what had happened to them, about what might happen to them, but sitting there on the bathroom floor with the water running in the tub, he couldn't think anything about himself and Elise. He and Elise just were. He didn't feel threatened, or sad, or particularly lonely, he didn't feel cut off from her or isolated, and it seemed to him that no matter what happened they would always be connected.

It wasn't a "We'll always be friends" idea, either. He wasn't going to marry anybody else. He'd lived fifteen years with Elise, from twenty-five to forty, and he wasn't interested in building another relationship like his relationship with Elise. In fact, it wasn't possible. Those years weren't available. So what he figured, as he got up off the bathroom floor and hung the robe on the top of the corner of the door, slid into the warm water in the tub, was that in some way or another he and Elise would stay together—there weren't any options.

There was a knock on the bedroom door, then the door opened and Roscoe said, "Edward? May I come in?"

"Wait a minute," Edward said. "I'm in the tub. I'll be right out."

"I'm not coming in there," Roscoe said. "I'll just sit out here, OK?"

"Yeah," Edward said. "Sure. What's up?" Edward had started to get up when he heard the door opening, but when Roscoe said he was staying in the bedroom, Edward had settled back into the tub and pulled a washcloth off the towel rack. "What's happening?" he said.

"I'm not feeling too good about this thing," Roscoe said from the bedroom. "I feel shitty, in fact." He seemed anxious. "Maybe we should do this later?"

"No," Edward said. "It's all right. What is it that you feel shitty about?"

"You and me and Elise," Roscoe said. "I mean, I love Elise, you know what I mean?"

Edward nodded his head.

"I guess you do, too," Roscoe said. "And she loves you. She loves me, too, I guess. Or she likes me a lot or something." Roscoe let that hang out in the air a minute. Then he went on. "I'm sorry I went into the thing about Ginger. You said that about Elise being my new wife, and I started thinking about her. About Ginger. It's like when anybody says 'wife,' all I can think about is Ginger. It's hard—"

"I know what you're talking about," Edward said.

"Elise told me what she was going to tell you," Roscoe said. "The thing about the three of us together. I mean, I don't know how together she wants to be, but I said it was OK with me. I mean, what have I got to lose?"

"I don't know what you've got to lose," Edward said. "But it's crazy to think about us together. I don't like it when she touches you. I didn't like it out there in the living room when she put her arm around you."

"I know," Roscoe said. "I felt real awkward."

"I don't know that awkward is what I felt," Edward said.

"Yeah," Roscoe said.

Edward was staring at the shower head, thinking how it would feel if the shower were on, spraying him with little sticks of hot water. He'd been anxious when Roscoe came into the bedroom, but he'd relaxed some, and he felt oddly at ease having this conversation with Roscoe in the next room. One of the things he was thinking about was that he liked Roscoe because Roscoe seemed to be so meek. He didn't want to hurt anybody or offend anybody or attack anybody or tell anybody how to do anything. Yet he was sure of himself at the same time. Still, Edward had a hard time imagining him walking into the bedroom like that.

"I don't think it would be too bad," Roscoe said.

"You and me holding hands, right?" Edward said. "I mean, you're a charming guy, Roscoe, you're really a swell guy, but I don't want you in my house twenty-four hours a day. Nothing personal. I used to have enough trouble just having Elise in the house twenty-four hours. I like to walk around naked, for example. If you're in the house, I can't walk around naked, you know what I mean?"

"What if I was blind?" Roscoe said.

"If you were blind, you'd still be looking at me with your skin or something," Edward said. "And besides, you're not blind. And I don't think it would be bright for you to get blind. It's like every-thing we've done since we were about two works against this kind of a deal. What if you had two fathers? Or two mothers? How do you explain it to anybody? I mean, God knows we don't explain much to many people, we barely talk to anybody, but even if we did it, we'd have to explain it to somebody. People at the office, people at the grocery store, people at the cleaner—Elise takes some shirts over there, and she's got to tell the guy that these are your shirts, and these are my shirts. So she puts them under two different names. Then sometimes you pick up my shirts, and other times I pick up yours. And the guy starts looking at us funny, looking at me funny when I go in there. He makes me feel like I'm a fool. And that's just the guy at the laundry. I can just see my brothers on hearing of this, offering to drive me to the doctor. It's just, I don't want to see you every day. She does, apparently."

"I think she does," Roscoe said. "Yes."

"Yes," Edward repeated. "And then we've got the problem of dialogue attribution. We're all sitting in the room, and Elise says something, and both of us answer her. You've got two problems off of that; one is that we say the same thing, and the other is that we say different things. And then there's her walking around naked, and you walking around naked—pretty soon we're some kind of nudist colony around here. And I just don't like her having some-body else. I mean, I don't have anybody else, why should she? That's stupid, sure, I know that, but it's still there. Underneath that polite and well-behaved exterior, you probably feel the same thing. Do you feel that?"

Roscoe didn't answer. Edward sat up in the tub, used the wash-cloth to wipe his face. Out the bathroom door all he could see was the corner of the bed, the desk against the far wall, and the edge of the open bedroom door.

"Roscoe?" Edward said.

"Yeah," Roscoe said. "I'm thinking. I guess I feel a little of it. But our situations are different. I haven't been living with her for fifteen years. She's not my wife. I mean, I'm not used to having her all to myself. I started this as her friend, knowing about you, knowing that she was married to you."

"Are you talking before or after the accident?" Edward said.

There was a snort from the next room. "OK," Roscoe said. "You get three for that, and you get to go again." He sighed and stretched his feet out in front of him so that Edward could see them by the corner of the bed. "Before Ginger died, we were having an affair. I know you know that, but I mean, it was different then than it is now. I don't know why I was having an affair. People do that. We saw each other, we liked each other, that's the way it went. I'm sorry about that." He paused again. Then he said, "Edward?"

"Still here," Edward said.

"Is this OK?" Roscoe said. "I don't have to to talk about this."

"Fuck you, Roscoe," Edward said.

"OK, I'll talk about it," Roscoe said.

"Thank you," Edward said.

Roscoe said, "I liked Elise. She was funny and charming, and she kind of broke my heart. But even when she was breaking my heart, I knew she wasn't going to replace Ginger. I guess I didn't *know* that, but I didn't think she would. Ginger was somebody I loved so much I couldn't believe it. She made a sad face and it killed me. I didn't want to be with her all the time, but I wanted her there. And I wanted to know she was there. Do you know what I mean? She was like the basis for everything. She was sort of my mother, as an adult. I always asked her, I wanted to know what she thought, I wanted her to be happy, I wanted her to be content. If she wasn't content, I just stopped everything and tried to fix her situation. This is paradoxical stuff. If I was so worried, what was I doing out with Elise? I don't know. It was sex, it was romance, it was new. It's hard to imagine, now, I guess, but at that time I was doing better, and I felt like I could help Elise. She wasn't doing real great with you, I mean, the sex stuff, the rest of it—I think she felt unneces-sary. Anyway, what I'm saying is that there was one kind of rela-tionship that went on before Ginger got killed, and there's another thing that's going on now. Probably we couldn't be friends like we are now if we hadn't done the other. But what we're doing now isn't the other. It's sort of the other, but it's a lot truer. Do you know what I mean?"

"No," Edward said. "What do you mean? Do you mean it's not done in neon? It's not thunder and lightning?"

"Something like that," Roscoe said. "It's not any of those things, but I do love her, I want to be with her. It's like, I've found the way I want to live. When I started out with Ginger there wasn't any question of how I wanted to live. I just lived the way everybody else lived. I didn't think about it. You know, you've got a wife, you've got a house, you've got a job, you get some cars, you wash the cars, you get a boat, you wash the boat—these things come at you like pop-up toys, and you pick some. It's not as if I did much thinking about any other ways to do anything. That's what I did. And it was OK. Don't get me wrong on that. If Ginger were alive, we'd still be doing it. Even if I thought the way I think now, we'd be doing it, because when it was me and her, it didn't matter what we did. It didn't matter to *me*. Whatever she wanted was all right—she wants more money, I'll make more money; she wants a house, we can get a house. I mean, none of it signified. The only thing that signified was seeing her there, smiling. Seeing that I was making her kind of happy. That was what I got from her, this kind of . . . glow. Anyway, so, I hadn't thought much about the way I lived. And then when she got killed, I had to. I didn't have any other reason to do what I was doing.

"Then for a while I went a little crazy. There was no system. If I ate, I ate what was there, and if nothing was there, I got in the car and went to the closest store and bought the first thing that I saw, and ate that. Elise thinks we broke off because of Ginger, but I don't think that's true. I had the guilt she talks about, but that isn't the reason I didn't want to see her—there wasn't any reason, but there wasn't any reason *to* see her either. And then, by the time I could feel things again, I had some stuff figured out. Like that Ginger was the only wife I was ever going to have, that I'd used up that feeling, and that I had to figure out some other way of living. And that there were some people I really liked—Elise, for one. I mean, it's not very often that you actually *like* people. You know what I mean? You get along with a lot of people, but you don't like them. So when you actually like somebody, it's not a small thing. The way we talk about friends now, we mean acquaintances—it's like the category of friends pretty much vanished. I've known this since high school, of course, but you just don't pay any attention. You just go along. You go over to people's houses, and you don't want to be there, but you're there anyway, because that's what you're supposed to do. Then you turn around and have them over to your house. Same thing. And I don't mean that you don't like these people at all, because you do; some part of the time when you're over at their house or they're at yours, you actually enjoy yourself. But that's not friendship, is it? It's something, but not friendship. So Elise was a friend, and I started thinking about that, and I thought that was something that could be preserved, that intimacy. I didn't have to hide anything from her."

Edward was looking at Roscoe's feet and thinking that he and Roscoe had a lot in common, that they even stretched their feet out in front of them the same way. And he was thinking, too, that they were both like the guy who built the Watts Towers—everything homemade, pasted together, bits of junk picked up off the ground and shoved into cracks.

"What was the question again?" Roscoe said. "Oh, I remember. It was about whether or not I wanted exclusive rights to Elise, wasn't it?"

"That was a long time ago," Edward said. He used the wash-cloth to wipe his face again, and then he stood up in the tub.

Roscoe said, "You want me to get out? I'll get out while you dress, OK?"

"That's fine," Edward said. "Or just stay there, go on—I've got my robe here."

"Your blue robe," Roscoe said.

Edward didn't like that. Didn't like Roscoe knowing about his robe. "I'll bet you've got one just like it."

"Nope," Roscoe said. "I always wanted one, but I never had one. Not since I was a kid. When I was a kid I had one. And I think I may get one, but I don't have one now."

"So I guess you want my wife and my robe, too?" Edward said.

"No," Roscoe said. "Bathrobes are covered by one of the commandments."

"The ninth," Edward said.

"I can't even remember what the commandments are," Roscoe said. "Some of them are real dumb, aren't they? Isn't it, like, don't kill anybody, don't maim anybody, and keep your shirttail tucked in? Something like that?"

"That's close," Edward said. He was drying himself with the first of the two towels he always used for that purpose.

"I guess what it comes down to is, I don't see that much difference between your position and mine, with respect to Elise, I mean. I know there is a difference, and that if it came down to the nut-cutting, I'd probably lose, but I guess I'm betting it won't come to that. In answer to the question, I don't have the proprietary feeling about her that you do. I might like to, but I don't. And that's OK. I can live with that."

"That's mighty white of you," Edward said.

"You don't want to use that expression, I don't think," Roscoe said.

Edward made a fright-face at himself in the bathroom mirror. "Yikes," he said. "My mother should be ashamed of herself. There must be some explanation—cleanliness, saintliness, something like that. She's my mother, so we give her the benefit of the doubt. OK?"

"Sure," Roscoe said. "Maybe it's the soul. Remember how the soul used to look like a bowling pin? Maybe that's what it's about."

"That's it," Edward said. "Get all of those little black dots off of there. It's OK, Mom. We've PR'd this one into oblivion. Say it with impunity." He took the second towel and went over his arms and legs quickly, then put on the robe. "I'm coming out," he said. "Fully clothed. No need to worry." He went into the bedroom, stepped over Roscoe's legs, and went into the closet. When he came out he was carrying jeans and a fresh oxford-cloth shirt. He said, "You might want to retire to the hall for the next part of this conversation, so we can carry on in relative anonymity."

"Only the grille cloth between us," Roscoe said, getting up out of the chair. "I'll tell you what—I want a Coke. Do you want a Coke? I'll get a couple of Cokes."

"Do we have Cokes?" Edward said.

"Yeah, Kinta and I went out and got some last night. You want regular Coke or Diet Coke?"

"Diet," Edward said.

He felt better when Roscoe was out of the room. He didn't want to feel better particularly, but he did. He had thought he was relaxed during their conversation, but when Roscoe left, he was suddenly more relaxed, which is how he knew that he hadn't been relaxed in the first place. He put on the jeans and shirt and went into the bathroom to look at his teeth. He used a toothbrush and some fresh water on them—no toothpaste. Then he rinsed his mouth with the mouthwash he had in the closet. It was blue, and when he spit it out into the basin it bubbled. Then there was a slight blue residue around the drain, so he had to turn on the water to get rid of that. Then he looked at his teeth again. They were still yellow. "Looks like you guys could use a coat of chip-free laser-optimized porcelain enamel," he said, addressing his teeth. "You ever wonder why you're so lonely in there? You ever hear of Clorox?" He watched himself button the collar buttons of his shirt, then tossed the towels over the shower curtain rod, got the hairbrush out of the cabinet and ran it through his hair, then brought out the hydrogen peroxide. He rinsed his mouth with that, spit into the sink, then opened his mouth and watched the peroxide bubble on his tongue. He rinsed a couple of times to get rid of the bubbles, then dried his face on one of the towels he had thrown over the curtain rod. "OK," he said to himself in the mirror. "Roscoe IV." He shook his head. "You shouldn't say that, Edward. You should behave your-self, Edward. They'll be gone soon, Edward."

In the living room, Roscoe had taken the chair he'd been in earlier. Edward's Diet Coke was on the coffee table on a carefully folded paper towel.

Edward sat on the couch. "OK—let's just divvy her up, what do you say? You take the top, and I'll take the bottom, or the other way around. I don't care. You take Mondays and Tuesdays, I'll take Wednesdays and Thursdays. I'll take the right eye, you can have the left. But I don't want to catch her looking at you with my eye, you hear? I don't want my eye to be an occasion of sin. How many pubic hairs has she got?"

Roscoe shook his head, then opened one eye a little and squinted at Edward.

"Slipped," Edward said. "It was OK up until the last part. I don't know—" He took a long swallow out of his drink, then held the can to his forehead, rubbing it lightly back and forth. "Maybe it's OK. Maybe after five years of this it'll make sense. If this is what she came up here to tell me about, she could have called. It's not like I hate it, it's like . . . I hate it." He looked away from Roscoe, looked around his living room. "But I don't have a better idea. I mean, I don't want to go back and do what we used to do, live the way we did. It wasn't so bad, it wasn't all that bad, but it's the way we *used* to do things. When I was down there last night, I was thinking that the place is nice. It's stupid-looking, but it's nice."

Roscoe hung his head. "It's OK. She misses you, though. She wants you to come down there sometimes, to be with her."

"I don't know," Edward said. "Maybe I can, maybe I can't. One of the things I've noticed is that for the last six months I haven't been running down there every five minutes. I guess it means I don't *need* that. Maybe it means I don't love her. She hasn't been running up here, so maybe that means she doesn't love me."

"Or maybe it's not that simple," Roscoe said.

"Yes, Roscoe," Edward said. "Maybe it's not that simple. I didn't think of that. You mean, like, maybe it's as complicated as a *human relationship?* Is that possible?"

"OK," Roscoe said. "I just didn't want us to lapse into any more dumbness than we had to lapse into."

"Aw, why don't we just go ahead and lapse," Edward said. "You lapse over there, and I'll lapse over here. We could have some rage in this lapse. Some deeply buried emotion, what do you say? Maybe we can get into a fistfight, bust up the place, and then we can be discovered by Elise and Kinta, and we can feel foolish but somehow cleansed—is it a deal?"

"I haven't had a fistfight since eighth grade," Roscoe said. "I shot this guy the finger and he comes over and we start this fight, and what we're really doing is St. Dominic's Championship Wrestling. So here's the way I was—as a kid, I mean. I could have beaten this guy up easy. I knew that, I could tell that when we were fighting. We were in this parking lot—did I already tell you this story?"

Edward shook his head.

"So anyway, there was this big hole there, they were doing some kind of construction next to the parking lot, and there was this hole that was eight feet deep and full of water because it had been raining, and we were kind of struggling right next to this hole, and I thought about throwing this kid in there, tripping him and dropping him in the hole. There were kids all around, people yelling, and you know what I did? I didn't throw him in. I figured that would end the fight, would bring the nuns, they'd fish him out of this hole, and then he'd tell them why we were fighting. He'd tell them that I'd shot him the finger, and then I'd get in *real* trouble. That's me all over. Anyway"—Roscoe paused a minute, studying the top of his Coke can—"I'm safe now. The kid's not telling anybody anything. He stuffed a shotgun in his mouth about a year later. God knows why. He had a lot of pimples, and he wasn't well liked. I guess that's it. I didn't like him much myself. He had a style problem, or something. Still . . . what happens is, you think about him years later, you wonder what was going through his head." Roscoe put his Coke can on his forehead, just as Edward had. "I mean, besides buckshot. That's pretty radical for the eighth grade."

"It's not radical later?" Edward said.

"No," Roscoe said. "Later it's only liberal." He took some condensation off the can with his palm and wiped his neck. "You see all these kid movies now, and you think you were a kid once, and you remember some of that, and then you think about this guy who blew his head off, and suddenly you feel sorry for him, even though you didn't feel sorry for him twenty-five years ago. All you felt then was that he was weird. It was hushed up, of course, at St. Dominic's. For all I know his father could have shot him. His father didn't like him much either, is what I heard."

"That must happen to everybody, there must be somebody like that. I knew a guy in high school did that—same thing. Shotgun. It must be a disease, a brain problem." Edward put his bare feet on the coffee table, letting his head lean to one side. He wasn't looking at Roscoe, but past him, under the table by the door, where he thought he saw a crumpled piece of paper, something the size of a thumbnail. He was tapping the side of his foot on the coffee table.

"You're not comfortable, right?" Roscoe said. Then, immediately, he said, "Jesus, that's a stupid thing to say."

"Don't sweat it. We had a lull there, right? We're working on the lull. It's not personal—I'm not comfortable with anybody much. I think nobody's comfortable, but a lot of people have more patience than me." He bent the tab on his Diet Coke until it broke off in his hand. He looked at it for a second, one side, then the other, saw a little sliver of aluminum like a piece of glass on his fingertip. "I've got aluminum in my drink now," he said. "Aluminum causes some dread disease, I don't remember which one. Wait a minute—" He leaned forward, hunching his shoulders. "Now look, am I crazy or something? I don't want to break the mood here, but it seems to me that you're doing everything that I'm doing. I mean, I did the thing with the can, and then you did the thing with the can." He put his can back on his forehead to illustrate. "Is this zany, or what?"

"Raise your arm, see if I do it, too." Roscoe waved at Edward, who, as instructed, had lifted a hand. "You're right. It's zany," Roscoe said. "Now, what if we consider this other thing a non-problem? We say we got this woman, we like her, she likes us, and we go situational from there? Couldn't we just forget the rest of this shit and watch TV, stuff like that? Where does it say we have to make the Big Decision?"

"Elise finds another boyfriend and you're out on your ass," Edward said. "That it?"

"You think so?" Roscoe said. "You're telling me to behave myself? You're powerful?"

Edward slid back into the sofa. "I'm just figuring your interest in this, in me."

"Oh," Roscoe said. "OK, fine. The deal is, there's this light in her face when you're around. It's not she's happy, but she thinks she's in the right place, where she belongs. So I have an interest, yes. I need your participation."

"That's pretty Soviet," Edward said. "I already told her it's OK with me. I don't want anything else. I'm not out there jumping on the Peace of Mind Club, flashing my card at the few remaining clean ones, I'm here, doing my stuff."

"Not enough. She reads that as, You aren't together."

"I'm together," Edward said. "I promise."

"Give me a break, will you? You'll want to be alone for twenty minutes, then you'll want wife, child, house—the usual."

"I don't know that," Edward said.

"Don't you just piddle around like a little old man? Isn't that what you're doing?"

"Yeah. Right," Edward said. "What is that, supposed to hurt? I'm supposed to feel inadequate because I don't power out in rhinestones and ride the hot young women? Then go hunting afterwards? Maybe blow the heads off some animals? Then come on back and eat a big, juicy steak, and then fuck the women some more? Bust some guy's ass at a business deal, then take a whiskey into the yard and have deep thoughts about America? Then go on back inside and watch some pals fuck the women for a while? I mean, what's the deal?" He spread his hands as if asking for an answer, then didn't wait, but changed his tone, started speaking softly, deliberately, as if explaining something to a child. "What I like is to walk from one room to another, mess around in that room for a while, walk back to the room I came out of, rest a while, then walk into a third room and get a Nestlé's Crunch ice cream bar and sit down on the couch for a minute, then go in the bathroom and wash my face, then read a magazine—*Consumer Reports* is good— then heat up a bagel in the microwave and go back in the other room and check out that hinge on the door to the closet that's been bothering me—see? That's what I like. That, and work. Work gets me out of the house, I see a few trees, some cars, other people— they tell their jokes and I tell mine. Both of us get our jokes from the television, only we watch different shows, so it's OK. And I pretend to be seriously engaged in whatever we're seriously engaged in on that particular day. Then I come home and walk around. Sometimes I'll go to the store and buy something. Ziploc bags are good. I've got this thing out in the kitchen that's got eighteen two-inch-square by four-inch-deep plastic drawers in it. That was a big find. It's like, yes, a little old man. So what?"

"So nothing," Roscoe said. "The only thing is, what about Elise? You owe her—"

"I don't owe shit," Edward said. "I did mine."

"Yeah, I know," Roscoe said. "People don't owe each other things, la-la-la. And when you get out of the sixties art-movie version of things, what you've got is people who want to be together, but aren't. Because somebody *believes* something. That's really swell."

What Edward was thinking was that he agreed with Roscoe and that he didn't agree with himself—or that he agreed with himself, but he *felt as if* he agreed with Roscoe. It was a situation in which he frequently found himself. It made him feel, in unequal measure, stupid and defiant, and it was obvious that the sense of having been caught out, of having a correct but limited view fueled the defiance. He couldn't say, *Yeah, you're right, it's OK with me,* because he'd already said that, and it wasn't enough. What he had to say was *Wow, what a great idea. OK, let's do it.* He didn't want to say that. He didn't know why—something about sharing Elise with Roscoe didn't work. Maybe he was afraid of it, maybe it was too modern, too awkward, too hurtful to think she'd found somebody else she liked that much . . . something. On the other hand, he didn't want to be afraid of something and be dumber than he was in order to cover the fear. He was thinking maybe if they let it alone it would sneak up on him, present itself as a thing accomplished, and he wouldn't have to worry.

Roscoe said, "Sounds to me like you're blocked on the thing. I mean, in practical terms, it doesn't amount to anything. All you've got to do is take it easy and like Elise. We can avoid each other, or see each other, whatever. I'd prefer the latter, of course. But either way, what we're talking about is some kind of pact, the three of us making a pact. Stay together, live as, you know, whatever you want to call us, and that's it. It is something you have to do in your head, though. You have to OK it in your head."

"That's a problem," Edward said.

"You'd rather do without?"

That angered Edward, but he made a joke out of it. "It's my famous 'No loaf is better than half' theory," he said.

"Well, it isn't something that anybody planned, you know? It fell out this way. I think if any of us had a choice, we wouldn't choose this. I'd rather be with Ginger. Elise would rather be with you. You'd rather have me gone. But none of that's happening. My thinking is, you take what you've got and make the best of it. You wait and you've got no chance. You complain and you lose."

Edward said, "If Elise wants to be with me, and I want you gone, what's to prevent us from getting together and losing you?"

"It's not nice," Roscoe said, grinning. He shut his eyes and stifled a nervous yawn. "Besides, she doesn't want that. She wants to be with you and be with me, too. That's what she tells me." This time he did yawn. He put his hand over his mouth and shook like a dog when he yawned. He said, "It seems to me the things people do are so complicated you can't ever understand them. It's like we never get close."

Edward got off the couch, went to the window, and looked into the street where some kids were banging their bicycles into each other. He was tired, too. "We could go out here and lord it over these kids," he said. "That's always fun. They think we're another species. It's great. You go out there, and they look at you like you're a sand mutant."

Roscoe joined Edward at the window, standing beside him, staring out at the kids. "My thinking is, you know, we're in here, in this dark little room, behind this shaded glass here, behind these blinds, and we're standing here, the two of us. They're out there. I mean, look how much space they've got and look how much space we've got. It's as if we can't handle it. We start out in the open, and as we get older, we find smaller and smaller spaces, smaller houses, smaller rooms, until we get to the pine room."

Edward turned around and put a hand on Roscoe's arm, braced him. "Why, that's poetical," Edward said. "It's not much fun, but it's poetical."

"Well, we're not out in the yard, are we?" Roscoe said.

"You want to go out in the yard? We can go out in the yard. We've got a yard. It's our yard. We could go out in it and point at things in the sky. We could play with the neighbor's cat. We could get our cars and bump them into each other. I mean, Roscoe, it's not that these things are unavailable to us." Edward pointed out the window. "See, the thing is, these kids out here don't care about gnats. Gnats are part of life for them. Gnats are just the way of things. I mean, a gnat comes along and bites you on the neck, and you slap him, and that's the way things are supposed to be. But they'll learn. They'll grow up and see gnats for what they really are, Roscoe. They'll discover the truth soon enough." He turned around and waved a hand at the room. "And look at us—sure, we've given up the street, the sky, the shifting air, the pungency of tulips, but . . . no gnats."

Roscoe sat down on the arm of the sofa, looked around the room.

"Oh, sure," Edward said. "Sometimes, late at night, you're in bed, lights out, you're enjoying the goose down, feeling parts of your body you'd forgotten, muscles shrinking inside you, bones falling through space, your head propped just right so you don't have to hold it up—you thought you were the Elephant Man in the early going—so you're getting used to that ring in the house, that faint, out-of-earshot, not unfriendly electrical ring that's maybe the refrigerator, the clock, the surge protector, something—it's not natural, you know, and the sheets are sweet and soft, and there's no light beating your eyelids to get in, and you let go of the arms so they feel separate, like they're not part of you, tools that have done work and are themselves aiming for sleep . . ." Edward stopped and turned to Roscoe, pointed at him with a forefinger. "You got all that?"

"Yeah," Roscoe said. "I'm in bed with my tools, and I used to be the Elephant Man."

"Right," Edward said. "So you're there and everything's quiet and nothing is moving and for a second it's perfect and then, out of nowhere, comes this fierce buzz like a tiny chain saw—does a rapid-descent procedure into your ear, hovers there, then shoots away trailing its whine." Edward held up a minute, letting the room sounds rise. "So once in a way one gets through the net, right? But by and large, we're gnatless. It's really great." He glanced at Roscoe, then looked back to the window, to the kids in the street. They had dumped their bikes into a kind of tepee pile and were sitting on the grass in front of the house across the street. One kid, towheaded, wearing a striped T-shirt, was systematically slapping the ground with a three-foot stick. "See here?" Edward said, pointing this kid out to Roscoe. "He's learning."

21

KINTA DANCED on the table at dinner. They had had a pleasant meal, most pleasant from Edward's point of view, because Elise and Roscoe and Kinta did all the talking. Edward was allowed to sit by and watch—nobody talked about him, nobody turned to him and asked him what he thought, no one seemed to take much notice of his presence. This was, of course, a mixed blessing, since along with being able to relax, Edward had to face the fact that he wasn't essential to the party, that these three people could get along quite comfortably without him. Elise and Kinta had apparently had a big discussion while shopping, had enjoyed themselves, and had decided to have a moderately fancy show of things at dinner to mark the end of the weekend and mark Edward's birthday, which had barely been mentioned since Elise arrived on Friday. So they had gotten a leg of lamb, several bottles of wine, mushrooms, French bread, and they had come home shortly after four o'clock and gone straight to the kitchen, where they stayed until eight, when dinner was served. Elise had gone into the closets and brought out the sterling, the crystal, and the linen, all of which she had left behind when she moved, and Kinta had prepared the dining table as if for a formal Christmas dinner, with fully enough equipment, it seemed to Edward, for twice as many guests.

It was shocking to have so much stuff out of the cabinets at one time, and a little distressing—one of the things that kept passing through his mind during the preparations for dinner, and during the dinner itself, was how much of his ordinary life had been disrupted in the short space of the afternoon, not to mention the weekend. He thought about washing all the dishes that were being used, about returning them to their cabinets, about trying to get everything back in place when Roscoe and Elise and Kinta left. Everything glittered at the table—the knives were brightly polished; the serving spoons were fish-eye lenses; the plates and saucers delivered their pale reflections; the wineglasses were pretty and sharp as they clicked on the tabletop, and in them even the wine rocked gently back and forth. It was a cluttered table, elegant and homely and genuine—nothing on it only for show. He thought about how people who make dinners, who invite guests for dinner have their own styles—this was Elise's. He didn't know what his style was. He didn't know what he would do if he were having people to dinner. Since Elise had been gone, he had not had anyone to dinner. Six months and no one to dinner.

He was thinking about that, thinking it sounded kind of grim, and listening to Roscoe tell a story about something that happened on an airplane—Edward missed the first part, so he didn't know where the airplane was, or where Roscoe was going.

"So we're sitting there in the plane," Roscoe said. "So we're about two hours late, and the flight crew is running out of ways to be polite and encouraging. There's a big huddle in the front of the plane, all the attendants in a little clutch. They're putting their heads together. There's some disagreement, apparently. One guy, who I figured was the head guy—I figured it because he wasn't one of the ones who did the drop-down masks and the lifeboats and the 'Where are the exits?' business—finally gives some instructions to the others, and two of them trot down the aisle past me to the back. A minute later they go the other direction carrying a box the size of a small computer. Then the head guy gets on the microphone and says that we're going to be delayed a little longer, and that they have some special things for us to help us pass the time. Then they come down the aisle passing out these little black and white plastic puzzles. Some dumb puzzle, I don't know what it was. Anyway, so

I'm sitting there in my seat looking at my puzzle, kind of fiddling with it, not even taking it out of its plastic wrapper, and I look up and the guy across the aisle from me, a black guy about forty-five years old, kind of grizzled-looking, like he's a poor guy from Haiti or someplace, well, he's ripping open his plastic wrapper, and he's trying to eat this puzzle." Roscoe looks around the table. "See, he thinks they've given him something to eat. And he's over there trying to eat this puzzle. He's got it between his teeth, and he's trying to bend it. I can hear his teeth clicking down on it. The damn thing is plastic. And what I'm doing is sitting there wondering whether or not I should tell him that it's a puzzle, not something to eat."

"That's an awful story," Elise said.

"Well, that's what I'm thinking," Roscoe said. "I'm thinking it's real sad that this guy doesn't know that this thing he's trying to eat is a puzzle. So I look away, I look at the guy next to me, who's fiddling with *his* puzzle, moving the little pieces around in it, and I hear this big crack, and I figure, *Oh shit, there goes a tooth*. So I start to turn around and look. I really don't want to see, but I'm already thinking about what we can do about his tooth, about the blood, I'm thinking about whether I should go into the back to the toilet and get some paper out of there, or whether I should go to the front and see if the attendant has some towel, or a dish towel, and I'm feeling guilty and stupid for not saying something. I'm about ready to push up out of the seat when I first see the guy, and he's sitting over there with this big smile on his face, chewing like crazy. I mean, he looks over at me and smiles, does a little thing like . . . tipping the puzzle at me, what's left of the puzzle, and gives me a big grin like he's saying, *Top of the morning*."

That's when Kinta got up. "This is Edward's birthday party," she said. "Edward hasn't said a word. The whole time. I hate this. Why don't we do something else? Why don't we do something more interesting?" And then she stood up on her chair and started gyrating, bump and grind, slowly unbuttoning the buttons of her blouse. She got to the third button down from the neck before anybody said anything. It was Edward. He said, "Thank you, Kinta," and motioned in a funny way for her to sit down.

"This is your present," Kinta said. "Elise and I worked it out."

Edward looked at Elise, giving her a skeptical look, a question about her complicity. She smiled at him and rocked her hand side to side as if to say that she was sort of involved, but not really involved.

Roscoe got up to take his plate out into the kitchen. "I think I hear my mother calling," he said.

"You guys must have had some hot dog for a mother," Kinta said. "I mean, I know about Edward, but you, too?" Elise was nodding agreement.

"Same woman," Roscoe said. "Edward and I were talking about it earlier. Watch this."

Edward wasn't quite sure what Roscoe was doing, but he had an idea, so when Roscoe raised his right arm, Edward was quick enough to get his up almost at the same time. When Roscoe wiggled his hand in a circle, Edward did the same. Roscoe looked under his dinner plate, and Edward looked under his. They did this routine for a few seconds, and then they finished up as Marx brothers—Roscoe doing a 360-degree turn and bowing, and Edward bowing with him as if he, too, had made the turn.

"Flesh of my flesh," Roscoe said, picking up his plate and going into the kitchen.

"What about my breasts?" Kinta said. "Doesn't anybody want to see my breasts?"

"Wonder what's on TV," Roscoe called out from the kitchen.

"Maybe now's not such a good time," Edward said.

"I wouldn't mind seeing them," Elise said. "You can show them to me."

Kinta got down off the chair and went around the table so that she was standing right in front of Elise, her back to Edward, and she finished unbuttoning her shirt and then held it open for Elise to see.

"They're very pretty," Elise said, reaching out to touch Kinta. "May I?"

"Sure," Kinta said. "I'd like that."

"I think I hear my grandmother calling," Roscoe said from the kitchen.

Edward watched Kinta's back as Elise touched one breast, and then the other. He thought he saw Kinta shiver, but he wasn't sure. The two of them were saying things to each other, incomplete things, making little noises as if asking and answering questions without words. It was as if in admiring Kinta's breasts, in remarking on things they both saw there, things they knew in common, they were making public their alliance. What had started as an uncomfortable, awkward joke had turned into this remarkable, lovely moment for the two of them, and neither wanted to give it up to go back to the party.

Edward felt that things had slipped their moorings, that it was suddenly too easy to discard hard-won proprieties, to act as if you weren't yourself. It wasn't only the sexual component that bothered him, although, to be sure, that made him nervous. It was also the degree of intimacy that was signaled by the sexual component—on an ordinary Sunday night, in an ordinary house, on an ordinary street, his estranged wife was fondling the breasts of their mutual friend Kinta. With no announcement, no significant provocation, no reason. He wanted to stop them. At the same time, he wanted to watch. He also just wanted to get away from them, to leave them, undisturbed, to their pleasure, and to free himself, to get away.

If he said anything, he was the awkward intruder, the fool. Watching made him feel farther apart from them, and inferior. Staring at his plate made him feel like a child. They were pulling rank on him, pulling gender, displaying their power and the ease with which they could achieve this intimacy. He wanted to stand up on the chair and unzip his fly, to say, *Hey! What about me! Doesn't anybody want to see me?* but he couldn't. Because it might be taken seriously. Because it would be understood, at least, as a signal of his weakness, as an acknowledgment that he'd been kneecapped. He was wondering how long the little Elise and Kinta show was going to go on when Roscoe poked his head around the kitchen door frame.

"Oh, my God," he said. "What are you doing? What is the

deal?" He rubbed his forehead with his palm, then rubbed his eyes, rubbed his whole face. When he looked up again, he said, half playfully, "Could you people *please* behave yourselves?"

"Yeah, you guys," Edward said.

Kinta turned and looked at Edward over her shoulder. She was buttoning her shirt. "What?" she said. "Is self-effacement your long suit?"

Edward shrugged. "No," he said. "I just wish I'd said it before he did. You people were headed for the planet Zirkon at warp speed. I kind of got momentarily lost in the burnoff from your solid rockets."

Elise was up, starting to clear the table. "So, let me see," she said. "We've got dessert yet to go, right?"

"I don't want any dessert," Edward said.

"Well, maybe the rest of us would like dessert," Kinta said. "I personally would like some dessert."

"Me, too," Roscoe said. "What is dessert?"

"The last act in the tragedy of dinner," Elise said.

"Melon balls," Kinta said. "I made them myself. Well, I didn't actually *make* them. I mean, God made them. I just delivered them. I scooped them into life. We've got melon balls in about four colors. We've got a leg up on the melon ball industry here tonight such as would curl the blood of melon ball enthusiasts internationally."

"We're long on melon balls," Edward said.

Kinta helped Elise clear the table, and Roscoe helped, and Edward watched them make their trips to the kitchen. He tried to calculate how long it would take them to serve the dessert, finish it off, clean the dishes, get their things together, and leave. He was trying to calculate that because he had the feeling that he didn't want them to leave. Having them there was awkward, but exciting—like an experiment, something going on in the lab. He felt undetached—that was new. He was eager for them to stay. He wanted to say something about that, wanted to invite them, wanted to explain to them that he felt something that was some shadow of a different attitude, an attitude he didn't quite have, but was close to having.

22

"IT ISN'T exactly giving everybody the heebie-geebies, is it?" Elise said. "This brave, new idea?" They were in the bedroom. She was getting her things together, packing, and Edward was sitting on the bed, watching. Kinta and Roscoe were out in the kitchen doing the dishes. They'd volunteered.

"I don't know what you want, Elise," Edward said. "You come in with some idea about us getting together, only it isn't *us* anymore, it's us and Roscoe. And you don't give me any details—do you know that you haven't once said what you want me to do? You haven't said, for example, why don't I move down there, or that you want to move back up here. I mean, you've said it, but you haven't really *said* it, you know? And I don't know what you're thinking. If you're thinking I should move down there, the three of us live together in the same house, then you're probably nuts. It'll never happen. On the other hand, if all you're thinking is that you'd like to visit more often, up here, I mean, then that's fine. I don't have any problem with that. I wouldn't mind if you stayed now."

"I didn't come with a plan," Elise said. "I mean, it's what I've been thinking, but I didn't come up here to talk to you about it, to try to sell it to you."

"So why did you come?"

She stopped what she was doing—straightening Edward's clothes in his closet—and stood there a second staring at the floor. "God knows," she said. "It's your birthday, but that isn't why. I guess I just wanted to see you. To spend a little time." She started working on the closet again. "I miss everything about this place, about you. I don't know why, it doesn't make any sense. I mean, you're a nice guy, and all that, you're an interesting problem, but you're not exactly Man of the Year. You're a little bit anal, right? And you're not a big romantic. I mean, you give new meaning to the concept of room temperature. So I don't know what the attraction is."

Edward watched her work on the closet. He'd always liked watching her doing what she took to be her chores—straightening, cleaning, arranging. And he was touched by the fact that she was doing it now without thinking about it, forgetting that she was in his house, that it wasn't hers, forgetting that the arrangement of his closet was no longer her territory. "You don't think I'd rip 'em up on *The Dating Game?*" he said.

"Bachelor number four. But don't sweat it. Bachelors one through three are inflatable. They wear black underwear." She turned around and looked at Edward. She was holding a jacket of his. "Did I ever tell you about the time I picked up this guy and took him home, and he was wearing black underwear, and I made him leave?" She shook her head. "No, I guess I didn't. It's just as well. That's the whole story. He was a geek."

Edward looked at the ceiling as if making a plea to God. "Let all my underwear be white," he said.

"You don't have any underwear," she said.

"Well, I'm going to get some, and it's going to be white," Edward said.

She put the jacket back in the closet, then straightened the shirts, spreading the hangers so that the shirts were equally spaced along the rod. "I guess I came back to tell you that I loved you," she said. "A lot of things have changed, but that hasn't." She finished in the closet and shut the door, then sat down on the chair facing the bed, the chair nobody ever sat in, the chair Edward often wondered why he had in the bedroom. It was the same chair Roscoe had been in earlier. She said, "The way I love you is different, though. I'm more like you were when I left, like you were the last three or four years we were together. The way I love you is much less demanding. For a while I thought that meant I didn't love you, but that was wrong. I don't want to go on record here as being one of those people who thinks there's only one man for one woman, and all that, but I think there's only one man for one woman. You for me."

"Paradoxically," Edward said.

"That's not what I mean," Elise said. "I don't mean only one is possible, I mean only one *is*."

"Let me call your friend in here, and you can say that again," Edward said.

"He knows," she said. "Jesus, I think you just don't want to understand this. You're trying not to understand it. Why don't you just take the easy way and look at it as a person with two friends, two boyfriends. You don't really care if you're first or second—it happens that you're first, and you know it, and I know it, and Roscoe knows it—but that doesn't really make any difference to you. What you care about is whether or not I love you. I do, so you're OK. It's the *idea* of three of us that's grating."

"Does that mean once you get over the idea, everything's fine?"

"Come on, Edward. I'm not a jerk. It's hard for me, too. I don't know how I got into it. I mean, I have the little mom that I carry around in my head just like everybody else. She's in there yelling, 'You can't do this. This is wrong, Elise. You're a bad person, Elise. You don't love anybody.' And then when I'm with you, she's always saying, 'See? You don't really love Roscoe.' And when I'm with Roscoe, and I have a good time, and I love him, she's in there saying, 'Yeah? So what about Edward? Where's your great love for Edward now?'" Elise tapped herself on the head with her forefinger. "She's a real joy, this mom."

Edward shook his head. "I don't know what any of this has to do with me," he said. "I was up here living away, having a great time—no, I mean it, I was doing fine. I was getting along fine. I sort of liked what I was doing. It was real quiet and simple. And then here you come with your entourage, so I endured you just like

I deal with everybody else, but half an hour ago, after dinner, when you were over there playing with Kinta's tits, it actually occurred to me that I liked having you around, all of you. What was that stuff with Kinta's tits, anyway?"

"I don't know," Elise said. "It was for you, but it was also for me—I don't think I've ever touched another woman's breasts before. I've always wanted to, but I've never done it. I mean, I haven't wanted to the way you want to, the way men want to—I don't want to get my hands on every pair of tits that comes down the pike—but just to feel her, to sense what it's like to be her, to have those particular breasts. . . . I don't know. I like Kinta. Underneath the 'I'll fuck anybody, anywhere' routine there's a real nice person. A decent person. She's not out to improve her lot no matter what the cost." Elise did a parody of a salacious look, eyeing Edward and wiggling her eyebrows. "And she has great nipples."

Edward sighed and smiled. "I know," he said.

"They're real long," Elise said. "When they stiffen."

Edward got off the bed and went into the bathroom, turned on the water.

Elise followed him, stood in the bathroom door. "I'd like to make love with her," she said. "I think Lurleen wants to do it with me, but I don't want to do it with her. But I could do it with Kinta."

"So why don't you take on Kinta, and then all four of us can live together, and you can have two boyfriends and one girlfriend?" Edward wet his hands and patted water onto his face, then looked at his teeth, then reached for the toothbrush, shook it in the stream of water from the tap, then brushed his teeth with plain water. He stopped in the middle of that, the toothbrush in his mouth, and he turned to Elise and said, "And let's get a dog, too, OK?"

"You're so disgusting," she said, pushing off the bathroom door frame.

When Edward finished brushing, he splashed more water on his forehead, then dried his face on the folded towel on the towel rack without unfolding the towel. He patted his hair, then went back into the bedroom. Elise was sitting on the bed, on her side of the bed. He said, "You notice that women always take the left-hand side of the bed? The side so that their left hand is to the outside? I don't know why that is. I'll bet when you sleep alone down there, you sleep on the left side of the bed."

She made some hand gestures trying to figure out which side of the bed she slept on, trying to reconstruct her bedroom there in the air, then said, "Yep. It's the same side as this." She stuck the bed beside her with her finger. "I think it's just because most people are right-handed, and men get to choose their side of the bed, and they choose the right-hand side so their right hand will be free in case of an attack. It's another sexist manifestation. The women defer to the men, and then we get used to it. It's like everything else."

"So when you and Kinta sleep together, which side are you going to take?"

"I'm probably not going to sleep with Kinta," Elise said. "Although I don't know why not. Women are falling in love with other women at a rate that ought to alarm the men. But the men don't even know what the game is. Most of them are still playing somewhere back in the fifties. The worst ones are the ones that are playing like they're in the fifties, but talking like they're not. I hate those guys—the self-righteous, hardworking, antisexist types who get all frothy over gender issues. They want to help us. Turns my stomach."

"It does?" Edward said.

"Sure," she said. "The *mea culpa* business is the power trip they've always been on, just turned around. Man taketh away, man giveth. If I meet one more guy who takes the full responsibility for two thousand years of sexual discrimination on his shoulders I think I'll bust his nuts right then and there. Hack them off and send them to *USA Today*. I mean, hasn't this earnestness stuff gone too far? You can't get at it by being earnest. The way things work now, it's like if you're earnest, it's OK to be stupid. It's a new rule. It's OK not to think very much, or very hard. It's OK to take the first thing that jumps into your mind. It's OK to make everything make sense, to force it to make sense, even though to do that you have to forget about two-thirds of what you know. Of what you've run into." She slid down on the bed, propping her head up on the pillow, one arm cocked behind her ear. "I'm sorry," she said. "I just started thinking about that a minute, and it got away from me."

Edward drew his lips together and turned down the corners of his mouth. "It's fine," he said.

"A lot of people aren't thinking," Elise said. "They've gone back in time. See, this is my version of things. The movement was this cultural aberration, and it's all over but it had to be done in public, and to do it in public, to get the support, it had to be wrong—too hot on one side, too simple on the other. But the fallout is terrific. It's everywhere. It's not headlines, it's real stuff. My thing is, I hope the big talkers don't get the credit, don't go down in history as the ones who did this. This one's everybody's."

"I wouldn't worry about history," Edward said.

"I know," she said. "But it'd be nice if history could get it right at least once. Now what we've got is geeks running around trying to make everything all better, trying to revise into respectability. So we can watch TV, jerk the wife around, teach our kids to have the fat asses at forty."

"Somebody pull your chain?" Edward said, giving her a circus-shock face. "What about you? You're poking around here like some queen of the modern, giving me the bullshit about our new life, the way we are, the way we're going to be, and I'm sitting here thinking, 'Roll me over in the clover.' I mean, you fucked Roscoe until you bled, God knows who else, now maybe you want Kinta—I may have a problem with some of this, you know? We have a hard time being nice to each other. I think we've just run this bitch into the ground. We sit here and talk, and you wait for me to finish, and I wait for you to finish, neither one of us cares shit about what the other is saying. We're running on basic training here. I don't see how we're ever going to get back to anything. Like, I used to sit around and look at you, and you'd be doing something stupid, and I didn't care, I loved you anyway. Because it was you, and because it was stupid. But we've gone bureaucratic, we're thinking a lot about things, and now we've got to do everything in triplicate." Edward was up and looking out the window. "In half an hour you're out of here, and I'm alone, and maybe I want to be, and maybe I don't, but it's not like I have a choice."

"You could come with us," she said.

"Shit I could," Edward said. "That's one of those things like 'We'll meet again here next year,' that's an Alan Alda thing. I mean, the reason he never stands on his head is he's afraid he'll stick to the floor." Edward turned and looked at Elise. "In the movies I come with you, you know what I mean? I know that."

She got off the bed and started straightening the cover. "So, fine," she said. "I'll go back home. You can stay up here. That'll be fine."

Edward turned and looked at her. She was bent over the bed, her back to him. He took a step toward her, put his foot on her ass, and half kicked, half shoved her onto the bed, facedown.

She was up instantly, screaming "Fuck you" and slapping at his face.

He tried to block her, tried to get her hands, her wrists, but he couldn't catch them. She was strong. She caught him once on the temple, then again on the chin, and he backed up, bumped into the table by the window, then into the window itself. She kept coming, swinging at his face. "Don't you fucking touch me," she screamed. "You fuck." She kicked him, catching him just below the knee, and swung at his face again, but this time he caught her arm, twisted it.

"Wait a minute," he said. "Am I crazy or something? I'm sorry, you hear me? I'm sorry."

"Fuck you're sorry."

She was twisting, trying to get out of his grip, but he had her tight around the arm, and she couldn't get away. She slugged his shoulder with her left hand, hitting him a couple of times at the base of the neck with her fist, until he caught that hand, too. "You didn't hear me?" he said, shaking her.

She went limp suddenly, as if hit by a ray from some kind of police weapon for neutralizing crazies. Everything washed out of her face all at once. She stood there, her wrists trapped in Edward's hands, and she looked at him—no expression.

"I am sorry," he said. "It was a stupid thing to do. I don't know why I did it—no, I do know. It was the way you said OK, that you would just go. It was like you were giving up too easy."

"Fine," she said.

"No, I mean it," Edward said. He tightened his grip on her wrists. "Don't just say 'fine,' please."

"I can't say anything else," Elise said. "What do you want me to say?"

"Say we aren't doing this," Edward said.

"Will you let me go?" Elise said.

She didn't try to pull out of his grip, didn't do anything except stand and wait, the question hanging between them. He wouldn't let her go. "What's this about?" he said. "I mean, all of this. Why am I doing this, why are you doing this?"

"What do you want, a textbook? I mean, you want to make it real simple?" She was more animated, meaner, as if his question had made her mad enough to talk. "You're the one who taught me that things don't mean the way they're supposed to, remember? You said if everything makes perfect sense, if all the ducks are in pretty rows, you can bet that whatever sense is made is wrong. You taught me that. You made me live it. Now I can't get away from it. Now nothing ever comes to anything, because anything it could come to could never be true."

Their faces were close. Edward saw the tears starting in her eyes, wet and glassy, a small gashlike bubble just above the lower lid in each eye. He spread her arms and pulled her closer to him, then released her wrists and put his arms around her.

She put her face on his shoulder. "I can't trust anything. I think real hard, I try real hard, and I end up in this situation, and I'm going freaky because I don't want to live this way anymore. But there isn't any way out. I can't do anything. No matter what I do, I lose. Everybody loses. I don't know what to do." She pulled back and looked at Edward, tears dropping from the corners of her eyes. "Do you understand? Do you know what I'm talking about?"

He nodded, reaching up to rub at the tears on her face with his thumb.

She dodged his hand, turning her head to one side. "You and me are *supposed* to be together," she said. "I mean, that's it. But he and I are supposed to be together, too. I feel that way about him. I can't put those things together." She backed away from him, wiped her eyes, turned her back to him as she did. "I *can,* but I can't," she said, facing him again. "I hate it. I wish it were five years ago when we loved each other, when we were just . . . together. When that's all there was. I want to go back, but I know I can't. It's so stupid. It's hard to believe I've gotten myself into this, that somewhere back there I made a choice, I took a step, I did something that started this, that came to this moment when we're standing here together in this bedroom." She brushed the last tear lines from her face and pulled her arms over her chest, swung herself back and forth. "I have no idea what it was, what thing it was that made this inevitable. That's the trouble with trying to do things by the brain. You get lost. I get lost. I guess I should've known that. When I came up here, I didn't know what to expect, I didn't know how you'd be, how you'd react, but I wanted to come, I wanted to see you. I didn't even know how I felt about us, about what we were supposed to be doing. I just came. I didn't think we were finished or anything."

"Are we?" Edward said.

Elise shook her head. "I don't know. Something's finished." She held herself tightly and rocked a minute, then swung her arms open, up in the air, as if she were surrendering. "I don't know— maybe nothing's finished. That's what I'm telling you. It's like, one minute everything's gone, and the next I love you a lot. I love everything about you. I love the way you smell, the way your eyes hood when you get tired. Back and forth. It's not like I'm afraid to live without you, I can do that. I don't have to have you right there twenty-four hours a day. But we've always been this team, it seems like always. You and me, you know, at the store. Or in the car. Going somewhere. All those other people in the other cars, they never mattered. Nothing mattered except you and me, in the car, inside that little ship. The rest of it didn't count. Now it's different. I mean, the only way to do this is get a bigger car." She did a queer little snicker, dropping her head, a tight smile spreading her mouth. "You know what I mean? It's got to be all three of us, but I know it can't. I mean, *I* think it can, but it's up to you, up to him."

Edward took a step toward her and she took a step back. He said, "Come on, Elise. Take it easy. We'll be fine. Everything's going to be fine."

"Now you're shutting down," she said. "You're quitting on me. You can't know that everything's going to be fine. You've got no reason to say that."

"Everything's always been fine," Edward said.

Elise sighed, letting her body sag, and then, after a second of stillness, jerked her shoulders up and shivered, giving her head a quick, awkward shake. "That's what I'm trying to tell you. It's not like always. It's not going to be. Most times I think I'll spend the rest of my life with Roscoe. That's what I'll get. At first we'll talk, you and me, then we won't talk so much and I'll see you once a year, then every three years, then I won't see you. I'll have a life, and you'll have a life, and all this time we spent together, all the *ways* we were together, all the things we did, the things we felt, will be like stuff lost somewhere. I'll remember it the way I remember things from when I was a kid. I won't be able to feel any of it. It'll be names, places, things—schematics. Every once in a while I'll see something, remember something we did together, and I'll feel a trace of it, a hint. Just like a feeling coming over you sometime when you're not doing anything else, when you're sitting on a couch somewhere, staring at a fireplace, and I'll think of you and a fireplace we used to have, and how you liked fires, or how you didn't, and it'll be better than what I have. I'll think it was better when I had you."

They repeated the dance, Edward stepping toward her, she stepping away. "Would you stop that?" he said. "Would you let me hold you? Why are you suddenly so skittish? Why is all this happening right now? Where's all this been? I mean, I've been up here six months, where the fuck have you been? Where've you been with all this love and affection and caring and need? Why now? Why are you bringing it up?"

"I've been living with it. I've been thinking. Trying to do what I can. I'm driving myself to this. It's like I'm on this road, and it only goes one way—it's a monorail thing, and I can't stop it. I can see you out the window, dropping away, sliding by me, stretching out in some kind of mirror reflection. I can see the place we used to be, I can remember it, feel it, feel the warmth of it, but I can't get there. It's been gone too long. Years. We never said that. Or if we said it, we didn't believe it. But it dried up years ago. We were like roommates living in this house together—"

"Wait a minute," Edward said. "This is the opposite of what you said two minutes ago, isn't it? We were made for each other, I thought. Destined. Nothing mattered but the two of us. What about the car and all that?"

"I don't know," she said. She tossed her head back and looked at the ceiling, blew air out of her mouth. "It's stupid, it's stupid. It's crazy. I'm whipping around in here. Yes. I said that. I liked that. I want that. Tell me how to get it. I don't want to worry anymore. I don't want to look at him and think he's not you, and I don't want to look at you and think you're not him. I don't want any of it. See, I thought it would settle itself. I don't want to have to settle it— that's too much to ask. To make some kind of choice. I can't do that. But it's like I'm making a choice anyway, like the choice is making itself, but I know I'm responsible, it's mine." She stopped and ran her hands through her hair in this particular way she had of doing it, picking at the hair. She was quiet for a minute, and then the trouble in her face lifted as if she suddenly were not confused, as if something had come to her. She said, "I would like it if you could understand this. See how it goes. I mean, it's like this all the time in here"—she tapped herself on the head, and then did a giggle, brushing the seat of her pants. "All the time. You see what I'm saying?"

This time when Edward stepped toward her she didn't move away. He put his arms around her, touched her back, strong and broad, muscled, and he felt that tenderness he had always had for her, felt that and filled himself with it, with the sweetness of knowing the person you liked best, the person you loved, meant no harm to anyone, could not mean harm. He held her close to him, her face turned to the side and pressed to his shirt, and he breathed in the clean, plain scent of her hair, and he shut his eyes and let himself sink into her, let his shoulders go, released his neck, let his arms slacken behind her, so that it seemed their bodies, already pressed together, settled into an even more intimate touch, seating themselves in each other, locking.

23

THEY STOOD holding each other for a minute. For Edward it could have been longer, could have been five minutes, or an hour, or an afternoon. When she started moving in a way that suggested it was time to separate, he was slow to react, and she was gentle in her insistence. She took a step away from him, then came back and gave him a careful, formal kiss, and then put her cheek to his, holding it there in a deliberate, delicate equilibrium long enough for him to feel the roughness of her skin, the warmth of it, and then she was across the room picking up her bag and her purse, and she said, "It's always this way, isn't it? We go to Paris. We spend the week in the basement. We get ready to leave Paris. We look out the window. We say, *Hey! This is pretty!* Then we leave."

"It does happen that way, doesn't it?" Edward said.

She led him out of the bedroom, down the hall, into the living room. "Yeah," she said. "I guess it's better than not noticing." She dropped her bags by the front door and yelled for Roscoe.

The departure was quick, almost surgical. Roscoe and Edward shook hands in the front yard. Elise kissed Kinta, then Edward. He walked her to her car, which was in the driveway in front of Roscoe's car. She gave him a look when she got the engine started, but that was it. Roscoe backed out and waited in the street, then Elise backed out, then the two of them drove away.

Edward and Kinta lingered outside a minute, then went in. Edward started straightening things up. He didn't want Kinta to help, so she sat on the couch in the living room watching the small television, listening to it through the earphones he connected for her.

He cleaned house. He started in the back bedroom, changing the sheets and the pillowcases, changing even the bedspread, then got down on his hands and knees in the back bathroom and scrubbed the tub. It was already clean, but he did it anyway. He shook Ajax into the toilet bowl, then went on to the sink, washing it, and splashing water around on the imitation marble, and then using one of Roscoe's towels to dry things off. He used the same towel to clean the mirror. He was working fast. When he reached for the wastebasket to take it out, he noticed that there wasn't anything in it, so he left it where it was between the toilet and the cabinet under the sink. He dropped the sheets, towels, and pillowcases in the hall, and cleaned up his own bedroom and bath. He was working from the extremities of the house toward the kitchen, a procedure he followed because it seemed logical—the cleaning equipment and the cleaning supplies were kept in the kitchen. He worked around Kinta in the living room, wiping tabletops, straightening chair cushions, dusting shelves, repositioning lamp cords, rotating plants, checking to see that the chair feet were in their indentations in the carpet. He was finished in the living room when he noticed Kinta wasn't watching television, she was watching him. He said, "What, there's nothing on?"

She swiveled her eyes toward the screen, then back toward him. "Where does it say that Edward goes into a cleaning frenzy? You know, if I were Dr. Ruth, I'd figure you were trying to clean something out of your system."

"If you were Dr. Ruth, you'd be a lot shorter," Edward said.

They stared at each other a minute. Kinta squinted at him. "Are you all right?" she said.

"I'm OK," he said. "I just want to get things back together here."

She nodded at him. He nodded back. Then they both made a joke out of it, nodding more vigorously than was necessary or appropriate, and then she went back to the TV, and Edward went about his business. He sprayed Lemon Pledge on the dining room table, which looked as if it had already been Lemon-Pledged. He reset the chairs around the table. He fixed the bowl and the salt and pepper shakers on the sideboard.

In the kitchen he wiped the stove and the cabinet tops, rinsed the coffee maker, shook the crumbs out of the toaster into the garbage bag, started the dishwasher, rinsed and then dried the kitchen sink, polished the chrome faucet and the hot and cold water handles, rearranged the few things inside the refrigerator, and then opened the louvered wood doors to the laundry room. He put Tide and bleach in the washer and then went back to the hall for the sheets and pillowcases and towels he'd collected there, brought them back and stuffed them into the washer and turned it on. Then he checked the back porch, taking a wet rag to wipe the tabletop out there. He got the vacuum cleaner out of its closet and steered it through the dining room, the living room, down the hall to the back bedroom. He vacuumed the bathroom, the bedroom, the hall, the other bedroom, the other bath, then rolled the thing out and started doing the living room. Kinta got up and came across the room and stopped him, turning off the vacuum. "I think you ought to be finished pretty soon, don't you?" she said. "We can do the dog and the cat, would you be interested in that?" She brushed her hand over the front of his shirt.

"I'm almost ready," Edward said.

She smiled and started rolling up the cord for the earphones. Edward restarted the vacuum. He was thinking about Elise and Roscoe sliding down the dark highway in tandem, Elise in the lead car, watching her rearview mirror, and Roscoe studying her silhouette in the lights of the oncoming traffic. Edward ran the vacuum under the chairs, but then he felt guilty about that, so he turned the chairs over onto their backs, one after the other, so he could vacuum thoroughly under them. He did the same thing to the sofa. He pushed the coffee table out of the way so he could get under it. He was working fast, sweating a lot. Every once in a while he stopped and wiped his brow on his shirtsleeve, then looked at the spot he'd made, proud of how wet it was. He ran the vacuum in a precise way so the pile on the carpet ended up having the look of a golf green—it stood up in parallel strips the width of the cleaner. He had to move all the chairs away from the dining table in order to clean under there. Then he did the kitchen, banging the head of the vacuum into the baseboards of the cabinets as he went along the edges of the floor. He started to take the vacuum out to the back porch, but then decided to use the broom out there, so he turned off the vacuum and wrapped the cord around his arm from his elbow to his hand, then hung the cord on the top cord hook on the handle of the vacuum, and put the vacuum away. He swept the porch until he collected a good pile of dust, which he swept out the door. Then he swept the three concrete steps that led up to the porch. He latched the screen door, put the broom away, went back into the kitchen, moved a few things around on the counters in there—the mason jars of beans and sugar and flour, the coffee maker and the coffee grinder; he pushed the toaster back up against the wall, wrung the water out of the sponge and placed it on the right rear corner of the lip of the sink, turned on the light in the stove hood, and turned off the overhead light, and then, moving through the house, turned off the lights in the dining room and the living room, and went into the hall, into his bedroom, looking for Kinta.

She was sitting on the still-made bed, bare-legged, reading a magazine. She had changed into one of his shirts, the same one she'd had on when Edward and Elise got back from the coast. "You feel better?" she said. "You look like you need a bath. You want me to give you a bath?"

Edward said, "Give me a bath?"

"Yeah," she said. "You're the only thing left around here that even knows dirt's name. Don't you think this is a little bit of an overreaction? All this cleaning?"

Edward started unbuttoning his shirt. He shook his head. "It's not that. It's just what I do when people leave. I always do it. When Elise was here all the time, she and I did it together."

"Oh," Kinta said.

"I didn't mean to upset you," Edward said. "I just meant that's what we did."

"Why don't you just go around and pee on everything? It'd be easier. If it's a territorial thing."

"Good idea," he said. He opened the closet and got out a fresh shirt and a pair of white cotton tennis shorts. He started for the bathroom.

"What are you doing?" she said. "You're not going to put that on now, are you?"

"I was," Edward said.

"It's stupid, Edward. Those are tennis shorts, right? It's ten o'clock Sunday night and you're climbing into your tennis shorts?"

"That's not a great idea?" he said, looking at the shorts in his hand.

"No," she said. "Why don't you wear the robe?" She got up and came around the bed, took the tennis shorts and the shirt out of his hand and put them back in the closet. She brought out his robe and tossed it on the bed, then started to undress him, holding his shirt while he slipped out of it, undoing the button of his jeans and unzipping them, sliding them down his legs, holding the bottom of each pants leg in turn as he stepped out of it. "Don't get nervous here, OK?" she said. "I know what I'm doing."

In a couple of seconds he was naked, and she was touching his thighs, rubbing his legs from the heels up, scratching his ankles, dragging her pointed nails along the sides of his legs. He watched her head as she pressed a cheek against his thigh and then kissed him, her hands at the backs of his legs, just below his ass.

He reached down and touched her hair, said, "Kinta."

"Shhh," she said, and she ran a hand up the front of his body until she could put her forefinger to his lips, and she smiled when she did that. "It's OK."

She stayed in front of him for several minutes, kissing him, touching him, and his resistance evaporated. He was thinking of Elise, of how much he loved her, and he was reacting to Kinta's touch, and these were two separate things going on at the same time in his head.

Then she stood up and said, "Come with me," and took his hand and led him into the bathroom. She put up the lid of the toilet seat and told him to sit, and he did, and she sat down on top of him, facing him. She kissed his face, his neck, his ear, whispered to him, "I want to, OK? This one's hers." She leaned away from him, holding herself with both hands behind his neck, looking at him to be sure he understood. He could see in her face what she meant, and she must have seen what she was looking for in his face, because then she came forward and kissed him, her mouth wide and wet, and she started moving her hips in a slow, small circle, and then she started to pee, and he felt her hot stream on his cock, on his thighs, splashing up on his belly, and he heard that glassy tinkle of her urine falling lazily into the water.

They made love for an hour after that, maybe a little longer, and when they were done Kinta took a shower and then crawled into bed and fell asleep at once. Edward was next to her in the bed, his arm around her, her head on his shoulder, and he listened to her breathing and the other sounds of the night, and in a few minutes he started thinking about Elise, about her smile, about the way she laughed when she realized that something she'd said was accidentally funny, about how her eyes looked when she was hurt, about her hands, and the muscles in her shoulders, and about the way she worked hard when she did her toenails, thought about her radiating strength all the time, and about how she apologized when she'd done something goofy, thought about her in that overdone apartment, alone in spite of Roscoe, toughing it out, trying to figure a way to play the game, trying to do right, thought about how difficult it was for her to do things, just ordinary things, and how much harder it must be for her now that she didn't have him to do them with, and then he wondered if it might not be easier without him, and thought it must be, or she would have come home, and then he felt sad about that, because he'd wanted to help her, to make things easier, to make her life something like a good dream, he'd wanted to do everything for her, still wanted that, but now he knew he couldn't, he wasn't her, she wasn't him, and he didn't know how that obvious distinction had escaped him, or how she had, if she had. There in the dark in the bed he felt how much he missed her, how much he had *already* missed her, and he had tears in his eyes, gathering there but not coming any further, and he felt his life was smaller than it used to be, that it would get only smaller, and then Kinta rolled over beside him, kissed his arm, and moved to her pillow, and she said, when she was resettled, "Edward. She loves you. I promise."

COLLIER FICTION

Ballard, J. G. *The Day of Creation.*   ISBN 0-02-041514-1

Barthelme, Frederick. *Two Against One.*   ISBN 0-02-030445-5

Beattie, Ann. *Where You'll Find Me.*   ISBN 0-02-016560-9

Cantor, Jay. *Krazy Kat.*   ISBN 0-02-042081-1

Carrère, Emmanuel. *The Mustache.*   ISBN 0-02-018870-6

Coover, Robert. *A Night at the Movies.*   ISBN 0-02-019120-0

Coover, Robert. *Whatever Happened to Gloomy
  Gus of the Chicago Bears?*   ISBN 0-02-042781-6

Dickinson, Charles. *With or Without.*   ISBN 0-02-019560-5

Handke, Peter. *Across.*   ISBN 0-02-051540-5

Handke, Peter. *Repetition.*   ISBN 0-02-020762-X

Handke, Peter. *Slow Homecoming.*   ISBN 0-02-051530-8

Handke, Peter. *3 X Handke.*   ISBN 0-02-020761-1

Handke, Peter. *2 X Handke.*   ISBN 0-02-051520-0

Havazelet, Ehud. *What Is It Then Between Us?*   ISBN 0-02-051750-5

Hawkes, John. *Whistlejacket.*   ISBN 0-02-043591-6

Hemingway, Ernest. *The Garden of Eden.*   ISBN 0-684-18871-6

Mathews, Harry. *Cigarettes.*   ISBN 0-02-013971-3

McIlvoy, Kevin. *The Fifth Station.*   ISBN 0-02-034622-0

Miller, John (Ed.). *Hot Type.*   ISBN 0-02-044701-9

Morrow, Bradford. *Come Sunday.*   ISBN 0-02-023001-X

Olson, Toby. *The Woman Who Escaped
  from Shame.*   ISBN 0-02-023231-4

Olson, Toby. *Utah.*   ISBN 0-02-098410-3

Pelletier, Cathie. *The Funeral Makers.*   ISBN 0-02-023610-7

Phillips, Caryl. *A State of Independence.*   ISBN 0-02-015080-6

Powers, Richard. *Prisoner's Dilemma.*   ISBN 0-02-036055-X

Pritchard, Melissa. *Spirit Seizures.*   ISBN 0-02-036070-3

Robison, Mary. *Believe Them.*   ISBN 0-02-036380-X

Rush, Norman. *Whites.*   ISBN 0-02-023841-X

Tallent, Elizabeth. *Time with Children.*   ISBN 0-02-045540-2

Theroux, Alexander. *An Adultery.*   ISBN 0-02-008821-3

Vargas Llosa, Mario. *Who Killed
  Palomino Molero?*   ISBN 0-02-022570-9

West, Paul. *Rat Man of Paris.*   ISBN 0-02-026250-7

West, Paul. *The Place in Flowers Where
  Pollen Rests.*   ISBN 0-02-038260-X

*Available from your local bookstore, or from Macmillan Publishing Company,
100K Brown Street, Riverside, New Jersey 08370*